Dorothy L. Sayers

The greatest detective novelist of the golden age was born in Oxford in 1893. She was one of the first women to be awarded a degree by Oxford University and she was a copywriter in an advertising agency from 1922 to 1929. Her aristocratic detective Lord Peter Wimsey became one of the world's most popular fictional heroes.

Dorothy L. Sayers also became famous for her religious plays, notably *The Man Born to Be King*, which was broadcast controversially during the war years, and her translation of Dante's *Divine Comedy*. She died in 1957.

New English Library is the paperback publisher of all her detective stories and of two new Lord Peter Wimsey novels by Jill Paton Walsh. *Thrones, Dominations* and *A Presumption of Death* are based closely on and include some of Dorothy L. Sayers' own work. Hodder and Stoughton's Sceptre imprint is the publisher of the revised and updated version of the definitive biography, *Dorothy L. Sayers: Her Life and Soul* by Barbara Reynolds.

BY DOROTHY L. SAYERS
IN NEW ENGLISH LIBRARY PAPERBACKS

Busman's Honeymoon

The Documents in the Case (*with Robert Eustace*)

Five Red Herrings

Gaudy Night

Hangman's Holiday

Have His Carcase

In the Teeth of the Evidence

Lord Peter Views the Body

Murder Must Advertise

The Nine Tailors

Striding Folly

Strong Poison

Unnatural Death

The Unpleasantness at the Bellona Club

Whose Body?

DOROTHY L. SAYERS
CLOUDS OF WITNESS

WITH A NEW INTRODUCTION
BY ELIZABETH GEORGE

NEW ENGLISH LIBRARY
Hodder & Stoughton

First published in Great Britain in 1926 by T. Fisher Unwin
First published in paperback by New English Library in 1970
Hodder and Stoughton: a division of Hodder Headline
A New English Library paperback

Introduction © Susan Elizabeth George 2003

The right of Dorothy L. Sayers to be identified as the Author
of the Work has been asserted in accordance with the
Copyright, Designs and Patents Act 1988.

1

A CIP catalogue record for this title
is available from the British Library

ISBN 978-0-450-00180-2

Typeset in Sabon by Hewer Text Ltd, Edinburgh
Printed and bound by
Clays Ltd, St Ives plc

Hodder and Stoughton
A division of Hodder Headline
338 Euston Road
London NW1 3BH

THE SOLUTION OF
THE RIDDLESDALE MYSTERY

WITH
A REPORT
OF THE TRIAL OF
THE DUKE OF DENVER

BEFORE THE HOUSE OF LORDS
FOR
MURDER

The inimitable stories of Tong-king never have any real ending, and this one, being in his most elevated style, has even less end than most of them. But the whole narrative is permeated with the odour of joss-sticks and honourable high-mindedness, and the two characters are both of noble birth. – *The Wallet of Kai-Lung*

I came to the wonderful detective novels of Dorothy L. Sayers in a way that would probably make that distinguished novelist spin in her grave. Years ago, actor Ian Carmichael starred in the film productions of a good chunk of them, which I eventually saw on my public television station in Huntington Beach, California. I recall the host of the show reciting the impressive, salient details of Sayers' life and career – early female graduate of Oxford, translator of Dante, among other things – and I was much impressed. But I was even more impressed with her delightful sleuth Lord Peter Wimsey, and I soon sought out her novels.

Because I had never been – and still am not today – a great reader of detective fiction, I had not heard of this marvellous character. I quickly became swept up in everything about him: from his foppish use of language to his family relations. In very short order, I found myself thoroughly attached to Wimsey, to his calm and omnipresent manservant Bunter, to the Dowager Duchess of Denver (was ever there a more deliciously alliterative title?), to the stuffy Duke and the unbearable Duchess of Denver, to Viscount St. George, to Charles Parker, to Lady Mary. . . . In Dorothy L. Sayers' novels, I found the sort of main character I loved when I turned to fiction: someone with a 'real' life, someone who wasn't just a hero who conveniently had no relations to mess up the workings of the novelist's plot.

Dorothy L. Sayers, as I discovered, had much to teach

me both as a reader and as a future novelist. While many detective novelists from the Golden Age of mystery kept their plots pared down to the requisite crime, suspects, clues, and red herrings, Sayers did not limit herself to so limited a canvas in her work. She saw the crime and its ensuing investigation as merely the framework for a much larger story, the skeleton – if you will – upon which she could hang the muscles, organs, blood vessels and physical features of a much larger tale. She wrote what I like to call the tapestry novel, a book in which the setting is realised (from Oxford, to the dramatic coast of Devon, to the flat bleakness of the Fens), in which throughout both the plot and the subplots the characters serve functions surpassing that of mere actors on the stage of the criminal investigation, in which themes are explored, in which life and literary symbols are used, in which allusions to other literature abound. Sayers, in short, did what I call 'taking no prisoners' in her approach to the detective novel. She did not write down to her readers; rather, she assumed that her readers would rise to her expectations of them.

I found in her novels a richness that I had not previously seen in detective fiction. I became absorbed in the careful application of detail that characterized her plots: whether she was educating me about bell ringing in *The Nine Tailors*, about the unusual uses of arsenic in *Strong Poison*, about the beauties of architectural Oxford in *Gaudy Night*. She wrote about everything from cryptology to vinology, making unforgettable that madcap period between wars that marked the death of an overt class system and heralded the beginning of an insidious one.

What continues to be remarkable about Sayers' work, however, is her willingness to explore the human condition. The passions felt by characters created eighty years ago are as real today as they were then. The motives behind people's behavior are no more complex now than they were in 1923 when Lord Peter Wimsey took his first public bow. Times have changed, rendering Sayers' England in so many ways unrecognizable to today's reader. But one of the true pleasures inherent to picking up a Sayers novel now is to see how the times in which we live alter our perceptions of the world around us, while doing nothing at all to alter the core of our humanity.

When I first began my own career as a crime novelist, I told people that I would rest content if my name was ever mentioned positively in the same sentence as that of Dorothy L. Sayers. I'm pleased to say that that occurred with the publication of my first novel. If I ever come close to offering the reader the details and delights that Sayers offered in her Wimsey novels, I shall consider myself a success indeed.

The reissuing of a Sayers novel is an event, to be sure. As successive generations of readers welcome her into their lives, they embark upon an unforgettable journey with an even more unforgettable companion. In time of dire and immediate trouble, one might well call upon a Sherlock Holmes for a quick solution to one's trials. But for the balm that reassures one about surviving the vicissitudes of life, one could do no better than to anchor onto a Lord Peter Wimsey.

Elizabeth George
Huntington Beach, California
May 27, 2003

1

'OF HIS MALICE AFORETHOUGHT'

'O, Who hath done this deed?'
OTHELLO

LORD PETER WIMSEY stretched himself luxuriously between the sheets provided by the Hôtel Meurice. After his exertions in the unravelling of the Battersea Mystery, he had followed Sir Julian Freke's advice and taken a holiday. He had felt suddenly weary of breakfasting every morning before his view over the Green Park; he had realised that the picking up of first editions at sales afforded insufficient exercise for a man of thirty-three; the very crimes of London were over-sophisticated. He had abandoned his flat and his friends and fled to the wilds of Corsica. For the last three months he had forsworn letters, newspapers, and telegrams. He had tramped about the mountains, admiring from a cautious distance the wild beauty of Corsican peasant-women, and studying the vendetta in its natural haunt. In such conditions murder seemed not only reasonable, but lovable. Bunter, his confidential man and assistant sleuth, had nobly sacrificed his civilised habits, had let his master go dirty and even unshaven, and had turned his faithful camera from the recording of finger-prints to that of craggy scenery. It had been very refreshing.

Now, however, the call of the blood was upon Lord Peter. They had returned late last night in a vile train to Paris, and had picked up their luggage. The autumn light, filtering through the curtains, touched caressingly the silver-topped bottles on the dressing-table, outlined an electric lamp-shade and the shape of the telephone. A noise of running water near by proclaimed that Bunter had turned on the bath (h. & c.) and was laying out scented soap, bath-salts, the huge bath-sponge, for which there had been no scope in Corsica, and the delightful flesh-brush with the long handle, which rasped you so agreeably all down the spine. 'Contrast,' philosophised Lord Peter sleepily, 'is life. Corsica – Paris – then London. . . . Good morning, Bunter.'

'Good morning, my lord. Fine morning, my lord. Your lordship's bath-water is ready.'

'Thanks,' said Lord Peter. He blinked at the sunlight.

It was a glorious bath. He wondered, as he soaked in it, how he could have existed in Corsica. He wallowed happily and sang a few bars of a song. In a soporific interval he heard the valet de chambre bringing in coffee and rolls. Coffee and rolls! He heaved himself out with a splash, towelled himself luxuriously, enveloped his long-mortified body in a silken bath-robe, and wandered back.

To his immense surprise he perceived Mr Bunter calmly replacing all the fittings in his dressing-case. Another astonished glance showed him the bags – scarcely opened the previous night – repacked, relabelled, and standing ready for a journey.

'I say, Bunter, what's up?' said his lordship. 'We're stayin' here a fortnight y'know.'

'Excuse me, my lord,' said Mr Bunter, deferentially, 'but, having seen *The Times* (delivered here every morning by air, my lord; and very expeditious I'm sure, all things considered), I made no doubt your lordship would be wishing to go to Riddlesdale at once.'

'Riddlesdale!' exclaimed Peter. 'What's the matter? Anything wrong with my brother?'

For answer Mr Bunter handed him the paper, folded open at the heading:

RIDDLESDALE INQUEST.

DUKE OF DENVER ARRESTED

ON MURDER CHARGE.

Lord Peter stared as if hypnotised.

'I thought your lordship wouldn't wish to miss anything,' said Mr Bunter, 'so I took the liberty—'

Lord Peter pulled himself together.

'When's the next train?' he asked.

'I beg your lordship's pardon – I thought your lordship would wish to take the quickest route. I took it on myself to book two seats in the aeroplane *Victoria*. She starts at 11.30.'

Lord Peter looked at his watch.

'Ten o'clock,' he said. 'Very well. You did quite right. Dear me! Poor old Gerald arrested for murder. Uncommonly worryin' for him, poor chap. Always hated my bein' mixed up with police-courts. Now he's there himself. Lord Peter Wimsey in the witness-box – very distressin' to feelin's of a brother. Duke of Denver in the dock – worse still. Dear me! Well, I suppose one must have breakfast.'

'Yes, my lord. Full account of the inquest in the paper, my lord.'

'Yes. Who's on the case, by the way?'

'Mr Parker, my lord.'

'Parker? That's good. Splendid old Parker! Wonder how he managed to get put on to it. How do things look, Bunter?'

'If I may say so, my lord, I fancy the investigation will prove very interesting. There are several extremely suggestive points in the evidence, my lord.'

'From a criminological point of view, I daresay it is interesting,' replied his lordship, sitting down cheerfully to his *café au lait*, 'but it's deuced awkward for my brother, all the same, havin' no turn for criminology, what?'

'Ah, well!' said Mr Bunter, 'they say, my lord, there's nothing like having a personal interest.'

'The inquest was held today at Riddlesdale, in the North Riding of Yorkshire, on the body of Captain Denis Cathcart, which was found at three o'clock on Thursday morning lying just outside the conservatory door of the Duke of Denver's shooting-box, Riddlesdale Lodge. Evidence was given to show that deceased had quarrelled with the Duke of Denver on the preceding evening, and was subsequently shot in a small thicket adjoining the house. A pistol belonging to the Duke was found near the scene of the crime. A verdict of murder was returned against the Duke of Denver. Lady Mary Wimsey, sister of the Duke, who was engaged to be married to the deceased, collapsed after giving evidence, and is now lying seriously ill at the Lodge. The Duchess of Denver hastened from town yesterday and was present at the inquest. Full report on p.12.'

'Poor old Gerald!' thought Lord Peter, as he turned to page 12; 'and poor old Mary! I wonder if she really was fond of the fellow. Mother always said not, but Mary never would let on about herself.'

The full report began by describing the little village of Riddlesdale, where the Duke of Denver had recently taken a small shooting-box for the season. When the tragedy occurred the Duke had been staying there with a party of guests. In the Duchess's absence Lady Mary

Wimsey had acted as hostess. The other guests were Colonel and Mrs Marchbanks the Hon. Frederick Arbuthnot, Mr and Mrs Pettigrew-Robinson, and the dead man, Denis Cathcart.

The first witness was the Duke of Denver, who claimed to have discovered the body. He gave evidence that he was coming into the house by the conservatory door at three o'clock in the morning of Thursday, October 14th, when his foot struck against something. He had switched on his electric torch and seen the body of Denis Cathcart at his feet. He had at once turned it over, and seen that Cathcart had been shot in the chest. He was quite dead. As Denver was bending over the body, he heard a cry in the conservatory, and, looking up, saw Lady Mary Wimsey gazing out horror-struck. She came out by the conservatory door and exclaimed at once. 'O God, Gerald, you've killed him!' (Sensation.)*

The Coroner: 'Were you surprised by that remark?'

Duke of D.: 'Well, I was so shocked and surprised at the whole thing. I think I said to her, "Don't look," and she said, "Oh, it's Denis! Whatever can have happened? Has there been an accident?" I stayed with the body, and sent her up to rouse the house.'

The Coroner: 'Did you expect to see Lady Mary Wimsey in the conservatory?'

Duke of D.: 'Really, as I say, I was astonished all round, don't you know, I didn't think about it.'

The Coroner: 'Do you remember how she was dressed?'

* This report, though substantially the same as that read by Lord Peter in *The Times*, has been corrected, amplified, and annotated from the shorthand report made at the time by Mr Parker.

Duke of D.: 'I don't think she was in her pyjamas.' (Laughter.) 'I think she had a coat on.'

The Coroner: 'I understand that Lady Mary Wimsey was engaged to the deceased?'

Duke of D.: 'Yes.'

The Coroner: 'He was well known to you?'

Duke of D.: 'He was the son of an old friend of my father's; his parents are dead. I believe he lived chiefly abroad. I ran across him during the war, and in 1919 he came to stay at Denver. He became engaged to my sister at the beginning of this year.'

The Coroner: 'With your consent, and with that of the family?'

Duke of D.: 'Oh, yes, certainly.'

The Coroner; 'What kind of man was Captain Cathcart?'

Duke of D.: 'Well – he was a Sahib and all that. I don't know what he did before he joined in 1914. I think he lived on his income; his father was well off. Crack shot, good at games, and so on. I never heard anything against him – till that evening.'

The Coroner: 'What was that?'

Duke of D.: 'Well – the fact is – it was deuced queer. He – If anybody but Tommy Freeborn had said it I should never have believed it.' (Sensation.)

The Coroner: 'I'm afraid I must ask your grace of what exactly you had to accuse the deceased.'

Duke of D.: 'Well, I didn't – I don't exactly accuse him. An old friend of mine made a suggestion. Of course I thought it must be all a mistake, so I went to Cathcart, and, to my amazement, he practically admitted it! Then we both got angry, and he told me to go to the devil, and rushed out of the house.' (Renewed sensation.)

The Coroner: 'When did this quarrel occur?'

Duke of D.: 'On Wednesday night. That was the last I saw of him.' (Unparalleled sensation.)

The Coroner: 'Please, please, we cannot have this disturbance. Now, will your grace kindly give me, as far as you can remember it, the exact history of this quarrel?'

Duke of D.: 'Well, it was like this. We'd had a long day on the moors and had dinner early, and about half-past nine we began to feel like turning in. My sister and Mrs Pettigrew-Robinson toddled on up, and we were havin' a last peg in the billiard-room when Fleming – that's my man – came in with the letters. They come rather any old time in the evening, you know, we being two and a half miles from the village. No – I wasn't in the billiard-room at the time – I was lockin' up the gun-room. The letter was from an old friend of mine I hadn't seen for years – Tom Freeborn – used to know him at the House—'

The Coroner: 'Whose house?'

Duke of D.: 'Oh, Christ Church, Oxford. He wrote to say he'd seen the announcement of my sister's engagement in Egypt.'

The Coroner: 'In Egypt?'

Duke of D.: 'I mean, *he* was in Egypt – Tom Freeborn, you see – that's why he hadn't written before. He engineers. He went out there after the war was over, you see, and, bein' somewhere up near the sources of the Nile, he doesn't get the papers regularly. He said, would I 'scuse him for interferin' in a very delicate matter, and all that, but did I know who Cathcart was? Said he'd met him in Paris during the war, and he lived by cheatin' at cards – said he could swear to it, with details of a row there'd been in some French place or other. Said he knew I'd want to chaw his head off – Freeborn's, I mean – for buttin' in, but he'd seen the man's photo in the paper, an' he thought I ought to know.'

The Coroner: 'Did this letter surprise you?'

Duke of D.: 'Couldn't believe it at first. If it hadn't been old Tom Freeborn I'd have put the thing in the fire straight off, and, even as it was, I didn't quite know what to think. I mean to say, Frenchmen get so excited about nothing. Only there was Freeborn, and he isn't the kind of man that makes mistakes.'

The Coroner: 'What did you do?'

Duke of D.: 'Well, the more I looked at it the less I liked it, you know. Still, I couldn't quite leave it at that, so I thought the best way was to go straight to Cathcart. They'd all gone up while I was sittin' thinkin' about it, so I went up and knocked at Cathcart's door. He said, "What's that?" or "Who the devil's that?" or somethin' of the sort, and I went in. "Look here," I said, "can I just have a word with you?" "Well, cut it short, then," he said. I was surprised – he wasn't usually rude. "Well," I said, "fact is, I've had a letter I don't like the look of, and I thought the best thing to do was to bring it straight away to you an' have the whole thing cleared up. It's from a man – a very decent sort – old college friend, who says he's met you in Paris." "Paris!" he said, in a most uncommonly unpleasant way. "Paris! What the hell do you want to come talkin' to me about Paris for?" "Well," I said, "don't talk like that, because it's misleadin' under the circumstances." "What are you drivin' at?" says Cathcart. "Spit it out and go to bed, for God's sake." I said, "Right oh! I will. It's a man called Freeborn, who says he knew you in Paris and that you made money cheatin' at cards." I thought he'd break out at that, but all he said was, "What about it?" "What about it?" I said. "Well, of course, it's not the sort of thing I'm goin' to believe like that, right bang-slap off, without any proofs." Then he said a funny thing. He said, "Beliefs don't matter – it's what one *knows* about people." "Do you mean to say you don't deny it?" I said. "It's no good my denying it," he said; "you must make up your own mind. Nobody could *dis*prove it." And then he suddenly jumped up, nearly knocking the table over, and said, "I don't care what you think or what you do, if you'll only get out. For God's sake leave me alone!" "Look here," I said, "you needn't take it that way. I don't say I do believe it – in fact," I said, "I'm sure there must be some mistake; only, you bein' engaged to Mary," I said, "I couldn't just let it go at that without looking into it, could I?" "Oh !" says Cathcart, "if that's what's worrying you, it needn't. That's off." I said, "What?" He said, "Our engagement." "Off?" I said. "But I was talking to Mary about it only yesterday." "I haven't told her yet," he said. "Well," I said, "I think that's damned cool. Who the hell do you think you are, to come here and jilt my sister?" Well, I said quite a lot, first and last. "You can get out," I said; "I've no use for swine like you." "I will," he said, and he pushed past me an' slammed downstairs and out of the front door, an' banged it after him.'

The Coroner: 'What did you do?'

Duke of D.: 'I ran into my bedroom, which has a window over the conservatory, and shouted out to him not to be a silly fool. It was pourin' with rain and beastly cold. He didn't come back, so I told Fleming to leave the conservatory door open – in case he thought better of it – and went to bed.'

The Coroner: 'What explanation can you suggest for Cathcart's behaviour?'

Duke of D.: 'None, I was simply staggered. But I think he must somehow have got wind of the letter, and knew the game was up.'

The Coroner: 'Did you mention the matter to anybody else?'

Duke of D.: 'No, It wasn't pleasant, and I thought I'd better leave it till the morning.'

The Coroner: 'So you did nothing further in the matter?'

Duke of D.: 'No. I didn't want to go out huntin' for the fellow. I was too angry. Besides, I thought he'd change his mind before long – it was a brute of a night and he'd only a dinner-jacket.'

The Coroner: 'Then you just went quietly to bed and never saw deceased again?'

Duke of D.: 'Not till I fell over him outside the conservatory at three in the morning.'

The Coroner: 'Ah yes. Now can you tell us how you came to be out of doors at that time?'

Duke of D. (hesitating): 'I didn't sleep well. I went out for a stroll.'

The Coroner: 'At three o'clock in the morning?'

Duke of D.: 'Yes.' With sudden inspiration: 'You see, my wife's away.' (Laughter and some remarks from the back of the room.)

The Coroner: 'Silence, please. . . . You mean to say that you got up at that hour of an October night to take a walk in the garden in the pouring rain?'

Duke of D.: 'Yes, just a stroll.' (Laughter.)

The Coroner: 'At what time did you leave your bed-room?'

Duke of D.: 'Oh – oh, about half-past two, I should think.'

The Coroner: 'Which way did you go out?'

Duke of D.: 'By the conservatory door.'

The Coroner: 'The body was not there when you went out?'

Duke of D.: 'Oh no!'

The Coroner: 'Or you would have seen it?'

Duke of D.: 'Lord, yes! I'd have had to walk over it.'

The Coroner: 'Exactly where did you go?'

Duke of D. (vaguely) : 'Oh, just round about.'

The Coroner: 'You heard no shot?'

Duke of D.: 'No.'

The Coroner: 'Did you go far away from the con-servatory door and the shrubbery?'

Duke of D.: 'Well – I was some way away. Perhaps that's why I didn't hear anything. It must have been.'

The Coroner: 'Were you as much as a quarter of a mile away?'

Duke of D.: 'I should think I was – oh yes, quite!'

The Coroner: 'More than a quarter of a mile away?'

Duke of D.: 'Possibly. I walked about briskly because it was cold.'

The Coroner: 'In which direction?'

Duke of D. (with visible hesitation): 'Round at the back of the house. Towards the bowling-green.'

The Coroner: 'The bowling-green?'

Duke of D. (more confidently): 'Yes.'

The Coroner: 'But if you were more than a quarter of a mile away, you must have left the grounds?'

Duke of D.: 'I – oh yes – I think I did. Yes, I walked about on the moor a bit, you know.'

The Coroner: 'Can you show us the letter you had from Mr Freeborn?'

Duke of D.: 'Oh, certainly – if I can find it. I thought I put it in my pocket, but I couldn't find it for that Scotland Yard fellow.'

The Coroner: 'Can you have accidentally destroyed it?'

Duke of D.: 'No – I'm sure I remember putting it – Oh'

– here the witness paused in very patent confusion, and grew red – 'I remember now. I destroyed it.'

The Coroner. 'That is unfortunate. How was that?'

Duke of D.: 'I had forgotten; it has come back to me now. I'm afraid it has gone for good.'

The Coroner : 'Perhaps you kept the envelope?'

Witness shook his head.

The Coroner: 'Then you can show the jury no proof of having received it?'

Duke of D.: 'Not unless Fleming remembers it.'

The Coroner: 'Ah yes! No doubt we can check it that way. Thank you, your grace. Call Lady Mary Wimsey.'

The noble lady, who was, until the tragic morning of October 14th, the fiancée of the deceased, aroused a murmur of sympathy on her appearance. Fair and slender, her naturally rose-pink cheeks ashy pale, she seemed overwhelmed with grief. She was dressed entirely in black, and gave her evidence in a very low tone which was at times almost inaudible.*

After expressing his sympathy, the Coroner asked, 'How long had you been engaged to the deceased?'

Witness: 'About eight months.'

The Coroner: 'Where did you first meet him?'

Witness: 'At my sister-in-law's house in London.'

The Coroner: 'When was that?'

Witness: 'I think it was June last year.'

The Coroner: 'You were quite happy in your engagement?'

Witness: 'Quite.'

The Coroner: 'You naturally saw a good deal of Captain Cathcart. Did he tell you much about his previous life?'

* From the newspaper report, *not* Mr Parker.

Witness: 'Not very much. We were not given to mutual confidences. We usually discussed subjects of common interest.'

The Coroner: 'You had many such subjects?'

Witness: 'Oh yes.'

The Coroner: 'You never gathered at any time that Captain Cathcart had anything on his mind?'

Witness: 'Not particularly. He had seemed a little anxious the last few days.'

The Coroner: 'Did he speak of his life in Paris?'

Witness: 'He spoke of theatres and amusements there. He knew Paris very well. I was staying in Paris with some friends last February, when he was there, and he took us about. That was shortly after our engagement.'

The Coroner: 'Did he ever speak of playing cards in Paris?'

Witness: 'I don't remember.'

The Coroner: 'With regard to your marriage – had any money settlements been gone into?'

Witness: 'I don't think so. The date of the marriage was not in any way fixed.'

The Coroner: 'He always appeared to have plenty of money?'

Witness: 'I suppose so; I didn't think about it.'

The Coroner: 'You never heard him complain of being hard up?'

Witness: 'Everybody complains of that, don't they?'

The Coroner: 'Was he a man of cheerful disposition?'

Witness: 'He was very moody, never the same two days together.'

The Coroner: 'You have heard what your brother says about the deceased wishing to break off the engagement. Had you any idea of this?'

Witness: 'Not the slightest.'

The Coroner: 'Can you think of any explanation now?'

Witness: 'Absolutely none.'

The Coroner: 'There had been no quarrel?'

Witness: 'No.'

The Coroner: 'So far as you knew, on the Wednesday evening, you were still engaged to deceased with every prospect of being married to him shortly?'

Witness: 'Ye-es. Yes, certainly, of course.'

The Coroner: 'He was not – forgive me this very painful question – the sort of man who would have been likely to lay violent hands on himself?'

Witness: 'Oh, I never thought – well, I don't know – I suppose he might have done. That would explain it, wouldn't it?'

The Coroner: 'Now, Lady Mary – please don't distress yourself, take your own time – will you tell us exactly what you heard and saw on Wednesday night and Thursday morning?'

Witness: 'I went up to bed with Mrs Marchbanks and Mrs Pettigrew-Robinson at about half-past nine, leaving all the men downstairs. I said good night to Denis, who seemed quite as usual. I was not downstairs when the post came. I went to my room at once. My room is at the back of the house. I heard Mr Pettigrew-Robinson come up at about ten. The Pettigrew-Robinsons sleep next door to me. Some of the other men came up with him. I did not hear my brother come upstairs. At about a quarter past ten I heard two men talking loudly in the passage, and then I heard someone run downstairs and bang the front door. Afterwards I heard rapid steps in the passage, and finally I heard my brother shut his door. Then I went to bed.'

The Coroner: 'You did not inquire the cause of the disturbance?'

Witness (indifferently): 'I thought it was probably some thing about the dogs.'

The Coroner: 'What happened next?'

Witness: 'I woke up at three o'clock.'

The Coroner: 'What wakened you?'

Witness: 'I heard a shot.'

The Coroner: 'You were not awake before you heard it?'

Witness: 'I may have been partly awake. I heard it very distinctly. I was sure it was a shot. I listened for a few minutes, and then went down to see if anything was wrong.'

The Coroner: 'Why did you not call your brother or some other gentleman?'

Witness (scornfully): 'Why should I? I thought it was probably only poachers, and I didn't want to make an unnecessary fuss at that unearthly hour.'

The Coroner: 'Did the shot sound close to the house?'

Witness: 'Fairly, I think – it is hard to tell when one is awakened by a noise – it always sounds so extra loud.'

The Coroner: 'It did not seem to be in the house or in the conservatory?'

Witness: 'No, it was outside.'

The Coroner: 'So you went downstairs by yourself. That was very plucky of you, Lady Mary. Did you go immediately?'

Witness: 'Not quite immediately. I thought it over for a few minutes; then I put on walking-shoes over bare feet, a heavy covert-coat, and a woolly cap. It may have been five minutes after hearing the shot that I left my bed-room. I went downstairs and through the billiard-room to the conservatory.'

The Coroner: 'Why did you go out that way?'

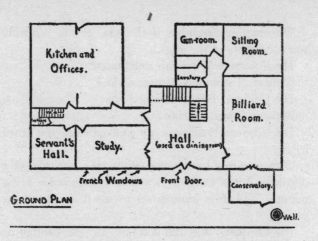

GROUND PLAN

Labels in ground plan:
Kitchen and Offices.
Gun-room.
Sitting Room.
lavatory
Billiard Room.
Servant's Hall.
Study.
Hall. (used as dining room)
French Windows
Front Door.
Conservatory.
Well.

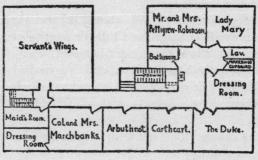

x.—Old Oak Chest.

Labels in upper plan:
Servant's Wings.
Mr. and Mrs. Pettigrew-Robinson.
Lady Mary
Bathroom.
Lav.
HOUSEMAID'S CUPBOARD
Dressing Room.
Maid's Room.
Dressing Room.
Col. and Mrs. Marchbanks.
Arbuthnot.
Cathcart.
The Duke.

Witness: 'Because it was quicker than unbolting either the front door or the back door.'

At this point a plan of Riddlesdale Lodge was handed to the jury. It is a roomy, two-storied house, built in a plain style, and leased by the present owner, Mr Walter Montague, to the Duke of Denver for the season, Mr Montague being in the States.

Witness (resuming): 'When I got to the conservatory door I saw a man outside bending over something on the ground. When he looked up I was astonished to see my brother.'

The Coroner: 'Before you saw who it was, what did you expect?'

Witness: 'I hardly know – it all happened so quickly. I thought it was burglars, I think.'

The Coroner: 'His grace has told us that when you saw him you cried out, "O God! you've killed him!" Can you tell us why you did that?'

Witness (very pale): 'I thought my brother must have come upon the burglar and fired at him in self-defence – that is, if I thought at all.'

The Coroner: 'Quite so. You knew that the Duke possessed a revolver?'

Witness: 'Oh yes – I think so.'

The Coroner: 'What did you do next?'

Witness: 'My brother sent me up to get help. I knocked up Mr Arbuthnot and Mr and Mrs Pettigrew-Robinson. Then I suddenly felt very faint, and went back to my bedroom and took some sal volatile.'

The Coroner: 'Alone?'

Witness: 'Yes, everybody was running about and calling out. I couldn't bear it – I–'

Here the witness, who up till this moment had given her evidence very collectedly, though in a low voice, collapsed suddenly, and had to be assisted from the room.

The next witness called was James Fleming, the man-servant. He remembered having brought the letters from Riddlesdale at 9.45 on Wednesday evening. He had taken three or four letters to the Duke in the gun-room. He could not remember at all whether one of them had had an Egyptian stamp. He did not collect stamps; his hobby was autographs.

The Hon. Frederick Arbuthnot then gave evidence. He had gone up to bed with the rest at a little before ten. He had heard Denver come up by himself some time later – couldn't say how much later – he was brushing his teeth at the time. (Laughter.) Had certainly heard loud voices and a row going on next door and in the passage. Had heard somebody go for the stairs hell-for-leather. Had stuck his head out and seen Denver in the passage. Had said, 'Hello, Denver, what's the row?' The Duke's reply had been inaudible. Denver had bolted into his bedroom and shouted out of the window, 'Don't be an ass, man!' He had seemed very angry indeed, but the Hon. Freddy attached no importance to that. One was always getting across Denver, but it never came to anything. More dust than kick in his opinion. Hadn't known Cathcart long – always found him all right – no, he didn't *like* Cathcart, but he was all right, you know, nothing wrong about him that he knew of. Good lord, no, he'd never heard it suggested he cheated at cards! Well, no, of course, he didn't go about looking out for people cheating at cards – it wasn't a thing one expected. He'd been had that way in a club at Monte once – he'd had no hand in bringing it to light – hadn't noticed anything till the fun began. Had not noticed anything particular in Cathcart's manner to Lady Mary, or hers to him. Didn't suppose he ever would notice anything; did not consider himself an observing sort of man. Was not interfering by nature; had thought Wednesday evening's dust-up none of his business. Had gone to bed and to sleep.

The Coroner: 'Did you hear anything further that night?'

Hon. Frederick: 'Not till poor little Mary knocked me up. Then I toddled down and found Denver in the conservatory, bathing Cathcart's head. We thought we ought to clean the gravel and mud off his face, you know.'

The Coroner: 'You heard no shot?'

Hon. Frederick: 'Not a sound. But I sleep pretty heavily.'

Colonel and Mrs Marchbanks slept in the room over what was called the study – more a sort of smoking-room really. They both gave the same account of a conversation which they had had at 11.30. Mrs Marchbanks had sat up to write some letters after the Colonel was in bed. They had heard voices and someone running about, but had paid no attention. It was not unusual for members of the party to shout and run about. At last the Colonel had said, 'Come to bed, my dear, it's half-past eleven, and we're making an early start tomorrow. You won't be fit for anything.' He said this because Mrs Marchbanks was a keen sportswoman and always carried her gun with the rest. She replied, 'I'm just coming.' The Colonel said, 'You're the only sinner burning the midnight oil – everybody's turned in.' Mrs Marchbanks replied, 'No, the Duke's still up; I can hear him moving about in the study.' Colonel Marchbanks listened and heard it too. Neither of them heard the Duke come up again. They had heard no noise of any kind in the night.

Mr Pettigrew-Robinson appeared to give evidence with extreme reluctance. He and his wife had gone to bed at ten. They had heard the quarrel with Cathcart. Mr Pettigrew-Robinson, fearing that something might be going to happen, opened his door in time to hear the Duke say, 'If you dare to speak to my sister again I'll break every bone in your body,' or words to that effect. Cathcart had rushed downstairs. The Duke was scarlet in the face. He had not seen Mr Pettigrew-Robinson, but had spoken a few words to Mr Arbuthnot, and rushed into his own bedroom. Mr Pettigrew-Robinson had run out, and said to Mr Arbuthnot, 'I say, Arbuthnot,' and

Mr Arbuthnot had very rudely slammed the door in his face. He had then gone to the Duke's door and said, 'I say, Denver.' The Duke had come out, pushing past him, without even noticing him, and gone to the head of the stairs. He had heard him tell Fleming to leave the conservatory door open, as Mr Cathcart had gone out. The Duke had then returned. Mr Pettigrew-Robinson had tried to catch him as he passed, and had said again, 'I say, Denver, what's up?' The Duke had said nothing, and had shut his bedroom door with great decision. Later on, however, at 11.30 to be precise, Mr Pettigrew-Robinson had heard the Duke's door open, and stealthy feet moving about the passage. He could not hear whether they had gone downstairs. The bathroom and lavatory were at his end of the passage, and, if anybody had entered either of them, he thought he should have heard. He had not heard the footsteps return. He had heard his travelling clock strike twelve before falling asleep. There was no mistaking the Duke's bedroom door, as the hinge creaked in a peculiar manner.

Mrs Pettigrew-Robinson confirmed her husband's evidence. She had fallen asleep before midnight, and had slept heavily. She was a heavy sleeper at the beginning of the night, but slept lightly in the early morning. She had been annoyed by all the disturbance in the house that evening, as it had prevented her from getting off. In fact, she had dropped off about 10.30, and Mr Pettigrew-Robinson had had to wake her an hour after to tell her about the footsteps. What with one thing and another she only got a couple of hours' good sleep. She woke up again at two, and remained broad awake till the alarm was given by Lady Mary. She could swear positively that she heard no shot in the night. Her window was next to Lady Mary's, on the opposite side from the conservatory.

She had always been accustomed from a child to sleep with her window open. In reply to a question from the Coroner, Mrs Pettigrew-Robinson said she had never felt there was a real, true affection between Lady Mary Wimsey and deceased. They seemed very off-hand, but that sort of thing was the fashion nowadays. She had never heard of any disagreement.

Miss Lydia Cathcart, who had been hurriedly summoned from town, then gave evidence about the deceased man. She told the Coroner that she was the Captain's aunt and his only surviving relative. She had seen very little of him since he came into possession of his father's money. He had always lived with his own friends in Paris, and they were such as she could not approve of.

'My brother and I never got on very well,' said Miss Cathcart, 'and he had my nephew educated abroad till he was eighteen. I fear Denis's notions were always quite French. After my brother's death Denis went to Cambridge, by his father's desire. I was left executrix of the will, and guardian till Denis came of age. I do not know why, after neglecting me all his life, my brother should have chosen to put such a responsibility upon me at his death, but I did not care to refuse. My house was open to Denis during his holidays from college, but he preferred, as a rule, to go and stay with his rich friends. I cannot now recall any of their names. When Denis was twenty-one he came into £10,000 a year. I believe it was in some kind of foreign property. I inherited a certain amount under the will as executrix, but I converted it all, at once, into good, sound British securities. I cannot say what Denis did with his. It would not surprise me at all to hear that he had been cheating at cards. I have heard that the persons he consorted with in Paris were most undesirable. I never met any of them. I have never been in France.'

John Hardraw, the gamekeeper, was next called. He and his wife inhabit a small cottage just inside the gate of Riddlesdale Lodge. The grounds, which measure twenty acres or so, are surrounded at this point by a strong paling; the gate is locked at night. Hardraw stated that he had heard a shot fired at about ten minutes to twelve on Wednesday night, close to the cottage, as it seemed to him. Behind the cottage are ten acres of preserved plantation. He supposed that there were poachers about; they occasionally came in after hares. He went out with his gun in that direction, but saw nobody. He returned home at one o'clock by his watch.

The Coroner: 'Did you fire your gun at any time?'

Witness: 'No.'

The Coroner: 'You did not go out again?'

Witness; 'I did not.'

The Coroner: 'Nor hear any other shots?'

Witness: 'Only that one; but I fell asleep after I got back, and was awakened up by the chauffeur going out for the doctor. That would be at about a quarter past three.'

The Coroner. 'Is it not unusual for poachers to shoot so very near the cottage?'

Witness: 'Yes, rather. If poachers do come, it is usually on the other side of the preserve, towards the moor.'

Dr Thorpe gave evidence of having been called to see deceased. He lived in Stapley, nearly fourteen miles from Riddlesdale. There was no medical man in Riddlesdale. The chauffeur had knocked him up at 3.45 a.m., and he had dressed quickly and come with him at once. They were at Riddlesdale Lodge at half-past four. Deceased, when he saw him, he judged to have been dead three or four hours. The lungs had been pierced by a bullet, and death had resulted from loss of blood and suffocation. Death would not have resulted immediately – deceased might have lingered some time. He had made a post-mortem investigation, and found that the bullet had been deflected from a rib. There was nothing to show whether the wound had been self-inflicted or fired from another hand, at close quarters. There were no other marks of violence.

Inspector Craikes from Stapley had been brought back in the car with Dr Thorpe. He had seen the body. It was then lying on its back, between the door of the conservatory and the covered well just outside. As soon as it became light, Inspector Craikes had examined the house and grounds. He had found bloody marks all along the path leading to the conservatory, and signs as though a body had been dragged along. This path ran into the main path leading from the gate to the front door. (Plan produced.) Where the two paths joined, a shrubbery began, and ran down on both sides of the path to the gate and the gamekeeper's cottage. The blood-tracks had led to a little clearing in the middle of the shrubbery, about half-way between the house and the gate. Here the inspector found a great pool of blood, a handkerchief soaked in blood, and a revolver. The handkerchief bore the initials D. C., and the revolver was a small weapon of American pattern, and bore no mark. The conservatory door was open when the Inspector arrived, and the key was inside.

Deceased, when he saw him, was in dinner-jacket and pumps, without hat or overcoat. He was wet through, and his clothes, besides being much blood-stained, were very muddy and greatly disordered through the dragging of the body. The pocket contained a cigar-case and a small flat pocket-knife. Deceased's bedroom had been searched for papers, etc., but so far nothing had been found to shed very much light on his circumstances.

The Duke of Denver was then recalled.

The Coroner: 'I should like to ask your grace whether you ever saw deceased in possession of a revolver?'

Duke of D.: 'Not since the war.'

The Coroner: 'You do not know if he carried one about with him?'

Duke of D.: 'I have no idea.'

The Coroner: 'You can make no guess, I suppose, to whom this revolver belongs?'

Duke of D. (in great surprise): 'That's my revolver – out of the study table drawer. How did you get hold of that?' (Sensation.)

The Coroner: 'You are certain?'

Duke of D.: 'Positive. I saw it there only the other day, when I was hunting out some photos of Mary for Cathcart, and I remember saying then that it was getting rusty lying about. There's the speck of rust.'

The Coroner: 'Did you keep it loaded?'

Duke of D.: 'Lord, no! I really don't know why it was there. I fancy I turned it out one day with some old Army stuff, and found it among my shooting things when I was up at Riddlesdale in August. I think the cartridges were with it.'

The Coroner: 'Was the drawer locked?'

Duke of D.: 'Yes, but the key was in the lock. My wife tells me I'm careless.'

The Coroner: 'Did anybody else know the revolver was there?'

Duke of D.: 'Fleming did, I think. I don't know of anybody else.'

Detective-Inspector Parker of Scotland Yard, having

only arrived on Friday, had been unable as yet to make any very close investigation. Certain indications led him to think that some person or persons had been on the scene of the tragedy in addition to those who had taken part in the discovery. He preferred to say nothing more at present.

The Coroner then reconstructed the evidence in chronological order. At, or a little after, ten o'clock there had been a quarrel between deceased and the Duke of Denver, after which deceased had left the house never to be seen alive again. They had the evidence of Mr Pettigrew-Robinson that the Duke had gone downstairs at 11.30, and that of Colonel Marchbanks that he had been heard immediately afterwards moving about in the study, the room in which the revolver produced in evidence was usually kept. Against this they had the Duke's own sworn statement that he had not left his bedroom till half-past two in the morning. The jury would have to consider what weight was to be attached to those conflicting statements. Then, as to the shots heard in the night; the gamekeeper had said he heard a shot at ten minutes to twelve, but he had supposed it to be fired by poachers. It was, in fact, quite possible that there had been poachers about. On the other hand, Lady Mary's statement that she had heard the shot at about three a.m. did not fit in very well with the doctor's evidence that when he arrived at Riddlesdale at 4.30 deceased had been already three or four hours dead. They would remember also that in Dr Thorpe's opinion, death had not immediately followed the wound. If they believed this evidence, therefore, they would have to put back the moment of death to between eleven p.m. and midnight, and this might very well have been the shot which the gamekeeper heard. In that case they had still to ask themselves about the shot which had awakened Lady Mary Wimsey. Of course, if they liked to put that down to poachers, there was no inherent impossibility.

They next came to the body of deceased, which had been discovered by the Duke of Denver at three a.m. lying outside the door of the small conservatory, near the covered well. There seemed little doubt, from the medical evidence, that the shot which killed deceased had been fired in the shrubbery, about seven minutes' distance from the house, and that the body of deceased had been dragged from that place to the house. Deceased had undoubtedly died as the result of being shot in the lungs. The jury would have to decide whether that shot was fired by his own hand or by the hand of another; and, if the latter, whether by accident, in self-defence, or by malice aforethought with intent to murder. As regards suicide, they must consider what they knew of deceased's character and circumstances. Deceased was a young man in the prime of his strength, and apparently of considerable fortune. He had had a meritorious military career, and was liked by his friends. The Duke of Denver had thought sufficiently well of him to consent to his own sister's engagement to deceased. There was evidence to show that the fiancés, though perhaps not demonstrative, were on excellent terms. The Duke affirmed that on the Wednesday night deceased had announced his intention of breaking off the engagement. Did they believe that deceased, without even communicating with the lady, or writing a word of explanation or farewell, would thereupon rush out and shoot himself? Again, the jury must consider the accusation which the Duke of Denver said he had brought against deceased. He had accused him of cheating at cards. In the kind of society to which the persons involved in this inquiry belonged, such a misdemeanour as cheating at cards was regarded as far more shameful than such sins as murder and adultery. Possibly the mere suggestion of such a thing, whether well-founded or not, might well cause a gentleman of sensitive honour to make away with himself. But was deceased honourable? Deceased had been educated in France, and French notions of the honest thing were very different from British ones. The Coroner himself had had business relations with French persons in his capacity as a solicitor, and could assure such of the jury as had never been in France that they ought to allow for these different standards. Unhappily, the alleged letter giving details of the accusation had not been produced to them. Next, they might ask themselves whether it was not more usual for a suicide to shoot himself in the head. They should ask themselves how deceased came by the revolver. And, finally, they must consider, in that case, who had dragged the body towards the house, and why the person had chosen to do so, with great labour to himself and at the risk of extinguishing any lingering remnant of the vital spark,* instead of arousing the household and fetching help.

If they excluded suicide, there remained accident, manslaughter, or murder. As to the first, if they thought it likely that deceased or any other person had taken out the Duke of Denver's revolver that night for any purpose, and that, in looking at, cleaning, shooting with, or otherwise handling the weapon, it had gone off and killed deceased accidentally, then they would return a verdict of death by misadventure accordingly. In that case, how did they explain the conduct of the person, whoever it was, who had dragged the body to the door?

* Verbatim.

The Coroner then passed on to speak of the law concerning manslaughter. He reminded them that no mere words however meaning or unmeaning, can be an efficient excuse for killing anybody, and that the conflict must be sudden and unpremeditated. Did they think, for example, that the Duke had gone out, wishing to induce his guest to return and sleep in the house, and that deceased had retorted upon him with blows or menaces of assault? If so, and the Duke, having a weapon in his hand, had shot deceased in self-defence, that was only manslaughter. But, in that case, they must ask themselves how the Duke came to go out to deceased with a lethal weapon in his hand? And this suggestion was in direct conflict with the Duke's own evidence.

Lastly, they must consider whether there was sufficient evidence of malice to justify a verdict of murder. They must consider whether any person had a motive, means, and opportunity for killing deceased; and whether they could reasonably account for that person's conduct on any other hypothesis. And, if they thought there *was* such a person, and that his conduct was in any way suspicious or secretive, or that he had wilfully suppressed evidence which might have had a bearing on the case, or (here the Coroner spoke with great emphasis, staring over the Duke's head) fabricated other evidence with intent to mislead – then all these circumstances might be sufficient to amount to a violent presumption of guilt against some party, in which case they were in duty bound to bring in a verdict of wilful murder against that party. And, in considering this aspect of the question, the Coroner added, they would have to decide in their own minds whether the person who had dragged deceased towards the conservatory door had done so with the object of obtaining assistance or of thrusting the body down the garden well, which, as they had heard from Inspector Craikes, was situated close by the spot where the body had been found. If the jury were satisfied that deceased had been murdered, but were not prepared to accuse any particular person on the evidence, they might bring in a verdict of murder against an unknown person, or persons; but, if they felt justified in laying the killing at any person's door, then they must allow no respect of persons to prevent them from doing their duty.

Guided by these extremely plain hints, the jury, without very long consultation, returned a verdict of wilful murder against Gerald, Duke of Denver.

2

THE GREEN-EYED CAT

And here's to the hound
With his nose unto the ground—'
            DRINK, PUPPY, DRINK

SOME people hold that breakfast is the best meal of the day. Others, less robust, hold that it is the worst, and that, of all breakfasts in the week, Sunday morning breakfast is incomparably the worst.

The party gathered about the breakfast-table at Riddlesdale Lodge held, if one might judge from their faces, no brief for that day miscalled of sweet refection and holy love. The only member of it who seemed neither angry nor embarrassed was the Hon. Freddy Arbuthnot, and he was silent, engaged in trying to take the whole skeleton out of a bloater at once. The very presence of that undistinguished fish upon the Duchess's breakfast-table indicated a disorganised household.

The Duchess of Denver was pouring out coffee. This was one of her uncomfortable habits. Persons arriving late for breakfast were thereby made painfully aware of their sloth. She was a long-necked, long-backed woman, who disciplined her hair and her children. She was never embarrassed, and her anger, though never permitted to be visible, made itself felt the more.

Colonel and Mrs Marchbanks sat side by side. They had nothing beautiful about them but a stolid mutual affection. Mrs Marchbanks was not angry, but she was embarrassed in the presence of the Duchess, because she could not feel sorry for her. When you felt sorry for people you called them 'poor old dear' or 'poor dear old man'. Since, obviously, you could not call the Duchess poor old dear, you were not being properly sorry for her. This distressed Mrs Marchbanks. The Colonel was both embarrassed and angry – embarrassed because, 'pon my soul, it was very difficult to know what to talk about in a house where your host had been arrested for murder; angry in a dim way, like an injured animal, because unpleasant things like this had no business to break in on the shooting-season.

Mrs Pettigrew-Robinson was not only angry, she was outraged. As a girl she had adopted the motto stamped upon the school notepaper: *Quocunque honesta*. She had always thought it *wrong* to let your mind *dwell* on anything that was not really nice. In middle life she still made a point of ignoring those newspaper paragraphs which bore such headlines as: 'ASSAULT UPON A SCHOOLTEACHER AT CRICKLEWOOD'; 'DEATH IN A PINT OF STOUT'; '£75 FOR A KISS'; or 'SHE CALLED HIM HUBBYKINS.' She said she could not see what *good* it did you to know about such things. She regretted having consented to visit Riddlesdale Lodge in the absence of the Duchess. She had never liked Lady Mary; she considered her a very objectionable specimen of the modern independent young woman; besides, there had been that very undignified incident connected with a Bolshevist while Lady Mary was nursing in London during the war. Nor had Mrs Pettigrew-Robinson at all cared for Captain Denis Cathcart. She did not like a young man to be handsome in that obvious kind of way. But, of course, since Mr Pettigrew-Robinson had wanted to come to Riddlesdale, it was her place to be with him. She was not to blame for the unfortunate result.

Mr Pettigrew-Robinson was angry, quite simply, because the detective from Scotland Yard had not accepted his help in searching the house and grounds for footprints. As an older man of some experience in these matters (Mr Pettigrew-Robinson was a county magistrate) he had gone out of his way to place himself at the man's disposal. Not only had the man been short with him, but he had rudely ordered him out of the conservatory, where he (Mr Pettigrew-Robinson) had been reconstructing the affair from the point of view of Lady Mary.

All these angers and embarrassments might have caused less pain to the company had they not been aggravated by the presence of the detective himself, a quiet young man in a tweed suit, eating curry at one end of the table next to Mr Murbles, the solicitor. This person had arrived from London on Friday, had corrected the local police, and strongly dissented from the opinion of Inspector Craikes. He had suppressed at the inquest information which, if openly given, might have precluded the arrest of the Duke. He had officiously detained the whole unhappy party, on the grounds that he wanted to re-examine everybody, and was thus keeping them miserably cooped up together over a horrible Sunday; and he had put the coping-stone on his offences by turning out to be an intimate friend of Lord Peter Wimsey's, and having, in consequence, to be accommodated with a bed in the gamekeeper's cottage and breakfast at the Lodge.

Mr Murbles, who was elderly and had a delicate digestion, had travelled up in a hurry on Thursday night. He had found the inquest very improperly conducted and his client altogether impracticable. He had spent all his time trying to get hold of Sir Impey Biggs, K.C., who had vanished for the week-end, leaving no address. He was eating a little dry toast, and was inclined to like the detective, who called him 'Sir', and passed him the butter.

'Is anybody thinking of going to church?' asked the Duchess.

'Theodore and I should like to go,' said Mrs Pettigrew-Robinson, 'if it is not too much trouble; or we could walk. It is not so *very* far.'

'It's two and a half miles, good,' said Colonel March-banks.

Mr Pettigrew-Robinson looked at him gratefully.

'Of course you will come in the car,' said the Duchess. 'I am going myself.'

'Are you, though?' said the Hon. Freddy. 'I say, won't you get a bit stared at, what?'

'Really, Freddy,' said the Duchess, 'does that matter?'

'Well,' said the Hon. Freddy, 'I mean to say, these bounders about here are all Socialists and Methodists. . . .'

'If they are Methodists,' said Mrs Pettigrew-Robinson, 'they will not be at church.'

'Won't they?' retorted the Hon. Freddy. 'You bet they will if there's anything to see. Why, it'll be better'n a funeral to 'em.'

'Surely,' said Mrs Pettigrew-Robinson, 'one has a *duty* in the matter, whatever our private feelings may be – especially at the present day, when people are so terribly *slack*.'

She glanced at the Hon. Freddy.

'Oh, don't you mind me, Mrs P.,' said that youth amiably. 'All *I* say is, if these blighters make things unpleasant, don't blame me.'

'Whoever thought of blaming you, Freddy?' said the Duchess.

'Manner of speaking,' said the Hon. Freddy.

'What do you think, Mr Murbles?' inquired her ladyship.

'I feel,' said the lawyer, carefully stirring his coffee, 'that, while your intention is a very admirable one, and does you very great credit, my dear lady, yet Mr Arbuthnot is right in saying it may involve you in some – er – unpleasant publicity. Er – I have always been a sincere Christian myself, but I cannot feel that our religion demands that we should make ourselves conspicuous – er – in such very painful circumstances.'

Mr Parker reminded himself of a dictum of Lord Melbourne.

'Well, after all,' said Mrs Marchbanks, 'as Helen so rightly says, does it matter? Nobody's really got anything to be ashamed of. There has been a stupid mistake, of course, but I don't see why anybody who wants to shouldn't go to church.'

'Certainly not, certainly not, my dear,' said the Colonel heartily. 'We might look in ourselves, eh dear? Take a walk that way I mean, and come out before the sermon. I think it's a good thing. Shows *we* don't believe old Denver's done anything wrong, anyhow.'

'You forget, dear,' said his wife, 'I've promised to stay at home with Mary, poor girl.'

'Of course, of course – stupid of me,' said the Colonel. 'How is she?'

'She was very restless last night, poor child,' said the Duchess.

'Perhaps she will get a little sleep this morning. It has been a shock to her.'

'One which may prove a blessing in disguise,' said Mrs Pettigrew-Robinson.

'My dear!' said her husband.

'Wonder when we shall hear from Sir Impey,' said Colonel Marchbanks hurriedly.

'Yes, indeed,' moaned Mr Murbles. 'I am counting on his influence with the Duke.'

'Of course,' said Mrs Pettigrew-Robinson, 'he must speak out – for everybody's sake. He must say what he was doing out of doors at that time. Or, if he does not, it must be discovered. Dear me! That's what these detectives are for, aren't they?'

'That is their ungrateful task,' said Mr Parker suddenly. He had said nothing for a long time, and everybody jumped.

'There,' said Mrs Marchbanks, 'I expect you'll clear it all up in no time, Mr Parker. Perhaps you've got the real mur – the culprit up your sleeve all the time.'

'Not quite,' said Mr Parker, 'but I'll do my best to get him. Besides,' he added, with a grin, 'I'll probably have some help on the job.'

'From whom?' inquired Mr Pettigrew-Robinson.

'Her grace's brother-in-law.'

'Peter?' said the Duchess. 'Mr Parker must be amused at the family amateur,' she added.

'Not at all,' said Parker. 'Wimsey would be one of the finest detectives in England if he wasn't lazy. Only we can't get hold of him.'

'I've wired to Ajaccio – poste restante,' said Mr Murbles, 'but I don't know when he's likely to call there. He said nothing about when he was coming back to England.'

'He's a rummy old bird,' said the Hon. Freddy tactlessly, 'but he oughter be here, what? What I mean to say is, if anything happens to old Denver, don't you see, he's the head of the family, ain't he – till little Pickled Gherkins comes of age.'

In the frightful silence which followed this remark, the sound of a walking-stick being clattered into an umbrella-stand was distinctly audible.

'Who's that, I wonder,' said the Duchess.

The door waltzed open.

'Mornin', dear old things,' said the newcomer cheerfully. 'How are you all? Hullo, Helen! Colonel, you owe me half a crown since last September year. Mornin', Mrs Marchbanks, Mornin' Mrs P. Well, Mr Murbles, how d'you like this bili – beastly weather? Don't trouble to get up, Freddy; I'd simply hate to inconvenience you. Parker, old man, what a damned reliable old bird you are! Always on the spot, like that patent ointment thing. I say, have you all finished? I meant to get up earlier, but I was snorin' so Bunter hadn't the heart to wake me. I nearly blew in last night, only we didn't arrive till 2 a.m. and I thought you wouldn't half bless me if I did. Eh, what, Colonel? Aeroplane. *Victoria* from Paris to London – North-Eastern to Northallerton – damn bad roads the rest of the way, and a puncture just below Riddlesdale. Damn bad bed at the "Lord in Glory"; thought I'd blow in for the last sausage here, if I was lucky. What? Sunday morning in an English family and no sausages? God bless my soul, what's the world coming to, eh, Colonel? I say, Helen, old Gerald's been an' gone an' done it this time, what? You've no business to leave him on his own, you know; he always gets into mischief. What's that? Curry? Thanks, old man. Here I say, you needn't be so stingy about it; I've been travelling for three days on end. Freddy, pass the toast. Beg pardon, Mrs Marchbanks? Oh, rather, yes; Corsica was perfectly amazin' – all black-eyed fellows with knives in their belts and jolly fine-looking girls. Old Bunter had a regular affair with the inn-keeper's daughter in one place. D'you know, he's an awfully susceptible old beggar. You'd never think it, would you? Jove! I am hungry. I say, Helen, I meant to get you some fetchin' crêpe-de-Chine undies from Paris, but I saw that old Parker was gettin' ahead of me over the bloodstains, so we packed up our things and buzzed off.'

Mrs Pettigrew-Robinson rose.

'Theodore,' she said, 'I think we ought to be getting ready for church.'

'I will order the car,' said the Duchess. 'Peter, of course I'm exceedingly glad to see you. Your leaving no address was most inconvenient. Ring for anything you want. It is a pity you didn't arrive in time to see Gerald.'

'Oh, that's all right,' said Lord Peter cheerfully; 'I'll look him up in quod. Y'know it's rather a good idea to keep one's crimes in the family; one has so many more facilities. I'm sorry for poor old Polly, though. How is she?'

'She must not be disturbed today,' said the Duchess with decision.

'Not a bit of it,' said Lord Peter; 'she'll keep. Today Parker and I hold high revel. Today he shows me all the bloody footprints – it's all right, Helen, that's not swearin', that's an adjective of quality. I hope they aren't all washed away, are they, old thing?'

'No.' said Parker, 'I've got most of them under flower-pots.'

'Then pass the bread and squish,' said Lord Peter, 'and tell me about it.'

The departure of the church-going element had in-duced a more humanitarian atmosphere. Mrs Marchbanks stumped off upstairs to tell Mary that Peter had come, and the Colonel lit a large cigar. The Hon. Freddy rose, stretched himself, pulled a leather arm-chair to the fireside, and sat down with his feet on the brass fender, while Parker marched round and poured himself out another cup of coffee.

'I suppose you've seen the papers,' he said.

'Oh yes, I read up the inquest,' said Lord Peter. 'Y'know, if you'll excuse my saying so, I think you rather mucked it between you.'

'It was disgraceful,' said Mr Murbles, 'disgraceful. The Coroner behaved most improperly. He had no business to give such a summing-up. With a jury of ignorant country fellows, what could one expect? And the details that were allowed to come out! If I could have got here earlier—'

'I'm afraid that was partly my fault, Wimsey,' said Parker penitently. 'Craikes rather resents me. The Chief Constable at Stapley sent to us over his head, and when the message came through I ran along to the Chief and asked for the job, because I thought if there should be any misconception or difficulty, you see, you'd just as soon I tackled it as anybody else. I had a few little arrangements to make about a forgery I've been looking into, and, what with one thing and another, I didn't get off till the night express. By the time I turned up on Friday, Craikes and the Coroner were already as thick as thieves, had fixed the inquest for that morning – which was ridiculous – and arranged to produce their blessed evidence as dramatically as possible. I only had time to skim over the ground (disfigured, I'm sorry to say, by the prints of Craikes and his local ruffians), and really had nothing for the jury.'

'Cheer up,' said Wimsey. 'I'm not blaming you. Besides, it all lends excitement to the chase.'

'Fact is,' said the Hon. Freddy, 'that we ain't popular with respectable Coroners. Giddy aristocrats and immoral Frenchmen. I say, Peter, sorry you've missed Miss Lydia Cathcart. You'd have loved her. She's gone back to Golders Green and taken the body with her.'

'Oh well,' said Wimsey. 'I don't suppose there was anything abstruse about the body.'

'No,' said Parker, 'the medical evidence was all right as far as it went. He was shot through the lungs, and that's all.'

'Though, mind you,' said the Hon. Freddy, 'he didn't shoot himself. I didn't say anything, not wishin' to upset old Denver's story, but, you know, all that stuff about his bein' so upset and go-to-blazes in his manner was all my whiskers.'

'How do you know?' said Peter.

'Why, my dear man, Cathcart'n I toddled up to bed together. I was rather fed up, havin' dropped a lot on some shares, besides missin' everything I shot at in the mornin', an' lost a bet I made with the Colonel about the number of toes on the kitchen cat, an' I said to Cathcart it was a hell of a damn-fool world, or words to that effect. "Not a bit of it," he said; "it's a damn good world. I'm goin' to ask Mary for a date to-morrow, an' then we'll go and live in Paris, where they understand sex." I said somethin' or other vague, and he went off whistlin'.'

Parker looked grave. Colonel Marchbanks cleared his throat.

'Well, well,' he said, 'there's no accounting for a man like Cathcart, no accounting at all. Brought up in France, you know. Not at all like a straightforward Englishman. Always up and down, up and down! Very sad, poor fellow. Well, well, Peter, hope you and Mr Parker will find out something about it. We mustn't have poor old

39

Denver cooped up in gaol like this, you know. Awfully unpleasant for him, poor chap, and with the birds so good this year. Well, I expect you'll be making a tour of inspection, eh, Mr Parker? What do you say to shoving the balls about a bit, Freddy?'

'Right you are,' said the Hon. Freddy; 'you'll have to give me a hundred, though, Colonel.'

'Nonsense, nonsense,' said that veteran, in high good humour; 'you play an excellent game.'

Mr Murbles having withdrawn, Wimsey and Parker faced each other over the remains of the breakfast.

'Peter,' said the detective, 'I don't know if I've done the right thing by coming. If you feel—'

'Look here, old man,' said his friend earnestly, 'let's cut out the considerations of delicacy. We're goin' to work this case like any other. If anything unpleasant turns up, I'd rather you saw it than anybody else. It's an uncommonly pretty little case, on its merits, and I'm goin' to put some damn good work into it.'

'If you're sure it's all right—'

'My dear man, if you hadn't been here I'd have sent for you. Now let's get to business. Of course, *I'm* settin' off with the assumption that old Gerald didn't do it.'

'I'm sure he didn't,' agreed Parker.

'No, no,' said Wimsey, 'that isn't your line. Nothing rash about you – nothing trustful. You are expected to throw cold water on my hopes and doubt all my conclusions.'

'Right ho!' said Parker. 'Where would you like to begin?'

Peter considered. 'I think we'll start from Cathcart's bedroom,' he said.

The bedroom was of moderate size, with a single window overlooking the front door. The bed was on the right-hand side, the dressing-table before the window. On the left was the fireplace, with an arm-chair before it, and a small writing-table.

'Everything's as it was,' said Parker. 'Craikes had that much sense.'

'Yes,' said Lord Peter. 'Very well. Gerald says that when he charged Cathcart with bein' a scamp, Cathcart jumped up, nearly knockin' the table over. That's the writin'-table, then, so Cathcart was sittin' in the arm-chair. Yes, he was – and he pushed it back violently and rumpled up the carpet. See! So far, so good. Now what was he doin' there? He wasn't readin', because there's no book about, and we know that he rushed straight out of the room and never came back. Very good. Was he writin'? No; virgin sheet of blottin'-paper—'

'He might have been writing in pencil,' suggested Parker.

'That's true, old Kill-Joy, so he might. Well, if he was he shoved the paper into his pocket when Gerald came in, because it isn't here; but he didn't, because it wasn't found on his body; so he wasn't writing.'

'Unless he threw the paper away somewhere else,' said Parker. 'I haven't been all over the grounds, you know, and at the smallest computation – if we accept the shot heard by Hardraw at 11.50 as *the* shot – there's an hour and a half unaccounted for.'

'Very well. Let's say there is nothing to show he was writing. Will that do? Well, then—'

Lord Peter drew out a lens and scrutinised the surface of the armchair carefully before sitting down in it.

'Nothing helpful there,' he said. 'To proceed, Cathcart sat where I am sitting. He wasn't writing; he – you're sure this room hasn't been touched?'

'Certain.'

'Then he wasn't smoking.'

'Why not? He might have chucked the stub of a cigar or cigarette into the fire when Denver came in.'

'Not a cigarette,' said Peter, 'or we should find traces somewhere – on the floor or in the grate. That light ash blows about so. But a cigar – well, he might have smoked a cigar without leaving a sign, I suppose. But I hope he didn't.'

'Why?'

'Because, old son, I'd rather Gerald's account had some element of truth in it. A nervy man doesn't sit down to the delicate enjoyment of a cigar before bed, and cherish the ash with such scrupulous care. On the other hand, if Freddy's right and Cathcart was feelin' unusually sleek and pleased with life, that's just the sort of thing he would do.'

'Do you think Mr Arbuthnot would have invented all that, as a matter of fact?' said Parker thoughtfully. 'He doesn't strike me that way. He'd have to be imaginative and spiteful to make it up, and I really don't think he's either.'

'I know,' said Lord Peter. 'I've known old Freddy all my life, and he wouldn't hurt a fly. Besides, he simply hasn't the wits to make up any sort of a story. But what bothers me is that Gerald most certainly hasn't the wits either to invent that Adelphi drama between him and Cathcart.'

'On the other hand,' said Parker, 'if we allow for a moment that he shot Cathcart, he had an incentive to invent it. He would be trying to get his head out of the – I mean, when anything important is at stake it's wonderful how it sharpens one's wits. And the story being so far-fetched does rather suggest an unpractised story-teller.'

'True, O King. Well, you've sat on all my discoveries

so far. Never mind. My head is bloody but unbowed. Cathcart was sitting here—'

'So your brother said.'

'Curse you, *I* say he was; at least, somebody was; he's left the impression of his sit-me-down-upon on the cushion.'

'That might have been earlier in the day.'

'Rot. They were out all day. You needn't overdo this Sadducee attitude, Charles. I say Cathcart was sitting here, and – hullo! hullo!'

He leaned forward and stared into the grate.

'There's some burnt paper here, Charles.'

'I know. I was frightfully excited about that yesterday, but I found it was just the same in several of the rooms. They often let the bedroom fires go out when every-body's out during the day, and relight them about an hour before dinner. There's only the cook, housemaid, and Fleming here, you see, and they've got a lot to do with such a large party.'

Lord Peter was picking the charred fragments over.

'I can find nothing to contradict your suggestion,' he sadly said, 'and this fragment of the *Morning Post* rather confirms it. Then we can only suppose that Cathcart sat here in a brown study, doing nothing at all. That doesn't get us much further, I'm afraid.' He got up and went to the dressing-table.

'I like these tortoiseshell sets,' he said, 'and the perfume is "*Baiser du Soir*" – very nice too. New to me. I must draw Bunter's attention to it. A charming manicure set, isn't it? You know, I like being clean and neat and all that, but Cathcart was the kind of man who always impressed you as bein' just a little *too* well turned out. Poor devil! And he'll be buried at Golders Green after all. I only saw him once or twice, you know. He impressed me as knowin' about everything there was to know. I was rather surprised at Mary's takin' to him, but, then, I know really awfully little about Mary. You see, she's five years younger than me. When the war broke out she'd just left school and gone to a place in Paris, and I joined up, and she came back and did nursing and social work, so I only saw her occasionally. At that time she was rather taken up with new schemes for puttin' the world to rights and hadn't a lot to say to me. And she got hold of some pacifist fellow who was a bit of a stunner, I fancy. Then I was ill, you know, and after I got the chuck from Barbara I didn't feel much like botherin' about other people's heart-to-hearts, and then I got mixed up in the Attenbury diamond case – and the result is I know uncommonly little about my own sister. But it looks as though her taste in men had altered. I know my mother said Cathcart had charm; that means he was attractive to women, I suppose. No man can see what makes that in another man, but mother is usually right. What's become of this fellow's papers?'

'He left very little here,' replied Parker. 'There's a cheque-book on Cox's Charing Cross branch, but it's a new one and not very helpful. Apparently he only kept a small current account with them for convenience when he was in England. The cheques are mostly to self, with an occasional hotel or tailor.'

'Any pass-book?'

'I think all his important papers are in Paris. He has a flat there, near the river somewhere. We're in communication with the Paris police. He had a room in Albany. I've told them to lock it up till I get there. I thought of running up to town tomorrow.'

'Yes, you'd better. Any pocket-book?'

'Yes; here you are. About £30 in various notes, a wine-merchant's card, and a bill for a pair of riding-breeches.'

'No correspondence?'

'Not a line.'

'No,' said Wimsey, 'he was the kind, I imagine, that didn't keep letters. Much too good an instinct of self-preservation.'

'Yes. I asked the servants about his letters, as a matter of fact. They said he got a good number, but never left them about. They couldn't tell me much about the ones he wrote, because all the outgoing letters are dropped into the post-bag, which is carried down to the post-office as it is and opened there, or handed over to the postman when – or if – he calls. The general impression was that he didn't write much. The housemaid said she never found anything to speak of in the waste-paper basket.'

'Well, that's uncommonly helpful. Wait a moment. Here's his fountain-pen. Very handsome – Onoto with complete gold casing. Dear me! entirely empty. Well, I don't know that one can deduce anything from that, exactly. I don't see any pencil about, by the way. I'm inclined to think you're wrong in supposing that he was writing letters.'

'I didn't suppose anything,' said Parker mildly. 'I daresay you're right.'

Lord Peter left the dressing-table, looked through the contents of the wardrobe, and turned over the two or three books on the pedestal beside the bed.

'*La Rôtisserie de la Reine Pédauque, L'Anneau d'Améthyste, South Wind* (our young friend works out very true to type), *Chronique d'un Cadet de Coutras* (tut-tut, Charles!), *Manon Lescaut.* H'm! Is there anything else in this room I ought to look at?'

'I don't think so. Where'd you like to go now?'

'We'll follow 'em down. Wait a jiff. Who are in the other rooms? Oh yes. Here's Gerald's room. Helen's at church. In we go. Of course, this has been dusted and cleaned up, and generally ruined for purposes of observation?'

'I'm afraid so. I could hardly keep the Duchess out of her bedroom.'

'No. Here's the window Gerald shouted out of. H'm! Nothing in the grate, here, naturally – the fire's been lit since. I say, I wonder where Gerald did put that letter to – Freeborn's, I mean.'

'Nobody's been able to get a word out of him about it,' said Parker. 'Old Mr Murbles had a fearful time with him. The Duke insists simply that he destroyed it. Mr Murbles says that's absurd. So it is. If he was going to bring that sort of accusation against his sister's fiancé he'd want *some* evidence of a method in his madness, wouldn't he? Or was he one of those Roman brothers who say simply: "As the head of the family I forbid the banns and that's enough"?'

'Gerald,' said Wimsey, 'is a good, clean, decent, thorough-bred public schoolboy, and a shocking ass. But I don't think he's so mediaeval as that.'

'But if he has the letter, why not produce it?'

'Why, indeed? Letters from old college friends in Egypt aren't, as a rule, compromising.'

'You don't suppose,' suggested Parker tentatively, 'that this Mr Freeborn referred in his letter to any old – er – entanglement which your brother wouldn't wish the Duchess to know about?'

Lord Peter paused, while absently examining a row of boots.

'That's an idea,' he said. 'There were occasions – mild

ones, but Helen would make the most of them.' He whistled thoughtfully. 'Still, when it comes to the gallows—'

'Do you suppose, Wimsey, that your brother really contemplates the gallows?' asked Parker.

'I think Murbles put it to him pretty straight,' said Lord Peter.

'Quite so. But does he actually realise – imaginatively – that it is possible to hang an English peer for murder on circumstantial evidence?'

Lord Peter considered this.

'Imagination isn't Gerald's strong point,' he admitted. 'I suppose they *do* hang peers? They can't be beheaded on Tower Hill or anything?'

'I'll look it up,' said Parker; 'but they certainly hanged Earl Ferrers in 1760.'

'Did they, though?' said Lord Peter. 'Ah well, as the old pagan said of the Gospels, after all, it was a long time ago, and we'll hope it wasn't true.'

'It's true enough,' said Parker; 'and he was dissected and anatomised afterwards. But that part of the treatment is obsolete.'

'We'll tell Gerald about it,' said Lord Peter, 'and persuade him to take the matter seriously. Which are the boots he wore Wednesday night?'

'These,' said Parker, 'but the fool's cleaned them.'

'Yes,' said Lord Peter bitterly. 'M'm! a good heavy lace-up boot – the sort that sends the blood to the head.'

'He wore leggings, too,' said Parker; 'these.'

'Rather elaborate peparations for a stroll in the garden. But, as you were just going to say, the night was wet. I must ask Helen if Gerald ever suffered from insomnia.'

'I did. She said she thought not as a rule, but that he occasionally had toothache, which made him restless.'

'It wouldn't send one out of doors on a cold night, though. Well, let's get downstairs.'

They passed through the billiard-room, where the Colonel was making a sensational break, and into the small conservatory which led from it.

Lord Peter looked gloomily round at the chrysanthemums and boxes of bulbs.

'These damned flowers look jolly healthy,' he said. 'Do you mean you've been letting the gardener swarm in here every day to water 'em?'

'Yes,' said Parker apologetically, 'I did. But he's had strict orders only to walk on these mats.'

'Good,' said Lord Peter. 'Take 'em up, then, and let's get to work.'

With his lens to his eye he crawled cautiously over the floor.

'They all came through this way, I suppose,' he said.

'Yes,' said Parker. 'I've identified most of the marks. People went in and out. Here's the Duke. He comes in from outside. He trips over the body.' (Parker had opened the outer door and lifted some matting, to show a trampled patch of gravel, discoloured with blood.) 'He kneels by the body. Here are his knees and toes. Afterwards he goes into the house, through the conservatory, leaving a good impression in black mud and gravel just inside the door.'

Lord Peter squatted carefully over the marks.

'It's lucky the gravel's so soft here,' he said.

'Yes. It's just a patch. The gardener tells me it gets very trampled and messy just here owing to his coming to fill cans from the water-trough. They fill the trough up from the well every so often, and then carry the water away in cans. It got extra bad this year, and they put down fresh gravel a few weeks ago.'

'Pity they didn't extend their labours all down the path while they were about it,' grunted Lord Peter, who was balancing himself precariously on a small piece of sacking. 'Well, that bears out old Gerald so far. Here's an elephant been over this bit of box border. Who's that?'

'Oh, that's a constable. I put him at eighteen stone. He's nothing. And this rubber sole with a patch on it is Craikes. He's all over the place. This squelchy-looking thing is Mr Arbuthnot in bedroom slippers, and the goloshes are Mr Pettigrew-Robinson. We can dismiss all those. But now here, just coming over the threshold, is a woman's foot in a strong shoe. I make that out to be Lady Mary's. Here it is again, just at the edge of the well. She came out to examine the body.'

'Quite so,' said Peter; 'and then she came in again, with a few grains of red gravel on her shoes. Well, that's all right. Hullo!'

On the outer side of the conservatory were some shelves for small plants, and, beneath these, a damp and dismal bed of earth, occupied, in a sprawling and lackadaisical fashion, by stringy cactus plants and a sporadic growth of maidenhair fern, and masked by a row of large chrysanthemums in pots.

'What've you got?' inquired Parker, seeing his friend peering into this green retreat.

Lord Peter withdrew his long nose from between two pots and said 'Who put what down here?'

Parker hastened to the place. There, among the cacti, was certainly the clear mark of some oblong object, with corners, that had been stood out of sight on the earth behind the pots.

'It's a good thing Gerald's gardener ain't one of those conscientious blighters that can't even let a cactus alone for the winter,' said Lord Peter, 'or he'd've tenderly lifted these little drooping heads – oh! damn and blast the beastly plant for a crimson porcupine! *You* measure it.'

Parker measured it.

'Two and a half feet by six inches,' he said. 'And fairly heavy, for it's sunk in and broken the plants about. Was it a bar of anything?'

'I fancy not,' said Lord Peter. 'The impression is deeper on the farther side. I think it was something bulky set up on edge, and leaned against the glass. If you ask for my private opinion I should guess that it was a suitcase.'

'A suitcase!' exclaimed Parker. 'Why a suitcase?'

'Why indeed? I think we may assume that it didn't stay here very long. It would have been exceedingly visible in the daytime. But somebody might very well have shoved it in here if they were caught with it – say at three o'clock in the morning – and didn't want it to be seen.'

'Then when did they take it away?'

'Almost immediately, I should say. Before daylight, anyhow, or even Inspector Craikes could hardly have failed to see it.'

'It's not the doctor's bag, I suppose?'

'No – unless the doctor's a fool. Why put a bag inconveniently in a damp and dirty place out of the way when every law of sense and convenience would urge him to pop it down handy by the body? No. Unless Craikes or the gardener has been leaving things about, it was thrust away there on Wednesday night by Gerald, by Cathcart – or, I suppose, by Mary. Nobody else could be supposed to have anything to hide.'

'Yes,' said Parker, 'one person.'

'Who's that?'

'The Person Unknown.'

'Who's he?'

For answer Mr Parker proudly stepped to a row of

wooden frames, carefully covered with matting. Stripping this away, with the air of a bishop unveiling a memorial, he disclosed a V-shaped line of footprints.

'These,' said Parker, 'belonged to nobody – to nobody I've ever seen or heard of, I mean.'

'Hurray!' said Peter.

> '*Then downwards from the steep hill's edge*
> *They tracked the footmarks small*

(only they're largish).'

'No such luck,' said Parker. 'It's more a case of:

> '*They followed from the earthy bank*
> *Those footsteps one by one,*
> *Into the middle of the plank;*
> *And farther there were none!*'

'Great poet, Wordsworth,' said Lord Peter; 'how often I've had that feeling. Now let's see. These footmarks – a man's No. 10 with worn-down heels and a patch on the left inner side – advance from the hard bit of the path which shows no footmarks; they come to the body – here, where that pool of blood is. I say, that's rather odd, don't you think? No? Perhaps not. There are no footmarks under the body? Can't say, it's such a mess. Well, the Unknown gets so far – here's a footmark deeply pressed in. Was he just going to throw Cathcart into the well? He hears a sound; he starts; he turns; he runs on tiptoe – into the shrubbery, by Jove!'

'Yes,' said Parker, 'and the tracks come out on one of the grass paths in the wood, and there's an end of them.'

'H'm! Well, we'll follow them later. Now where did they come from?'

Together the two friends followed the path away from the house. The gravel, except for the little patch before the conservatory, was old and hard, and afforded but little trace, particularly as the last few days had been rainy. Parker, however, was able to assure Wimsey that there had been definite traces of dragging and blood-stains.

'What sort of bloodstains? Smears?'

'Yes, smears mostly. There were pebbles displaced, too, all the way – and now here is something odd.'

It was the clear impression of the palm of a man's hand heavily pressed into the earth of a herbaceous border, the fingers pointing towards the house. On the path the gravel had been scraped up in two long furrows. There was blood on the grass border between the path and the bed, and the edge of the grass was broken and trampled.

'I don't like that,' said Lord Peter.

'Ugly, isn't it?' agreed Parker.

'Poor devil!' said Peter. 'He made a determined effort to hang on here. That explains the blood by the con-servatory door. But what kind of a devil drags a corpse that isn't quite dead?'

A few yards farther the path ran into the main drive. This was bordered with trees, widening into a thicket. At the point of intersection of the two paths were some further indistinct marks, and in another twenty yards or so they turned aside into the thicket. A large tree had fallen at some time and made a little clearing, in the midst of which a tarpaulin had been carefully spread out and pegged down. The air was heavy with the smell of fungus and fallen leaves.

'Scene of the tragedy,' said Parker briefly, rolling back the tarpaulin.

Lord Peter gazed down sadly. Muffled in an overcoat and a thick grey scarf, he looked, with his long, narrow face, like a melancholy adjutant stork. The writing body of the fallen man had scraped up the dead leaves and left a depression in the sodden ground. At one place the darker earth showed where a great pool of blood had soaked into it, and the yellow leaves of Spanish poplar were rusted with no autumnal stain.

'That's where they found the handkerchief and revolver,' said Parker. 'I looked for finger-marks, but the rain and mud had messed everything up.'

Wimsey took out his lens, lay down, and conducted a personal tour of the whole space slowly on his stomach, Parker moving mutely after him.

'He paced up and down for some time,' said Lord Peter. 'He wasn't smoking. He was turning something over in his mind, or waiting for somebody. What's this? Aha! Here's our No. 10 foot again, coming in through the trees on the farther side. No signs of a struggle. That's odd! Cathcart was shot close up, wasn't he?'

'Yes; it singed his shirt-front.'

'Quite so. Why did he stand still to be shot at?'

'I imagine,' said Parker, 'that if he had an appointment with No. 10 Boots it was somebody he knew, who could get close to him without arousing suspicion.'

'Then the interview was a friendly one – on Cathcart's side, anyhow. But the revolver's a difficulty. How did No. 10 get hold of Gerald's revolver?'

'The conservatory door was open,' said Parker dubiously.

'Nobody knew about that except Gerald and Fleming,' retorted Lord Peter. 'Besides, do you mean to tell me that No. 10 walked in here, went to the study, fetched the revolver, walked back here, and shot Cathcart? It seems a clumsy method. If he wanted to do any shooting, why didn't he come armed in the first place?'

'It seems more probable that Cathcart brought the revolver,' said Parker.

'Then why no signs of a struggle?'

'Perhaps Cathcart shot himself,' said Parker.

'Then why should No. 10 drag him into a conspicuous position and then run away?'

'Wait a minute,' said Parker. 'How's this? No. 10 has an appointment with Cathcart – to blackmail him, let's say. He somehow gets word of his intention to him between 9.45 and 10.15. That would account for the alteration in Cathcart's manner, and allow both Mr Arbuthnot and the Duke to be telling the truth. Cathcart rushes violently out after his row with your brother. He comes down here to keep his appointment. He paces up and down waiting for No. 10. No. 10 arrives and parleys with Cathcart. Cathcart offers him money. No. 10 stands out for more. Cathcart says he really hasn't got it. No. 10 says in that case he blows the gaff. Cathcart retorts, "In that case you can go to the devil. I'm going there myself." Cathcart, who has previously got hold of the revolver, shoots himself. No. 10 is seized with remorse. He sees that Cathcart isn't quite dead. He picks him up and part drags, part carries him to the house. He is smaller than Cathcart and not very strong, and finds it a hard job. They have just got to the conservatory door when Cathcart has a final haemorrhage and gives up the ghost. No. 10 suddenly becomes aware that his position in somebody else's grounds, alone with a corpse at 3 a.m., wants some explaining. He drops Cathcart – and bolts. Enter the Duke of Denver and falls over the body. Tableau.'

'That's good,' said Lord Peter; 'that's very good. But when do you suppose it happened? Gerald found the body at 3 a.m.; the doctor was here at 4.30, and said Cathcart had been dead several hours. Very well. Now, how about that shot my sister heard at three o'clock?'

'Look here, old man,' said Parker, 'I don't want to appear rude to your sister. May I put it like this? I suggest that that shot at 3 a.m. was poachers.'

'Poachers by all means,' said Lord Peter. 'Well, really, Parker, I think that hangs together. Let's adopt that explanation provisionally. The first thing to do is now to find No. 10, since he can bear witness that Cathcart committed suicide; and that, as far as my brother is concerned, is the only thing that matters a rap. But for the satisfaction of my own curiosity I'd like to know: What was No. 10 blackmailing Cathcart about? Who hid a suitcase in the conservatory? And what was Gerald doing in the garden at 3 a.m.?'

'Well,' said Parker, 'suppose we begin by tracing where No. 10 came from.'

'Hi, hi!' cried Wimsey, as they returned to the trail. 'Here's something – here's real treasure-trove, Parker!'

From amid the mud and the fallen leaves he retrieved a tiny, glittering object – a flash of white and green between his finger-tips.

It was a little charm such as women hang upon a bracelet – a diminutive diamond cat with eyes of bright emerald.

3

MUDSTAINS AND BLOODSTAINS

*'Other things are all very well in their way, but give me
Blood . . . We say, "There it is! that's Blood!" It is an
actual matter of fact. We point it out. It admits of no
doubt . . . We must have blood, you know.'*

DAVID COPPERFIELD

'HITHERTO,' said Lord Peter, as they picked their painful
way through the little wood on the trail of Gent's No.
10's, 'I have always maintained that those obliging
criminals who strew their tracks with little articles of
personal adornment – here he is, on a squashed fungus –
were an invention of detective fiction for the benefit of
the author. I see that I have still something to learn about
my job.'

'Well, you haven't been at it very long, have you?' said
Parker. 'Besides, we don't know that the diamond cat is
the criminal's. It may belong to a member of your own
family, and have been lying here for days. It may belong
to Mr What's-his-name in the States, or to the last tenant
but one, and have been lying here for years. This broken
branch may be our friend – I think it is.'

'I'll ask the family,' said Lord Peter, 'and we could find
out in the village if anyone's ever inquired for a lost cat.
They're pukka stones. It ain't the sort of thing one would
drop without making a fuss about – I've lost him altogether.'

'It's all right – I've got him. He's tripped over a root.'

'Serve him glad,' said Lord Peter viciously, straightening his back. 'I say, I don't think the human frame is very thoughtfully constructed for this sleuth-hound business. If one could go on all-fours, or had eyes in one's knees, it would be a lot more practical.'

'There are many difficulties inherent in a teleological view of creation,' said Parker placidly. 'Ah! here we are at the park palings.'

'And here's where he got over,' said Lord Peter, pointing to a place where the *chevaux de frise* on the top was broken away. 'Here's the dent where his heels came down, and here's where he fell forward on hands and knees. Hum! Give us a back, old man, would you? Thanks. An old break, I see. Mr Montagne-now-in-the-States should keep his palings in better order. No. 10 tore his coat on the spikes all the same; he left a fragment of Burberry behind him. What luck! Here's a deep, damp ditch on the other side, which I shall now proceed to fall into.'

A slithering crash proclaimed that he had carried out his intention. Parker, thus callously abandoned, looked round, and, seeing that they were only a hundred yards or so from the gate, ran along and was let out, decorously, by Hardraw, the gamekeeper, who happened to be coming out of the lodge.

'By the way,' said Parker to him, 'did you ever find any signs of any poachers on Wednesday night after all?'

'Nay,' said the man, 'not so much as a dead rabbit. I reckon t'lady wor mistaken, an 'twore the shot I heard as killed t'Captain.'

'Possibly,' said Parker. 'Do you know how long the spikes have been broken off the palings over there?'

'A month or two, happen. They should 'a' bin put right, but the man's sick.'

'The gate's locked at night, I suppose?'

'Aye.'

'Anybody wishing to get in would have to waken you?'

'Aye, that he would.'

'You didn't see any suspicious character loitering about outside these palings last Wednesday, I suppose?'

'Nay, sir, but my wife may ha' done. Hey, lass!'

Mrs Hardraw, thus summoned, appeared at the door with a small boy clinging to her skirts.

'Wednesday?' said she. 'Nay, I saw no loiterin' folks. I keep a look-out for tramps and such, as it be such a lonely place. Wednesday. Eh, now, John, that wad be t'day t'young mon called wi' t'motor-bike.'

'Young man with a motor-bike?'

'I reckon 'twas. He said he'd had a puncture and asked for a bucket o' watter.'

'Was that all the asking he did?'

'He asked what were t'name o' t'place and whose house it were.'

'Did you tell him the Duke of Denver was living here?'

'Aye, sir, and he said he supposed as many gentlemen came up for t'shooting.'

'Did he say where he was going?'

'He said he'd coom oop fra' Weirdale an' were makin' a trip into Coomberland.'

'How long was he here?'

'Happen half an hour. An' then he tried to get his machine started, an' I see him hop-hoppitin' away towards King's Fenton.'

She pointed away to the right, where Lord Peter might be seen gesticulating in the middle of the road.

'What sort of a man was he?'

Like most people, Mrs Hardraw was poor at definition. She thought he was youngish and tallish, neither dark nor fair, in such a long coat as motor-bicyclists use, with a belt round it.

'Was he a gentleman?'

Mrs Hardraw hesitated, and Mr Parker mentally classed the stranger as 'Not quite quite.'

'You didn't happen to notice the number of the bicycle?'

Mrs Hardraw had not. 'But it had a side-car,' she added.

Lord Peter's gesticulations were becoming quite violent, and Mr Parker hastened to rejoin him.

'Come on, gossiping old thing,' said Lord Peter unreasonably. 'This is a beautiful ditch.

> From such a ditch as this,
> When the soft wind did gently kiss the trees
> And they did make no noise, from such a ditch
> Our friend, methinks, mounted the Troyan walls,
> And wiped hts soles upon the greasy mud.

Look at my trousers!'

'It's a bit of a climb from this side,' said Parker.

'It is. He stood here in the ditch, and put one foot into this place where the paling's broken away and one hand on the top, and hauled himself up. No. 10 must have been a man of exceptional height, strength, and agility. I couldn't get my foot up, let alone reaching the top with my hand. I'm five foot nine. Could you?'

Parker was six foot, and could just touch the top of the wall with his hand.

'I *might* do it – on one of my best days,' he said, 'for an adequate object, or after adequate stimulant.'

'Just so,' said Lord Peter. 'Hence we deduce No. 10's exceptional height and strength.'

'Yes,' said Parker. 'It's a bit unfortunate that we had to

deduce his exceptional shortness and weakness just now, isn't it?'

'Oh!' said Peter. 'Well – well, as you so rightly say, that *is* a bit unfortunate.'

'Well, it may clear up presently. He didn't have a confederate to give him a back or a leg, I suppose?'

'Not unless the confederate was a being without feet or any visible means of support,' said Peter, indicating the solitary print of a pair of patched 10s. 'By the way, how did he make straight in the dark for the place where the spikes were missing? Looks as though he belonged to the neighbourhood, or had reconnoitered previously.'

'Arising out of that reply,' said Parker, 'I will now relate to you the entertaining "gossip" I have had with Mrs Hardraw.'

'Humph!' said Wimsey at the end of it. 'That's interesting. We'd better make inquiries at Riddlesdale and King's Fenton. Meanwhile we know where No. 10 came from; now where did he go after leaving Cathcart's body by the well?'

'The footsteps went into the preserve,' said Parker. 'I lost them there. There is a regular carpet of dead leaves and bracken.'

'Well, but we needn't go through all that sleuth grind again,' objected his friend. 'The fellow went in, and, as he presumably is not there still, he came out again. He didn't come out through the gate or Hardraw would have seen him; he didn't come out the same way he went in or he would have left some traces. Therefore he came out elsewhere. Let's walk round the wall.'

'Then we'll turn to the left,' said Parker, 'since that's the side of the preserve, and he apparently went through there.'

'True, O King! and as this isn't a church, there's no

harm in going round it widdershins. Talking of church, there's Helen coming back. Get a move on, old thing.'

They crossed the drive, passed the cottage, and then, leaving the road, followed the paling across some open grass fields. It was not long before they found what they sought. From one of the iron spikes above them dangled forlornly a strip of material. With Parker's assistance Wimsey scrambled up in a state of almost lyric excitement.

'Here we are,' he cried. 'The belt of a Burberry! No sort of precaution here. Here are the toe-prints of a fellow sprinting for his life. He tore off his Burberry! he made desperate leaps – one, two, three – at the palings. At the third leap he hooked it on to the spikes. He scrambled up, scoring long, scrabbling marks on the paling. He reached the top. Oh, here's a blood-stain run into this crack. He tore his hands. He dropped off. He wrenched the coat away, leaving the belt dangling—'

'I wish you'd drop off,' grumbled Parker. 'You're breaking my collar-bone.'

Lord Peter dropped off obediently, and stood there holding the belt between his fingers. His narrow grey eyes wandered restlessly over the field. Suddenly he seized Parker's arm and marched briskly in the direction of the wall on the farther side – a low erection of unmortared stone in the fashion of the country. Here he hunted along like a terrier, nose foremost, the tip of his tongue caught absurdly between his teeth, then jumped over, and, turning to Parker, said:

'Did you ever read *The Lay of the Last Minstrel*?'

'I learnt a good deal of it at school,' said Parker. 'Why?'

'Because there was a goblin page-boy in it,' said Lord Peter, 'who was always yelling "Found! Found! Found!"

at the most unnecessary moments. I always thought him a terrible nuisance, but now I know how he felt. See here.'

Close under the wall, and sunk heavily into the narrow and muddy lane which ran up here at right angles to the main road, was the track of a side-car combination.

'Very nice too,' said Mr Parker approvingly. 'New Dunlop tyre on the front wheel. Old tyre on the back. Gaiter on the side-car tyre. Nothing could be better. Tracks come in from the road and go back to the road. Fellow shoved the machine in here in case anybody of an inquisitive turn of mind should pass on the road and make off with it, or take its number. Then he went round on shank's mare to the gap he'd spotted in the daytime and got over. After the Cathcart affair he took fright, bolted into the preserve, and took the shortest way to his bus, regardless. Well, now.'

He sat down on the wall, and drawing out his note-book, began to jot down a description of the man from the data already known.

'Things begin to look a bit more comfortable for old Jerry,' said Lord Peter. He leaned on the wall and began whistling softly, but with great accuracy, that elaborate passage of Bach which begins 'Let Zion's children'.

'I wonder,' said the Hon. Freddy Arbuthnot, 'what damn silly fool invented Sunday afternoon.'

He shovelled coals on to the library fire with a vicious clatter, waking Colonel Marchbanks, who said, 'Eh? Yes, quite right,' and fell asleep again instantly.

'Don't *you* grumble, Freddy,' said Lord Peter, who had been occupied for some time in opening and shutting all the drawers of the writing-table in a thoroughly irritating manner, and idly snapping to and fro the catch of the

French window. 'Think how dull old Jerry must feel. S'pose I'd better write him a line.'

He returned to the table and took a sheet of paper. 'Do people use this room much to write letters in, do you know?'

'No idea,' said the Hon. Freddy. 'Never write 'em myself. Where's the point of writin' when you can wire? Encourages people to write back, that's all. I think Denver writes here when he writes anywhere, and I saw the Colonel wrestlin' with pen and ink a day or two ago, didn't you, Colonel?' (The Colonel grunted, answering to his name like a dog that wags its tail in its sleep.) 'What's the matter? Ain't there any ink?'

'I only wondered,' replied Peter placidly. He slipped a paper-knife under the top sheet of the blotting-pad and held it up to the light. 'Quite right, old man. Give you full marks for observation. Here's Jerry's signature, and the Colonel's, and a big, sprawly hand, which I should judge to be feminine.' He looked at the sheet again, shook his head, folded it up, and placed it in his pocket-book, 'Doesn't seem to be anything there,' he commented, 'but you never know. "Five something of fine something" – grouse, probably! "oe – is fou" – is found, I suppose. Well, it can't do any harm to keep it.' He spread out his paper and began:

'DEAR JERRY, – Here I am, the family sleuth on the trail, and it's damned exciting—'

The Colonel snored.

Sunday afternoon. Parker had gone with the car to King's Fenton, with orders to look in at Riddlesdale on the way and inquire for a green-eyed cat, also for a young man with a side-car. The Duchess was lying down. Mrs Pettigrew-Robinson had taken her husband for a brisk walk. Upstairs, somewhere, Mrs Marchbanks enjoyed a perfect communion of thought with her husband.

Lord Peter's pen gritted gently over the paper, stopped, moved on again, stopped altogether. He leaned his long chin on his hands and stared out of the window, against which there came sudden little swishes of rain, and from time to time a soft, dead leaf. The Colonel snored; the fire tinkled; the Hon. Freddy began to hum and tap his fingers on the arms of his chair. The clock moved slothfully on to five o'clock, which brought tea-time and the Duchess.

'How's Mary?' asked Lord Peter, coming suddenly into the fire-light.

'I'm really worried about her,' said the Duchess. 'She is giving way to her nerves in the strangest manner. It is so unlike her. She will hardly let anybody come near her. I have sent for Dr Thorpe again.'

'Don't you think she'd be better if she got up an' came downstairs a bit?' suggested Wimsey. 'Gets broodin' about things all by herself, I shouldn't wonder. Wants a bit of Freddy's intellectual conversation to cheer her up.'

'You forget; poor girl,' said the Duchess, 'she was engaged to Captain Cathcart. Everybody isn't as callous as you are.'

'Any more letters, your grace?' asked the footman, appearing with the post-bag.

'Oh, are you going down now?' said Wimsey. 'Yes, here you are – and there's one other, if you don't mind waitin' a minute while I write it. Wish I could write at the rate people do on the cinema,' he added, scribbling rapidly as he spoke. ' "DEAR LILIAN – Your father has killed Mr William Snooks, and unless you send me £1,000 by bearer, I shall disclose all to your husband.

– Sincerely, EARL OF DIGGLESBRAKE". That's the style; and all done in one scrape of the pen. Here you are, Fleming.'

The letter was addressed to her grace the Dowager Duchess of Denver.

From the *Morning Post* of Monday, November –, 19–

'ABANDONED MOTOR-CYCLE

'A singular discovery was made yesterday by a cattle-drover. He is accustomed to water his animals in a certain pond lying a little off the road about twelve miles south of Ripley. On this occasion he saw that one of them appeared to be in difficulties. On going to the rescue, he found the animal entangled in a motor-cycle, which had been driven into the pond and abandoned. With the assistance of a couple of workmen he extricated the machine. It is a Douglas, with dark-grey side-car. The number-plates and licence-holder have been carefully removed. The pond is a deep one, and the outfit was entirely submerged. It seems probable, however, that it could not have been there for more than a week, since the pond is much used on Sundays and Mondays for the watering of cattle. The police are making search for the owner. The front tyre of the bicycle is a new Dunlop, and the side-car tyre has been repaired with a gaiter. The machine is a 1914 model, much worn.'

'That seems to strike a chord,' said Lord Peter musingly. He consulted a time-table for the time of the next train to Ripley, and ordered the car.

'And send Bunter to me,' he added.

That gentleman arrived just as his master was struggling into an overcoat.

'What was that thing in last Thursday's paper about a number-plate, Bunter?' inquired his lordship.

Mr Bunter produced, apparently by legerdemain, a cutting from an evening paper:

'Number-plate Mystery

'The Rev. Nathaniel Foulis, of St. Simon's, North Fellcote, was stopped at six o'clock this morning for riding a motor-cycle without number-plates. The reverend gentleman seemed thunderstruck when his attention was called to the matter. He explained that he had been sent for in great haste at 4 a.m. to administer the Sacrament to a dying parishioner six miles away. He hastened out on his motor-cycle, which he confidingly left by the roadside while executing his sacred duties. Mr Foulis left the house at 5.30 without noticing that anything was wrong. Mr Foulis is well known in North Fellcote and the surrounding country, and there seems little doubt that he has been the victim of a senseless practical joke. North Fellcote is a small village a couple of miles north of Ripley.'

'I'm going to Ripley, Bunter,' said Lord Peter.

'Yes, my lord. Does your lordship require me?'

'No,' said Lord Peter, 'but – who has been lady's maiding my sister, Bunter?'

'Ellen, my lord – the housemaid.'

'Then I wish you'd exercise your powers of conversation on Ellen.'

'Very good, my lord.'

'Does she mend my sister's clothes, and brush her skirts, and all that?'

'I believe so, my lord.'

'Nothing she may think is of any importance, you know, Bunter.'

'I wouldn't suggest such a thing to a woman, my lord. It goes to their heads, if l may say so.'

'When did Mr Parker leave for town?'

'At six o'clock this morning, my lord.'

Circumstances favoured Mr Bunter's inquiries. He bumped into Ellen as she was descending the back stairs with an armful of clothing. A pair of leather gauntlets was jerked from the top of the pile, and, picking them up, he apologetically followed the young woman into the servants' hall.

'There,' said Ellen, flinging her burden on the table, 'and the work I've had to get them, I'm sure. Tantrums, that's what I call it, pretending you've got such a headache you can't let a person into the room to take your things down to brush, and, as soon as they're out of the way, 'opping out of bed and trapesing all over the place. 'Tisn't what I call a headache, would you, now? But there! I daresay you don't get them like I do. Regular fit to split, my head is sometimes – couldn't keep on my feet, not if the house was burning down. I just have to lay down and keep laying – something cruel it is. And gives a person such wrinkles in one's forehead.'

'I'm sure I don't see any wrinkles,' said Mr Bunter, 'but perhaps I haven't looked hard enough.' An interlude followed, during which Mr Bunter looked hard enough and close enough to distinguish wrinkles. 'No,' said he, 'wrinkles? I don't believe I'd see any if I was to take his lordship's big microscope he keeps up in town.'

'Lor' now, Mr Bunter,' said Ellen, fetching a sponge and a bottle of benzine from the cupboard, 'what would his lordship be using a thing like that for, now?'

'Why, in our hobby, you see, Miss Ellen, which is criminal investigation, we might want to see something magnified extra big – as it might be handwriting in a forgery case, to see if anything's been altered or rubbed out, or if different kinds of ink have been used. Or we might want to look at the roots of a lock of hair, to see if it's been torn out or fallen out. Or take bloodstains, now; we'd want to know if it was animal's blood or human blood, or maybe only a glass of port.'

'Now is it really true, Mr Bunter,' said Ellen, laying a tweed skirt out upon the table and unstoppering the benzine, 'that you and Lord Peter can find out all that?'

'Of course, we aren't analytical chemists,' Mr Bunter replied, 'but his lordship's dabbled in a lot of things – enough to know when anything looks suspicious, and if we've any doubts we send to a very famous scientific gentleman.' (He gallantly intercepted Ellen's hand as it approached the skirt with a benzine-soaked sponge.) 'For instance, now, here's a stain on the hem of this skirt, just at the bottom of the side-seam. Now, supposing it was a case of murder, we'll say, and the person that had worn this skirt was suspected, I should examine that stain.' (Here Mr Bunter whipped a lens out of his pocket.) 'Then I might try it at one edge with a wet handkerchief.' (He suited the action to the word.) 'And I should find, you see, that it came off red. Then I should turn the skirt inside-out, I should see that the stain went right through, and I should take my scissors' (Mr Bunter produced a small, sharp pair) 'and snip off a tiny bit of the inside edge of the seam, like this' (he did so) 'and pop it into a little pill-box, so' (the pill-box appeared magically from an inner pocket), 'and seal it up both sides with a wafer, and write on the top "Lady Mary Wimsey's skirt," and the date. Then I should send it straight off to the analytical gentleman in London, and he'd look through his microscope, and tell me right off that it was rabbit's blood, maybe, and how many days it had been there, and that would be the end of that,' finished Mr Bunter triumphantly, replacing his nail-scissors and thoughtlessly pocketing the pill-box with its contents.

'Well, he'd be wrong, then,' said Ellen, with an engaging toss of the head, 'because it's bird's blood, and not rabbit's at all, because her ladyship told me so; and wouldn't it be quicker just to go and ask the person than get fiddling round with your silly old microscope and things?'

'Well, I only mentioned rabbits for an example,' said Mr Bunter. 'Funny she should have got a stain down there. Must have regularly knelt in it.'

'Yes. Bled a lot, hasn't it, poor thing? Somebody must 'a' been shootin' careless-like. 'Twasn't his grace, nor yet the Captain, poor man. Perhaps it was Mr Arbuthnot. He shoots a bit wild sometimes. It's a nasty mess, anyway, and it's so hard to clean off, being left so long. I'm sure I wasn't thinking about cleaning nothing the day the poor Captain was killed; and then the Coroner's inquest – 'orrid, it was – and his grace being took off like that! Well, there, it upsets me. I suppose I'm a bit sensitive. Anyhow, we was all at sixes and sevens for a day or two, and then her ladyship shuts herself up in her room and won't let me go near the wardrobe. "Ow !" she says, "do leave that wardrobe door alone. Don't you know it squeaks, and my head's so bad and my nerves so bad I can't stand it," she says. "I was only going to brush your skirts, my lady", I says. "Bother my skirts", says her ladyship, "and do go away, Ellen. I shall scream if I see you fidgeting about there. You get on my nerves", she says, Well, I didn't see why I should go on, not after being spoken to like that. It's very nice to be a ladyship, and all your tempers coddled and called nervous prostration. I know I was dreadfully cut up about poor Bert, my young man what was killed in the war – nearly cried my eyes out, I did; but, law! Mr Bunter, I'd be ashamed to go on so. Besides, between you and I and the gate-post, Lady Mary wasn't that fond of the Captain. Never appreciated him, that's what I said to cook at the time, and she agreed with me. He had a way with him, the Captain had. Always quite the gentleman, of course, and never said anything as wasn't his place – I don't mean that – but I mean as it was a pleasure to do anythink for him. Such a handsome man as he was, too, Mr Bunter.'

'Ah!' said Mr Bunter. 'So on the whole her ladyship was a bit more upset than you expected her to be?'

'Well, to tell you the truth, Mr Bunter, I think it's just temper. She wanted to get married and away from home. Drat this stain! It's regular dried in. She and his grace could never get on, and when he was away in London during the war she had a rare old time, nursing officers, and going about with all kinds of queer people his grace didn't approve of. Then she had some sort of a love-affair with some quite low-down sort of fellow, so cook says; I think he was one of them dirty Russians as wants to blow us all to smithereens – as if there hadn't been enough people blown up in the war already! Anyhow, his grace made a dreadful fuss, and stopped supplies, and sent for her ladyship home, and ever since then she's been just mad to be off with somebody. Full of notions, she is. Makes me tired, I can tell you. Now, I'm sorry for his grace. I can see what he thinks. Poor gentleman! And then to be taken up for murder and put in gaol, just like one of them nasty tramps. Fancy!'

Ellen, having exhausted her breath and finished cleaning off the bloodstains, paused and straightened her back.

'Hard work it is,' she said, 'rubbing; I quite ache.'

'If you would allow me to help you,' said Mr Bunter, appropriating the hot water, the benzine bottle, and the sponge.

He turned up another breadth of the skirt.

'Have you got a brush handy,' he asked, 'to take this mud off?'

'You're as blind as a bat, Mr Bunter,' said Ellen, giggling. 'Can't you see it just in front of you?'

'Ah yes,' said the valet. 'But that's not as hard a one as I'd like. Just you run and get me a real hard one, there's a dear good girl, and I'll fix this for you.'

'Cheek!' said Ellen. 'But,' she added, relenting before the admiring gleam in Mr Bunter's eye, 'I'll get the clothesbrush out of the hall for you. That's as hard as a brick-bat, that is.'

No sooner was she out of the room than Mr Bunter produced a pocket-knife and two more pill-boxes. In a twinkling of an eye he had scraped the surface of the skirt in two places and written two fresh labels:

'Gravel from Lady Mary's skirt, about 6 in. from hem.'

'Silver sand from hem of Lady Mary's skirt.'

He added the date, and had hardly pocketed the boxes when Ellen returned with the clothes-brush. The cleaning process continued for some time, to the accompaniment of desultory conversation. A third stain on the skirt caused Mr Bunter to stare critically.

'Hullo!' he said. 'Her ladyship's been trying her hand at cleaning this herself.'

'What?' cried Ellen. She peered closely at the mark, which at one edge was smeared and whitened, and had a slightly greasy appearance.

'Well, I never,' she exclaimed, 'so she has! Whatever's

that for, I wonder? And her pretending to be so ill, she couldn't raise her head off the pillow. She's a sly one, she is.'

'Couldn't it have been done before?' suggested Mr Bunter.

'Well, she might have been at it between the day the Captain was killed and the inquest,' agreed Ellen, 'though you wouldn't think that was a time to choose to begin learning domestic work. *She* ain't much hand at it, anyhow, for all her nursing. I never believed that came to anything.'

'She's used soap,' said Mr Bunter, benzining away resolutely. 'Can she boil water in her bedroom?'

'Now, whatever should she do that for, Mr Bunter?' exclaimed Ellen, amazed. 'You don't think she keeps a kettle? I bring up her morning tea. Ladyships don't want to boil water.'

'No,' said Mr Bunter, 'and why didn't she get it from the bathroom?' He scrutinised the stain more carefully still. 'Very amateurish,' he said; 'distinctly amateurish. Interrupted, I fancy. An energetic young lady, but not ingenious.'

The last remarks were addressed in confidence to the benzine bottle. Ellen had put her head out of the window to talk to the gamekeeper.

The Police Superintendent at Ripley received Lord Peter at first frigidly, and later, when he found out who he was, with a mixture of the official attitude to private detectives and the official attitude to a Duke's son.

'I've come to you,' said Wimsey, 'because you can do this combin'-out business a sight better'n an amateur like myself. I suppose your fine organisation's hard at work already, what?'

'Naturally,' said the Superintendent, 'but it's not altogether easy to trace a motor-cycle without knowing the number. Look at the Bournemouth Murder.' He shook his head regretfully and accepted a Villar y Villar.

'We didn't think at first of connecting him with the number-plate business,' the Superintendent went on in a careless tone which somehow conveyed to Lord Peter that his own remarks within the last half hour had established the connection in the official mind for the first time. 'Of course, if he'd been seen going through Ripley *without* a number-plate he'd have been noticed and stopped, whereas with Mr Foulis's he was as safe as – as the Bank of England,' he concluded in a burst of originality.

'Obviously,' said Wimsey. 'Very agitatin' for the parson, poor chap. So early in the mornin', too. I suppose it was just taken to be a practical joke?'

'Just that,' agreed the Superintendent, 'but, after hearing what you have to tell us, we shall use our best efforts to get the man. I expect his grace won't be any too sorry to hear he's found. You may rely on us, and if we find the man or the number-plates—'

'Lord bless us and save us, man,' broke in Lord Peter with unexpected vivacity, 'you're not goin' to waste your time lookin' for the number-plates. What d'you s'pose he'd pinch the curate's plates for if he wanted to advertise his own about the neighbourhood? Once you drop on them you've got his name and address; s'long as they're in his trousers pocket you're up a gum-tree. Now, forgive me, Superintendent, for shovin' along with my opinion, but I simply can't bear to think of you takin' all that trouble for nothin' – draggin' ponds an' turnin' over rubbish-heaps to look for number-plates that ain't there. You just scour the railway stations for a young man six foot one or two with a No. 10 shoe, and dressed in a Burberry that's lost its belt, and with a deep scratch on one of his hands. And look here, here's my address, and I'll be very grateful if you'll let me know anything that turns up. So awkward for my brother, y'know, all this. Sensitive man; feels it keenly. By the way, I'm a very uncertain bird – always hoppin' about; you might wire me any news in duplicate, to Riddlesdale and to town – 110 Piccadilly. Always delighted to see you, by the way, if ever you're in town. You'll forgive me slopin' off now, won't you? I've got a lot to do.'

Returning to Riddlesdale, Lord Peter found a new visitor seated at the tea-table. At Peter's entry he rose into towering height, and extended a shapely, expressive hand that would have made an actor's fortune. He was not an actor, but he found this hand useful, nevertheless, in the exploitation of dramatic moments. His magnificent build and the mobility of his head and mask were impressive; his features were flawless; his eyes ruthless. The Dowager Duchess had once remarked: 'Sir Impey Biggs is the handsomest man in England, and no woman will ever care twopence for him.' He was, in fact, thirty-eight, and a bachelor, and was celebrated for his rhetoric and his suave but pitiless dissection of hostile witnesses. The breeding of canaries was his unexpected hobby, and besides their song he could appreciate no music but revue airs. He answered Wimsey's greeting in his beautiful, resonant, and exquisitely controlled voice. Tragic irony, cutting contempt, or a savage indignation were the emotions by which Sir Impey Biggs swayed court and jury; he prosecuted murderers of the innocent, defended in actions for criminal libel, and, moving others, was himself as stone. Wimsey expressed himself delighted to see him in a voice, by contrast, more husky and hesitant even than usual.

'You just come from Jerry?' he asked. 'Fresh toast, please, Fleming. How is he? Enjoyin' it? I never knew a fellow like Jerry for gettin' the best possible out of any situation. I'd rather like the experience myself, you know; only I'd hate bein' shut up and watchin' the other idiots bunglin' my case. No reflection on Murbles and you, Biggs. I mean myself – I mean the man who'd be me if I was Jerry. You follow me?'

'I was just saying to Sir Impey,' said the Duchess, 'that he really must make Gerald say what he was doing in the garden at three in the morning. If only I'd been at Riddlesdale none of this would have happened. Of course, *we* all know that he wasn't doing any harm, but we can't expect the jurymen to understand that. The lower orders are so prejudiced. It is absurd of Gerald not to realise that he must speak out. He has *no* consideration.'

'I am doing my very best to persuade him, Duchess,' said Sir Impey, 'but you must have patience. Lawyers enjoy a little mystery, you know. Why, if everybody came forward and told the truth, the whole truth, and nothing but the truth straight out, we should all retire to the workhouse.'

'Captain Cathcart's death is very mysterious,' said the Duchess, 'though when I think of the things that have come out about him it really seems quite providential, as far as my sister-in-law is concerned.'

'I s'pose you couldn't get 'em to bring it in "Death by the Visitation of God," could you, Biggs?' suggested Lord Peter. 'Sort of judgement for wantin' to marry into our family, what?'

'I have known less reasonable verdicts,' returned Biggs drily. 'It's wonderful what you can suggest to a jury if you try. I remember once at the Liverpool Assizes—'

He steered skilfully away into a quiet channel of

reminiscence. Lord Peter watched his statuesque profile against the fire; it reminded him of the severe beauty of the charioteer of Delphi and was about as communicative.

It was not until after dinner that Sir Impey opened his mind to Wimsey. The Duchess had gone to bed, and the two men were alone in the library. Peter, scrupulously in evening dress, had been valeted by Bunter, and had been more than usually rambling and cheerful all evening. He now took a cigar, retired to the largest chair, and effaced himself in a complete silence.

Sir Impey Biggs walked up and down for some halfhour, smoking. Then he came across with determination, brutally switched on a reading-lamp right into Peter's face, sat down opposite to him, and said:

'Now, Wimsey, I want to know all you know.'

'Do you, though?' said Peter. He got up, disconnected the reading-lamp, and carried it away to a side-table.

'No bullying of the witness, though,' he added, and grinned.

'I don't care so long as you wake up,' said Biggs, unperturbed. 'Now then.'

Lord Peter removed his cigar from his mouth, considered it with his head on one side, turned it carefully over, decided that the ash could hang on to its parent leaf for another minute or two, smoked without speaking until collapse was inevitable, took the cigar out again, deposited the ash entire in the exact centre of the ashtray, and began his statement, omitting only the matter of the suitcase and Bunter's information obtained from Ellen.

Sir Impey Biggs listened with what Peter irritably described as a cross-examining countenance, putting a sharp question every now and again. He made a few notes, and, when Wimsey had finished, sat tapping his note-book thoughtfully.

'I think we can make a case out of this,' he said, 'even if the police don't find your mysterious man. Denver's silence is an awkward complication, of course.' He hooded his eyes for a moment. 'Did you say you'd put the police on to find the fellow?'

'Yes.'

'Have you a very poor opinion of the police?'

'Not for that kind of thing. That's in their line; they have all the facilities, and do it well.'

'Ah! You expect to find the man, do you?'

'I hope to.'

'Ah! What do you think is going to happen to my case if you *do* find him, Wimsey?'

'What do I—'

'See here, Wimsey,' said the barrister, 'you are not a fool, and it's no use trying to look like a country police-man. You are really trying to find this man?'

'Certainly.'

'Just as you like, of course, but my hands are rather tied already. Has it ever occurred to you that perhaps he'd better not be found?'

Wimsey stared at the lawyer with such honest astonishment as actually to disarm him.

'Remember this,' said the latter earnestly, 'that if once the police get hold of a thing or a person it's no use relying on my, or Murble's, or anybody's professional discretion. Everything's raked out into the light of common day, and very common it is. Here's Denver accused of murder, and he refuses in the most categorical way to give me the smallest assistance.'

'Jerry's an ass. He doesn't realise—'

'Do you suppose,' broke in Biggs, 'I have not made it my business to *make* him realise? All he says is, "They can't hang me; I didn't kill the man, though I think it's a jolly good thing he's dead. It's no business of theirs what I was doing in the garden." Now I ask you, Wimsey, is that a reasonable attitude for a man in Denver's position to take up?'

Peter muttered something about 'Never had any sense.'

'Had anybody told Denver about this other man?'

'Something vague was said about footsteps at the inquest, I believe.'

'That Scotland Yard man is your personal friend, I'm told?'

'Yes.'

'So much the better. He can hold his tongue.'

'Look here, Biggs, this is all damned impressive and mysterious, but what are you gettin' at? Why shouldn't I lay hold of the beggar if I can?'

'I'll answer that question by another.' Sir Impey leaned forward a little. 'Why is Denver screening him?'

Sir Impey Biggs was accustomed to boast that no witness could perjure himself in his presence undetected. As he put the question, he released the other's eyes from his, and glanced down with finest cunning at Wimsey's long, flexible mouth and nervous hands. When he glanced up again a second later he met the eyes passing, guarded and inscrutable, through all the changes expressive of surprised enlightenment; but by that time it was too late; he had seen a little line at the corner of the mouth fade out, and the fingers relax ever so slightly. The first movement had been one of relief.

'B'Jove!' said Peter, 'I never thought of that. What sleuths you lawyers are. If that's so, I'd better be careful, hadn't I? Always was a bit rash. My mother says—'

'You're a clever devil, Wimsey,' said the barrister. 'I may be wrong, then. Find your man by all means. There's just one other thing I'd like to ask. Whom are *you* screening?'

'Look here, Biggs,' said Wimsey, 'you're not paid to ask that kind of question here, you know. You can jolly well wait till you get into court. It's your job to make the best of the stuff we serve up to you, not to give us the third degree. Suppose I murdered Cathcart myself—'

'You didn't.'

'I know I didn't, but if I did I'm not goin' to have you askin' questions and lookin' at me in that tone of voice. However, just to oblige you, I don't mind sayin' plainly that I don't know who did away with the fellow. When I do I'll tell you.'

'You will?'

'Yes, I will, but not till I'm sure. You people can make such a little circumstantial evidence go such a damn long way, you might hang me while I was only in the early stages of suspectin' myself.'

'H'm!' said Biggs. 'Meanwhile, I tell you candidly, I am taking the line that they can't make out a case.'

'Not proven, eh? Well, anyhow, Biggs, I swear my brother shan't hang for lack of my evidence.'

'Of course not,' said Biggs, adding inwardly: 'but you hope it won't come to that.'

A spurt of rain splashed down the wide chimney and sizzled on the logs.

> 'Craven Hotel,
> 'Strand, WC.,
> *'Tuesday*.

'MY DEAR WIMSEY, – A line as I promised, to report progress, but it's precious little. On the journey up I sat next to Mrs Pettigrew-Robinson, and opened and shut the window for her and looked after her parcels. She mentioned that when your sister roused the household on Thursday morning she went first to Mr Arbuthnot's room – a circumstance which the lady seemed to think odd, but which is natural enough when you come to think of it, the room being directly opposite the head of the staircase. It was Mr Arbuthnot who knocked up the Pettigrew-Robinsons, and Mr P. ran downstairs immediately. Mrs P. then saw that Lady Mary was looking very faint, and tried to support her. Your sister threw her off – rudely, Mrs P. says – declined "in a most savage manner" all offers of assistance, rushed to her own room, and locked herself in. Mrs Pettigrew-Robinson listened at the door "to make sure," as she says, "that everything was all right," but, hearing her moving about and slamming cupboards, she concluded that she would have more chance of poking her finger into the pie downstairs, and departed.

'If Mrs Marchbanks had told me this, I admit I should have thought the episode worth looking into, but I feel strongly that if I were dying I should still lock the door between myself and Mrs Pettigrew-Robinson. Mrs P. was quite sure that at no time had Lady Mary anything in her hand. She was dressed as described at the inquest – a long coat over her pyjamas (sleeping suit was Mrs P.'s expression), stout shoes, and a woolly cap, and she kept these garments on throughout the subsequent visit of the doctor. Another odd little circumstance is that Mrs Pettigrew-Robinson (who was awake, you remember, from 2 a.m. onwards) is certain that just *before* Lady Mary knocked on Mr Arbuthnot's door she heard a door slam somewhere in the passage. I don't know what to make of this – perhaps there's nothing in it, but I just mention it.

'I've had a rotten time in town. Your brother-in-law-elect was a model of discretion. His room in Albany is a desert from a detecting point of view; no papers except a few English bills and receipts, and invitations. I looked up a few of his inviters, but they were mostly men who had met him at the club or knew him in the Army, and could tell me nothing about his private life. He is known at several night-clubs. I made the round of them last night – or, rather, this morning. General verdict: generous but impervious. By the way, poker seems to have been his great game. No suggestion of anything crooked. He won pretty consistently on the whole, but never very spectacularly.

'I think the information we want must be in Paris. I have written to the Sûreté and the Crédit Lyonnais to produce his papers, especially his account and cheque-book.

'I'm pretty dead with yesterday's and today's work. Dancing all night on top of a journey is a jolly poor joke. Unless you want me, I'll wait here for the papers, or I may run over to Paris myself.

'Cathcart's books here consist of a few modern French novels of the usual kind, and another copy of *Manon* with what the catalogues call "curious" plates. He must have had a life somewhere, mustn't he?

'The enclosed bill from a beauty specialist in Bond Street may interest you. I called on her. She says he came regularly every week when he was in England.

'I drew quite blank at King's Fenton on Sunday – oh, but I told you that. I don't think the fellow ever went there. I wonder if he slunk off up into the moor. Is it worth rummaging about, do you think? Rather like looking for a needle in a bundle of hay. It's odd about that diamond cat. You've got nothing out of the household, I suppose? It doesn't seem to fit No. 10, somehow – and yet you'd think somebody would have heard about it in the village if it had been lost. Well, so long,

'Yours ever,

'CH. PARKER.'

4

– AND HIS DAUGHTER, MUCH-AFRAID

'The women also looked pale and wan.'
THE PILGRIM'S PROGRESS

MR BUNTER brought Parker's letter up to Lord Peter in bed on the Wednesday morning. The house was almost deserted, everybody having gone to attend the police-court proceedings at Northallerton. The thing would be purely formal, of course, but it seemed only proper that the family should be fully represented. The Dowager Duchess, indeed, was there – she had promptly hastened to her son's side and was living heroically in furnished lodgings, but the younger Duchess thought her mother-in-law more energetic than dignified. There was no knowing what she might do if left to herself. She might even give an interview to a newspaper reporter. Besides, at these moments of crisis a wife's right place is at her husband's side. Lady Mary was ill, and nothing could be said about that, and if Peter chose to stay smoking cigarettes in his pyjamas while his only brother was undergoing public humiliation, that was only what might be expected. Peter took after his mother. How that eccentric strain had got into the family her grace could easily guess; the Dowager came of a good Hampshire family, but there was foreign blood at the roots of her family tree. Her own duty was clear, and she would do it.

Lord Peter was awake, and looked rather fagged, as though he had been sleuthing in his sleep. Mr Bunter wrapped him solicitously in a brilliant Oriental robe, and placed the tray on his knees.

'Bunter,' said Lord Peter rather fretfully, 'your *café au lait* is the one tolerable incident in this beastly place.'

'Thank you, my lord. Very chilly again this morning, my lord, but not actually raining.'

Lord Peter frowned over his letter.

'Anything in the paper, Bunter?'

'Nothing urgent, my lord. A sale next week at Northbury Hall – Mr Fleetwhite's library, my lord – a Caxton *Confession Amantis*—'

'What's the good of tellin' me that when we're stuck up here for God knows how long? I wish to heaven I'd stuck to books and never touched crime. Did you send those specimens up to Lubbock?'

'Yes, my lord,' said Bunter gently. Dr Lubbock was the 'analytical gentleman.'

'Must have facts,' said Lord Peter, 'facts. When I was a small boy I always hated facts. Thought of 'em as nasty, hard things, all knobs. Uncompromisin'.'

'Yes, my lord. My old mother—'

'Your mother, Bunter? I didn't know you had one. I always imagined you were turned out ready-made so to speak. 'Scuse me. Infernally rude of me. Beg your pardon, I'm sure.'

'Not at all, my lord. My mother lives in Kent, my lord, near Maidstone. Seventy-five, my lord, and an extremely active woman for her years, if you'll excuse my mentioning it. I was one of seven.'

'That is an invention, Bunter. I know better. You are unique. But I interrupted you. You were goin' to tell me about your mother.'

'She always says, my lord, that facts are like cows. If

84

you look them in the face hard enough they generally run away. She is a very courageous woman, my lord.'

Lord Peter stretched out his hand impulsively, but Mr Bunter was too well trained to see it. He had, indeed, already begun to strop a razor. Lord Peter suddenly bundled out of bed with a violent jerk and sped across the landing to the bathroom.

Here he revived sufficiently to lift up his voice in 'Come unto these Yellow Sands.' Thence, feeling in a Purcellish mood, he passed to 'I attempt from Love's Sickness to Fly,' with such improvement of spirits that, against all custom, he ran several gallons of cold water into the bath and sponged himself vigorously. Wherefore, after a rough towelling, he burst explosively from the bathroom, and caught his shin somewhat violently against the lid of a large oak chest which stood at the head of the staircase – so violently, indeed, that the lid lifted with the shock and shut down with a protesting bang.

Lord Peter stopped to say something expressive and to caress his leg softly with the palm of his hand. Then a thought struck him. He set down his towels, soap, sponge, loofah, bath-brush, and other belongings, and quietly lifted the lid of the chest.

Whether, like the heroine of *Northanger Abbey*, he expected to find anything gruesome inside was not apparent. It is certain that, like her, he beheld nothing more startling than certain sheets and counterpanes neatly folded at the bottom. Unsatisfied, he lifted the top one of these gingerly and inspected it for a few moments in the light of the staircase window. He was just returning it to its place, whistling softly the while, when a little hiss of indrawn breath caused him to look up with a start.

His sister was at his elbow. He had not heard her come, but she stood there in her dressing-gown, her hands clutched together on her breast. Her blue eyes were dilated till they looked almost black and her skin seemed nearly the colour of her ash-blonde hair. Wimsey stared at her over the sheet he held in his arms, the terror in her face passed over into his, stamping them suddenly with the mysterious likeness of blood-relationship.

Peter's own impression was that he stared 'like a stuck pig' for about a minute. He knew, as a matter of fact, that he had recovered himself in a fraction of a second. He dropped the sheet into the chest and stood up.

'Hullo, Polly, old thing,' he said, 'where've you been hidin' all this time? First time I've seen you. 'Fraid you've been havin' a pretty thin time of it.'

He put his arm round her, and felt her shrink.

'What's the matter?' he demanded. 'What's up, old girl? Look here, Mary, we've never seen enough of each other, but I am your brother. Are you in trouble? Can't I—'

'Trouble?' she said. 'Why, you silly old Peter, of course I'm in trouble. Don't you know they've killed my man and put my brother in prison? Isn't that enough to be in trouble about?' She laughed, and Peter suddenly thought 'She's talking like somebody in a blood-and-thunder novel.' She went on more naturally. 'It's all right, Peter, truly – only my head's so bad. I really don't know what I'm doing. What are you after? You made such a noise, I came out. I thought it was a door banging.'

'You'd better toddle back to bed,' said Lord Peter. 'You're gettin' all cold. Why do girls wear such mimsy little pyjimjams in this damn cold climate? There, don't you worry. I'll drop in on you later and we'll have a jolly old pow-wow, what?'

'Not today – not today, Peter. I'm going mad, I think.' ('Sensation fiction again,' thought Peter.) 'Are they trying Gerald today?'

'Not exactly trying,' said Peter, urging her gently along to her room. 'It's just formal, y'know. The jolly old magistrate bird hears the charge read, and then old Murbles pops up and says please he wants only formal evidence given as he has to instruct counsel. That's Biggy, y'know. Then they hear the evidence of arrest, and Murbles says old Gerald reserves his defence. That's all till the Assizes – evidence before the Grand Jury – a lot of bosh! That'll be early next month, I suppose. You'll have to buck up, and be fit by then.'

Mary shuddered.

'No – no! Couldn't I get out of it? I couldn't go through it all again. I should be sick. I'm feeling awful. No, don't come in. I don't want you. Ring the bell for Ellen. No, let go; go away! I don't want you, Peter!'

Peter hesitated, a little alarmed.

'Much better not, my lord, if you'll excuse me,' said Bunter's voice at his ear. 'Only produce hysterics,' he added, as he drew his master gently from the door. 'Very distressing for both parties, and altogether unproductive of results. Better to wait for the return of her grace, the Dowager.'

'Quite right,' said Peter. He turned back to pick up his paraphernalia, but was dexterously forestalled. Once again he lifted the lid of the chest and looked in.

'What did you say you found on that skirt, Bunter?'

'Gravel, my lord, and silver sand.'

'Silver sand.'

Behind Riddlesdale Lodge the moor stretched starkly away and upward. The heather was brown and wet, and the little streams had no colour in them. It was six o'clock, but there was no sunset. Only a paleness had moved behind the thick sky from east to west all day. Lord Peter, tramping back after a long and fruitless search for tidings of the man with the motor-cycle, voiced the dull suffering of his gregarious spirit. 'I wish old Parker was here,' he muttered, and squelched down a sheep-track.

He was making, not directly for the Lodge, but for a farmhouse about two and a half miles distant from it, known as Grider's Hole. It lay almost due north of Riddlesdale village, a lonely outpost on the edge of the moor, in a valley of fertile land between two wide swells of heather. The track wound down from the height called Whemmeling Fell, skirted a vile swamp, and crossed the little River Ridd about half a mile before reaching the farm. Peter had small hope of hearing any news at Grider's Hole, but he was filled with a sudden determination to leave no stone unturned. Privately, however, he felt convinced that the motor-cycle had come by the high road, Parker's investigations notwithstanding, and perhaps passed directly through King's Fenton without stopping or attracting attention. Still, he had said he would search the neighbourhood, and Grider's Hole was in the neighbourhood. He paused to relight his pipe, then squelched steadily on. The path was marked with stout white posts at regular intervals, and presently with hurdles. The reason for this was apparent as one came to the bottom of the valley, for only a few yards on the left began the stretch of rough, reedy tussocks, with slobbering black bog between them, in which anything heavier than a water-wagtail would speedily suffer change into a succession of little bubbles. Wimsey stooped for an empty sardine tin which lay, horribly battered, at his feet, and slung it idly into the quag. It struck the surface with a noise like a wet kiss, and vanished instantly. With that instinct which prompts one, when depressed, to wallow in every circumstance of gloom, Peter leaned sadly upon the hurdles and abandoned himself to a variety of shallow considerations upon (1) The vanity of human wishes; (2) Mutability; (3) First love; (4) The decay of idealism; (5) The aftermath of the Great War; (6) Birth-control; and (7) The fallacy of free-will. This was his nadir, however. Realising that his feet were cold and his stomach empty, and that he had still some miles to go, he crossed the stream on a row of slippery stepping-stones and approached the gate of the farm, which was not an ordinary five-barred one, but solid and uncompromising. A man was leaning over it, sucking a straw. He made no attempt to move at Wimsey's approach. 'Good evening,' said that nobleman in a sprightly manner, laying his hand on the catch. 'Chilly, ain't it?'

The man made no reply, but leaned more heavily, and breathed. He wore a rough coat and breeches, and his leggings were covered with manure.

'Seasonable, of course, what?' said Peter. 'Good for the sheep, I daresay. Makes their wool curl, and so on.'

The man removed the straw and spat in the direction of Peter's right boot.

'Do you lose many animals in the bog?' went on Peter, carelessly unlatching the gate, and leaning upon it in the opposite direction. 'I see you have a good wall around the house. Must be a bit dangerous in the dark, what, if you're thinkin' of takin' a little evenin' stroll with a friend?'

The man spat again, pulled his hat over his forehead, and said briefly:

'What doost 'a want?'

'Well,' said Peter, 'I thought of payin' a little friendly call on Mr – on the owner of this farm, that is to say. Country neighbours, and all that. Lonely kind of country, don't you see. Is he in, d'ye think?'

The man grunted.

'I'm glad to hear it,' said Peter; 'it's so uncommonly jolly findin' all you Yorkshire people so kind and hospitable, what? Never mind who you are, always a seat at the fireside and that kind of thing. Excuse me, but do you know you're leanin' on the gate so as I can't open it? I'm sure it's a pure oversight, only you mayn't realise that just where you're standin' you get the maximum of leverage. What an awfully charmin' house this is, isn't it? All so jolly stark and grim and all the rest of it. No creepers or little rose-grown porches or anything suburban of that sort. Who lives in it?'

The man surveyed him up and down for some moments, and replied, 'Mester Grimethorpe.'

'No, does he now?' said Lord Peter. 'To think of that. Just the fellow I want to see. Model farmer, what? Wherever I go throughout the length and breadth of the North Riding I hear of Mr Grimethorpe. "Grimethorpe's butter is the best"; "Grimethorpe's fleeces Never go to pieces"; "Grimethorpe's pork Melts on the fork"; "For Irish stews Take Grimethorpe's ewes"; "A tummy lined with Grimethorpe's beef, Never, never comes to grief". It has been my life's ambition to see Mr Grimethorpe in the flesh. And you no doubt are his sturdy henchman and right-hand man. You leap from bed before the breaking day, To milk the kine amid the scented hay. You, when the shades of evening gather deep, Home from the mountain lead the mild-eyed sheep. You, by the ingle's red and welcoming blaze, Tell your sweet infants tales of olden days. A wonderful life, though a trifle monotonous p'raps in the winter. Allow me to clasp your honest hand.'

Whether the man was moved by this lyric outburst, or whether the failing light was not too dim to strike a pale sheen from the metal in Lord Peter's palm, at any rate he moved a trifle back from the gate.

'Thanks awfully, old bean,' said Peter, stepping briskly past him. 'I take it I shall find Mr Grimethorpe in the house?'

The man said nothing till Wimsey had proceeded about a dozen yards up the flagged path, then he hailed him, but without turning round.

'Mester!'

'Yes, old thing?' said Peter affably, returning.

'Happen he'll set dog on tha.'

'You don't say so?' said Peter. 'The faithful hound welcomes the return of the prodigal. Scene of family rejoicing. "My own long-lost boy!" Sobs and speeches, beer all round for the delighted tenantry. Glees by the old fireside, till the rafters ring and all the smoked hams tumble down to join in the revelry. Good night, sweet Prince, until the cows come home and the dogs eat Jezebel in the portion of Jezreel when the hounds of spring are on winter's traces. I suppose,' he added to himself, 'they will have finished tea.'

As Lord Peter approached the door of the farm his spirits rose. He enjoyed paying this kind of visit. Although he had taken to detecting as he might, with another conscience or constitution, have taken to Indian hemp – for its exhilarating properties – at a moment when life seemed dust and ashes, he had not primarily the detective temperament. He expected next to nothing from inquiries at Grider's Hole, and, if he had, he might probably have extracted all the information he wanted by a judicious display of Treasury notes to the glum man at the gate. Parker would in all likelihood have done so; he was paid to detect and to do nothing else, and neither his natural gifts nor his education (at Barrow-in-Furness Grammar School) prompted him to stray into side-tracks at the back of an ill-regulated imagination. But to Lord Peter the world presented itself as an entertaining labyrinth of side-issues. He was a respectable scholar in five or six languages, a musician of some skill and more understanding, something of an expert in toxicology, a collector of rare editions, an entertaining man-about-town, and a common sensationalist. He had been seen at half-past twelve on a Sunday morning walking in Hyde Park in a top-hat and frock-coat, reading the *News of the World*. His passion for the unexplored led him to hunt up obscure pamphlets in the British Museum, to unravel the emotional history of income-tax collectors, and to find out where his own drains led to. In this case, the fascinating problem of a Yorkshire farmer who habitually set the dogs on casual visitors imperatively demanded investigation in a personal interview. The result was unexpected.

His first summons was unheeded, and he knocked again. This time there was a movement, and a surly voice called out:

'Well, let 'un in then, dang 'un – and dang *thee*,' emphasised by the sound of something falling or thrown across the room.

The door was opened unexpectedly by a little girl of about seven, very dark and pretty, and rubbing her arm as though the missile had caught her there. She stood defensively, blocking the threshold, till the same voice growled impatiently:

'Well, who is it?'

'Good evening,' said Wimsey, removing his hat. 'I hope you'll excuse me dropping in like this. I'm livin' at Riddlesdale Lodge.'

'What of it?' demanded the voice. Above the child's head Wimsey saw the outline of a big, thick-set man smoking in the inglenook of an immense fireplace. There was no light but the firelight, for the window was small, and dusk had already fallen. It seemed to be a large room, but a high oak settle on the farther side of the chimney ran out across it, leaving a cavern of impenetrable blackness beyond.

'May I come in?' said Wimsey.

'If tha must,' said the man ungraciously. 'Shoot door, lass; what art starin' at? Go to thi moother and bid her mend thi manners for thee.'

This seemed a case of the pot lecturing the kettle on cleanliness, but the child vanished hurriedly into the blackness behind the settle, and Peter walked in.

'Are you Mr Grimethorpe?' he asked politely.

'What if I am?' retorted the farmer. '*I've* no call to be ashamed o' my name.'

'Rather not,' said Lord Peter, 'nor of your farm. Delightful place, what? My name's Wimsey, by the way – Lord Peter Wimsey, in fact, the Duke of Denver's brother, y'know. I'm sure I hate interruptin' you – you must be busy with the sheep and all that – but I thought you wouldn't mind if I just ran over in a neighbourly way. Lonely sort of country, ain't it? I like to know the people next door, and all that sort of thing. I'm used to London, you see, where people live pretty thick on the ground. I suppose very few strangers ever pass this way?'

'None,' said Mr Grimethorpe, with decision.

'Well, perhaps it's as well,' pursued Lord Peter. 'Makes one appreciate one's home circle more, what?

Often think one sees too many strangers in town. Nothing like one's family when all's said and done – cosy, don't you know. You a married man, Mr Grimethorpe?'

'What the hell's that to you?' growled the farmer, rounding on him with such ferocity that Wimsey looked about quite nervously for the dogs before-mentioned.

'Oh, nothin',' he replied, 'only I thought that charmin' little girl might be yours.'

'And if I thought she weren't,' said Mr Grimethorpe, 'I'd strangle the bitch and her mother together. What hast got to say to that?'

As a matter of fact, the remark, considered as a conversational formula, seemed to leave so much to be desired that Wimsey's natural loquacity suffered a severe check. He fell back, however, on the usual resource of the male, and offered Mr Grimethorpe a cigar, thinking to himself as he did so:

'What a hell of a life the woman must lead.'

The farmer declined the cigar with a single word, and was silent. Wimsey lit a cigarette for himself and became meditative, watching his companion. He was a man of about forty-five, apparently, rough, harsh, and weather-beaten, with great ridgy shoulders and short, thick thighs – a bull-terrier with a bad temper. Deciding that delicate hints would be wasted on such an organism, Wimsey adopted a franker method.

'To tell the truth, Mr Grimethorpe,' he said, 'I didn't blow in without any excuse at all. Always best to provide oneself with an excuse for a call, what? Though it's so perfectly delightful to see you – I mean, no excuse might appear necessary. But fact is, I'm looking for a young man – a – an acquaintance of mine – who said he'd be roamin' about this neighbourhood some time or other about now. Only I'm afraid I may have missed him. You see, I've only just got over from Corsica – interestin' country and all that, Mr Grimethorpe, but a trifle out of the way – and from what my friend said I think he must have turned up here about a week ago and found me out. Just my luck. But he didn't leave his card, so I can't be quite sure, you see. You didn't happen to come across him by any chance? Tall fellow with big feet on a motor-cycle with a side-car. I thought he might have come rootin' about here. Hullo! d'you know him?'

The farmer's face had become swollen and almost black with rage.

'What day sayst tha?' he demanded thickly.

'I should think last Wednesday night or Thursday morning,' said Peter, with a hand on his heavy malacca cane.

'I knew it,' growled Mr Grimethorpe. '– the slut, and all these dommed women wi' their dirty ways. Look here, mester. The tyke were a friend o' thine? Well, I wor at Stapley Wednesday and Thursday – tha knew that, didn't tha? And so did thi friend, didn't 'un? An if I hadn't, it'd a bin the worse for 'un. He'd a been in Peter's Pot if I'd 'a' cot 'un, an that's where tha'll be thesen in a minute, blast tha! And if I find 'un sneakin' here again, I'll blast every boon in a's body and send 'un to look for thee there.'

And with these surprising words he made for Peter's throat like a bull-dog.

'That won't do,' said Peter, disengaging himself with an ease which astonished his opponent, and catching his wrist in a grip of mysterious and excruciating agony. ''Tisn't wise, y'know – might murder a fellow like that. Nasty business, murder. Coroner's inquest and all that sort of thing. Counsel for the Prosecution askin' all sorts of inquisitive questions, and a feller puttin' a string round your neck. Besides, your method's a bit primitive. Stand still, you fool, or you'll break your arm. Feelin' better? That's right. Sit down. You'll get into trouble one of these days, behavin' like that when you're asked a civil question.'

'Get out o' t'house,' said Mr Grimethorpe sullenly.

'Certainly,' said Peter. 'I have to thank you for a very entertain' evenin', Mr Grimethorpe. I'm sorry you can give me no news of my friend—'

Mr Grimethorpe sprang up with a blasphemous ejaculation, and made for the door, shouting 'Jabez!' Lord Peter stared after him for a moment, and then stared round the room.

'Something fishy here,' he said. 'Fellow knows somethin'. Murderous sort of brute. I wonder—'

He peered round the settle, and came face to face with a woman – a dim patch of whiteness in the thick shadow.

'You?' she said, in a low, hoarse gasp. 'You? You are mad to come here. Quick, quick! He has gone for the dogs.'

She placed her two hands on his breast, thrusting him urgently back. Then, as the firelight fell upon his face, she uttered a stifled shriek and stood petrified – a Medusa-head of terror.

Medusa was beautiful, says the tale, and so was this woman; a broad white forehead under massed, dusky hair, black eyes glowing under straight brows, a wide, passionate mouth – a shape so wonderful that even in that strenuous moment sixteen generations of feudal privilege stirred in Lord Peter's blood. His hands closed over hers instinctively, but she pulled herself hurriedly away and shrank back.

'Madam,' said Wimsey, recovering himself, 'I don't quite—'

A thousand questions surged up in his mind, but before he could frame them a long yell, and another, and then another came from the back of the house.

'Run, run!' she said. 'The dogs! My God, my God, what will become of me? Go, if you don't want to see me killed. Go, go! Have pity!'

'Look here,' said Peter, 'can't I stay and protect—'

'You can stay and murder me,' said the woman. 'Go!'

Peter cast Public School tradition to the winds, caught up his stick, and went. The brutes were at his heels as he fled. He struck the foremost with his stick, and it dropped back, snarling. The man was still leaning on the gate, and Grimethorpe's hoarse voice was heard shouting to him to seize the fugitive. Peter closed with him; there was a scuffle of dogs and men, and suddenly Peter found himself thrown bodily over the gate. As he picked himself up and ran, he heard the farmer cursing the man and the man retorting that he couldn't help it; then the woman's voice, uplifted in a frightened wail. He glanced over his shoulder. The man and the woman and a second man who had now joined the party, were beating the dogs back, and seemed to be persuading Grimethorpe not to let them through. Apparently their remonstrances had some effect, for the farmer turned moodily away, and the second man called the dogs off, with much whip-cracking and noise. The woman said something, and her husband turned furiously upon her and struck her to the ground.

Peter made a movement to go back, but a strong conviction that he could only make matters worse for her arrested him. He stood still, and waited till she had picked herself up and gone in, wiping the blood and dirt from her face with her shawl. The farmer looked round, shook his fist at him, and followed her into the house.

Jabez collected the dogs and drove them back, and Peter's friend returned to lean over the gate.

Peter waited till the door had closed upon Mr and Mrs Grimethorpe; then he pulled out his handkerchief and, in the half-darkness, signalled cautiously to the man, who slipped through the gate and came slowly down to him.

'Thanks very much,' said Wimsey, putting money into his hand. 'I'm afraid I've done unintentional mischief.'

The man looked at the money and at him.

' 'Tes t'mester's way wi' them as cooms t'look at t'missus,' he said. 'Tha's best keep away if so be tha wutna' have her blood on tha heid.'

'See here,' said Peter, 'did you by any chance meet a young man with a motor-cycle wanderin' round here last Wednesday or thereabouts?'

'Naay. Wednesday? T'wod be day t'mester went to Stapley, Ah reckon, after machines. Naay, Ah seed nowt.'

'All right. If you find anybody who did, let me know. Here's my name, and I'm staying at Riddlesdale Lodge. Good night; many thanks.' The man took the card from him and slouched back without a word of farewell.

Lord Peter walked slowly, his coat collar turned up and his hat pulled over his eyes. This cinematographic episode had troubled his logical faculty. With an effort, he sorted out his ideas and arranged them in some kind of order.

'First item,' said he, 'Mr Grimethorpe. A gentleman who will stick at nothing. Hefty. Unamiable. Inhospitable. Dominant characteristic – jealousy of his very astonishing wife. Was at Stapley last Wednesday and Thursday buying machinery. (Helpful gentleman at the gate corroborates this, by the way, so that at this stage of the proceedings one may allow it to be a sound alibi.) Did not, therefore, see our mysterious friend with the side-car *if* he was there. But is disposed to think he *was* there, and has very little doubt about what he came for. Which raises an interestin' point. Why the side-car? Awkward thing to tour about with. Very good. But if our friend came after Mrs G. he obviously didn't take her. Good again.

'Second item, Mrs Grimethorpe. Very singular item. By Jove!' He paused meditatively to reconstruct a thrilling moment. 'Let us at once admit that if No. 10 came for the purpose suspected he had every excuse for it. Well! Mrs G. goes in terror of her husband, who thinks nothing of knocking her down on suspicion. I wish to God – but I'd only have made things worse. Only thing you can do for the wife of a brute like that is to keep away from her. Hope there won't be murder done. One's enough at a time. Where was I?'

'Yes – well, Mrs Grimethorpe knows something – and she knows somebody. She took me for somebody who had every reason for not coming to Grider's Hole. Where was she, I wonder, while I was talking to Grimethorpe? She wasn't in the room. Perhaps the child warned her. No, that won't wash; I told the child who I was. Aha! Wait a minute. Do I see light? She looked out of the window and saw a bloke in an aged Burberry. No. 10 is a bloke in an aged Burberry. Now let's suppose for a moment she takes me for No. 10. What does she do? She sensibly keeps out of the way – can't think why I'm such a fool as to turn up. Then, when Grimethorpe runs out shoutin' for the kennelman, she nips down with her life in her hands to warn her – her – shall we say boldly her lover? – to get away. She finds it isn't her lover, but only a gaping ass of (I fear) a very comin'-on disposition. New compromisin' position. She tells the ass to save himself and herself by clearin' out. Ass clears – not too gracefully. The next instalment of this enthrallin' drama will be shown in this theatre – when? I'd jolly well like to know.'

He tramped on for some time.

'All the same,' he retorted upon himself, 'all this throws no light on what No. 10 was doing at Riddlesdale Lodge.'

At the end of his walk he had reached no conclusion.

'Whatever happens,' he said to himself, 'and if it can be done without danger to her life, I must see Mrs Grimethorpe again.'

5

THE RUE ST HONORE AND
THE RUE DE LA PAIX

'I think it was the cat.'
H.M.S. PINAFORE

MR PARKER sat disconsolate in a small *apartement* in the Rue St Honoré. It was three o'clock in the afternoon. Paris was full of subdued but cheerful autumn sunlight, but the room faced north, and was depressing, with its plain, dark furniture and its deserted air. It was a man's room, well appointed after the manner of a discreet club; a room that kept its dead owner's counsel imperturbably. Two large saddlebag chairs in crimson leather stood by the cold hearth. On the mantelpiece was a bronze clock, flanked by two polished German shells, a stone tobacco-jar, and an Oriental brass bowl containing a long-cold pipe. There were several excellent engravings in narrow pearwood frames, and the portrait in oils of a rather florid lady of the period of Charles II. The window-curtains were crimson, and the floor covered with a solid Turkey carpet. Opposite the fireplace stood a tall mahogany book-case with glass doors, containing a number of English and French classics, a large collection of books on history and international politics, various French novels, a number of works on military and sporting subjects, and a famous French edition of the *Decameron* with the additional plates. Under the window stood a large bureau.

Parker shook his head, took out a sheet of paper, and

began to write a report. He had breakfasted on coffee and rolls at seven; he had made an exhaustive search of the flat; he had interviewed the concierge, the manager of the Crédit Lyonnais, and the Prefect of Police for the Quartier, and the result was very poor indeed.

Information obtained from Captain Cathcart's papers:

Before the war Denis Cathcart had undoubtedly been a rich man. He had considerable investments in Russia and Germany and a large share in a prosperous vineyard in Champagne. After coming into his property at the age of twenty-one he had concluded his three years' residence at Cambridge, and had then travelled a good deal, visiting persons of importance in various countries, and apparently studying with a view to a diplomatic career. During the period from 1913 to 1918 the story told by the books became intensely interesting, baffling, and depressing. At the outbreak of war he had taken a commission in the 15th – shires. With the help of the cheque-book, Parker reconstructed the whole economic life of a young British officer – clothes, horses, equipment, travelling, wine and dinners when on leave, bridge debts, rent of the flat in the Rue St Honoré, club subscriptions, and what not. This outlay was strictly moderate and proportioned to his income. Receipted bills, neatly docketed, occupied one drawer of the bureau, and a careful comparison of these with the cheque-book and the returned cheques revealed no discrepancy. But, beyond these, there appeared to have been another heavy drain upon Cathcart's resources. Beginning in 1913, certain large cheques, payable to self, appeared regularly at every quarter, and sometimes at shorter intervals. As to the destination of these sums, the bureau preserved the closest discretion; there were no receipts, no memoranda of their expenditure.

The great crash which in 1914 shook the credits of the world was mirrored in little in the pass-book. The credits from Russian and German sources stopped dead; those from the French shares slumped to a quarter of the original amount, as the tide of war washed over the vineyards and carried the workers away. For the first year or so there were substantial dividends from the capital invested in French *rentes*; then came an ominous entry of 20,000 francs on the credit side of the account, and, six months after, another of 30,000 francs. After that the landslide followed fast. Parker could picture those curt notes from the Front, directing the sale of Government securities, as the savings of the past six years whirled away in the maelstrom of rising prices and collapsing currencies. The dividends grew less and less and ceased; then, more ominous still, came a series of debits representing the charges of renewal of promissory notes.

About 1918 the situation had become acute, and several entries showed a desperate attempt to put matters straight by gambling in foreign exchanges. There were purchases, through the bank, of German marks, Russian roubles, and Roumanian lei. Mr Parker sighed sympathetically, when he saw this, thinking of £12 worth of these delusive specimens of the engraver's art laid up in his own desk at home. He knew them to be waste paper, yet his tidy mind could not bear the thought of destroying them. Evidently Cathcart had found marks and roubles very broken reeds.

It was about this time that Cathcart's pass-book began to reveal the paying in of various sums in cash, some large, some small, at irregular dates and with no particular consistency. In December, 1919, there had been one of these amounting to as much as 35,000 francs.

Parker at first supposed that these sums might represent dividends from some separate securities which Cathcart was handling for himself without passing them through the bank. He made a careful search of the room in the hope of finding either the bonds themselves or at least some memorandum concerning them, but the search was in vain, and he was forced to conclude either that Cathcart had deposited them in some secret place or that the credits in question represented some different source of income.

Cathcart had apparently contrived to be demobilised almost at once (owing, no doubt, to his previous frequentation of distinguished governmental personages), and to have taken a prolonged holiday upon the Riviera. Subsequently a visit to London coincided with the acquisition of £700, which, converted into francs at the then rate of exchange, made a very respectable item in the account. From that time on, the outgoings and receipts presented a similar aspect and were more or less evenly balanced, the cheques to self becoming rather larger and more frequent as time went on, while during 1921 the income from the vineyard began to show signs of recovery.

Mr Parker noted down all this information in detail, and leaning back in his chair, looked round the flat. He felt, not for the first time, distaste for his profession, which cut him off from the great masculine community whose members take each other for granted and respect privacy. He relighted his pipe, which had gone out, and proceeded with his report.

Information obtained from Monsieur Turgeot, the manager of the Crédit Lyonnais, confirmed the evidence of the pass-book in every particular. Monsieur Cathcart had recently made all his payments in notes, usually in notes of small denominations. Once or twice he had had an overdraft – never very large, and always made up within a few months. He had, of course, suffered a diminution of income, like everybody else, but the account had never given the bank any uneasiness. At the moment it was some 14,000 francs on the right side. Monsieur Cathcart was always very agreeable, but not communicative – *très correct*.

Information obtained from the concierge:

One did not see much of Monsieur Cathcart, but he was *très gentil*. He never failed to say, '*Bon jour, Bourgois*,' when he came in or out. He received visitors sometimes – gentlemen in evening dress. One made card-parties. Monsieur Bourgois had never directed any ladies to his rooms; except once, last February, when he had given a lunch-party to some ladies *très comme il faut* who brought with them his fiancée, *une jolie blonde*. Monsieur Cathcart used the flat as a *pied à terre*, and often he would shut it up and go away for several weeks or months. He was *un jeune homme très rangé*. He had never kept a valet. Madame Leblanc, the cousin of one's late wife, kept his *apartement* clean. Madame Leblanc was very respectable. But certainly monsieur might have Madam Leblanc's address.

Information obtained from Madame Leblanc:

Monsieur Cathcart was a charming young man, and very pleasant to work for. Very generous and took a great interest in the family. Madame Leblanc was desolated to hear that he was dead, and on the eve of his marriage to the daughter of the English milady. Madame Leblanc had seen Mademoiselle last year when she visited Monsieur Cathcart in Paris; she considered the young lady very fortunate. Very few young men were as serious as Monsieur Cathcart, especially when they were so good-looking. Madame Leblanc had had experience of young men, and she could relate many histories if she were disposed, but none of Monsieur Cathcart. He would not always be using his rooms; he had the habit of letting her know when he would be at home, and she then went round to put the flat in order. He kept his things very tidy; he was not like English gentlemen in that respect. Madame Leblanc had known many of them, who kept their affairs *sens dessus dessous*. Monsieur Cathcart was always very well dressed; he was particular about his bath; he was like a woman for his toilet, the poor gentleman. And so he was dead. *Le pauvre garçon!* Really it had taken away Madame Leblanc's appetite.

Information obtained from Monsieur the Prefect of Police:

Absolutely nothing. Monsieur Cathcart had never caught the eye of the police in any way. With regard to the sums of money mentioned by Monsieur Parker, if monsieur would give him the numbers of some of the notes, efforts would be made to trace them.

Where had the money gone? Parker could think only of two destinations – an irregular establishment or a blackmailer. Certainly a handsome man like Cathcart might very well have a woman or two in his life, even without the knowledge of the concierge. Certainly a man who habitually cheated at cards – if he did cheat at cards – might very well have got himself into the power of somebody who knew too much. It was noteworthy that his mysterious receipts in cash began just as his economies were exhausted; it seemed likely that they represented irregular gains from gambling – in the casinos, on the exchange, or, if Denver's story had any truth in it, from crooked play. On the whole, Parker rather inclined to the blackmailing theory. It fitted in with the rest of the business, as he and Lord Peter had reconstructed it at Riddlesdale.

Two or three things, however, still puzzled Parker. Why should the blackmailer have been trailing about the Yorkshire moors with a cycle and side-car? Whose was the green-eyed cat? It was a valuable trinket. Had Cathcart offered it as part of his payment? That seemed somehow foolish. One could only suppose that the blackmailer had tossed it away with contempt. The cat was in Parker's possession, and it occurred to him that it might be worth while to get a jeweller to estimate its value. But the side-car was a difficulty, the cat was a difficulty, and, more than all, Lady Mary was a difficulty.

Why had Lady Mary lied at the inquest? For that she had lied Parker had no manner of doubt. He disbelieved the whole story of the second shot which had awakened her. What had brought her to the conservatory door at three o'clock in the morning? Whose was the suitcase – if it was a suitcase – that had lain concealed among the cactus plants? Why this prolonged nervous breakdown, with no particular symptoms, which prevented Lady Mary from giving evidence before the magistrate or answering her brother's inquiries? Could Lady Mary have been present at the interview in the shrubbery? If so, surely Wimsey and he would have found her footprints. Was she in league with the blackmailer? That was an unpleasant thought. Was she endeavouring to help her fiancé? She had an allowance of her own – a generous one, as Parker knew from the Duchess. Could she have tried to assist Cathcart with money? But in that case, why not tell all she knew? The worst about Cathcart – always supposing that card-sharping were the worst – was now matter of public knowledge, and the man himself was dead. If she knew the truth, why did she not come forward and save her brother?

And at this point he was visited by a thought even more unpleasant. If, after all, it had not been Denver whom Mrs Marchbanks had heard in the library, but someone else – someone who had likewise an appointment with the blackmailer – someone who was on his side as against Cathcart – who knew that there might be danger in the interview. Had he himself paid proper attention to the grass lawn between the house and the thicket? Might Thursday morning perhaps have revealed here and there a trodden blade that rain and sap had since restored to uprightness? Had Peter and he found *all* the footsteps in the wood? Had some more trusted hand fired that shot at close quarters? Once again – *whose was the green-eyed cat?*

Surmises and surmises, each uglier than the last, thronged into Parker's mind. He took up a photograph of Cathcart with which Wimsey had supplied him, and looked at it long and curiously. It was a dark, handsome face; the hair was black, with a slight wave, the nose large and well shaped, the big, dark eyes at once pleasing and arrogant. The mouth was good, though a little thick, with a hint of sensuality in its close curves; the chin showed a cleft. Frankly, Parker confessed to himself, it did not attract him; he would have been inclined to dismiss the man as a 'Byronic blighter', but experience told him that this kind of face might be powerful with a woman, either for love or hatred.

Coincidences usually have the air of being practical jokes on the part of Providence. Mr Parker was shortly to be favoured – if the term is a suitable one – with a special display of this Olympian humour. As a rule, that kind of thing did not happen to him; it was more in Wimsey's line. Parker had made his way from modest beginnings to a respectable appointment in the C.I.D. rather by a combination of hard work, shrewdness, and caution than by spectacular displays of happy guesswork or any knack for taking fortune's tide at the flood. This time, however, he was given a 'leading' from above, and it was only part of the nature of things and men that he should have felt distinctly ungrateful for it.

He finished his report, replaced everything tidily in the desk and went round to the police-station to arrange with the Prefect about the keys and the fixing of the seals. It was still early evening and not too cold; he determined, therefore, to banish gloomy thoughts by a *café-cognac* in the Boul' Mich', followed by a stroll through the Paris of the shops. Being of a kindly, domestic nature, indeed, he turned over in his mind the idea of buying something Parisian for his elder sister, who was unmarried and lived a rather depressing life in Barrow-in-Furness. Parker knew that she would take pathetic delight in some filmy scrap of lace underwear which no one but herself would ever see. Mr Parker was not the kind of man to be deterred by the difficulty of buying ladies' underwear in a foreign language; he was not very imaginative. He remembered that a learned judge had one day asked in court what a camisole was, and recollected that there had seemed to be nothing particularly embarrassing about the garment when explained. He determined that he would find a really Parisian shop, and ask for a camisole. That would give him a start, and then mademoiselle would show him other things without being asked further.

Accordingly, towards six o'clock, he was strolling along the Rue de la Paix with a little carton under his arm. He had spent rather more money than he intended, but he had acquired knowledge. He knew for certain what a camisole was, and he had grasped for the first time in his life that crêpe-de-Chine had no recognisable relation to crape, and was astonishingly expensive for its bulk. The young lady had been charmingly sympathetic, and without actually insinuating anything, had contrived to make her customer feel just a little bit of a dog. He felt that his French accent was improving. The street was crowded with people, slowly sauntering past the brilliant shop windows. Mr Parker stopped and gazed nonchalantly over a gorgeous display of jewellery, as though hesitating between a pearl necklace valued at 80,000 francs and a pendant of diamonds and aquamarines set in platinum.

And there, balefully winking at him from under a label inscribed '*Bonne fortune*' hung a green-eyed cat.

The cat stared at Mr Parker, and Mr Parker stared at the cat. It was no ordinary cat. It was a cat with a personality. Its tiny arched body sparkled with diamonds, and its platinum paws, set close together, and its erect and glittering tail were instinct in every line with the sensuous delight of friction against some beloved object. Its head, cocked slightly to one side, seemed to demand a titillating finger under the jaw. It was a minute work of art, by no journeyman hand. Mr Parker fished in his pocket-book. He looked from the cat in his hand to the cat in the window. They were alike. They were astonishingly alike. They were identical. Mr Parker marched into the shop.

'I have here,' said Mr Parker to the young man at the counter, 'a diamond cat, which greatly resembles one which I perceive in your window. Could you have the obligingness to inform me what would be the value of such a cat?'

The young man replied instantly:

'But certainly, monsieur. The price of the cat is 5,000 francs. It is, as you perceive, made of the finest materials. Moreover, it is the work of an artist; it is worth more than the market value of the stones.'

'It is, I suppose, a mascot?'

'Yes, monsieur; it brings great good luck, especially at cards. Many ladies buy these little objects. We have here other mascots, but all of this special design are of similar quality and price. Monsieur may rest assured that his cat is a cat of pedigree.'

'I suppose that such cats are everywhere obtainable in Paris,' said Mr Parker nonchalantly.

'But no monsieur. If you desire to match your cat I recommend you to do it quickly. Monsieur Briquet had only a score of these cats to begin with, and there are now only three left, including the one in the window. I believe that he will not make any more. To repeat a thing often is to vulgarise it. There will, of course, be other cats—'

'I don't want another cat,' said Mr Parker, suddenly interested. 'Do I understand you to say that cats such as this are only sold by Monsieur Briquet? That my cat originally came from this shop?'

'Undoubtedly, monsieur, it is one of our cats. These little animals are made by a workman of ours – a genius who is responsible for many of our finest articles.'

'It would, I imagine, be impossible to find out to whom this cat was originally sold?'

'If it was sold over the counter for cash it would be difficult, but if it was entered in our books it might not be impossible to discover, if monsieur desired it.'

'I do desire it very much,' said Parker, producing his card. 'I am an agent of the British police, and it is of great importance that I should know to whom this cat originally belonged.'

'In that case,' said the young man, 'I shall do better to inform monsieur the proprietor.'

He carried away the card into the back premises, and presently emerged with a stout gentleman, whom he introduced as Monsieur Briquet.

In Monsieur Briquet's private office the books of the establishment were brought out and laid on the desk.

'You will understand, monsieur,' said Monsieur Briquet, 'that I can only inform you of the names and addresses of such purchasers of these cats as have had an account sent them. It is, however, unlikely that an object of such value was paid for in cash. Still, with rich Anglo-Saxons, such an incident may occur. We need not go back further than the beginning of the year, when these cats were made.' He ran a podgy finger down the pages of the ledger. 'The first purchase was on January 19th.'

Mr Parker noted various names and addresses, and at the end of half an hour Monsieur Briquet said in a final manner:

'That is all, monsieur. How many names have you there?'

'Thirteen,' said Parker.

'And there are still three cats in stock – the original number was twenty – so that four must have been sold for cash. If monsieur wishes to verify the matter we can consult the day-book.'

The search in the day-book was longer and more tiresome, but eventually four cats were duly found to have been sold; one on January 31st, another on February 6th, the third on May 17th, and the last on August 9th.

Mr Parker had risen, and embarked upon a long string of compliments and thanks, when a sudden association of ideas and dates prompted him to hand Cathcart's photograph to Monsieur Briquet and ask whether he recognised it.

Monsieur Briquet shook his head.

'I am sure he is not one of our regular customers,' he said, 'and I have a very good memory for faces. l make a point of knowing anyone who has any considerable account with me. And this gentleman has not everybody's face. But we will ask my assistants.'

The majority of the staff failed to recognise the photograph, and Parker was on the point of putting it back in his pocket-book when a young lady, who had just finished selling an engagement ring to an obese and elderly Jew, arrived, and said, without any hesitation:

'*Mais oui, je l'ai vu, ce monsieur-là*. It is the Englishman who bought a diamond cat for the *jolie blonde*.'

'Mademoiselle,' said Parker eagerly, 'I beseech you to do me the favour to remember all about it.'

'*Parfaitement*,' said she. 'It is not the face one would forget, especially when one is a woman. The gentleman bought a diamond cat and paid for – no, I am wrong. It was the lady who bought it, and I remember now to have been surprised that she should pay like that at once in money, because ladies do not usually carry such large sums. The gentleman bought too. He bought a diamond and tortoiseshell comb for the lady to wear, and then she said she must give him something *pour porter bonheur*, and asked me for a mascot that was good for cards. I showed her some jewels more suitable for a gentleman, but she saw these cats and fell in love with them, and said he should have a cat and nothing else; she was sure it would bring him good hands. She asked me if it was not

113

so, and I said, "Undoubtedly, and monsieur must be sure never to play without it", and he laughed very much, and promised always to have it upon him when he was playing.'

'And how was she, this lady?'

'Blonde, monsieur, and very pretty; rather tall and svelte, and very well dressed. A big hat and dark blue costume. *Quoi encore? Voyons* – yes, she was a foreigner.'

'English?'

'I do not know. She spoke French very, very well, almost like a French person, but she had just the little suspicion of accent.'

'What language did she speak with the gentleman?'

'French, monsieur. You see, we were speaking together, and they both appealed to me continually, and so all the talk was in French. The gentleman spoke French *à merveille*, it was only by his clothes and a *je ne sais quoi* in his appearance that I guessed he was English. The lady spoke equally fluently, but one remarked just the accent from time to time. Of course, I went away from them once or twice to get goods from the window, and they talked then; I do not know in what language.'

'Now, mademoiselle, can you tell me how long ago this was?'

'*Ah, mon Dieu, ça c'est plus difficile. Monsieur sait que les jours se suivent et se ressemblent. Voyons.*'

'We can see by the day-book,' put in Monsieur Briquet, 'on what occasion a diamond comb was sold with a diamond cat.'

'Of course,' said Parker hastily. 'Let us go back.'

They went back and turned to the January volume, where they found no help. But on February 6th they read:

| Peigne en écaille et diamants | f.7,500 |
| Chat en diamants (Dessin C-5) | f.5,000 |

'That settles it,' said Parker gloomily.

'Monsieur does not appear content,' suggested the jeweller.

'Monsieur,' said Parker, 'I am more grateful than I can say for your very great kindness, but I will frankly confess that, of all the twelve months in the year, I had rather it had been any other.'

Parker found this whole episode so annoying to his feelings that he bought two comic papers and, carrying them away to Boudet's at the corner of the Rue Auguste Léopold, read them solemnly through over his dinner, by way of settling his mind. Then, returning to his modest hotel, he ordered a drink and sat down to compose a letter to Lord Peter. It was a slow job, and he did not appear to relish it very much. His concluding paragraph was as follows:

'I have put all these things down for you without any comment. You will be able to draw your own inferences as well as I can – better, I hope, for my own are perplexing and worrying me no end. They may be all rubbish – I hope they are; I daresay something will turn up at your end to put quite a different interpretation upon the facts. But I do feel that they must be cleared up. I would offer to hand over the job, but another man might jump at conclusions even faster than I do, and make a mess of it. But of course, if you say so, I will be taken suddenly ill at any moment. Let me know. If you think I'd better go on grubbing about over here, can you get hold of a photograph of Lady Mary Wimsey, and find out if possible about the diamond comb and the green-eyed cat – also at exactly what date Lady

Mary was in Paris in February. Does she speak French as well as you do? Let me know how you are getting on.

'Yours ever,

'CHARLES PARKER.'

He re-read the letter and report carefully and sealed them up. Then he wrote to his sister, did up his parcel neatly, and rang for the valet de chambre.

'I want this letter sent off at once, registered,' he said, 'and the parcel is to go tomorrow as a *colis postal*.'

After which he went to bed, and read himself to sleep with a commentary on the Epistle to the Hebrews.

Lord Peter's reply arrived by return:

'DEAR CHARLES, – Don't worry. I don't like the look of things myself frightfully, but I'd rather you tackled the business than anyone else. As you say, the ordinary police bloke doesn't mind whom he arrests, provided he arrests someone, and is altogether a most damnable fellow to have poking into one's affairs. I'm putting my mind to getting my brother cleared – that *is* the first consideration, after all, and really anything else would be better than having Jerry hanged for a crime he didn't commit. Whoever did it, it's better the right person should suffer than the wrong. So go ahead.

'I enclose two photographs – all I can lay hands on for the moment. The one in nursing-kit is rather rotten, and the other's all smothered up in a big hat.

'I had a damn queer little adventure here on Wednesday, which I'll tell you about when we meet. I've found a woman who obviously knows more than she ought, and a most promising ruffian – only I'm afraid he's got an alibi. Also I've got a faint suggestion of a clue about No. 10. Nothing much happened at Northallerton, except that Jerry was of course committed for trial. My mother is here, thank God! and I'm hoping she'll get some sense out of Mary, but she's been worse the last two days – Mary, I mean, not my mother – beastly sick and all that sort of thing. Dr Thingummy – who is an ass – can't make it out. Mother says it's as clear as noonday, and she'll stop it if I have patience a day or two. I made her ask about the comb and the cat. M. denies the cat altogether, but admits to a diamond comb bought in Paris – says she can't remember where she bought it, has lost the bill, but it didn't cost anything like 7,500 francs. She was in Paris from February 2nd to February 20th. My chief business now is to see Lubbock and clear up a little matter concerning silver sand.

'The Assizes will be the first week in November – in fact, the end of next week. This rushes things a bit, but it doesn't matter, because they can't try him there; nothing will matter but the Grand Jury, who are bound to find a true bill on the face of it. After that we can hang matters up as long as we like. It's going to be a deuce of a business. Parliament sitting and all. Old Biggs is fearfully perturbed under that marble outside of his. I hadn't really grasped what a fuss it was to try peers. It's only happened about once in every sixty years, and the procedure's about as old as Queen Elizabeth. They have to appoint a Lord High Steward for the occasion, and God knows what. They have to make it frightfully clear in the Commission that it *is* only for the occasion, because, somewhere about Richard II's time, the L.H.S. was such a terrifically big pot that he got to ruling the roost. So when Henry IV came to the throne, and the office came into the hands of the Crown, he jolly well kept it there, and now they only appoint a man *pro tem.* for the Coronation and shows like Jerry's. The King always pretends not to know there isn't a L.H.S. till the time comes, and is no end surprised at having to think of somebody to take on the job. Did you know all this? I didn't. I got it out of Biggy.

'Cheer up. Pretend you don't know that any of these people are relations of mine. My mother sends you her kindest regards and what not, and hopes she'll see you again soon. Bunter sends something correct and respectful; I forgot what.

'Yours in the brotherhood of detection,

'P. W.'

It may as well be said at once that the evidence from the photographs was wholly inconclusive.

6

MARY QUITE CONTRARY

*'I am striving to take into public life what any man gets
from his mother.'*

LADY ASTOR

ON the opening day of the York Assizes, the Grand Jury
brought in a true bill against Gerald, Duke of Denver, for
murder. Gerald, Duke of Denver, being accordingly produced in the court, the Judge affected to discover – what,
indeed, every newspaper in the country had been announcing to the world for the last fortnight – that he, being but a
common or garden judge with a plebeian jury, was incompetent to try a peer of the realm. He added, however, that he
would make it his business to inform the Lord Chancellor
(who also, for the last fortnight, had been secretly calculat-
ing the accommodation in the Royal Gallery and choosing
lords to form the Select Committee). Order being taken
accordingly, the noble prisoner was led away.

A day or two later, in the gloom of a London afternoon,
Mr Charles Parker rang the bell of a second-floor flat at
No. 110A Piccadilly. The door was opened by Bunter,
who informed him with a gracious smile that Lord Peter
had stepped out for a few minutes but was expecting
him, and would he kindly come in and wait.

'We only came up this morning,' added the valet, 'and
are not quite straight yet, sir, if you will excuse us. Would
you feel inclined for a cup of tea?'

Parker accepted the offer, and sank luxuriously into a corner of the chesterfield. After the extraordinary discomfort of French furniture there was solace in the enervating springiness beneath him, the cushions behind the head, and Wimsey's excellent cigarettes. What Bunter had meant by saying that things were 'not quite straight yet' he could not divine. A leaping wood fire was merrily reflected in the spotless surface of the black baby grand; the mellow calf bindings of Lord Peter's rare editions glowed softly against the black and primrose walls; the vases were filled with tawny chrysanthemums; the latest editions of all the papers were on the table – as though the owner had never been absent.

Over his tea Mr Parker drew out the photographs of Lady Mary and Denis Cathcart from his breast pocket. He stood them up against the teapot and stared at them, looking from one to the other as if trying to force a meaning from their faintly smirking, self-conscious gaze. He referred again to his Paris notes, ticking off various points with a pencil. 'Damn!' said Mr Parker, gazing at Lady Mary. 'Damn – damn – damn—'

The train of thought he was pursuing was an extraordinarily interesting one. Image after image, each rich in suggestions, crowded into his mind. Of course, one couldn't think properly in Paris – it was so uncomfortable and the houses were central heated. Here, where so many problems had been unravelled, there was a good fire. Cathcart had been sitting before the fire. Of course, he wanted to think out a problem. When cats sat staring into the fire they were thinking out problems. It was odd he should not have thought of that before. When the green-eyed cat sat before the fire one sank right down into a sort of rich, black, velvety suggestiveness which was most important. It was luxurious to be able to think so lucidly as this, because otherwise it would be a pity to exceed the speed limit – and the black moors were reeling by so fast. But now he had really got the formula he wouldn't forget it again. The connection was just there – close, thick, richly coherent.

'The glass-blower's cat is bompstable,' said Mr Parker aloud and distinctly.

'I'm charmed to hear it,' replied Lord Peter, with a friendly grin. 'Had a good nap, old man?'

'I – what?' said Mr Parker. 'Hullo! Watcher mean, nap? I had got hold of the most important train of thought, and you've put it out of my head. What was it? Cat – cat – cat –' He groped wildly.

'You *said* "The glass-blower's cat is bompstable,"' retorted Lord Peter. 'It's a perfectly rippin' word, but I don't know what you mean by it.'

'Bompstable?' said Mr Parker, blushing slightly. 'Bomp – oh, well, perhaps you're right – I may have dozed off. But, you know, I thought I'd just got the clue to the whole thing. I attached the greatest importance to that phrase. Even now – No, now I come to think of it, my train of thought doesn't seem quite to hold together. What a pity. I thought it was so lucid.'

'Never mind,' said Lord Peter. 'Just back?'

'Crossed last night. Any news?'

'Lots.'

'Good?'

'No.'

Parker's eyes wandered to the photographs.

'I don't believe it,' he said obstinately. 'I'm damned if I'm going to believe a word of it.'

'A word of what?'

'Of whatever it is.'

'You'll have to believe it, Charles, as far as it goes,'

said his friend softly, filling his pipe with decided little digs of the fingers. 'I didn't say' – dig – 'that Mary' – dig – 'shot Cathcart' – dig, dig – 'but she has lied' – dig – 'again and again.' – Dig, dig – 'She knows who did it' – dig – 'she was prepared for it' – dig – 'she's malingering and lying to keep the fellow shielded' – dig – 'and we shall have to make her speak.' Here, he struck a match and lit the pipe in a series of angry little puffs.

'If you can think,' said Mr Parker, with some heat, 'that that woman' – he indicated the photographs – 'had any hand in murdering Cathcart, I don't care what your evidence is, you – hang it all, Wimsey, she's your own sister.'

'Gerald is my brother,' said Wimsey quietly. 'You don't suppose I'm exactly enjoying this business, do you? But I think we shall get along very much better if we try to keep our tempers.'

'I'm awfully sorry,' said Parker. 'Can't think why I said that – rotten bad form – beg pardon, old man.'

'The best thing we can do,' said Wimsey, 'is to look the evidence in the face, however ugly. And I don't mind admittin' that some of it's a positive gargoyle.

'My mother turned up at Riddlesdale on Friday. She marched upstairs at once and took possession of Mary, while I drooped about in the hall and teased the cat, and generally made a nuisance of myself. *You* know. Presently old Dr Thorpe called. I went and sat on the chest on the landing. Presently the bell rings and Ellen comes upstairs. Mother and Thorpe popped out and caught her just outside Mary's room, and they jibber-jabbered a lot and presently mother came barging down the passage to the bathroom with her heels tapping and her earrings simply dancing with irritation. I sneaked after 'em to the bathroom door, but I couldn't see anything, because they were blocking the doorway, but I heard mother say, "There, now, what did I tell you"; and Ellen said, "Lawks! your grace, who'd 'a' thought it?"; and my mother said, "All l can say is, if l had to depend on you people to save me from being murdered with arsenic or that other stuff with the name like anemones* – you know what I mean – that that very attractive-looking man with the preposterous beard used to make away with his wife and mother-in-law (who was vastly the more attractive of the two, poor thing), I might be being cut up and analysed by Dr Spilsbury now – such a horrid, distasteful job he must have of it, poor man, and the poor little rabbits, too."' Wimsey paused for breath, and Parker laughed in spite of his anxiety.

'I won't vouch for the exact words,' said Wimsey, 'but it was to that effect – you know my mother's style. Old Thorpe tried to look dignified, but mother ruffled up like a little hen and said, looking beadily at him: "In *my* day we called that kind of thing hysterics and naughtiness. *We* didn't let girls pull the wool over our eyes like that. I suppose *you* call it a neurosis, or a supposed desire, or a reflex, and coddle it. You might have let that silly child make herself really ill. You are all perfectly ridiculous, and no more fit to take care of yourselves than a lot of babies – not but what there are plenty of poor little things in the slums that look after whole families and show more sense than the lot of you put together. I am very angry with Mary, advertising herself in this way, and she's not to be pitied." You know,' said Wimsey, 'I think there's often a great deal in what one's mother says.'

'I believe you,' said Parker.

* Antimony? The Duchess appears to have had Dr Pritchard's case in mind.

'Well, I got hold of mother afterwards and asked her what it was all about. She said Mary wouldn't tell her anything about herself or her illness; just asked to be let alone. Then Thorpe came along and talked about nervous shock – said he couldn't understand these fits of sickness, or the way Mary's temperature hopped about. Mother listened, and told him to go and see what the temperature was now. Which he did, and in the middle mother called him away to the dressing-table. But, bein' a wily old bird, you see, she kept her eyes on the looking-glass, and nipped round just in time to catch Mary stimulatin' the thermometer to terrific leaps on the hot-water bottle.'

'Well, I'm damned!' said Parker.

'So was Thorpe. All mother said was, that if he wasn't too old a bird yet to be taken in by that hoary trick he'd no business to be gettin' himself up as a grey-haired family practitioner. So then she asked the girl about the sick fits – when they happened, and how often, and was it after meals or before, and so on, and at last she got out of them that it generally happened a bit after breakfast, and occasionally at other times. Mother said she couldn't make it out at first, because she'd hunted all over the room for bottles and things, till at last she asked who made the bed, thinkin', you see, Mary might have hidden something under the mattress. So Ellen said she usually made it while Mary had her bath. "When's that?" says mother. "Just before her breakfast," bleats the girl. "God forgive you all for a set of nincompoops," says my mother. "Why didn't you say so before?" So away they all trailed to the bathroom, and there, sittin' up quietly on the bathroom shelf among the baths salts and the Elliman's embrocation and the Krushchen feelings and the toothbrushes and things, was the family bottle of ipecacuanha – three-quarters empty! Mother said – well, I told you what she said. By the way, how do you spell ipecacuanha?'

Mr Parker spelt it.

'Damn you!' said Lord Peter. 'I *did* think I'd stumped you that time. I believe you went and looked it up beforehand. *No* decent-minded person would know how to spell ipecacuanha out of his own head. Anyway, as you were saying, it's easy to see which side of the family has the detective instinct.'

'I didn't say so—'

'I know. Why didn't you? I think my mother's talents deserve a little acknowledgment. I said so to her, as a matter of fact, and she replied in these memorable words: "My dear child, you can give it a long name if you like, but I'm an old-fashioned woman and I call it mother-wit, and it's so rare for a man to have it that if he does you write a book about him and call him Sherlock Holmes." However, apart from all that, I said to mother (in private, of course), "It's all very well, but I can't believe that Mary has been going to all this trouble to make herself horribly sick and frighten us all just to show off. Surely she isn't that sort." Mother looked at me as steady as an owl, and quoted a whole lot of examples of hysteria, ending up with the servant-girl who threw paraffin about all over somebody's house to make them think it was haunted, and finished up – that if all these new-fangled doctors went out of their way to invent subconsciousness and kleptomania, and complexes and other fancy descriptions to explain away when people had done naughty things, she thought one might just as well take advantage of the fact.'

'Wimsey,' said Parker, much excited, 'did she mean she suspected something?'

'My dear old chap,' replied Lord Peter, 'whatever can be known about Mary by putting two and two together my mother knows. I told her all *we* knew up to that point, and she took it all in, in her funny way, you know, never answering anything directly, and then she put her head on one side and said: "If Mary had listened to me, and done something useful instead of that V.A.D. work, which never came to much, if you ask me – not that I have anything against V.A.D.s in a general way, but that silly woman Mary worked under was the most terrible snob on God's earth – and there were very much more sensible things which Mary might really have done well, only that she was so crazy to get to London – I shall always say it was the fault of that ridiculous club – what could you expect of a place where you ate such horrible food, all packed into an underground cellar painted pink and talking away at the tops of their voices, and never any evening dress – only Soviet jumpers and side-whiskers. Anyhow, I've told that silly old man what to say about it, and they'll never be able to think of a better explanation for themselves." Indeed, you know,' said Peter, 'I think if any of them start getting inquisitive, they'll have mother down on them like a ton of bricks.'

'What do you really think yourself?' asked Parker.

'I haven't come yet to the unpleasantest bit of the lot,' said Peter. 'I've only just heard it, and it did give me a nasty jar, I'll admit. Yesterday I got a letter from Lubbock saying he would like to see me, so I trotted up here and dropped in on him this morning. You remember I sent him a stain off one of Mary's skirts which Bunter had cut out for me? I had taken a squint at it myself, and didn't like the look of it, so I sent it up to Lubbock, *ex abundantia cauteloe*; and I'm sorry to say he confirms me. It's human blood, Charles, and I'm afraid it's Cathcart's.'

'But – I've lost the thread of this a bit.'

'Well, the skirt must have got stained the day Cathcart – died, as that was the last day on which the party was out on the moors, and if it had been there earlier Ellen would have cleaned it off. Afterwards Mary strenuously resisted Ellen's efforts to take the skirt away, and made an amateurish effort to tidy it up herself with soap. So I think we may conclude that Mary knew the stains were there, and wanted to avoid discovery. She told Ellen that the blood was from a grouse – which must have been a deliberate untruth.'

'Perhaps,' said Parker, struggling against hope to make out a case for Lady Mary, 'she only said, "Oh! one of the birds must have bled," or something like that.'

'I don't believe,' said Peter, 'that one could get a great patch of human blood on one's clothes like that and not know what it was. She must have knelt right in it. It was three or four inches across.'

Parker shook his head dismally, and consoled himself by making a note.

'Well, now,' went on Peter, 'on Wednesday night everybody comes in and dines and goes to bed except Cathcart, who rushes out and stays out. At 11.50 the gamekeeper, Hardraw, hears a shot which may very well have been fired in the clearing where the – well, let's say the accident – took place. The time also agrees with the medical evidence about Cathcart having already been dead three or four hours when he was examined at 4.30. Very well. At 3 a.m. Jerry comes home from somewhere or other and finds the body. As he is bending over it, Mary arrives in the most apropos manner from the house in her coat and cap and walking-shoes. Now what is her story? She says that at three o'clock she was awakened by a shot. Now nobody else heard that shot, and we have the evidence of Mrs Pettigrew-Robinson, who slept in the next room to Mary, with her window open according to her immemorial custom, that she lay broad awake from 2 a.m. till a little after 3 a.m., when the alarm was given, and heard no shot. According to Mary, the shot was loud enough to waken her on the other side of the building. It's odd, isn't it, that the person already awake should swear so positively that she heard nothing of a noise loud enough to waken a healthy young sleeper next door? And, in any case, *if* that was the shot that killed Cathcart, he can barely have been dead when my brother found him – and again, in that case, how was there time for him to be carried up from the shrubbery to the conservatory?'

'We've been over all this ground,' said Parker, with an expression of distaste. 'We agreed we couldn't attach any importance to the story of the shot.'

'I'm afraid we've got to attach a great deal of importance to it,' said Lord Peter gravely. 'Now, what does Mary do? Either she thought the shot—'

'There was no shot.'

'I know that. But I'm examining the discrepancies of her story. She said she did not give the alarm because she thought it was probably only poachers. But, if it was poachers, it would be absurd to go down and investigate. So she explains that she thought it might be burglars. Now how does she dress to go and look for burglars? What would you or I have done? I think we would have taken a dressing-gown, a stealthy kind of pair of slippers, and perhaps a poker or a stout stick – not a pair of walking-shoes, a coat, and a cap, of all things!'

'It was a wet night,' mumbled Parker.

'My dear chap, if it's burglars you're looking for you don't expect to go and hunt them round the garden. Your first thought is that they're getting into the house, and your idea is to slip down quietly and survey them from the staircase or behind the dining-room door. Anyhow, fancy a present-day girl, who rushes about bareheaded in all weathers, stopping to embellish herself in a cap for a burglar-hunt – damn it all, Charles, it won't wash, you know! And she walks straight off to the conservatory and comes upon the corpse, exactly as if she knew where to look for it beforehand.'

Parker shook his head again.

'Well, now. She sees Gerald stooping over Cathcart's body. What does she say? Does she ask what's the matter? Does she ask who it is? She exclaims: "O God! Gerald, you've killed him", and *then* she says, as if on second thoughts, "Oh, it's Denis! What has happened? Has there been an accident?" Now, does that strike you as natural?'

'No. But it rather suggests to me that it wasn't Cathcart she expected to see there, but somebody else.'

'Does it? It rather sounds to me as if she was pretending not to know who it was. First she says, "You've killed him!" and then, recollecting that she isn't supposed to know who "he" is, she says, "Why it's Denis!"'

'In any case, then, if her first exclamation was genuine, she didn't expect to find the man dead.'

'No – no – we must remember that. The death *was* a surprise. Very well. Then Gerald sends Mary up for help. And here's where a little bit of evidence comes in that you picked up and sent along. Do you remember what Mrs Pettigrew-Robinson said to you in the train?'

'About the door slamming on the landing, do you mean?'

'Yes. Now I'll tell you something that happened to me the other morning. I was burstin' out of the bathroom in my usual breezy way when I caught myself a hell of a whack on that old chest on the landin', and the lid lifted up and shut down, *plonk*! That gave me an idea, and I thought I'd have a squint inside. I'd got the lid up and was lookin' at some sheets and stuff that were folded up at the bottom, when I heard a sort of gasp, and there was Mary, starin' at me, as white as a ghost. She gave me a turn, by Jove, but nothin' like the turn I'd given her. Well, she wouldn't say anything to me, and got hysterical, and I hauled her back to her room. But I'd seen something on those sheets.'

'What?'

'Silver sand.'

'Silver—'

'D'you remember those cacti in the greenhouse, and the place where somebody'd put a suitcase or something down?'

'Yes.'

'Well, there was a lot of silver sand scattered about – the sort people stick round some kinds of bulbs and things.'

'And that was inside the chest too?'

'Yes. Wait a moment. After the noise, Mrs Pettigrew-Robinson heard, Mary woke up Freddy and then the Pettigrew-Robinsons – and then what?'

'She locked herself into her room.'

'Yes. And shortly afterwards she came down and joined the others in the conservatory, and it was at this point everybody remembered noticing that she was wearing a cap and coat and walking-shoes over pyjamas and bare feet.'

'You are suggesting,' said Parker, 'that Lady Mary was already awake and dressed at three o'clock, that she went out by the conservatory door with her suitcase, expecting to meet the – the murderer of her – damn it, Wimsey!'

'We needn't go so far as that,' said Peter; 'we decided that she *didn't* expect to find Cathcart dead.'

'No. Well, she went, presumably to meet somebody.'

'Shall we say, *pro tem.*, she went to meet No. 10?' suggested Wimsey softly.

'I suppose we may as well say so. When she turned on the torch and saw the Duke stooping over Cathcart she thought – by Jove, Wimsey, I was right after all! When she said, "You've killed him!" she meant No. 10 – she thought it was No. 10's body.'

'Of course!' cried Wimsey. 'I'm a fool! Yes. Then she said, "It's Denis – what has happened?" That's quite clear. And, meanwhile, what did she do with the suit-case?'

'I see it all now,' cried Parker. 'When she saw that the body wasn't the body of No. 10 she realised that No. 10 must be the murderer. So her game was to prevent anybody knowing that No. 10 had been there. So she shoved the suitcase behind the cacti. Then, when she went upstairs, she pulled it out again, and hid it in the oak chest on the landing. She couldn't take it to her room, of course, because if anybody'd heard her come upstairs it would seem odd that she should run to her room before calling the others. Then she knocked up Arbuthnot and the Pettigrew-Robinsons – she'd be in the dark, and they'd be flustered and wouldn't see exactly what she had on. Then she escaped from Mrs P., ran into her room, took off the skirt in which she had knelt by Cathcart's side, and the rest of her clothes, and put on her pyjamas and the cap, which someone might have noticed, and the coat, which they *must* have noticed, and the shoes, which had probably left foot-marks already.

Then she could go down and show herself. Meantime she'd concocted the burglar story for the Coroner's benefit.'

'That's about it,' said Peter. 'I suppose she was so desperately anxious to throw us off the scent of No. 10 that it never occurred to her that her story was going to help implicate her brother.'

'She realised it at the inquest,' said Parker eagerly. 'Don't you remember how hastily she grasped at the suicide theory?'

'And when she found that she was simply saving her – well, No. 10 – in order to hang her brother, she lost her head, took to her bed, and refused to give any evidence at all. Seems to me there's an extra allowance of fools in my family,' said Peter gloomily.

'Well, what could she have done, poor girl?' asked Parker. He had been growing almost cheerful again. 'Anyway, she's cleared—'

'After a fashion,' said Peter, 'but we're not out of the wood yet by a long way. Why is she hand-in-glove with No. 10, who is at least a blackmailer if not a murderer? How did Gerald's revolver come on the scene? And the green-eyed cat? How much did Mary know of that meeting between No. 10 and Denis Cathcart? And if she was seeing and meeting the man she might have put the revolver into his hands any time.'

'No, no,' said Parker. 'Wimsey, don't think such ugly things as that.'

'Hell!' cried Peter, exploding. 'I'll have the truth of this beastly business if we all go to the gallows together!'

At this moment Bunter entered with a telegram addressed to Wimsey. Lord Peter read as follows:

'Party traced London; seen Marylebone Friday. Further information from Scotland Yard. – POLICE-SUPERIN-TENDENT GOSLING, Ripley.'

'Good egg!' cried Wimsey. 'Now we're gettin' down to it. Stay here, there's a good man, in case anything turns up. I'll run round to the Yard now. They'll send you up dinner, and tell Bunter to give you a bottle of the Chateau Yquem – it's rather decent. So long.'

He leapt out of the flat, and a moment later his taxi buzzed away up Piccadilly.

7

THE CLUB AND THE BULLET

'*He is dead, and by my hand. It were better that I were dead myself, for the guilty wretch I am.*'

ADVENTURES OF SEXTON BLAKE

HOUR after hour Mr Parker sat waiting for his friend's return. Again and again he went over the Riddlesdale Case, checking his notes here, amplifying them there, involving his tired brain in speculations of the most fantastic kind. He wandered about the room, taking down here and there a book from the shelves, strumming a few unskilful bars upon the piano, glancing through the weeklies, fidgeting restlessly. At length he selected a volume from the criminological section of the book-shelves, and forced himself to read with attention that most fascinating and dramatic of poison trials – the Seddon Case. Gradually the mystery gripped him, as it invariably did, and it was with a start of astonishment that he looked up at a long and vigorous whirring of the door-bell, to find that it was already long past midnight.

His first thought was that Wimsey must have left his latchkey behind, and he was preparing a facetious greeting when the door opened – exactly as in the beginning of a Sherlock Holmes story – to admit a tall and beautiful young woman, in an extreme state of nervous agitation, with halo of golden hair, violet-blue eyes, and disordered apparel all complete; for as she threw back her heavy travelling-coat he observed that she wore evening dress, with light green silk stockings and heavy brogue shoes thickly covered with mud.

'His lordship has not yet returned, my lady,' said Mr Bunter, 'but Mr Parker is here waiting for him, and we are expecting him at any minute now. Will your ladyship take anything?'

'No, no,' said the vision hastily, 'nothing, thanks. I'll wait. Good evening, Mr Parker. Where's Peter?'

'He has been called out, Lady Mary,' said Parker. 'I can't think why he isn't back yet. Do sit down.'

'Where did he go?'

'To Scotland Yard – but that was about six o'clock. I can't imagine—'

Lady Mary made a gesture of despair.

'I knew it. Oh, Mr Parker, what am I to do?'

Mr Parker was speechless.

'I *must* see Peter,' cried Lady Mary. 'It's a matter of life and death. Can't you send for him?'

'But I don't know where he is,' said Parker. 'Please, Lady Mary—'

'He's doing something dreadful – he's all *wrong*,' cried the young woman, wringing her hands with desperate vehemence. 'I must see him – tell him – Oh! did anybody ever get into such dreadful trouble! I – oh!—'

Here the lady laughed loudly and burst into tears.

'Lady Mary – I beg you – please don't,' cried Mr Parker anxiously, with a strong feeling that he was being incompetent and rather ridiculous. 'Please sit down. Drink a glass of wine. You'll be ill if you cry like that. If it is crying,' he added dubiously to himself. 'It *sounds* like hiccups. Bunter!'

Mr Bunter was not far off. In fact, he was just outside the door with a small tray. With a respectful 'Allow me, sir,' he stepped forward to the writhing Lady Mary and presented a small phial to her nose. The effect was startling. The patient gave two or three fearful whoops, and sat up, erect and furious.

'How *dare* you, Bunter!' said Lady Mary. 'Go away at once!'

'Your ladyship had better take a drop of brandy,' said Mr Bunter, replacing the stopper in the smelling-bottle, but not before Parker had caught the pungent reek of ammonia. 'This is the 1800 Napoleon brandy, my lady. Please don't snort so, if I may make the suggestion. His lordship would be greatly distressed to think that any of it should be wasted. Did your ladyship dine on the way up? No? Most unwise, my lady, to undertake a long journey on a vacant interior. I will take the liberty of sending in an omelette for your ladyship. Perhaps you would like a little snack of something yourself, sir, as it is getting late?'

'Anything you like,' said Mr Parker, waving him off hurriedly. 'Now, Lady Mary, you're feeling better, aren't you? Let me help you off with your coat.'

No more of an exciting nature was said until the omelette was disposed of, and Lady Mary comfortably settled on the chesterfield. She had by now recovered her poise. Looking at her, Parker noticed how her recent illness (however produced) had left its mark upon her. Her complexion had nothing of the brilliance which he remembered; she looked strained and white, with purple hollows under her eyes.

'I am sorry I was so foolish just now, Mr Parker,' she said, looking into his eyes with a charming frankness and confidence, 'but I was dreadfully distressed, and I came up from Riddlesdale so hurriedly.'

'Not at all,' said Parker meaninglessly. 'Is there anything I can do in your brother's absence?'

'I suppose you and Peter do everything together?'

'I think I may say that neither of us knows anything about this investigation which he has not communicated to the other.'

'If I tell you, it's the same thing?'

'Exactly the same thing. If you can bring yourself to honour me with your confidence—'

'Wait a minute, Mr Parker. I'm in a difficult position. I don't quite know what I ought – Can you tell me just how far you've got – what you have discovered?'

Mr Parker was a little taken aback. Although the face of Lady Mary had been haunting his imagination ever since the inquest, and although the agitation of his feelings had risen to boiling-point during this romantic interview, the official instinct of caution had not wholly deserted him. Holding, as he did, proof of Lady Mary's complicity in the crime, whatever it was, he was not so far gone as to fling all his cards on the table.

'I'm afraid,' he said, 'that I can't quite tell you that. You see, so much of what we've got is only suspicion as yet. I might accidentally do great mischief to an innocent person.'

'Ah! You definitely suspect somebody, then?'

'*In*definitely would be a better word for it,' said Mr Parker with a smile. 'But if you have anything to tell us which may throw light on the matter, I beg you to speak. We may be suspecting a totally wrong person.'

'I shouldn't be surprised,' said Lady Mary, with a sharp, nervous little laugh. Her hands strayed to the table and began pleating the orange envelope into folds. 'What do you want to know?' she asked suddenly, with a change of tone. Parker was conscious of a new hardness in her manner – a something braced and rigid.

He opened his note-book, and as he began his questioning his nervousness left him; the official reasserted himself.

'You were in Paris last February?'

Lady Mary assented.

'Do you recollect going with Captain Cathcart – oh! by the way, you speak French, I presume?'

'Yes, very fluently.'

'As well as your brother – practically without accent?'

'Quite as well. We always had French governesses as children, and mother was very particular about it.'

'I see. Well, now, do you remember going with Captain Cathcart on February 6th to a jeweller's in the Rue de la Paix and buying, or his buying for you, a tortoise-shell comb set with diamonds and a diamond and platinum cat with emerald eyes?'

He saw a lurking awareness come into the girl's eyes.

'Is that the cat you have been making inquiries about in Riddlesdale?' she demanded.

It being never worth while to deny the obvious, Parker replied 'Yes.'

'It was found in the shrubbery, wasn't it?'

'Had you lost it? Or was it Cathcart's?'

'If I said it was his—'

'I should be ready to believe you. *Was* it his?'

'No' – a long breath – 'it was mine.'

'When did you lose it?'

'That night.'

'Where?'

'I suppose in the shrubbery. Wherever you found it. I didn't miss it till later.'

'Is it the one you bought in Paris?'

'Yes.'

'Why did you say before that it was not yours?'

'I was afraid.'

'And now?'

'I am going to speak the truth.'

Parker looked at her again. She met his eye frankly,

but there was a tenseness in her manner which showed that it had cost her something to make up her mind.

'Very well,' said Parker, 'we shall all be glad of that, for I think there were one or two points at the inquest on which you didn't tell the truth, weren't there?'

'Yes.'

'Do believe,' said Parker, 'that I am sorry to have to ask these questions. The terrible position in which your brother is placed—'

'In which I helped to place him.'

'I don't say that.'

'I do. I helped to put him in gaol. Don't say I didn't, because I did.'

'Well,' said Parker, 'don't worry. There's plenty of time to put it all right again. Shall I go on?'

'Yes.'

'Well, now, Lady Mary, it wasn't true about hearing that shot at three o'clock was it?'

'No.'

'Did you hear the shot at all?'

'Yes.'

'When?'

'At 11.50.'

'What was it, then, Lady Mary, you hid behind the plants in the conservatory?'

'I hid nothing there.'

'And in the oak chest on the landing?'

'My skirt.'

'You went out – why? – to meet Cathcart?'

'Yes.'

'Who was the other man?'

'What other man?'

'The other man who was in the shrubbery. A tall, fair man dressed in a Burberry?'

'There was no other man.'

'Oh, pardon me, Lady Mary. We saw his footmarks all the way up from the shrubbery to the conservatory.'

'It must have been some tramp. I know nothing about him.'

'But we have proof that he was there – of what he did, and how he escaped. For heaven's sake, and your brother's sake, Lady Mary, tell us the truth – for that man in the Burberry was the man who shot Cathcart.'

'No,' said the girl, with a white face, 'that is impossible.'

'Why impossible?'

'I shot Denis Cathcart myself.'

'So that's how the matter stands, you see, Lord Peter,' said the Chief of Scotland Yard, rising from his desk with a friendly gesture of dismissal. 'The man was undoubtedly seen at Marylebone on the Friday morning, and, though we have unfortunately lost him again for the moment, I have no doubt whatever that we shall lay hands on him before long. The delay has been due to the unfortunate illness of the porter Morrison, whose evidence has been so material. But we are wasting no time now.'

'I'm sure I may leave it to you with every confidence, Sir Andrew,' replied Wimsey, cordially shaking hands. 'I'm diggin' away too; between us we ought to get somethin' – you in your small corner and I in mine, as the hymn says – or is it a hymn? I remember readin' it in a book about missionaries when I was small. Did you want to be a missionary in your youth? I did. I think most kids do some time or another, which is odd, seein' how unsatisfactory most of us turn out.'

'Meanwhile,' said Sir Andrew Mackenzie, 'if you run across the man yourself, let us know. I would never deny your extraordinary good fortune, or it may be good judgement, in running across the criminals we may be wanting.'

'If I catch the bloke,' said Lord Peter, 'I'll come and shriek under your windows till you let me in, if it's the middle of the night and you in your little night-shirt. And talking of night-shirts reminds me that we hope to see you down at Denver one of these days, as soon as this business is over. Mother sends kind regards, of course.'

'Thanks very much,' replied Sir Andrew. 'I hope you feel that all is going well. I had Parker in here this morning to report, and he seemed a little dissatisfied.'

'He's been doing a lot of ungrateful routine work,' said Wimsey, 'and being altogether the fine, sound man he always is. He's been a damn good friend to me, Sir Andrew, and it's a real privilege to be allowed to work with him. Well, so long, Chief.'

He found that his interview with Sir Andrew Mackenzie had taken up a couple of hours, and that it was nearly eight o'clock. He was just trying to make up his mind where to dine when he was accosted by a cheerful young woman with bobbed red hair, dressed in a short checked skirt, brilliant jumper, corduroy jacket, and a rakish green velvet tam-o'-shanter.

'Surely,' said the young woman, extending a shapely, ungloved hand, 'it's Lord Peter Wimsey. How're you? And how's Mary?'

'B'Jove!' said Wimsey gallantly, 'it's Miss Tarrant. How perfectly rippin' to see you again. Absolutely delightful. Thanks, Mary ain't as fit as she might be – worryin' about this murder business, y'know. You've heard that we're what the poor so kindly and tactfully call "in trouble", I expect, what?'

'Yes, of course,' replied Miss Tarrant eagerly, 'and, of course, as a good socialist, I can't help rejoicing rather when a peer gets taken up, because it does make him look so silly, you know, and the House of Lords is silly, isn't it? But, really, I'd rather it was anybody else's brother. Mary and I were such great friends, you know, and, of course, *you* do investigate things, don't you, not just live on your estates in the country and shoot birds? So I suppose that makes a difference.'

'That's very kind of you,' said Peter. 'If you can prevail upon yourself to overlook the misfortune of my birth and my other deficiencies, p'raps you would honour me by comin' along and havin' a bit of dinner somewhere, what?'

'Oh, I'd have *loved* to,' cried Miss Tarrant, with enormous energy, 'but I've promised to be at the club tonight. There's a meeting at nine. Mr Coke – the Labour leader, you know – is going to make a speech about converting the Army and Navy to Communism. We expect to be raided, and there's going to be a grand hunt for spies before we begin. But look here, do come along and dine with me there, and, if you like, I'll try to smuggle you in to the meeting, and you'll be seized and turned out. I suppose I oughtn't to have told you anything about it, because you ought to be a deadly enemy, but I can't believe you're dangerous.'

'I'm just an ordinary capitalist, I expect,' said Lord Peter, 'highly obnoxious.'

'Well, come to dinner, anyhow. I *do* so want to hear all the news.'

Peter reflected that the dinner at the Soviet Club would be worse than execrable, and was just preparing an excuse when it occurred to him that Miss Tarrant might be able to tell him a good many of the things that he didn't know, and really ought to know, about his own sister. Accordingly, he altered his polite refusal into a polite acceptance, and, plunging after Miss Tarrant, was led at a reckless pace and by a series of grimy short cuts into Gerrard Street, where an orange door, flanked by windows with magenta curtains, sufficiently indicated the Soviet Club.

The Soviet Club, being founded to accommodate free thinking rather than high living, had that curious amateur air which pervades all worldly institutions planned by unworldly people. Exactly why it made Lord Peter instantly think of mission teas he could not say, unless it was that all the members looked as though they cherished a purpose in life, and that the staff seemed rather sketchily trained and strongly in evidence. Wimsey reminded himself that in so democratic an institution one could hardly expect the assistants to assume that air of superiority which marks the servants in a West End club. For one thing, they would not be such capitalists. In the dining-room below the resemblance to a mission tea was increased by the exceedingly heated atmosphere, the babel of conversation, and the curious inequalities of the cutlery. Miss Tarrant secured seats at a rather crumby table near the serving-hatch, and Peter wedged himself in with some difficulty next to a very large, curly-haired man in a velvet coat, who was earnestly conversing with a thin, eager young woman in a Russian blouse, Venetian beads, a Hungarian shawl, and a Spanish comb, looking like a personification of the United Front of the 'Internationale.'

Lord Peter endeavoured to please his hostess by a question about the great Mr Coke, but was checked by an agitated 'Hush!'

'*Please* don't shout about it,' said Miss Tarrant, leaning across till her auburn mop positively tickled his eyebrows. 'It's *so* secret.'

'I'm awfully sorry,' said Wimsey apologetically. 'I say, d'you know you're dipping those jolly little beads of yours in the soup?'

'Oh, am I?' cried Miss Tarrant, withdrawing hastily. 'Oh, thank you so much. Especially as the colour runs. I hope it isn't arsenic or anything.' Then, leaning forward again, she whispered hoarsely:

'The girl next me is Erica Heath-Warburton – the writer, you know.'

Wimsey looked with a new respect at the lady in the Russian blouse. Few books were capable of calling up a blush to his cheek, but he remembered that one of Miss Heath-Warburton's had done it. The authoress was just saying impressively to her companion:

'– ever know a sincere emotion to express itself in a subordinate clause?'

'Joyce has freed us from the superstition of syntax,' agreed the curly man.

'Scenes which make emotional history,' said Miss Heath-Warburton, 'should ideally be expressed in a series of animal squeals.'

'The D. H. Lawrence formula,' said the other.

'Or even Dada,' said the authoress.

'We need a new notation,' said the curly-haired man, putting both elbows on the table and knocking Wimsey's bread on to the floor. 'Have you heard Robert Snoates recite his own verse to the tom-tom and the penny whistle?'

Lord Peter with difficulty detached his attention from this fascinating discussion to find that Miss Tarrant was saying something about Mary.

'One misses your sister very much,' she said. 'Her wonderful enthusiasm. She spoke so well at meetings. She had such a *real* sympathy with the worker.'

'It seems astonishing to me,' said Wimsey, 'seeing Mary's never had to do a stroke of work in her life.'

'Oh,' cried Miss Tarrant, 'but she *did* work. She worked

144

for us. Wonderfully! She was secretary to our Propaganda Society for nearly six months. And then she worked so hard for Mr Goyles. To say nothing of her nursing in the war. Of course, I don't approve of England's attitude in the war, but nobody would say the work wasn't hard.'

'Who is Mr Goyles?'

'Oh, one of our leading speakers – quite young, but the Government are really afraid of him. I expect he'll be here tonight. He has been lecturing in the North, but I believe he's back now.'

'I say, do look out,' said Peter. 'Your beads are in your plate again.'

'Are they? Well, perhaps they'll flavour the mutton. I'm afraid the cooking isn't very good here, but the subscription's so small, you see. I wonder Mary never told you about Mr Goyles. They were so *very* friendly, you know, some time ago. Everybody thought she was going to marry him – but it seemed to fall through. And then your sister left town. Do you know about it?'

'That was the fellow, was it? Yes – well, my people didn't altogether see it, you know. Thought Mr Goyles wasn't quite the son-in-law they'd take to. Family row and so on. Wasn't there myself; besides, Mary'd never listen to *me*. Still, that's what I gathered.'

'Another instance of the absurd, old-fashioned tyranny of parents,' said Miss Tarrant warmly. 'You wouldn't think it would still be possible – in post-war times.'

'I don't know,' said Wimsey, 'that you could exactly call it that. Not parents exactly. My mother's a remarkable woman. I don't think she interfered. Fact, I fancy she wanted to ask Mr Goyles to Denver. But my brother put his foot down.'

'Oh well, what can you expect?' said Miss Tarrant scornfully. 'But I don't see what business it was of his.'

'Oh, none,' agreed Wimsey. 'Only, owin' to my late father's circumscribed ideas of what was owin' to women, my brother has the handlin' of Mary's money till she marries with his consent. I don't say it's a good plan – I think it's a rotten plan. But there it is.'

'Monstrous!' said Miss Tarrant, shaking her head so angrily that she looked like shock-headed Peter. 'Barbarous! Simply feudal, you know. But, after all, what's money?'

'Nothing, of course,' said Peter. 'But if you've been brought up to havin' it it's a bit awkward to drop it suddenly. Like baths, you know.'

'I can't understand how it could have made any difference to Mary,' persisted Miss Tarrant mournfully. 'She liked being a worker. We once tried living in a workman's cottage for eight weeks, five of us, on eighteen shillings a week. It was a *marvellous* experience – on the very *edge* of the New Forest.'

'In the winter?'

'Well – no, we thought we'd better not *begin* with winter. But we had nine wet days, and the kitchen chimney smoked all the time. You see, the wood came out of the forest, so it was all damp.'

'I see. It must have been uncommonly interestin'.'

'It was an experience I shall *never* forget,' said Miss Tarrant. 'One felt so *close* to the earth and the primitive things. If only we could abolish industrialism. I'm afraid, though, we shall never get it put right without a "bloody revolution", you know. It's very terrible, of course, but salutary and inevitable. Shall we have coffee? We shall have to carry it upstairs ourselves, if you don't mind. The maids don't bring it up after dinner.'

Miss Tarrant settled her bill and returned, thrusting a cup of coffee into his hand. It had already overflowed into the saucer, and as he groped his way round a screen and up a steep and twisted staircase it overflowed quite an amount more.

Emerging from the basement, they almost ran into a young man with fair hair who was hunting for letters in a dark little row of pigeonholes. Finding nothing, he retreated into the lounge. Miss Tarrant uttered an exclamation of pleasure.

'Why, there *is* Mr Goyles,' she cried.

Wimsey glanced across, and at the sight of the tall, slightly stooping figure with the untidy hair and the gloved right hand he gave an irrepressible little gasp.

'Won't you introduce me?' he said.

'I'll fetch him,' said Miss Tarrant. She made off across the lounge and addressed the young agitator, who started, looked across at Wimsey, shook his head, appeared to apologise, gave a hurried glance at his watch, and darted out by the entrance. Wimsey sprang forward in pursuit.

'Extraordinary,' cried Miss Tarrant, with a blank face. 'He says he has an appointment – but he can't surely be missing the—'

'Excuse me,' said Peter. He dashed out, in time to perceive a dark figure retreating across the street. He gave chase. The man took to his heels, and seemed to plunge into the dark little alley which leads into the Charing Cross Road. Hurrying in pursuit, Wimsey was almost blinded by a sudden flash and smoke nearly in his face. A crashing blow on the left shoulder and a deafening report whirled his surroundings away. He staggered violently, and collapsed on to a second-hand brass bedstead.

8

MR PARKER TAKES NOTES

*'A man was taken to the Zoo and shown the giraffe.
After gazing at it a little in silence: "I don't believe it,"
he said.'*

PARKER'S first impulse was to doubt his own sanity; his next, to doubt Lady Mary's. Then, as the clouds rolled away from his brain, he decided that she was merely not speaking the truth.

'Come, Lady Mary,' he said encouragingly, but with an accent of reprimand as to an over-imaginative child, 'you can't expect us to believe that, you know.'

'But you must,' said the girl gravely; 'it's a fact, I shot him. I did, really. I didn't exactly mean to do it; it was a – well, a sort of accident.'

Mr Parker got up and paced about the room.

'You have put me in a terrible position, Lady Mary,' he said. 'You see, I'm a police officer. I never really imagined—'

'It doesn't matter,' said Lady Mary. 'Of course you'll have to arrest me, or detain me, or whatever you call it. That's what I came for. I'm quite ready to go quietly – that's the right expression, isn't it? I'd like to explain about it, though, first. Of course I ought to have done it long ago, but I'm afraid I lost my head. I didn't realise that Gerald would get blamed. I hoped they'd bring it in suicide. Do I make a statement to you now? Or do I do it at the police-station?'

Parker groaned.

'They won't – they won't punish me so badly if it was an accident, will they?' There was a quiver in the voice.

'No, of course not – of course not. But if only you had spoken earlier! No,' said Parker, stopping suddenly short in his distracted pacing and sitting down beside her. 'It's impossible – absurd.' He caught the girl's hand, suddenly, in his own. 'Nothing will convince me,' he said. 'It's absurd. It's not like you.'

'But an accident—'

'I don't mean that – you know I don't mean that. But that you should keep silence—'

'I was afraid. I'm telling you now.'

'No, no, no,' cried the detective. 'You're lying to me. Nobly, I know; but it's not worth it. No man could be worth it. Let him go, I implore you. Tell the truth. Don't shield this man. If he murdered Denis Cathcart—'

'*No!*' The girl sprang to her feet, wrenching her hand away. 'There was no other man. How dare you say it or think it! I killed Denis Cathcart, I tell you, and you *shall* believe it. I swear to you that there was no other man.'

Parker pulled himself together.

'Sit down, please. Lady Mary, you are determined to make this statement?'

'Yes.'

'Knowing that I have no choice but to act upon it?'

'If you will not hear it I shall go straight to the Police.'

Parker pulled out his note-book. 'Go on,' he said.

With no other sign of emotion than a nervous fidgeting with her gloves, Lady Mary began her confession in a clear, hard voice, as though she were reciting it by heart.

'On the evening of Wednesday, October 13th, I went upstairs at half-past nine. I sat up writing a letter. At a quarter past ten I heard my brother and Denis quarrelling in the passage. I heard my brother call Denis a cheat, and tell him that he was never to speak to me again. I heard Denis run out. I listened for some time, but did not hear him return. At half-past eleven I became alarmed. I changed my dress and went out to try and find Denis and bring him in. I feared he might do something desperate. After some time I found him in the shrubbery. I begged him to come in. He refused, and he told me about my brother's accusation and the quarrel. I was very much horrified, of course. He said where was the good of denying anything, as Gerald was determined to ruin him, and asked me to go away and marry him and live abroad. I said I was surprised that he should suggest such a thing in the circumstances. We both became very angry. I said "Come in now. Tomorrow you can leave by the first train." He seemed almost crazy. He pulled out a pistol and said that he'd come to the end of things, that his life was ruined, that we were a lot of hypocrites, and that I had never cared for him, or I shouldn't have minded what he'd done. Anyway, he said, if I wouldn't come with him it was all over, and he might as well be hanged for a sheep as a lamb – he'd shoot me and himself. I think he was quite out of his mind. He pulled out a revolver; I caught his hand; we struggled; I got the muzzle right up against his chest, and – either I pulled the trigger or it went off itself – I'm not clear which. It was all in such a whirl.'

She paused. Parker's pen took down the words, and his face showed growing concern. Lady Mary went on:

'He wasn't quite dead. I helped him up. We struggled back nearly to the house. He fell once—'

'Why,' asked Parker, 'did you not leave him and run into the house to fetch help?'

Lady Mary hesitated.

'It didn't occur to me. It was a nightmare. I could only think of getting him along. I think – *I think I wanted him to die.*'

There was a dreadful pause.

'He did die. He died at the door. I went into the conservatory and sat down. I sat for hours and tried to think. I hated him for being a cheat and a scoundrel. I'd been taken in, you see – made a fool of by a common sharper. I was glad he was dead. I must have sat there for hours without a coherent thought. It wasn't till my brother came along that I realised what I'd done, and that I might be suspected of murdering him. I was simply terrified. I made up my mind all in a moment that I'd pretend I knew nothing – that I'd heard a shot and come down. You know what I did.'

'Why, Lady Mary,' said Parker, in a perfectly toneless voice, 'why did you say to your brother "Good God, Gerald, you've killed him"?'

Another hesitant pause.

'I never said that. I said, "Good God, Gerald, he's killed, then", I never meant to suggest anything but suicide.'

'You admitted to those words at the inquest?'

'Yes –' Her hands knotted the gloves into all manner of shapes. 'By that time I had decided on a burglary story, you see.'

The telephone bell rang, and Parker went to the instrument. A voice came thinly over the wire:

'Is that 110A Piccadilly? This is Charing Cross Hospital. A man was brought in tonight who says he is Lord Peter Wimsey. He was shot in the shoulder, and struck his head in falling. He has only just recovered consciousness. He was brought in at 9.15. No, he will probably do very well now. Yes, come round by all means.'

'Peter has been shot,' said Parker. 'Will you come round with me to Charing Cross Hospital? They say he is in no danger: still—'

'Oh, quick!' cried Lady Mary.

Gathering up Mr Bunter as they hurried through the hall, detective and self-accused rushed hurriedly out into Piccadilly, and, picking up a belated taxi at Hyde Park Corner, drove madly away through the deserted streets.

9

GOYLES

'"and the moral of that is –" said the Duchess.'
ALICE'S ADVENTURES IN WONDERLAND

A PARTY of four were assembled next morning at a very late breakfast, or very early lunch, in Lord Peter's flat. Its most cheerful member, despite a throbbing shoulder and a splitting headache, was undoubtedly Lord Peter himself, who lay upon the chesterfield surrounded with cushions and carousing upon tea and toast. Having been brought home in an ambulance, he had instantly fallen into a healing sleep, and had woken at nine o'clock aggressively clear and active in mind. In consequence, Mr Parker had been dispatched in a hurry, half-fed and burdened with the secret memory of last night's disclosures, to Scotland Yard. Here he had set in motion the proper machinery for catching Lord Peter's assassin. 'Only don't you say anything about the attack on me,' said his lordship. 'Tell 'em he's to be detained in connection with the Riddlesdale case. That's good enough for them.' It was now eleven, and Mr Parker had returned, gloomy and hungry, and was consuming a belated omelette and a glass of claret.

Lady Mary Wimsey was hunched up in the window-seat. Her bobbed golden hair made a little blur of light about her in the pale autumn sunshine. She had made an attempt to breakfast early, and now sat gazing out into Piccadilly. Her first appearance that morning had been made in Lord Peter's dressing-gown, but she now wore a serge skirt and jade-green jumper, which had been brought to town for her by the fourth member of the party, now composedly eating a mixed grill and sharing the decanter with Parker.

This was a rather short, rather plump, very brisk elderly lady, with bright black eyes like a bird's, and very handsome white hair exquisitely dressed. Far from looking as though she had just taken a long night journey, she was easily the most composed and trim of the four. She was, however, annoyed, and said so at considerable length. This was the Dowager Duchess of Denver.

'It is not so much, Mary, that you went off so abruptly last night – just before dinner, too – inconveniencing and alarming us very much – indeed, poor Helen was totally unable to eat her dinner, which was extremely distressing to her feelings, because, you know, she always makes such a point of never being upset about anything – I really don't know why, for some of the greatest men have not minded showing their feelings, I don't mean Southerners necessarily, but as Mr Chesterton very rightly points out – Nelson, too, who was certainly English if he wasn't Irish or Scotch, I forget, but United Kingdom, anyway (if that means anything nowadays with a Free State – such a ridiculous title, especially as it always makes one think of the Orange Free State, and I'm sure they wouldn't care to be mixed up with that, being so very green themselves). And going off without even proper clothes, and taking the car, so that I had to wait till the 1.15 from Northallerton – a ridiculous time to start, and such a bad train, too, not getting up till 10.30. Besides, if you *must* run off to town, why do it in that unfinished manner? If you had only looked up the trains before starting, you would have seen you would have half an hour's wait at Northallerton, and you could quite easily have packed a bag. It's so much better to do things neatly and thoroughly – even stupid things. And it was very stupid of you indeed to dash off like that, to embarrass and bore poor Mr Parker with a lot of twaddle – though I suppose it was Peter you meant to see. You know, Peter, if you will haunt low places full of Russians and sucking Socialists taking themselves seriously, you ought to know better than to encourage them by running after them, however futile, and given to drinking coffee and writing poems with no shape to them, and generally ruining their nerves. And in any case, it makes not the slightest difference; I could have told Peter all about it myself, if he doesn't know already, as he probably does.'

Lady Mary turned very white at this and glanced at Parker, who replied rather to her than to the Dowager:

'No. Lord Peter and I haven't had time to discuss anything yet.'

'Lest it should ruin my shattered nerves and bring a fever to my aching brow,' added that gentleman amiably. 'You're a kind, thoughtful soul, Charles, and I don't know what I should do without you. I wish that rotten old second-hand dealer had been a bit brisker about takin' in his stock-in-trade for the night, though. Perfectly 'stror'nary number of knobs there are on a brass bedstead. Saw it comin', y'know, an' couldn't stop myself. However, what's a mere brass bedstead? The great detective, though at first stunned and dizzy from his brutal treatment by the fifteen veiled assassins all armed with meat-choppers, soon regained his senses, thanks to his sound constitution and healthy manner of life. Despite the severe gassing he had endured in the underground room – eh? A telegram? Oh, thanks, Bunter.'

Lord Peter appeared to read the message with great inward satisfaction, for his long lips twitched at the corners, and he tucked the slip of paper away in his pocket-book with a little sigh of satisfaction. He called to Bunter to take away the breakfast-tray and to renew the cooling bandage about his brow. This done, Lord Peter leaned back among his cushions, and with an air of malicious enjoyment launched at Mr Parker the inquiry:

'Well, now, how did you and Mary get on last night? Polly, did you tell him you'd done the murder?'

Few things are more irritating than to discover, after you have been at great pains to spare a person some painful intelligence, that he has known it all along and is not nearly so much affected by it as he properly should be. Mr Parker quite simply and suddenly lost his temper. He bounded to his feet, and exclaimed, without the least reason: 'Oh, it's perfectly hopeless trying to do anything!'

Lady Mary sprang from the window-seat.

'Yes, I did,' she said. 'It's quite true. Your precious case is finished, Peter.'

The Dowager said, without the least discomposure: 'You must allow your brother to be the best judge of his own affairs, my dear.'

'As a matter of fact,' replied his lordship, 'I rather fancy Polly's right. Hope so, I'm sure. Anyway, we've got the fellow, so now we shall know.'

Lady Mary gave a sort of gasp, and stepped forward with her chin up and her hands tightly clenched. It caught at Parker's heart to see overwhelming catastrophe so bravely faced. The official side of him was thoroughly bewildered, but the human part ranged itself instantly in support of that gallant defiance.

'Whom have they got?' he demanded, in a voice quite unlike his own.

'The Goyles person,' said Lord Peter carelessly. 'Uncommon quick work, what? But since he'd no more original idea than to take the boat-train to Folkestone they didn't have much difficulty.'

'It isn't true,' said Lady Mary. She stamped. 'It's a lie. He wasn't there. He's innocent. I killed Denis.'

'Fine,' thought Parker, 'fine! Damn Goyles, anyway, what's he done to deserve it?'

Lord Peter said: 'Mary, don't be an ass.'

'Yes,' said the Dowager placidly. 'I was going to suggest to you, Peter, that this Mr Goyles – such a terrible name, Mary dear, I can't say I ever cared for it, even if there had been nothing else against him – especially as he would sign himself Geo. Goyles – G. e. o. you know, Mr Parker, for George, and I never *could* help reading it as Gargoyles – I very nearly wrote to you, my dear, mentioning Mr Goyles, and asking if you could see him in town, because there was something, when I came to think of it, about that ipecacuanha business that made me feel he might have something to do with it.'

'Yes,' said Peter, with a grin, 'you always did find him a bit sickenin', didn't you?'

'How can you, Wimsey?' growled Parker reproachfully, with his eyes on Mary's face.

'Never mind him,' said the girl. 'If you can't be a gentleman, Peter—'

'Damn it all!' cried the invalid explosively. 'Here's a fellow who, without the slightest provocation, plugs a bullet into my shoulder, breaks my collar-bone, brings me up head foremost on a knobbly, second-hand brass bedstead and vamooses, and when, in what seems to me jolly mild, parliamentary language, I call him a sickenin' feller, my own sister says I'm no gentleman. Look at me! In my own house, forced to sit here with a perfectly beastly headache, and lap up toast and tea, while you people distend and bloat yourselves on mixed grills and omelettes and a damn good vintage claret—'

'Silly boy,' said the Duchess, 'don't get so excited. And it's time for your medicine. Mr Parker, kindly touch the bell.'

Mr Parker obeyed in silence. Lady Mary came slowly across, and stood looking at her brother.

'Peter,' she said, 'what makes you say that *he* did it?'

'Did what?'

'Shot – you?' The words were only a whisper.

The entrance of Mr Bunter at this moment with a cooling draught dissipated the tense atmosphere. Lord Peter quaffed his potion, had his pillows re-arranged, submitted to have his temperature taken and his pulse counted, asked if he might not have an egg for his lunch, and lit a cigarette. Mr Bunter retired, people distributed themselves into more comfortable chairs, and felt happier.

'Now, Polly, old girl,' said Peter, 'cut out the sob-stuff. I accidentally ran into this Goyles chap last night at your Soviet Club. I asked that Miss Tarrant to introduce me, but the minute Goyles heard my name, he made tracks. I rushed out after him, only meanin' to have a word with him, when the idiot stopped at the corner of Newport Court, potted me, and bunked. Silly-ass thing to do. I knew who he was. He couldn't help gettin' caught.'

'Peter –' said Mary in a ghastly voice.

'Look here, Polly,' said Wimsey. 'I did think of you. Honest injun, I did. I haven't had the man arrested. I've made no charge at all – have I, Parker? What did you tell 'em to do when you were down at the Yard this morning?'

'To detain Goyles pending inquiries, because he was

wanted as a witness in the Riddlesdale case,' said Parker slowly.

'He knows nothing about it,' said Mary, doggedly now. 'He wasn't anywhere near. He is innocent of *that*!'

'Do you think so?' said Lord Peter gravely. 'If you know he is innocent, why tell all those lies to screen him? It won't do, Mary. You know he was there – and you think he is guilty.'

'No!'

'Yes,' said Wimsey, grasping her with his sound hand as she shrank away. 'Mary, have you thought what you are doing? You are perjuring yourself and putting Gerald in peril of his life, in order to shield from justice a man whom you suspect of murdering your lover and who has most certainly tried to murder me.'

'Oh,' cried Parker, in an agony, 'all this interrogation is horribly irregular.'

'Never mind him,' said Peter. 'Do you really think you're doing the right thing, Mary?'

The girl looked helplessly at her brother for a minute or two. Peter cocked up a whimsical, appealing eye from under his bandages. The defiance melted out of her face.

'I'll tell the truth,' said Lady Mary.

'Good egg,' said Peter, extending a hand. 'I'm sorry. I know you like the fellow, and we appreciate your decision enormously. Truly, we do. Now, sail ahead, old thing, and you take it down, Parker.'

'Well, it really all started years ago with George. You were at the Front then, Peter, but I suppose they told you about it – and put everything in the worst possible light.'

'I wouldn't say that, dear,' put in the Duchess. 'I think I told Peter that your brother and I were not altogether pleased with what we had seen of the young man – which was not very much, if you remember. He invited himself down one weekend when the house was very full, and he seemed to make a point of consulting nobody's convenience but his own. And you know, dear, you even said yourself you thought he was unnecessarily rude to poor old Lord Mountweazle.'

'He said what he thought,' said Mary. 'Of course, Lord Mountweazle, poor dear, doesn't understand that the present generation is accustomed to discuss things with its elders, not just kow-tow to them. When George gave his opinion, he thought he was just contradicting.'

'To be sure,' said the Dowager, 'when you flatly deny everything a person says it does sound like contradiction to the uninitiated. But all I remember saying to Peter was that Mr Goyles's manners seemed to me to lack polish, and that he showed a lack of independence in his opinions.'

'A lack of independence?' said Mary, wide-eyed.

'Well, dear, I thought so. What oft was thought and frequently much better expressed, as Pope says – or was it somebody else? But the worse you express yourself these days the more profound people think you – though that's nothing new. Like Browning and those quaint metaphysical people, when you never know whether they really mean their mistress or the Established Church, so bridegroomy and biblical – to say nothing of dear S. Augustine – the Hippo man, I mean, not the one who missionised over here, though I daresay he was delightful too, and in those days I suppose they didn't have annual sales of work and tea in the parish room, so it doesn't seem quite like what we mean nowadays by missionaries – he knew all about it – you remember about that mandrake – or is that the thing you had to get a big black dog for? Manichee, that's the word. What was his name? Was it Faustus? Or am I mixing him up with the old man in the opera?'

'Well, anyway,' said Mary, without stopping to disentangle the Duchess's sequence of ideas, 'George was the only person I really cared about – he still is. Only it did seem so hopeless. Perhaps you didn't say much about him, mother, but Gerald said *lots* – dreadful things!'

'Yes,' said the Duchess, 'he said what he thought. The present generation does, you know. To the uninitiated, I admit, dear, it does sound a little rude.'

Peter grinned, but Mary went on unheeding.

'George had simply *no* money. He'd really given everything he had to the Labour Party one way and another, and he'd lost his job in the Ministry of Information: they found he had too much sympathy with the Socialists abroad. It was awfully unfair. Anyhow, one couldn't be a burden on him; and Gerald was a beast, and he said he'd absolutely stop my allowance if I didn't send George away. So I did, but of course it didn't make a bit of difference to the way we both felt. I will say for mother she was a bit more decent. She said she'd help us if George got a job; but, as I pointed out, if George got a job we shouldn't *need* helping!'

'But, my dear, I could hardly insult Mr Goyles by suggesting that he should live on his mother-in-law,' said the Dowager.

'Why not?' said Mary. 'George doesn't believe in those old-fashioned ideas about property. Besides, if you'd given it to me, it would be *my* money. We believe in men and women being equal. Why should the one always be the bread-winner more than the other?'

'I can't imagine, dear,' said the Dowager. 'Still, I could hardly expect poor Mr Goyles to live on unearned increment when he didn't believe in inherited property.'

'That's a fallacy,' said Mary, rather vaguely. 'Anyhow,' she added hastily, 'that's what happened. Then, after the war, George went to Germany to study Socialism and Labour questions there, and nothing seemed any good. So when Denis Cathcart turned up, I said I'd marry him.'

'Why?' asked Peter. 'He never sounded to me a bit the kind of bloke for you. I mean, as far as I could make out, he was Tory and diplomatic and – well, quite crusted old tawny, so to speak. I shouldn't have thought you had an idea in common.'

'No; but then he didn't care twopence whether I had any ideas or not. I made him promise he wouldn't bother me with diplomats and people, and he said no, I could do as I liked, provided I didn't compromise him. And we were to live in Paris and go our own ways and not bother. And anything was better than staying here, and marrying somebody in one's own set, and opening bazaars and watching polo and meeting the Prince of Wales. So I said I'd marry Denis, because I didn't care about him, and I'm pretty sure he didn't care a halfpenny about me, and we should have left each other alone. I did so want to be left alone!'

'Was Jerry all right about your money?' inquired Peter.

'Oh yes. He said Denis was no great catch – I do wish Gerald wasn't so vulgar, in that flat, early-Victorian way – but he said that, after George, he could only thank his stars it wasn't worse.'

'Make a note of that, Charles,' said Wimsey.

'Well, it seemed all right at first, but, as things went on, I got more and more depressed. Do you know, there was something a little alarming about Denis. He was so extraordinarily reserved. I know I wanted to be left alone, but – well, it was uncanny! He was correct. Even when he went off the deep end and was passionate – which didn't often happen – he was correct about it.

Extraordinary. Like one of those odd French novels, you know, Peter: frightfully hot stuff, but absolutely impersonal.'

'Charles, old man!' said Lord Peter.

'M'm?'

'That's important. You realise the bearing of that?'

'No.'

'Never mind. Drive on, Polly?'

'Aren't I making your head ache?'

'Damnably; but I like it. Do go on. I'm not sprouting a lily with anguish moist and fever-dew, or anything like that. I'm getting really thrilled. What you've just said is more illuminating than anything I've struck for a week.'

'Really!' Mary stared at Peter with every trace of hostility vanished. 'I thought you'd never understand that part.'

'Lord!' said Peter. 'Why not?'

Mary shook her head. 'Well, I'd been corresponding all the time with George, and suddenly he wrote to me at the beginning of this month to say he'd come back from Germany, and had got a job on the *Thunderclap* – the Socialist weekly, you know – at a beginning screw of £4 a week, and wouldn't I chuck these capitalists and so on, and come and be an honest working woman with him. He could get me a secretarial job on the paper. I was to type and so on for him, and help him get his articles together. And he thought between us we should make £6 or £7 a week, which would be heaps to live on. And I was getting more frightened of Denis every day. So I said I would. But I knew there'd be an awful row with Gerald. And really I was rather ashamed – the engagement had been announced and there'd be a ghastly lot of talk and people trying to persuade me. And Denis might have made things horribly uncomfortable for Gerald – he was rather that sort. So we decided the best thing to do would be just to run away and get married first, and escape the wrangling.'

'Quite so,' said Peter. 'Besides, it would look rather well in the paper, wouldn't it? "PEER'S DAUGHTER WEDS SOCIALIST – ROMANTIC SIDE-CAR ELOPEMENT – '£6 a WEEK PLENTY,' SAYS HER LADYSHIP".'

'Pig!' said Lady Mary.

'Very good,' said Peter, 'I get you! So it was arranged that the romantic Goyles should fetch you away from Riddlesdale – why Riddlesdale? It would be twice as easy from London or Denver.'

'No. For one thing he had to be up North. And everybody knows one in town, and – anyhow, we didn't want to wait.'

'Besides, one would miss the Young Lochinvar touch. Well, then, why at the unearthly hour of 3 a.m.?'

'He had a meeting on Wednesday night at North-allerton. He was going to come straight on and pick me up, and run me down to town to be married by special licence. We allowed ample time. George had to be at the office next day.'

'I see. Well, I'll go on now, and you stop me if I'm wrong. You went up at 9.30 on Wednesday night. You packed a suitcase. You – did you think of writing any sort of letter to comfort your sorrowing friends and relations?'

'Yes, I wrote one. But I—'

'Of course. Then you went to bed, I fancy, or, at any rate, turned the clothes back and lay down.'

'Yes. I lay down. It was a good thing I did, as it happened—'

'True, you wouldn't have had much time to make the bed look probable in the morning, and we should have

164

heard about it. By the way, Parker, when Mary confessed her sins to you last night, did you make any notes?'

'Yes,' said Parker, 'if you can read my shorthand.'

'Quite so,' said Peter. 'Well, the rumpled bed disposes of your story about never having gone to bed at all, doesn't it?'

'And I thought it was such a good story!'

'Want of practice,' replied her brother kindly. 'You'll do better, next time. It's just as well, really, that it's so hard to tell a long, consistent lie. *Did* you, as a matter of fact, hear Gerald go out at 11.30, as Pettigrew-Robinson (damn his ears!) said?'

'I fancy I did hear somebody moving about,' said Mary, 'but I didn't think much about it.'

'Quite right,' said Peter, 'when I hear people movin' about the house at night, I'm much too delicate-minded to think anything at all.'

'Of course,' interposed the Duchess, 'particularly in England, where it is so oddly improper to think. I will say for Peter that, if he can put a continental interpretation on anything, he will – so considerate of you, dear, as soon as you took to doing it in silence and not mentioning it, as you so intelligently did as a child. You were really a very observant little boy, dear.'

'And still is,' said Mary, smiling at Peter with surprising friendliness.

'Old bad habits die hard,' said Wimsey. 'To proceed. At three o'clock you went down to meet Goyles. Why did he come all the way up to the house? It would have been safer to meet him in the lane.'

'I knew I couldn't get out of the lodge-gate without waking Hardraw, and so I'd have to get over the palings somewhere. I might have managed alone, but not with a heavy suitcase. So, as George would have to climb over, anyhow, we thought he'd better come and help carry the suitcase. And then we couldn't miss each other by the conservatory door. I sent him a little plan of the path.'

'Was Goyles there when you got downstairs?'

'No – at least – no, I didn't see him. But there was poor Denis's body, and Gerald bending over it. My first idea was that Gerald had killed George. That's why I said, "O God! you've killed him!" ' (Peter glanced across at Parker and nodded.) 'Then Gerald turned him over, and I saw it was Denis – and then I'm sure I heard something moving a long way off in the shrubbery – a noise like twigs snapping – and it suddenly came over me, where was George? Oh, Peter, I saw everything then, so clearly. I saw that Denis must have come on George waiting there, and attacked him – I'm sure Denis must have attacked him. Probably he thought he was a burglar. Or he found out who he was and tried to drive him away. And in the struggle George must have shot him. It was awful!'

Peter patted his sister on the shoulder. 'Poor kid,' he said.

'I didn't know what to do,' went on the girl. 'I'd so awfully little time, you see. My one idea was that nobody must suspect anybody had been there. So I had quickly to invent an excuse for being there myself. I shoved my suitcase behind the centre plants to start with. Jerry was taken up with the body and didn't notice – you know, Jerry never *does* notice things till you shove them under his nose. But I knew if there'd been a shot Freddy and the Marchbankses must have heard it. So I pretended I'd heard it too, and rushed down to look for burglars. It was a bit lame, but the best thing I could think of. Gerald sent me up to alarm the house, and I had the story all ready by the time I reached the landing. Oh, and I was quite proud of myself for not forgetting the suitcase!'

'You dumped it into the chest,' said Peter.

'Yes. I had a horrible shock the other morning when I found you looking in.'

'Nothing like the shock I had when I found the silver sand there.'

'Silver sand?'

'Out of the conservatory.'

'Good gracious!' said Mary.

'Well, go on. You knocked up Freddy and the Pettigrew-Robinsons. Then you had to bolt into your room to destroy your farewell letter and take your clothes off.'

'Yes, I'm afraid I didn't do that very naturally. But I couldn't expect anybody to believe that I went burglarhunting in a complete set of silk undies and a carefully knotted tie with a gold safety-pin.'

'No. I see your difficulty.'

'It turned out quite well, too, because they were all quite ready to believe that I wanted to escape from Mrs Pettigrew-Robinson – except Mrs P. herself, of course.'

'Yes; even Parker swallowed that, didn't you, old man?'

'Oh, quite, quite so,' said Parker gloomily.

'I made a dreadful mistake about that shot,' resumed Lady Mary. 'You see, I explained it all so elaborately – and then I found that nobody had heard a shot at all. And afterwards they discovered that it had all happened in the shrubbery – and the time wasn't right, either. Then at the inquest I *had* to stick to my story – and it got to look worse and worse – and then they put the blame on Gerald. In my wildest moments I'd never thought of that. Of course, I see now how my wretched evidence helped.'

'Hence the ipecacuanha,' said Peter.

'I'd got into such a frightful tangle,' said poor Lady

Mary, 'I thought I had better shut up altogether for fear of making things still worse.'

'And did you still think Goyles had done it?'

'I – I didn't know what to think,' said the girl. 'I don't now. Peter, who else *could* have done it?'

'Honestly, old thing,' said his lordship, 'if he didn't do it, I don't know who did.'

'He ran away, you see,' said Lady Mary.

'He seems rather good at shootin' and runnin' away,' said Peter grimly.

'If he hadn't done that to you,' said Mary slowly, 'I'd never have told you. I'd have died first. But, of course, with his revolutionary doctrines – and when you think of Red Russia and all the blood spilt in riots and insurrections and things – I suppose it does teach a contempt for human life.'

'My dear,' said the Duchess, 'it seems to me that Mr Goyles shows no especial contempt for his own life. You must try to look at the thing fairly. Shooting people and running away is not very heroic – according to *our* standards.'

'The thing I don't understand,' struck in Wimsey hurriedly, 'is how Gerald's revolver got into the shrubbery.'

'The thing I should like to know about,' said the Duchess, 'is, was Denis really a card-sharper?'

'The thing *I* should like to know about,' said Parker, 'is the green-eyed cat.'

'Denis *never* gave me a cat,' said Mary. 'That was a tarradiddle.'

'Were you ever in a jeweller's with him in the Rue de la Paix?'

'Oh yes; heaps of times. And he gave me a diamond and tortoise-shell comb. But never a cat.'

'Then we may disregard the whole of last night's elaborate confession,' said Lord Peter, looking through Parker's notes, with a smile. 'It's really not bad, Polly, not bad at all. You've a talent for romantic fiction – no, I mean it! Just here and there you need more attention to detail. For instance, you *couldn't* have dragged that badly wounded man all up the path to the house without getting blood all over your coat, you know. By the way, did Goyles know Cathcart at all?'

'Not to my knowledge.'

'Because Parker and I had an alternative theory, which would clear Goyles from the worst part of the charge, anyhow, Tell her, old man; it was your idea.'

Thus urged, Parker outlined the blackmail and suicide theory.

'That sounds plausible,' said Mary – 'academically speaking, I mean; but it isn't a bit like George – I mean blackmail is so *beastly*, isn't it?'

'Well,' said Peter, 'I think the best thing is to go and see Goyles. Whatever the key to Wednesday night's riddle is, he holds it. Parker, old man, we're nearing the end of the chase.'

10

NOTHING ABIDES AT THE NOON

*'Alas!' said Hiya, 'the sentiments which this person
expressed with irreproachable honourableness, when
the sun was high in the heavens and the probability of
secretly leaving an undoubtedly well-appointed home
was engagingly remote, seem to have an entirely different significance when recalled by night in a damp
orchard, and on the eve of their fulfilment.'*

THE WALLET OF KAI-LUNG

'And his short minute, after noon, is night.'

DONNE

MR GOYLES was interviewed the next day at the police-
station. Mr Murbles was present, and Mary insisted on
coming. The young man began by blustering a little, but
the solicitor's dry manner made its impression.

'Lord Peter Wimsey identifies you,' said Mr Murbles,
'as the man who made a murderous attack upon him last
night. With remarkable generosity, he has forborne to
press the charge. Now we know further that you were
present at Riddlesdale Lodge on the night when Captain
Cathcart was shot. You will no doubt be called as a
witness in the case. But you would greatly assist justice
by making a statement to us now. This is a purely
friendly and private interview, Mr Goyles. As you see,
no representative of the police is present. We simply ask
for your help. I ought, however, to warn you that,

whereas it is, of course, fully competent for you to refuse to answer any of our questions, a refusal might lay you open to the gravest imputations.'

'In fact,' said Goyles, 'it's a threat. If I don't tell you, you'll have me arrested on suspicion of murder.'

'Dear me, no, Mr Goyles,' returned the solicitor. 'We should merely place what information we hold in the hands of the police, who would then act as they thought fit. God bless my soul, no – anything like a threat would be highly irregular. In the matter of the assault upon Lord Peter, his lordship will, of course, use his own discretion.'

'Well,' said Goyles sullenly, 'it's a threat, call it what you like. However, I don't mind speaking – especially as you'll be jolly well disappointed. I suppose you gave me away, Mary.'

Mary flushed indignantly.

'My sister has been extraordinarily loyal to you, Mr Goyles,' said Lord Peter. 'I may tell you, indeed, that she put herself into a position of grave personal inconvenience – not to say danger – on your behalf. You were traced to London in consequence of your having left unequivocal traces in your exceedingly hasty retreat. When my sister accidentally opened a telegram addressed to me at Riddlesdale by my family name she hurried immediately to town, to shield you if she could, at any cost to herself. Fortunately I had already received a duplicate wire at my flat. Even then I was not certain of your identity when I accidentally ran across you at the Soviet Club. Your own energetic efforts, however, to avoid an interview gave me complete certainty, together with an excellent excuse for detaining you. In fact, I'm uncommonly obliged to you for your assistance.'

Mr Goyles looked resentful.

'I don't know how you could think, George –' said Mary.

'Never mind what I think,' said the young man, roughly. 'I gather you've told 'em all about it now, anyhow. Well, I'll tell you my story as shortly as I can, and you'll see I know damn all about it. If you don't believe me I can't help it. I came along at about a quarter to three, and parked the 'bus in the lane.'

'Where were you at 11.50?'

'On the road from Northallerton. My meeting didn't finish till 10.45. I can bring a hundred witnesses to prove it.'

Wimsey made a note of the address where the meeting had been held, and nodded to Goyles to proceed.

'I climbed over the wall and walked through the shrubbery.'

'You saw no person, and no body?'

'Nobody, alive or dead.'

'Did you notice any blood or footprints on the path?'

'No. I didn't like to use my torch, for fear of being seen from the house. There was just light enough to see the path. I came to the door of the conservatory just before three. As I came up I stumbled over something. I felt it, and it was like a body. I was alarmed. I thought it might be Mary – ill or fainted or something. I ventured to turn on my light. Then I saw it was Cathcart, dead.'

'You are sure he was dead?'

'Stone dead.'

'One moment,' interposed the solicitor. 'You say you saw that it was Cathcart. Had you known Cathcart previously?'

'No, never. I meant that I saw it was a dead man, and learnt afterwards that it was Cathcart.'

'In fact, you do not, now, know of your own knowledge, that it was Cathcart?'

'Yes – at least, I recognised the photographs in the papers afterwards.'

'It is very necessary to be accurate in making a statement, Mr Goyles. A remark such as you made just now might give a most unfortunate impression to the police or to a jury.'

So saying, Mr Murbles blew his nose, and resettled his pince-nez.

'What next?' inquired Peter.

'I fancied I heard somebody coming up the path. I did not think it wise to be found there with the corpse, so I cleared out.'

'Oh,' said Peter, with an indescribable expression, 'that was a very simple solution. You left the girl you were going to marry to make for herself the unpleasant discovery that there was a dead man in the garden and that her gallant wooer had made tracks. What did you expect *her* to think?'

'Well, I thought she'd keep quiet for her own sake. As a matter of fact, I didn't think very clearly about anything. I knew I'd broke in where I had no business, and that if I was found with a murdered man it might look jolly queer for me.'

'In fact,' said Mr Murbles, 'you lost your head, young man, and ran away in a very foolish and cowardly manner.'

'You needn't put it that way,' retorted Mr Goyles. 'I was in a very awkward and stupid situation to start with.'

'Yes,' said Lord Peter ironically, 'and 3 a.m. is a nasty chilly time of day. Next time you arrange an elopement, make it for six o'clock in the evening, or twelve o'clock at night. You seem better at framing conspiracies than carrying them out. A little thing upsets your nerves,

Mr Goyles. I don't really think, you know, that a person of your temperament should carry fire-arms. What in the world, you blitherin' young ass, made you loose off that pop-gun at me last night? You *would* have been in a damned awkward situation then, if you'd accidentally hit me in the head or the heart or anywhere that mattered. If you're so frightened of a dead body, why go about shootin' at people? Why, why, why? That's what beats me. If you're tellin' the truth now, you never stood in the slightest danger. Lord! and to think of the time and trouble we've had to waste catchin' you – you ass! And poor old Mary, workin' away and half killin' herself, because she thought at least you wouldn't have run away unless there was somethin' to run from!'

'You must make allowance for a nervous temperament,' said Mary in a hard voice.

'If you knew what it felt like to be shadowed and followed and badgered –' began Mr Goyles.

'But I thought you Soviet Club people enjoyed being suspected of things,' said Lord Peter. 'Why, it ought to be the proudest moment of your life when you're really looked on as a dangerous fellow.'

'It's the sneering of men like you,' said Goyles passionately, 'that does more to breed hatred between class and class—'

'Never mind about that,' interposed Mr Murbles. 'The law's the law for everybody, and you have managed to put yourself in a very awkward position, young man.' He touched a bell on the table, and Parker entered with a constable. 'We shall be obliged to you,' said Mr Murbles, 'if you will kindly have this young man kept under observation. We make no charge against him so long as he behaves himself, but he must not attempt to abscond before the Riddlesdale case comes up for trial.'

'Certainly not, sir,' said Mr Parker.

'One moment,' said Mary. 'Mr Goyles, here is the ring you gave me. Good-bye. When next you make a public speech calling for decisive action I will come and applaud it. You speak so well about that sort of thing. But otherwise, I think we had better not meet again.'

'Of course,' said the young man bitterly, 'your people have forced me into this position, and you turn round and sneer at me too.'

'I didn't mind thinking you were a murderer,' said Lady Mary spitefully, 'but I *do* mind your being such an ass.'

Before Mr Goyles could reply, Mr Parker, bewildered but not wholly displeased, manoeuvred his charge out of the room. Mary walked over to the window, and stood biting her lips.

Presently Lord Peter came across to her. 'I say, Polly, old Murbles has asked us to lunch. Would you like to come? Sir Impey Biggs will be there.'

'I don't want to meet him today. It's very kind of Mr Murbles—'

'Oh, come along, old thing. Biggs is some celebrity, you know, and perfectly toppin' to look at, in a marbly kind of way. He'll tell you all about his canaries—'

Mary giggled through her obstinate tears.

'It's perfectly sweet of you, Peter, to try and amuse the baby. But I can't. I'd make a fool of myself. I've been made enough of a fool of for one day.'

'Bosh,' said Peter. 'Of course, Goyles didn't show up very well this morning, but, then, he was in an awfully difficult position. *Do* come.'

'I hope Lady Mary consents to adorn my bachelor establishment,' said the solicitor, coming up. 'I shall esteem it a very great honour. I really do not think I have entertained a lady in my chambers for twenty years – dear me, twenty years indeed it must be.'

'In that case,' said Lady Mary, 'I simply *can't* refuse.'

Mr Murbles inhabited a delightful old set of rooms in Staple Inn, with windows looking out upon the formal garden, with its odd little flower-beds and tinkling fountain. The chambers kept up to a miracle the old-fashioned law atmosphere which hung about his own prim person. His dining-room was furnished in mahogany, with a Turkey carpet and crimson curtains. On his sideboard stood some pieces of handsome Sheffield plate and a number of decanters with engraved silver labels round their necks. There was a bookcase full of large volumes bound in law calf, and an oil-painting of a harsh-featured judge over the mantelpiece. Lady Mary felt a sudden gratitude for this discreet and solid Victorianism.

'I fear we may have to wait a few moments for Sir Impey,' said Mr Murbles, consulting his watch. 'He is engaged in Quangle & Hamper v. *Truth*, but they expect to be through this morning – in fact, Sir Impey fancied that midday would see the end of it. Brilliant man, Sir Impey. He is defending *Truth*.'

'Astonishin' position for a lawyer, what?' said Peter.

'The newspaper,' said Mr Murbles, acknowledging the pleasantry with a slight unbending of the lips, 'against these people who profess to cure fifty-nine different diseases with the same pill. Quangle & Hamper produced some of their patients in court to testify to the benefits they'd enjoyed from the cure. To hear Sir Impey handling them was an intellectual treat. His kindly manner goes a long way with the old ladies. When he suggested that one of them should show her leg to the Bench the sensation in court was really phenomenal.'

'And did she show it?' inquired Lord Peter.

'Panting for the opportunity, my dear Lord Peter, panting for the opportunity.'

'I wonder they had the nerve to call her.'

'Nerve?' said Mr Murbles. 'The nerve of men like Quangle & Hamper has not its fellow in the universe, to adopt the expression of the great Shakespeare. But Sir Impey is not the man to take liberties with. We are really extremely fortunate to have secured his help. – Ah, I think I hear him!'

A hurried footstep on the stair indeed announced the learned counsel, who burst in, still in wig and gown, and full of apology.

'Extremely sorry, Murbles,' said Sir Impey. 'We became excessively tedious at the end, I regret to say. I really did my best, but dear old Dowson is getting as deaf as a post, you know, and terribly fumbling in his movements. – And how are you, Wimsey? You look as if you'd been in the wars. Can we bring an action for assault against anybody?'

'Much better than that,' put in Mr Murbles; 'attempted murder, if you please.'

'Excellent, excellent,' said Sir Impey.

'Ah, but we've decided not to prosecute,' said Mr Murbles, shaking his head.

'Really! Oh, my dear Wimsey, this will never do. Lawyers have to live, you know. Your sister? I hadn't the pleasure of meeting you at Riddlesdale, Lady Mary. I trust you are fully recovered.'

'Entirely, thank you,' said Mary with emphasis.

'Mr Parker – of course, your name is very familiar. Wimsey, here, can't do a thing without you, I know. Murbles, are these gentlemen full of valuable information? I am immensely interested in this case.'

'Not just this moment, though,' put in the solicitor.

'Indeed, no. Nothing but that excellent saddle of mutton has the slightest attraction for me just now. Forgive my greed.'

'Well, well,' said Mr Murbles, beaming mildly, 'let's make a start. I fear, my dear young people, I am old-fashioned enough not to have adopted the modern practice of cocktail-drinking.'

'Quite right too,' said Wimsey emphatically. 'Ruins the palate and spoils the digestion. Not an English custom – rank sacrilege in this old Inn. Came from America – result, prohibition. That's what happens to people who don't understand how to drink. God bless me, sir, why, you're giving us the famous claret. It's a sin so much as to mention a cocktail in its presence.'

'Yes,' said Mr Murbles, 'yes, that's the Lafite '75. It's very seldom, very seldom, I bring it out for anybody under fifty years of age – but you, Lord Peter, have a discrimination which would do honour to one of twice your years.'

'Thanks very much, sir; that's a testimonial I deeply appreciate. May I circulate the bottle, sir?'

'Do, do – we will wait on ourselves, Simpson, thank you. After lunch,' continued Mr Murbles, 'I will ask you to try something really curious. An odd old client of mine died the other day, and left me a dozen of '47 port.'

'Gad!' said Peter. ''47! It'll hardly be drinkable, will it, sir?'

'I very greatly fear,' replied Mr Murbles, 'that it will not. A great pity. But I feel that some kind of homage should be paid to so notable an antiquity.'

'It would be something to say that one had tasted it,' said Peter. 'Like goin' to see the divine Sarah, you know. Voice gone, bloom gone, savour gone – but still a classic.'

'Ah,' said Mr Murbles. 'I remember her in her great days. We old fellows have the compensation of some wonderful memories.'

'Quite right, sir,' said Peter, 'and you'll pile up plenty more yet. But what was this old gentle man doing to let a vintage like that get past its prime?'

'Mr Featherstone was a very singular man,' said Mr Murbles. 'And yet – I don't know. He may have been profoundly wise. He had the reputation for extreme avarice. Never bought a new suit, never took a holiday, never married, lived all his life in the same dark, narrow chambers he occupied as a briefless barrister. Yet he inherited a huge income from his father, all of which he left to accumulate. The port was laid down by the old man, who died in 1860, when my client was thirty-four. He – the son, I mean – was ninety-six when he deceased. He said no pleasure ever came up to the anticipation, and so he lived like a hermit – doing nothing, but planning all the things he might have done. He wrote an elaborate diary, containing, day by day, the record of this visionary existence which he had never dared put to the test of actuality. The diary described minutely a blissful wedded life with the woman of his dreams. Every Christmas and Easter Day a bottle of the '47 was solemnly set upon his table and solemnly removed, unopened, at the close of his frugal meal. An earnest Christian, he anticipated great happiness after death, but, as you see, he put the pleasure off as long as possible. He died with the words, "He is faithful that promised" – feeling to the end the need of assurance. A very singular man, very singular indeed – far removed from the adventurous spirits of the present generation.'

'How curious and pathetic,' said Mary.

'Perhaps he had at some time set his heart on something unattainable,' said Parker.

'Well, I don't know,' said Mr Murbles. 'People used to say that the dream-lady had not always been a dream, but that he never could bring himself to propose.'

'Ah,' said Sir Impey briskly, 'the more I see and hear in the courts the more I am inclined to feel that Mr Featherstone chose the better part.'

'And are determined to follow his example – in that respect at any rate? Eh, Sir Impey!' replied Mr Murbles, with a mild chuckle.

Mr Parker glanced towards the window. It was beginning to rain.

Truly enough the '47 port was a dead thing; the merest ghost of its old flame and flavour hung about it. Lord Peter held his glass poised a moment.

'It is like the taste of a passion that has passed its noon and turned to weariness,' he said, with sudden gravity. 'The only thing to do is to recognise bravely that it is dead, and put it away.' With a determined movement, he flung the remainder of the wine into the fire. The mocking smile came back to his face:

> 'What I like about Clive
> Is that he is no longer alive—
> There is a great deal to be said
> For being dead.

What classic pith and brevity in those four lines! – However, in the matter of this case, we've a good deal to tell you, sir.'

With the assistance of Parker, he laid before the two men of law the whole train of the investigation up to date, Lady Mary coming loyally up to the scratch with her version of the night's proceedings.

'In fact, you see,' said Peter, 'this Mr Goyles has lost a lot by *not* being a murderer. We feel he would have cut a fine, sinister figure as a midnight assassin. But things bein' as they are, you see, we must make what we can of him as a witness, what?'

'Well, Lord Peter,' said Mr Murbles slowly, 'I congratulate you and Mr Parker on a great deal of industry and ingenuity in working the matter out.'

'I think we may say we have made some progress,' said Parker.

'If only negatively,' added Peter.

'Exactly,' said Sir Impey, turning on him with staggering abruptness. 'Very negatively indeed. And, having seriously hampered the case for the defence, what are you going to do next?'

'That's a nice thing to say,' cried Peter indignantly, 'when we've cleared up such a lot of points for you!'

'I daresay,' said the barrister, 'but they're the sort of points which are much better left muffled up.'

'Damn it all, we want to get at the truth!'

'Do you?' said Sir Impey drily. 'I don't. I don't care twopence about the truth. I want a case. It doesn't matter to me who killed Cathcart, provided I can prove it wasn't Denver. It's really enough if I can throw reasonable doubt on its being Denver. Here's a client comes to me with a story of a quarrel, a suspicious revolver, a refusal to produce evidence of his statements, and a totally inadequate and idiotic alibi. I arrange to obfuscate the jury with mysterious footprints, a discrepancy as to time, a young woman with a secret, and a general vague suggestion of something between a burglary and a *crime passionel*. And here you come explaining the footprints, exculpating the unknown man, abolishing the discrepancies, clearing up the motives of the young woman, and most carefully throwing back suspicion to where it rested in the first place. What *do* you expect?'

'I've always said,' growled Peter, 'that the professional advocate was the most immoral fellow on the face of the earth, and now I know for certain.'

'Well, well,' said Mr Murbles, 'all this just means that we mustn't rest upon our oars. You must go on, my dear boy, and get more evidence of a positive kind. If this Mr Goyles did not kill Cathcart we must be able to find the person who did.'

'Anyhow,' said Biggs, 'there's one thing to be thankful for – and that is, that you were still too unwell to go before the Grand Jury last Thursday, Lady Mary' – Lady Mary blushed – 'and the prosecution will be building their case on a shot fired at 3 a.m. Don't answer any questions if you can help it, and we'll spring it on 'em.'

'But will they believe anything she says at the trial after that?' asked Peter dubiously.

'All the better if they don't. She'll be their witness. You'll get a nasty heckling, Lady Mary, but you mustn't mind that. It's all in the game. Just stick to your story and we'll deliver the goods. See!' Sir Impey wagged a menacing finger.

'I see,' said Mary. 'And I'll be heckled like anything. Just go on stubbornly saying, "I am telling the truth now." That's the idea isn't it?'

'Exactly so,' said Biggs. 'By the way, Denver still refuses to explain his movements, I suppose?'

'Cat-e-gori-cally,' replied the solicitor. 'The Wimseys are a very determined family,' he added, 'and I fear that, for the present, it is useless to pursue that line of investigation. If we could discover the truth in some other way, and confront the Duke with it, he might then be persuaded to add his confirmation.'

'Well, now,' said Parker, 'we have, as it seems to me, still three lines to go upon. First, we must try to establish the Duke's alibi from external sources. Secondly, we can examine the evidence afresh with a view of finding the real murderer. And thirdly, the Paris police may give us some light upon Cathcart's past history.'

'And I fancy I know where to go next for information on the second point,' said Wimsey, suddenly. 'Grider's Hole.'

'Whew-w!' Parker whistled. 'I was forgetting that. That's where that bloodthirsty farmer fellow lives, isn't it, who set the dogs on you?'

'With the remarkable wife. Yes. See here, how does this strike you? This fellow is ferociously jealous of his wife, and inclined to suspect every man who comes near her. When I went up there that day, and mentioned that a friend of mine might have been hanging about there the previous week, he got frightfully excited and threatened to have the fellow's blood. Seemed to know who I was referrin' to. Now, of course, with my mind full of No. 10 – Goyles, you know – I never thought but that he was the man. But supposin' it was Cathcart? You see, we know now, Goyles hadn't even been in the neighbourhood till the Wednesday, so you wouldn't expect what's-his-name – Grimethorpe – to know about him, but Cathcart might have wandered over to Grider's Hole any day and been seen. And look here! Here's another thing that fits in. When I went up there Mrs Grimethorpe evidently mistook me for somebody she knew, and hurried down to warn me off. Well, of course, I've been thinkin' all the time she must have seen my old cap and Burberry from the window and mistaken me for Goyles, but, now I come to think of it, I told the kid who came to the door that I was from Riddlesdale Lodge. If

183

the child told her mother, she must have thought it was Cathcart.'

'No, no, Wimsey, that won't do,' put in Parker; 'she must have known Cathcart was dead by that time.'

'Oh, damn it! Yes, I suppose she must. Unless that surly old devil kept the news from her. By Jove; that's just what he would do if he'd killed Cathcart himself. He'd never say a word to her – and I don't suppose he would let her look at a paper, even if they took one in. It's a primitive sort of place.'

'But didn't you say Grimethorpe had an alibi?'

'Yes, but we didn't really test it.'

'And how do you suppose he knew Cathcart was going to be in the thicket that night?'

Peter considered.

'Perhaps he sent for him,' suggested Mary.

'That's right, that's right,' cried Peter eagerly. 'You remember we thought Cathcart must somehow or other have heard from Goyles, making an appointment – but suppose the message was from Grimethorpe, threatening to split on Cathcart to Jerry.'

'You are suggesting, Lord Peter,' said Mr Murbles, in a tone calculated to chill Peter's blithe impetuosity, 'that, at the very time Mr Cathcart was betrothed to your sister, he was carrying on a disgraceful intrigue with a married woman very much his social inferior.'

'I beg your pardon, Polly,' said Wimsey.

'It's all right,' said Mary. 'I – as a matter of fact, it wouldn't surprise me frightfully. Denis was always – I mean, he had rather Continental ideas about marriage and that sort of thing. I don't think he'd have thought that mattered very much. He'd probably have said there was a time and place for everything.'

'One of those watertight compartment minds,' said

Wimsey thoughtfully. Mr Parker, despite his long acquaintance with the seamy side of things in London, had his brows set in a gloomy frown of as fierce a provincial disapproval as ever came from Barrow-in-Furness.

'If you can upset this Grimethorpe's alibi,' said Sir Impey, fitting his right-hand finger-tips neatly between the fingers of his left hand, 'we might make some sort of a case of it. What do you think, Murbles?'

'After all,' said the solicitor, 'Grimethorpe and the servant both admit that he, Grimethorpe, was not at Grider's Hole on Wednesday night. If he can't prove he was at Stapley he may have been at Riddlesdale.'

'By Jove!' cried Wimsey; 'driven off alone, stopped somewhere, left the gee, sneaked back, met Cathcart, done him in, and toddled home next day with a tale about machinery.'

'Or he may even have been to Stapley,' put in Parker; 'left early or gone late, and put in the murder on the way. We shall have to check the precise times very carefully.'

'Hurray!' cried Wimsey. 'I think I'll be gettin' back to Riddlesdale.'

'I'd better stay here,' said Parker. 'There may be something from Paris.'

'Right you are. Let me know the minute anything comes through. I say, old thing!'

'Yes?'

'Does it occur to you that what's the matter with this case is that there are too many clues? Dozens of people with secrets and elopements bargin' about all over the place—'

'I hate you, Peter,' said Lady Mary.

11

MERIBAH

'Oh-ho, my friend! You are gotten into Lob's pond.'
    JACK THE GIANT-KILLER

LORD PETER broke his journey north at York, whither the Duke of Denver had been transferred after the Assizes, owing to the imminent closing-down of North-allerton Gaol. By dint of judicious persuasion, Peter contrived to obtain an interview with his brother. He found him looking ill at ease, and pulled down by the prison atmosphere, but still unquenchably defiant.

'Bad luck, old man,' said Peter, 'but you're keepin' your tail up fine. Beastly slow business, all this legal stuff, what? But it gives us time, an' that's all to the good.'

'It's a confounded nuisance,' said his grace. 'And I'd like to know what Murbles means. Comes down and tries to bully me – damned impudence! Anybody'd think he suspected me.'

'Look here, Jerry,' said his brother earnestly, 'why can't you let up on that alibi of yours! It'd help no end, you know. After all, if a fellow won't say what he's been doin'—'

'It ain't my business to prove anything,' retorted his grace, with dignity. 'They've got to show I was there, murderin' the fellow. I'm not bound to say where I was. I'm presumed innocent, aren't I, till they prove me guilty? I call it a disgrace. Here's a murder committed, and they aren't taking the slightest trouble to find the real criminal. I give 'em my word of honour, to say nothin' of an oath, that I didn't kill Cathcart – though, mind you, the swine deserved it – but they pay no attention. Meanwhile, the real man's escapin' at his confounded leisure. If I were only free, I'd make a fuss about it.'

'Well, why the devil don't you cut it short, then?' urged Peter. 'I don't mean here and now to me' – with a glance at the warder, within earshot – 'but to Murbles. Then we could get to work.'

'I wish you'd jolly well keep out of it,' grunted the Duke. 'Isn't it all damnable enough for Helen, poor girl, and mother, and everyone, without you makin' it an opportunity to play Sherlock Holmes? I'd have thought you'd have had the decency to keep quiet, for the family's sake. I may be in a damned rotten position, but I ain't makin' a public spectacle of myself, by Jove!'

'Hell!' said Lord Peter, with such vehemence that the wooden-faced warder actually jumped. 'It's you that's making' the spectacle! It need never have started, but for you. Do you think *I* like havin' my brother and sister dragged through the Courts, and reporters swarmin' over the place, and paragraphs and news-bills with your name staring at me from every corner, and all this ghastly business, endin' up in a great show in the House of Lords, with a lot of people togged up in scarlet and ermine, and all the rest of the damnfool jiggery-pokery? People are beginnin' to look oddly at me in the Club, and I can jolly well hear 'em whisperin' that "Denver's attitude looks jolly fishy, b'gad!" Cut it out, Jerry.'

'Well, we're in for it now,' said his brother, 'and thank heaven there are still a few decent fellows left in the peerage who'll know how to take a gentleman's word, even if my own brother can't see beyond his rotten legal evidence.'

As they stared angrily at one another, that mysterious sympathy of the flesh which we call family likeness sprang out from its hiding-place, stamping their totally dissimilar features with an elfish effect of mutual caricature. It was as though each saw himself in a distorting mirror, while the voices might have been one voice with its echo.

'Look here, old chap,' said Peter, recovering himself, 'I'm frightfully sorry. I didn't mean to let myself go like that. If you won't say anything, you won't. Anyhow, we're all working like blazes, and we're sure to find the right man before very long.'

'You'd better leave it to the police,' said Denver. 'I know you like playin' at detectives, but I do think you might draw the line somewhere.'

'That's a nasty one,' said Wimsey. 'But I don't look on this as a game, and I can't say I'll keep out of it, because I know I'm doin' valuable work. Still, I can – honestly, I can – see your point of view. I'm jolly sorry you find me such an irritatin' sort of person. I suppose it's hard for you to believe I feel anything. But I do, and I'm goin' to get you out of this, if Bunter and I both perish in the attempt. Well, so long – that warder's just wakin' up to say, "Time, gentlemen," Cheer-oh, old thing! Good luck!'

He rejoined Bunter outside.

'Bunter,' he said, as they walked through the streets of the old city, 'is my manner *really* offensive, when I don't mean it to be?'

'It is possible, my lord, if your lordship will excuse my saying so, that the liveliness of your lordship's manner may be misleading to persons of limited—'

'Be careful, Bunter!'

'Limited imagination, my lord.'

'Well-bred English people never have imagination, Bunter.'

'Certainly not, my lord. I meant nothing disparaging.'

'Well, Bunter – oh, lord! there's a reporter! Hide me, quick!'

'In here, my lord.'

Mr Bunter whisked his master into the cool emptiness of the cathedral.

'I venture to suggest, my lord,' he urged in a hurried whisper, 'that we adopt the attitude and external appearance of prayer, if your lordship will excuse me.'

Peeping through his fingers, Lord Peter saw a verger hastening towards them, rebuke depicted on his face. At this moment, however, the reporter entered in headlong pursuit, tugging a note-book from his pocket. The verger leapt swiftly on this new prey.

'The winder h'under which we stand,' he began in a reverential monotone, 'is called the Seven Sisters of York. They say—'

Master and man stole quietly out.

For his visit to the market town of Stapley Lord Peter attired himself in an aged Norfolk suit, stockings with sober tops, an ancient hat turned down all round, stout shoes, and carried a heavy ashplant. It was with regret that he abandoned his favourite stick – a handsome malacca, marked off in inches for detective convenience, and concealing a sword in its belly and a compass in its head. He decided, however, that it would prejudice the natives against him, as having a town-bred, not to say supercilious, air about it. The sequel to this commend-able devotion to his art forcibly illustrated the truth of Gertrude Rhead's observation, 'All this self-sacrifice is a sad mistake.'

The little town was sleepy enough as he drove into it in one of the Riddlesdale dog-carts, Bunter beside him, and the under-gardener on the back seat. For choice, he would have come on a market-day, in the hope of meeting Grimethorpe himself, but things were moving fast now, and he dared not lose a day. It was a raw, cold morning, inclined to rain.

'Which is the best inn to put up at, Wilkes?'

'There's t' "Bricklayers' Arms," my lord – a fine, well-thought-of place, or t' "Bridge and Bottle," i' t' square, or t' "Rose and Crown," t'other side o' square.'

'Where do the folks usually put up on market-days?'

'Mebbe "Rose and Crown" is most popular, so to say – Tim Watchett, t' landlord, is a rare gossip. Now Greg Smith ower t'way at "Bridge and Bottle," he's nobbut a grimly, surly man, but he keeps good drink.'

'H'm – I fancy, Bunter, our man will be more attracted by surliness and good drink than by a genial host. The "Bridge and Bottle" for us, I fancy, and, if we draw blank there, we'll toddle over to the "Rose and Crown," and pump the garrulous Watchett.'

Accordingly they turned into the yard of a large, stony-faced house, whose long-unpainted sign bore the dim outline of a 'Bridge Embattled,' which local etymology had (by a natural association of ideas) transmogrified into the 'Bridge and Bottle'. To the grumpy ostler who took the horse, Peter, with his most companionable manner, addressed himself:

'Nasty raw morning, isn't it?'

'Eea.'

'Give him a good feed. I may be here some time.'

'Ugh!'

'Not many people about today, what?'

'Ugh!'

'But I expect you're busy enough market-days.'

'Eea.'

'People come in from a long way round, I suppose.'

'Co-oop!' said the ostler. The horse walked three steps forward.

'Wo!' said the ostler. The horse stopped, with the shafts free of the tugs; the man lowered the shafts, to grate viciously on the gravel.

'Coom on oop!' said the ostler, and walked calmly off into the stable, leaving the affable Lord Peter as thoroughly snubbed as that young sprig of the nobility had ever found himself.

'I am more and more convinced,' said his lordship, 'that this is Farmer Grimethorpe's usual house of call. Let's try the bar. Wilkes, I shan't want you for a bit. Get yourself lunch if necessary. I don't know how long we shall be.'

'Very good, my lord.'

In the bar of the 'Bridge and Bottle' they found Mr Greg Smith gloomily checking a long invoice. Lord Peter ordered drinks for Bunter and himself. The landlord appeared to resent this as a liberty, and jerked his head towards the barmaid. It was only right and proper that Bunter, after respectfully returning thanks to his master for his half-pint, should fall into conversation with the girl, while Lord Peter paid his respects to Mr Smith.

'Ah!' said his lordship, 'good stuff, that, Mr Smith. I was told to come here for real good beer, and, by Jove! I've been sent to the right place.'

'Ugh!' said Mr Smith, ''tisn't what it was. Nowt's good these times.'

'Well, I don't want better. By the way, is Mr Grimethorpe here today?'

'Eh?'

'Is Mr Grimethorpe in Stapley this morning, d'you know?'

'How'd I know?'

'I thought he always put up here.'

'Ah!'

'Perhaps I mistook the name. But I fancied he'd be the man to go where the best beer is.'

'Ay?'

'Oh, well, if you haven't seen him, I don't suppose he's come over today.'

'Coom where?'

'Into Stapley.'

'Doesn't 'e live here? He can go and coom without my knowing.'

'Oh, of course!' Wimsey staggered under the shock, and then grasped the misunderstanding. 'I don't mean Mr Grimethorpe of Stapley, but Mr Grimethorpe of Grider's Hole.'

'Why didn't tha say so? Oh, him? Ay.'

'He's here today?'

'Nay, I knaw nowt about 'un.'

'He comes in on market-days, I expect.'

'Sometimes.'

'It's longish way. One can put up for the night, I suppose?'

'Doosta want t'stay t'night?'

'Well, no, I don't think so. I was thinking about my friend. Mr Grimethorpe. I daresay he often has to stay the night.'

'Happen a does.'

'Doesn't he stay here, then?'

'Naay.'

'Oh!' said Wimsey, and thought impatiently: 'If all these natives are as oyster-like I *shall* have to stay the night. . . . Well, well,' he added aloud, 'next time he drops in say I asked after him.'

'And who mought tha be?' inquired Mr Smith in a hostile manner.

'Oh, only Brooks of Sheffield,' said Lord Peter, with a happy grin. 'Good morning. I won't forget to recommend your beer.'

Mr Smith grunted. Lord Peter strolled slowly out, and before long Mr Bunter joined him, coming out with a brisk step and the lingering remains of what, in anyone else, might have been taken for a smirk.

'Well?' inquired his lordship. 'I hope the young lady was more communicative than that fellow.'

'I found the young person' ('Snubbed again,' muttered Lord Peter) 'perfectly amiable, my lord, but unhappily ill-informed. Mr Grimethorpe is not unknown to her, but he does not stay here. She has sometimes seen him in company with a man called Zedekiah Bone.'

'Well,' said his lordship, 'suppose you look for Bone, and come and report progress to me in a couple of hours' time. I'll try the "Rose and Crown". We'll meet at noon under that thing.'

'That thing,' was a tall erection in pink granite, neatly tooled to represent a craggy rock, and guarded by two petrified infantry-men in trench helmets. A thin stream of water gushed from a bronze knob half way up, a roll of honour was engraved on the octagonal base, and four gaslamps on cast-iron standards put the finishing touch to a very monument of incongruity. Mr Bunter looked carefully at it, to be sure of recognising it again, and moved respectfully away. Lord Peter walked ten brisk steps in the direction of the 'Rose and Crown,' then a thought struck him.

'Bunter!'

Mr Bunter hurried back to his side.

'Oh, nothing!' said his lordship. 'Only I've just thought of a name for it.'

'For—'

'That memorial,' said Lord Peter. 'I choose to call it "Meribah".'

'Yes, my lord. The waters of strife. Exceedingly apt, my lord. Nothing harmonious about it, if I may say so. Will there be anything further, my lord?'

'No, that's all.'

Mr Timothy Watchett of the 'Rose and Crown' was certainly a contrast to Mr Greg Smith. He was a small, spare sharp-eyed man of about fifty-five, with so twinkling and humorous an eye and so alert a cock of the head that Lord Peter summed up his origin the moment he set eyes on him.

'Morning, landlord,' said he genially, 'and when did *you* last see Piccadilly Circus?'

''Ard to say, sir. Gettin' on for thirty-five year, I reckon. Many's the time I said to my wife, "Liz I'll tike you ter see the 'Olborn Empire afore I die." But, with one thing and another, time slips aw'y. One day's so like another – blowed if I ever remember 'ow old I'm gettin', sir.'

'Oh, well, you've lots of time yet,' said Lord Peter.

'I 'ope so, sir. I ain't never wot you may call got used ter these Northerners. That slow, they are, sir – it fair giv' me the 'ump when I first come. And the w'y they speak – that took some gettin' used to. Call that English, I useter say, give me the Frenchies in the Chantycleer Restaurong, I ses. But there, sir, custom's everything. Blowed if I didn't ketch myself a-syin' "yon side the square" the other day. Me!'

'I don't think there's much fear of your turning into a Yorkshire man,' said Lord Peter, 'didn't I know you the minute I set eyes on you? In Mr Watchett's bar I said to myself, "My foot is on my native paving-stones".'

'That's raight, sir. And, bein' there, sir, what can I 'ave the pleasure of offerin' you? . . . Excuse me, sir, but 'aven't I seen your fice somewhere?'

'I don't think so,' said Peter; 'but that reminds me. Do you know one Mr Grimethorpe?'

'I know five Mr Grimethorpes. W'ich of 'em was you meanin', sir?'

'Mr Grimethorpe of Grider's Hole.'

The landlord's cheerful face darkened.

'Friend of yours, sir?'

'Not exactly. An acquaintance.'

'There naow!' cried Mr Watchett, smacking his hand down upon the counter. 'I knowed as I knowed your fice! Don't you live over at Riddlesdale, sir?'

'I'm stayin' there.'

'I knowed it,' retorted Mr Watchett triumphantly. He dived behind the counter and brought up a bundle of newspapers, turning over the sheets excitedly with a well-licked thumb. 'There! Riddlesdale! that's it, of course.'

He smacked open a *Daily Mirror* of a fortnight or so ago. The front page bore a heavy block headline: THE RIDDLESDALE MYSTERY. And beneath was a life-like snapshot entitled, '*Lord Peter Wimsey, the Sherlock Holmes of the West End, who is devoting all his time and energies to proving the innocence of his brother, the Duke of Denver,*' Mr Watchett gloated.

'You won't mind my syin' 'ow proud I am to 'ave you in my bar, my lord – 'Ere, Jem, you attend ter them gentlemen; don't you see they're wytin'? – Follered all yer caises I 'ave, my lord, in the pipers – jest like a book they are. An' ter think—'

'Look here, old thing,' said Lord Peter, 'd'you mind not talkin' quite so loud. Seein' dear old Felix is out of the bag, so to speak, do you think you could give me some information and keep your mouth shut, what?'

'Come be'hind into the bar-parlour, my lord. No-body'll 'ear us there,' said Mr Watchett eagerly, lifting up the flap. 'Jem,'ere! Bring a bottle of – what'll you 'ave, my lord?'

'Well, I don't know how many places I may have to visit,' said his lordship dubiously.

'Jem, bring a quart of the old ale – It's special, that's wot it is, my lord. I ain't never found none like it, except it might be once at Oxford. Thanks, Jem. Naow you get along sharp and attend to the customers. Naow, my lord.'

Mr Watchett's information amounted to this. That Mr Grimethorpe used to come to the 'Rose and Crown' pretty often, especially on market-days. About ten days previously he had come in lateish, very drunk and quarrelsome, with his wife, who seemed, as usual, ter-rified of him. Grimethorpe had demanded spirits, but Mr Watchett had refused to serve him. There had been a row, and Mrs Grimethorpe had endeavoured to get her husband away. Grimethorpe had promptly knocked her down, with epithets reflecting upon her virtue, and Mr Watchett had at once called upon the potmen to turn Grimethorpe out, refusing to have him in the house again. He had heard it said on all sides that Grime-thorpe's temper, always notoriously bad, had become positively diabolical of late.

'Could you hazard, so to speak, a calculation as to how long, or since when?'

'Well, my lord, come to think of it, especially since the middle of last month – p'r'aps a bit earlier.'

'M'm!'

'Not that I'd go for to insinuate anythink, nor your lordship, neither, of course,' said Mr Watchett quickly.

'Certainly not,' said Lord Peter. 'What about?'

'Ah!' said Mr Watchett, 'there it is, wot abaht?'

'Tell me,' said Lord Peter, 'do you recollect Grimethorpe comin' into Stapley on October 13th – a Wednesday, it was?'

'That would be the day of the – ah! to be sure! Yes, I do recollect it, for I remember thinking it was odd him comin' here except on a market-day. Said he 'ad ter look at some machinery – drills and such, that's raight. 'E was 'ere raight enough.'

'Do you remember what time he came in?'

'Well, naow, I've a fancy 'e was 'ere ter lunch. The waitress'd know. 'Ere, Bet!' he called through the side door, 'd'yer 'appen to recollect whether Mr Grimethorpe lunched 'ere October the 13th – Wednesday it were, the d'y the pore gent was murdered over at Riddlesdale?'

'Grimethorpe o' Grider's Hole?' said the girl, a well-grown young Yorkshire woman. 'Yes! 'E took loonch, and coom back to sleep. Ah'm not mistook, for ah waited on 'un, an took up 'is watter i' t'morning, and 'e only gied me tuppence.'

'Monstrous!' said Lord Peter. 'Look here, Miss Elizabeth, you're sure it was the thirteenth? Because I've got a bet on it with a friend, and I don't want to lose the money if I can help it. You're positive it was Wednesday night he slept here? I could have sworn it was Thursday.'

'Naay, sir, t'wor Wednesday for I remember hearing the men talking o' t'murder i' t'bar, an' telling Mester Grimethorpe next daay.'

'Sounds conclusive. What did Mr Grimethorpe say about it?'

'There now,' cried the young woman, ''tis queer you should ask that; everyone noticed how strange he acted. He turned all white like a sheet, and looked at both his hands, one after the other, and then he pushes 'es hair off's forehead – dazed-like. We reckoned he hadn't got over the drink. He's more often drunk than not. Ah wouldn't be his wife for five hundred pounds.'

'I should think not,' said Peter; 'you can do a lot better than that. Well, I suppose I've lost my money, then. By the way, what time did Mr Grimethorpe come in to bed?'

'Close on two i' t'morning,' said the girl, tossing her head. 'He were locked oot, 'an Jem had to go down and let un in.'

'That so?' said Peter. 'Well, I might try to get out on a technicality, eh, Mr Watchett? Two o'clock is Thursday, isn't it? I'll work that for all it's worth. Thanks frightfully. That's all I want to know.'

Bet grinned and giggled herself away, comparing the generosity of the strange gentleman with the stinginess of Mr Grimethorpe. Peter rose.

'I'm no end obliged, Mr Watchett,' he said. 'I'll just have a word with Jem. Don't say anything, by the way.'

'Not me,' said Mr Watchett; 'I know wot's wot. Good luck, my lord.'

Jem corroborated Bet. Grimethorpe had returned at about 1.50 a.m. on October 14th, drunk, and plastered with mud. He had muttered something about having run up against a man called Watson.

The ostler was next interrogated. He did not think that anybody could get a horse and trap out of the stable at night without his knowing it. He knew Watson. He was a carrier by trade, and lived in Windon Street. Lord Peter rewarded his informant suitably, and set out for Windon Street.

But the recital of his quest would be tedious. At a quarter-past noon he joined Bunter at the Meribah memorial.

'Any luck?'

'I have secured certain information, my lord, which I have duly noted. Total expenditure on beer for self and witnesses 7s. 2d., my lord.'

Lord Peter paid the 7s. 2d. without a word, and they adjourned to the 'Rose and Crown'. Being accommodated in a private parlour, and having ordered lunch, they proceeded to draw up the following schedule:

GRIMETHORPE'S MOVEMENTS. *Wednesday, October 13th, to Thursday, October 14th.*

October 13th:

12.30 p.m.	Arrives 'Rose and Crown'.
1.00 p.m.	Lunches.
3.00 p.m.	Orders two drills from man called Gooch in Trimmer's Lane.
4.30 p.m.	Drink with Gooch to clinch bargain.
5.00 p.m.	Calls at house of John Watson, carrier, about delivering some dog-food. Watson absent. Mrs Watson says W. expected back that night. G. says will call again.
5.30 p.m.	Calls on Mark Dolby, grocer, to complain about some tinned salmon.
5.45 p.m.	Calls on Mr Hewitt, optician, to pay bill for spectacles and dispute the amount.
6.00 p.m.	Drinks with Zedekiah Bone at 'Bridge and Bottle.'
6.45 p.m.	Calls again on Mrs Watson. Watson not yet home.

| 7.00 p.m. | Seen by Constable Z15 drinking with several men at 'Pig and Whistle'. Heard to use threatening language with regard to some person unknown. |
| 7.20 p.m. | Seen to leave 'Pig and Whistle' with two men (not yet identified). |

October 14th:

1.15 a.m.	Picked up by Watson, carrier, about a mile out on road to Riddlesdale, very dirty and ill-tempered, and not quite sober.
1.45 a.m.	Let into 'Rose and Crown' by James Johnson, potman.
9.00 a.m.	Called by Elizabeth Dobbin.
9.30 a.m.	In Bar of 'Rose and Crown'. Hears of man murdered at Riddlesdale. Behaves suspiciously.
10.15 a.m.	Cashes cheque £129 17s. 8d. at Lloyds Bank.
10.30 a.m.	Pays Gooch for drills.
11.05 a.m.	Leaves 'Rose and Crown' for Grider's Hole.

Lord Peter looked at this for a few minutes, and put his finger on the great gap of six hours after 7.20.

'How far to Riddlesdale, Bunter?'

'About thirteen and three-quarter miles, my lord.'

'And the shot was heard at 10.55. It couldn't be done on foot. Did Watson explain why he didn't get back from his round till two in the morning?'

'Yes, my lord. He says he reckons to be back about eleven, but his horse cast a shoe between King's Fenton and Riddlesdale. He had to walk him quietly into Riddlesdale – about 3½ miles – getting there about ten, and knock up the blacksmith. He turned in to the "Lord in Glory" till closing time, and then went home with a friend and had a few more. At 12.40 he started off home, and picked Grimethorpe up a mile or so out, near the cross roads.'

'Sounds circumstantial. The blacksmith and the friend ought to be able to substantiate it. But we simply must find those men at the "Pig and Whistle".'

'Yes, my lord. I will try again after lunch.'

It was a good lunch. But that seemed to exhaust their luck for the day, for by three o'clock the men had not been identified, and the scent seemed cold.

Wilkes, the groom, however, had his own contribution to the inquiry. He had met a man from King's Fenton at lunch, and they had, naturally, got to talking over the mysterious murder at the Lodge, and the man had said that he knew an old man living in a hut on the Fell, who said that on the night of the murder he'd seen a man walking over Whemmeling Fell in the middle of the night. 'And it coom to me, all of a sooden, it might be his grace,' said Wilkes brightly.

Further inquiries elicited that the old man's name was Groot, and that Wilkes could easily drop Lord Peter and Bunter at the beginning of the sheep-path which led up to his hut.

Now, had Lord Peter taken his brother's advice, and paid more attention to English country sports than to incunabula and criminals in London – or had Bunter been brought up on the moors, rather than in a Kentish village – or had Wilkes (who was a Yorkshire man bred and born, and ought to have known better) not been so outrageously puffed up with the sense of his own importance in suggesting a clue, and with impatience to have that clue followed up without delay – or had any

one of the three exercised common sense – this preposterous suggestion would never have been made, much
less carried out, on a November day in the North Riding.
As it was, however, Lord Peter and Bunter left the trap at
the foot of the moor-path at ten minutes to four, and,
dismissing Wilkes, climbed steadily up to the wee hut on
the edge of the fell.

The old man was extremely deaf, and, after half an
hour of interrogation, his story did not amount to
much. On a night in October, which he thought might
be the night of the murder, he had been sitting by his
peat fire when – about midnight, as he guessed – a tall
man had loomed up out of the darkness. He spoke like
a Southerner, and said he had got lost on the moor.
Old Groot had come to his door and pointed out the
track down towards Riddlesdale. The stranger had
then vanished, leaving a shilling in his hand. He could
not describe the stranger's dress more particularly than
that he wore a soft hat and an overcoat, and, he
thought, leggings. He was pretty sure it was the night
of the murder, because afterwards he had turned it
over in his mind and made out that it might have been
one of yon folk at the Lodge – possibly the Duke. He
had only arrived at this result by a slow process of
thought, and had not 'come forward', not knowing
whom or where to come to.

With this the inquirers had to be content, and, pre-
senting Groot with half a crown, they emerged upon the
moor at something after five o'clock.

'Bunter,' said Lord Peter through the dusk, 'I am
abso-bally-lutely positive that the answer to all this
business is at Grider's Hole.'

'Very possibly, my lord.'

Lord Peter extended his finger in a south-easterly direction. 'That is Grider's Hole,' he said. 'Let's go.'

'Very good, my lord.'

So, like two Cockney innocents, Lord Peter and Bunter set forth at a brisk pace down the narrow moor-track towards Grider's Hole, with never a glance behind them for the great white menace rolling silently down through the November dusk from the wide loneliness of Whemmeling Fell.

'Bunter!'

'Here, my lord!'

The voice was close at his ear.

'Thank God! I thought you'd disappeared for good. I say, we ought to have known.'

'Yes, my lord.'

It had come on them from behind, in a single stride, thick, cold, choking – blotting each from the other, though they were only a yard or two apart.

'I'm a fool, Bunter,' said Lord Peter.

'Not at all, my lord.'

'Don't move; go on speaking.'

'Yes, my lord.'

Peter groped to the right and clutched the other's sleeve.

'Ah! Now what are we to do?'

'I couldn't say, my lord, having no experience. Has the – er – phenomenon any habits, my lord?'

'No regular habits, I believe. Sometimes it moves. Other times it stays in one place for days. We can wait all night, and see if it lifts at daybreak.'

'Yes, my lord. It is unhappily somewhat damp.'

'Somewhat – as you say,' agreed his lordship, with a short laugh.

Bunter sneezed, and begged pardon politely.

'If we go on going south-east,' said his lordship, 'we shall get to Grider's Hole all right, and they'll jolly well *have* to put us up for the night – or give us an escort. I've got my torch in my pocket, and we can go by compass – oh, hell!'

'My lord?'

'I've got the wrong stick. This beastly ash! No compass, Bunter – we're done in.'

'Couldn't we keep on going downhill, my lord?'

Lord Peter hesitated. Recollections of what he had heard and read surged up in his mind to tell him that uphill or downhill seems much the same thing in a fog. But man walks in a vain shadow. It is hard to believe that one is really helpless. The cold was icy. 'We might try,' he said weakly.

'I have heard it said, my lord, that in a fog one always walked around in a circle,' said Mr Bunter, seized with a tardy diffidence.

'Not on a slope, surely,' said Lord Peter, beginning to feel bold out of sheer contrariness.

Bunter, being out of his element, had, for once, no good counsel to offer.

'Well, we can't be much worse off than we are,' said Lord Peter. 'We'll try it, and keep on shouting.'

He grasped Bunter's hand, and they strode gingerly forward into the thick coldness of the fog.

How long that nightmare lasted neither could have said. The world might have died about them. Their own shouts terrified them; when they stopped shouting the dead silence was more terrifying still. They stumbled over tufts of thick heather. It was amazing how, deprived of sight, they exaggerated the inequalities of the ground. It was with very little confidence that they could distinguish uphill from downhill. They were shrammed through with cold, yet the sweat was running from their faces with strain and terror.

Suddenly – from directly before them as it seemed, and only a few yards away – there rose a long, horrible shriek – and another – and another.

'My God! What's that?'

'It's a horse, my lord.'

'Of course.' They remembered having heard horses scream like that. There had been a burning stable near Poperinghe—

'Poor devil,' said Peter. He started off impulsively in the direction of the sound, dropping Bunter's hand.

'Come back, my lord,' cried the man in a sudden agony. And then, with a frightened burst of enlightenment:

'For God's sake stop, my lord – the bog!'

A sharp shout in the utter blackness.

'Keep away there – don't move – it's got me!'

And a dreadful sucking noise.

12

THE ALIBI

'When actually in the embrace of a voracious and powerful wild animal, the desirability of leaving a limb is not a matter to be subjected to lengthy consideration.'
THE WALLET OF KAI-LUNG

'I TRIPPED right into it,' said Wimsey's voice steadily, out of the blackness. 'One sinks very fast. You'd better not come near, or you'll go too. We'll yell a bit. I don't think we can be very far from Grider's Hole.'

'If your lordship will keep shouting,' returned Mr Bunter, 'I think – I can – get to you,' he panted, untying with his teeth the hard knot of a coil of string.

'Oy!' cried Lord Peter obediently. 'Help! Oy! Oy!'

Mr Bunter groped towards the voice, feeling cautiously before him with his walking-stick.

'Wish you'd keep away, Bunter,' said Lord Peter peevishly. 'Where's the sense of both of us –?' He squelched and floundered again.

'Don't do that, my lord,' cried the man entreatingly. 'You'll sink farther in.'

'I'm up to my thighs now,' said Lord Peter.

'I'm coming,' said Bunter. 'Go on shouting. Ah, here's where it gets soggy.'

He felt the ground carefully, selected a tussocky bit which seemed reasonably firm, and drove his stick well into it.

'Oy! Hi! Help!' said Lord Peter, shouting lustily.

Mr Bunter tied one end of the string to the walking-stick, belted his Burberry tightly about him, and, laying himself cautiously down upon his belly, advanced, clue in hand, like a very Gothic Theseus of a late and degenerate school.

The bog heaved horribly as he crawled over it, and slimy water squelched up into his face. He felt with his hands for tussocks of grass, and got support from them when he could.

'Call out again, my lord!'

'Here!' The voice was fainter and came from the right. Bunter had lost his line a little, hunting for tussocks. 'I daren't come faster,' he explained. He felt as though he had been crawling for years.

'Get out while there's time,' said Peter. 'I'm up to my waist. Lord! this is rather a beastly way to peg out.'

'You won't peg out,' grunted Bunter. His voice was suddenly quite close. 'Your hands now.'

For a few agonising minutes two pairs of hands groped over the invisible slime. Then:

'Keep yours still,' said Bunter. He made a slow, circling movement. It was hard work keeping his face out of the mud. His hands slithered over the slobbery surface – and suddenly closed on an arm.

'Thank God!' said Bunter. 'Hang on here, my lord.'

He felt forward. The arms were perilously close to the sucking mud. The hands crawled clingingly up his arms and rested on his shoulders. He grasped Wimsey beneath the armpits and heaved. The exertion drove his own knees deep into the bog. He straightened himself hurriedly. Without using his knees he could get no purchase, but to use them meant certain death. They could only hang on desperately till help came – or till the strain became too great. He could not even shout; it was almost

207

more than he could do to keep his mouth free of water. The dragging strain on his shoulders was intolerable; the mere effort to breathe meant an agonising crick in the neck.

'You must go on shouting, my lord.'

Wimsey shouted. His voice was breaking and fading.

'Bunter, old thing,' said Lord Peter, 'I'm simply beastly sorry to have let you in for this.'

'Don't mention it, my lord,' said Bunter, with his mouth in the slime. A thought struck him.

'What became of your stick, my lord?'

'I dropped it. It should be somewhere near, if it hasn't sunk in.' Bunter cautiously released his left hand and felt about.

'Hi! Hi! Help!'

Bunter's hand closed over the stick, which, by a happy accident, had fallen across a stable tuft of grass. He pulled it over to him, and laid it across his arms, so that he could just rest his chin upon it. The relief to his neck was momentarily so enormous that his courage was renewed. He felt he could hang on for ever.

'Help!'

Minutes passed like hours.

'See that?'

A faint, flickering gleam somewhere away to the right. With desperate energy both shouted together.

'Help! Help! Oy! Oy! Help!'

An answering yell. The light swayed – came nearer – a spreading blur in the fog.

'We *must* keep it up,' panted Wimsey. They yelled again.

'Where be?'

'Here!'

'Hello!' A pause. Then:

'Here be stick,' said a voice, suddenly near.

'Follow the string!' yelled Bunter. They heard two voices, apparently arguing. Then the string was twitched.

'Here! Here! Two of us! Make haste!'

More consultation.

'Hang on, canst a?'

'Yes, if you're quick.'

'Fetchin' hurdle. Two on 'ee, sayst a?'

'Yes.'

'Deep in?'

'One of us.'

'Aw reet. Jem's comin'.'

A splattering noise marked the arrival of Jem with a hurdle. Then came an endless wait. Then another hurdle, the string twitching, and the blur of the lantern bobbing violently about. Then a third hurdle was flung down, and the light came suddenly out of the mist. A hand caught Bunter by the ankle.

'Where's t' other?'

'Here – nearly up to his neck. Have you a rope?'

'Aye, sure. Jem! T'rope!'

The rope came snaking out of the fog. Bunter grasped it, and passed it round his master's body.

'Now – coom tha back and heave.'

Bunter crawled cautiously backwards upon the hurdle. All three set hands upon the rope. It was like trying to heave the earth out of her course.

''Fraid I'm rooted to Australia,' panted Peter apologetically. Bunter sweated and sobbed.

'It's aw reet – he's coomin'!'

With slow heavings the rope began to come towards them. Their muscles cracked.

Suddenly, with a great *plop!* the bog let go its hold. The three at the rope were hurled head over heels upon the hurdles. Something unrecognisable in slime lay flat, heaving helplessly. They dragged at him in a kind of frenzy, as though he might be snatched back from them again. The evil bog stench rose thickly round them. They crossed the first hurdle – the second – the third – and rose staggeringly to their feet on firm ground.

'What a beastly place,' said Lord Peter faintly. ''Pologise, stupid of me to have forgotten – what'sy name?'

'Well, tha's loocky,' said one of their rescuers. 'We thowt we heerd someun a-shouting. There be few folks as cooms oot o' Peter's Pot dead or alive, I reckon.'

'Well, it has nearly potted Peter that time,' said his lordship, and fainted.

To Lord Peter the memory of his entry that night into the farmhouse at Grider's Hole always brought with it a sensation of nightmare. The coils of fog rolled in with them as the door opened, and through them the firelight leapt steamily. A hanging lamp made a blur. The Medusa-head of Mrs Grimethorpe, terribly white against her black hair, peered over him. A hairy paw caught her by the shoulder and wrenched her aside.

'Shameless! A mon – ony mon – that's a' tha thinks on. Bide till tha's wanted. What's this?'

Voices – voices – ever so many fierce faces peering down all round.

'Peter's Pot? An' what were 'ee a-wanting on t'moor this time night? No good. Nobody but a fool or a thief'ud coom oop 'ere i' t' fog.'

One of the men, a farm labourer with wry shoulders and a thin, malicious face suddenly burst into tuneless song:

> *'I been a-courtin' Mary Jane
> On Ilka' Moor baht 'at.'*

'Howd toong!' yelled Grimethorpe, in a fury. 'Doost want Ah should break ivery bwoan i' thi body!' He turned on Bunter. 'Tak thesen off, Ah tell tha. Tha'art here for no good.'

'But, William –' began his wife. He snapped round at her like a dog, and she shrank back.

'Naay now, naay now,' said a man, whom Wimsey dimly recognised as the fellow who had befriended him on his previous visit, 'tha mun' taak them in for t'night, racken, or there'll be trouble wi' t' folk down yonder at t' Lodge, lat aloan what police 'ull saay. Ef t' fellow 'm coom to do harm, 'ee's doon it already – to 'unself. Woan't do no more tonight – look at un. Bring 'un to fire, mon,' he added to Bunter, and then, turning to the farmer again, ''Tes tha'll be in Queer Street ef 'e wor to goo an' die on us wi' noomony or rhoomaticks.'

This reasoning seemed partly to convince Grimethorpe. He made way, grumbling, and the two chilled and exhausted men were brought near the fire. Somebody brought two large, steaming tumblers of spirits. Wimsey's brain seemed to clear, then swim again drowsily, drunkenly.

Presently he became aware that he was being carried upstairs and put to bed. A big, old-fashioned room, with a fire on the hearth and a huge, grim four-poster. Bunter was helping him out of soaked clothes; rubbing him. Another man appeared from time to time to help him. From below came the bellowing sound of Grimethorpe's voice, blasphemously uplifted. Then the harsh, brassy singing of the wry-shouldered man:

> *'Then woorms will coom an' ate thee oop*
> *On Ilkla' Moor baht 'at . . .*
> *Then doocks will coom an' ate oop woorms*
> *On Ilkla' Moor . . .'*

Lord Peter rolled into bed.

'Bunter – where – you all right? Never said thank you – dunno what. I'm doing – anywhere to sleep – what?'

He drifted away into oblivion. The old song came up mockingly, and wound its horrible fancies into his dreams:

> *Then we shall coom an' ate oop doocks*
> *On Ilkla' Moor baht 'at . . .*

> *An' that is how – an' that is how – is how . . .*

When Wimsey next opened his eyes a pale November sun was struggling in at the window. It seemed that the fog had fulfilled its mission and departed. For some time he lay, vaguely unaware of how he came to be where he was; then the outlines of recollection straightened themselves, the drifting outposts of dreams were called back, the burden of his preoccupation settled down as usual. He became aware of an extreme bodily lassitude, and of the dragging pain of wrenched shoulder muscles. Examining himself perfunctorily, he found a bruised and tender zone beneath the armpits and round his chest and back, where the rescuing rope had hauled at him. It was painful to move, so he lay back and closed his eyes once more.

Presently the door opened to admit Bunter, neatly clothed and bearing a tray from which rose a most excellent odour of ham and eggs.

'Hullo, Bunter?'

'Good morning, my lord! I trust your lordship has rested.'

'Feel as fit as a fiddle, thanks – come to think of it, why fiddle? – except for a general feeling of havin' been violently massaged by some fellow with cast-iron fingers and knobbly joints. How about you?'

'The arms are a trifle fatigued, thank you, my lord; otherwise, I am happy to say, I feel no trace of the misadventure. Allow me, my lord.'

He set the tray tenderly upon Lord Peter's ready knees.

'They must be jolly well dragged out of their sockets,' said his lordship, 'holdin' me up all that ghastly long time. I'm so beastly deep in debt to you already, Bunter, it's not a bit of use tryin' to repay it. You know I won't forget, anyhow, don't you? All right, I won't be embarrassin' or anything – thanks awfully, anyhow. That's that. What? Did they give you anywhere decent to sleep? I didn't seem to be able to sit up an' take notice last night.'

'I slept excellently, I thank your lordship.' Mr Bunter indicated a kind of truckle-bed in a corner of the room. 'They would have given me another room, my lord, but in the circumstances, I preferred to remain with your lordship, trusting you would excuse the liberty. I told them that I feared the effects of prolonged immersion upon your lordship's health. I was uneasy, besides, about the intention of Grimethorpe. I feared he might not feel altogether hospitably disposed, and that he might be led into some hasty action if we were not together.'

'I shouldn't wonder. Most murderous-lookin' fellow I ever set eyes on. I'll have to talk to him this morning – or to Mrs Grimethorpe. I'd take my oath she could tell us something, what?'

'I should say there was very little doubt of it, my word,'

'Trouble is,' pursued Wimsey, with his mouth full of egg, 'I don't know how to get at her. That jolly husband of hers seems to cherish the most unpleasant suspicions of anything that comes this way in trousers. If he found out we'd been talking to her, what you may call privately, he might, as you say, be hurried by his feelin's into doin' something regrettable.'

'Just so, my lord.'

'Still, the fellow must go an' look after his bally old farm some time, and then, p'raps, we'll be able to tackle her. Queer sort of woman – damn fine one, what? Wonder what she made of Cathcart?' he added musingly.

Mr Bunter volunteered no opinion on this delicate point.

'Well, Bunter, I think I'll get up. I don't suppose we're altogether welcome here. I didn't fancy the look in our host's eye last night.'

'No, my lord. He made a deal of opposition about having your lordship conveyed to this room.'

'Why, whose room is it?'

'His own and Mrs Grimethorpe's, my lord. It appeared most suitable, there being a fireplace, and the bed already made up. Mrs Grimethorpe showed great kindness, my lord, and the man Jake pointed out to Grimethorpe that it would doubtless be to his pecuniary advantage to treat your lordship with consideration.'

'H'm. Nice, graspin' character, ain't he? Well, it's up and away for me. O Lord! I *am* stiff. I say, Bunter, have I any clothes to put on?'

'I have dried and brushed your lordship's suit to the best of my ability, my lord. It is not as I should wish to see it, but I think your lordship will be able to wear it to Riddlesdale.'

'Well, I don't suppose the streets will be precisely crowded,' retorted his lordship. 'I *do* so want a hot bath. How about shavin' water?'

'I can procure that from the kitchen, my lord.'

Bunter padded away, and Lord Peter, having pulled on a shirt and trousers with many grunts and groans, roamed over to the window. As usual with hardy country dwellers, it was tightly shut, and a thick wedge of paper had been rammed in to keep the sash from rattling. He removed this and flung up the sash. The wind rollicked in, laden with peaty moor scents. He drank it in gladly. It was good to see the jolly old sun after all – he would have hated to die a sticky death in Peter's Pot. For a few minutes he stood there, returning thanks vaguely in his mind for the benefits of existence. Then he withdrew to finish dressing. The wad of paper was still in his hand, and he was about to fling it into the fire, when a word caught his eye. He unrolled the paper. As he read it his eyebrows went up and his mouth pursed itself into an indescribable expression of whimsical enlightenment. Bunter, returning with the hot water, found his master transfixed, the paper in one hand, and his socks in the other, and whistling a complicated passage of Bach under his breath.

'Bunter,' said his lordship, 'I am, without exception, the biggest ass in Christendom. When a thing is close under my nose I can't see it. I get a telescope, and look for the explanation in Stapley. I deserve to be crucified upside-down, as a cure for anaemia of the brain. Jerry! Jerry! But, naturally, of course, you rotten ass, isn't it obvious? Silly old blighter. Why couldn't he tell Murbles or me?'

Mr Bunter advanced, the picture of respectful inquiry.

'Look at it – look at it!' said Wimsey, with a hysterical squeak of laughter. 'Oh Lord! O Lord! Stuck into the window frame for anybody to find. *Just* like Jerry. Signs his name to the business in letters a foot long, leaves it conspicuously about, and then goes away and is chival-rously silent.'

Mr Bunter put the jug down upon the washstand in case of accident, and took the paper.

It was the missing letter from Tommy Freeborn.

No doubt about it. There it was – the evidence which established the truth of Denver's evidence. More – which established his alibi for the night of the 13th.

Not Cathcart – Denver.

Denver suggesting that the shooting party should return in October to Riddlesdale, where they had opened the grouse season in August. Denver sneaking hurriedly out at 11.30 to walk two miles across the fields on a night when Farmer Grimethorpe had gone to buy machinery. Denver carelessly plugging a rattling sash on a stormy night with an important letter bearing his title on it for all to see. Denver padding back at three in the morning like a homing tom-cat, to fall over his guest's dead body by the conservatory. Denver, with his kind, stupid, English-gentleman ideas about honour, going obstinately off to prison, rather than tell his solicitor where he had been. Denver misleading them all into the wildest and most ingenious solutions of a mystery which now stood out clear as seven sunbeams. Denver, whose voice the wo-man had thought she recognised on the memorable day when she flung herself into the arms of his brother. Denver calmly setting in motion the enormous, creaking machinery of a trial by his noble peers in order to safeguard a woman's reputation.

This very day, probably, a Select Committee of lords was sitting 'to inspect the Journals of this House upon former trials of peers in criminal cases, in order to bring the Duke of Denver to a speedy trial, and to report to the House what they should think proper thereupon.' There they were: moving that an address be presented to His Majesty by the lords with white staves, to acquaint His Majesty of the date proposed for the trial; arranging for fitting up the Royal Gallery at Westminster; humbly requesting the attendance of a sufficient police force to keep clear the approaches leading to the House; petitioning His Majesty graciously to appoint a Lord High Steward; ordering, in sheep-like accordance with precedent, that all lords be summoned to attend in their robes; that every lord, in giving judgement, disclose his opinion upon his honour, laying his right hand upon his heart; that the Sergeant-at-Arms be within the House to make proclamations in the King's name for keeping silence – and so on, and on, unendingly. And there, jammed in the window-sash, was the dirty little bit of paper which, discovered earlier, would have made the whole monstrous ceremonial unnecessary.

Wimsey's adventure in the bog had unsettled his nerves. He sat down on the bed and laughed, with the tears streaming down his face.

Mr Bunter was speechless. Speechlessly he produced a razor – and to the end of his days Wimsey never knew how or from whom he had so adequately procured it – and began to strop it thoughtfully upon the palm of his hand.

Presently Wimsey pulled himself together and staggered for a little cooling draught of moor air. As he did so, a loud hullabaloo smote his ear, and he perceived, in the courtyard below, Farmer Grimethorpe striding among his dogs; when they howled he struck at them with a whip, and they howled again. Suddenly he glanced up at the window, with an expression of such livid hatred that Wimsey stepped hurriedly back as though struck.

While Bunter shaved him he was silent.

* * *

The interview before Lord Peter was a delicate one; the situation, however one looked at it, unpleasant. He was under a considerable debt of gratitude to his hostess; on the other hand, Denver's position was such that minor considerations really had to go to the wall. His lordship had, nevertheless, never felt quite such a cad as he did while descending the staircase at Grider's Hole.

In the big farm kitchen he found a stout country-woman, stirring a pot of stew. He asked for Mr Grime-thorpe, and was told that he had gone out.

'Can I speak to Mrs Grimethorpe, please?'

The woman looked doubtfully at him, wiped her hands on her apron, and, going into the scullery, shouted, 'Mrs Grimethorpe!' A voice replied from some-where outside.

'Gentleman wants see tha.'

'Where is Mrs Grimethorpe?' broke in Peter hurriedly.

'I' t'dairy, recken.'

'I'll go to her there,' said Wimsey, stepping briskly out. He passed through a stone-paved scullery, and across a yard, in time to see Mrs Grimethorpe emerging from a dark doorway opposite.

Framed there, the cold sunlight just lighting upon her still, dead-white face and heavy, dark hair, she was more wonderful than ever. There was no trace of Yorkshire descent in the long, dark eyes and curled mouth. The curve of nose and cheekbones vouched for an origin immensely remote; coming out of the darkness, she might have just risen from her far tomb in the Pyramids, dropping the dry and perfumed grave-bands from her fingers.

Lord Peter pulled himself together.

'Foreign,' he said to himself matter-of-factly. 'Touch of Jew perhaps, or Spanish, is it? Remarkable type. Don't blame Jerry. Couldn't live with Helen myself. Now for it.'

He advanced quickly.

'Good morning,' she said, 'are you better?'

'Perfectly all right, thank you – thanks to your kindness, which I do not know how to repay.'

'You will repay any kindness best by going at once,' she answered in her remote voice. 'My husband does not care for strangers, and 'twas unfortunate the way you met before.'

'I will go directly. But I must first beg for the favour of a word with you.' He peered past her into the dimness of the dairy. 'In there, perhaps?'

'What do you want with me?'

She stepped back, however, and allowed him to follow her in.

'Mrs Grimethorpe, I am placed in a most painful position. You know that my brother, the Duke of Denver, is in prison, awaiting his trial for a murder which took place on the night of October 13th?'

Her face did not change. 'I have heard so.'

'He has, in the most decided manner, refused to state where he was between eleven and three on that night. His refusal has brought him into great danger of his life.'

She looked at him steadily.

'He feels bound in honour not to disclose his whereabouts, though I know that, if he chose to speak, he could bring a witness to clear him.'

'He seems to be a very honourable man.' The cold voice wavered a trifle, then steadied again.

'Yes. Undoubtedly, from his point of view, he is doing the right thing. You will understand, however, that, as his brother, I am naturally anxious to have the matter put in its proper light.'

'I don't understand why you are telling me all this. I suppose, if the thing is disgraceful, he doesn't want it known.'

'Obviously. But to us – to his wife and young son, and to his sister and myself – his life and safety are matters of the first importance.'

'Of more importance than his honour?'

'The secret is a disgraceful one in a sense, and will give pain to his family. But it would be an infinitely greater disgrace that he should be executed for murder. The stigma in that case would involve all those who bear his name. The shame of the truth will, I fear, in this very unjust society of ours, rest more upon the witness to his alibi than upon himself.'

'Can you in that case expect the witness to come forward?'

'To prevent the condemnation of an innocent man? Yes, I think I may venture to expect even that.'

'I repeat – why are you telling me all this?'

'Because, Mrs Grimethorpe, you know, even better than I, how innocent my brother is of this murder. Believe me, I am deeply distressed at having to say these things to you.'

'I know nothing about your brother.'

'Forgive me, that is not true.'

'I know nothing. And surely, if the Duke will not speak, you should respect his reasons.'

'I am not bound in any way.'

'I am afraid I cannot help you. You are wasting time. If you cannot produce your missing witness, why do you not set about finding the real murderer? If you do so you surely need not trouble about this alibi. Your brother's movements are his own business.'

'I could wish,' said Wimsey, 'you had not taken up this

attitude. Believe me, I would have done all I could to spare you. I have been working hard to find, as you say, the real murderer, but with no success. The trial will probably take place at the end of the month.'

Her lips twitched a little at that, but she said nothing.

'I had hoped that with your help we might agree on some explanation – less than the truth, perhaps, but sufficient to clear my brother. As it is, I fear I shall have to produce the proof I hold, and let matters take their course.'

That, at last, struck under her guard. A dull flush crept up her cheeks; one hand tightened upon the handle of the churn, where she had rested it.

'What do you mean by proof?'

'I can prove that on the night of the 13th my brother slept in the room I occupied last night,' said Wimsey, with calculated brutality.

She winced. 'It is a lie. You cannot prove it. He will deny it. I shall deny it.'

'He was not there?'

'No.'

'Then how did this come to be wedged in the sash of the bedroom window?'

At the sight of the letter she broke down, crumpling up in a heap against the table. The set lines of her face distorted themselves into a mere caricature of terror.

'No, no, no! It is a lie! God help me!'

'Hush!' said Wimsey peremptorily. 'Someone will hear you.' He dragged her to her feet. 'Tell the truth, and we will see if we can find a way out. It is true – he was here that night?'

'You know it.'

'When did he come?'

'At a quarter past twelve.'

'Who let him in?'

'He had the keys.'

'When did he leave you?'

'A little after two.'

'Yes, that fits in all right. Three quarters of an hour to go and three quarters to come back. He stuck this into the window, I suppose, to keep it from rattling?'

'There was a high wind – I was nervous. I thought every sound was my husband coming back.'

'Where was your husband?'

'At Stapley.'

'Had he suspected this?'

'Yes, for some time.'

'Since my brother was here in August?'

'Yes. But he could get no proof. If he had had proof he would have killed me. You have seen him. He is a devil.'

'M'm.'

Wimsey was silent. The woman glanced fearfully at his face and seemed to read some hope there, for she clutched him by the arm.

'If you call me to give evidence,' she said, 'he will know. He *will* kill me. For God's sake, have pity. That letter is my death-warrant. Oh, for the mother that bore you, have mercy upon me. My life is a hell, and when I die I shall go to hell for my sin. Find some other way – you can – you must.'

Wimsey gently released himself.

'Don't do that, Mrs Grimethorpe. We might be seen. I am deeply sorry for you, and, if I can get my brother out of this without bringing you in, I promise you I will. But you see the difficulty. Why don't you leave this man? He is openly brutal to you.'

She laughed.

'Do you think he'd leave me alive while the law was slowly releasing me? Knowing him, do you think so?'

Wimsey really did not think so.

'I will promise you this, Mrs Grimethorpe. I will do all I can to avoid having to use your evidence. But if there should be no other way, I will see that you have police protection from the moment that the subpoena is served on you.'

'And for the rest of my life?'

'When you are once in London we will see about freeing you from this man.'

'No. If you call upon me, I am a lost woman. But you will find another way?'

'I will try, but I can promise nothing. I will do everything that is possible to protect you. If you care at all for my brother—'

'I don't know. I am so horribly afraid. He was kind and good to me. He was – so different. But I am afraid – I'm afraid.'

Wimsey turned. Her terrified eyes had seen the shadow cross the threshold. Grimethorpe was at the door, glowering in upon them.

'Ah, Mr Grimethorpe,' exclaimed Wimsey cheerfully, 'there you are. Awfully pleased to see you and thank you, don'tcherknow, for puttin' me up. I was just saying so to Mrs Grimethorpe, an' asking her to say good-bye to you for me. Must be off now, I'm afraid. Bunter and I are ever so grateful to you both for all your kindness. Oh, and I say, could you find me the stout fellows who hauled us out of that Pot of yours last night – if it is yours. Nasty, damp thing to keep outside the front door, what? I'd like to thank 'em.'

'Dom good thing for unwelcome guests,' said the man ferociously. 'An' tha'd better be off afore Ah throws thee out.'

'I'm just off,' said Peter. 'Good-bye again, Mrs Grime-thorpe, and a thousand thanks.'

He collected Bunter, rewarded his rescuers suitably, took an affectionate farewell of the enraged farmer, and departed, sore in body and desperately confused in mind.

13

MANON

'"That one word, my dear Watson, should have told me the whole story, had I been the ideal reasoner which you are so fond of depicting".'
        MEMOIRS OF SHERLOCK HOLMES

'THANK God,' said Parker. 'Well, that settles it.'

'It does – and yet again, it doesn't,' retorted Lord Peter. He leaned back against the fat silk cushion in the sofa corner meditatively.

'Of course, it's disagreeable having to give this woman away,' said Parker sensibly and pleasantly, 'but these things have to be done.'

'I know. It's all simply awfully nice and all that. And Jerry, who's got the poor woman into this mess, has to be considered first, I know. And if we don't restrain Grimethorpe quite successfully, and he cuts her throat for her, it'll be simply rippin' for Jerry to think of all his life.. . . Jerry! I say, you know, what frightful idiots we were not to see the truth right off! I mean – of course, my sister-in-law is an awfully good woman, and all that, but Mrs Grimethorpe – whew! I told you about the time she mistook me for Jerry. One crowded, split second of glorious all-overishness. I ought to have known then. Our voices are alike, of course, and she couldn't see in that dark kitchen. I don't believe there's an ounce of any feeling left in the woman except sheer terror – but, ye gods! What eyes and skin! Well, never mind. Some undeserving fellows have all the luck. Have you got any really good stories! No? Well, I'll tell you some – enlarge your mind and all that. Do you know the rhyme about the young man at the War Office?'

Mr Parker endured five stories with commendable patience, and then suddenly broke down.

'Hurray!' said Wimsey. 'Splendid man! I love to see you melt into a refined snigger from time to time. I'll spare you the really outrageous one about the young housewife and the traveller in bicycle-pumps. You know, Charles, I really *should* like to know who did Cathcart in. Legally, it's enough to prove Jerry innocent, but, Mrs Grimethorpe or no Mrs Grimethorpe, it doesn't do us credit in a professional capacity. "The father weakens, but the governor is fixed"; that is, as a brother I am satisfied – I may say light-hearted – but as a sleuth I am cast down, humiliated, thrown back upon myself, a lodge in a garden of cucumbers. Besides, of all defences an alibi is the most awkward to establish, unless a number of independent and disinterested witnesses combine to make it thoroughly airtight. If Jerry sticks to his denial, the most they can be sure of is that *either* he *or* Mrs Grimethorpe is being chivalrous.'

'But you've got the letter.'

'Yes. But how are we going to prove that it came that evening? The envelope is destroyed. Fleming remembers nothing about it. Jerry might have received it days earlier. Or it might be a complete fake. Who is to say that I didn't put it in the window myself and pretend to find it. After all, I'm hardly what you would call disinterested.'

'Bunter saw you find it.'

'He didn't, Charles. At that precise moment he was out of the room fetching shaving-water.'

'Oh, was he?'

'Moreover, only Mrs Grimethorpe can swear to what is really the important point – the moment of Jerry's arrival and departure. Unless he was at Grider's Hole before 12.30 at least, it's immaterial whether he was there or not.'

'Well,' said Parker, 'can't we keep Mrs Grimethorpe up our sleeve, so to speak—'

'Sounds a bit abandoned,' said Lord Peter, 'but we will keep her with pleasure if you like.'

'– and meanwhile,' pursued Mr Parker unheeding, 'do our best to find the actual criminal?'

'Oh yes,' said Lord Peter, 'and that reminds me. I made a discovery at the Lodge – at least, I think so. Did you notice that somebody had been forcing one of the study windows?'

'No, really?'

'Yes; I found distinct marks. Of course, it was a long time after the murder, but there were scratches on the catch all right – the sort of thing a penknife would leave.'

'What fools we were not to make an examination at the time!'

'Come to think of it, why should you have? Anyhow, I asked Fleming about it, and he said he did remember, now he came to think of it, that on the Thursday morning he'd found the window open, and couldn't account for it. And here's another thing. I've had a letter from my friend Tim Watchett. Here it is:

'MY LORD, – About our conversation. I have found a Man who was with the Party in question at the "Pig and Whistle" on the night of the 13th ult. and he tells me that the Party borrowed his bicycle, and same was found afterwards in the ditch where Party was picked up with the Handlebars bent and wheels buckled.

'Trusting to the Continuance of your esteemed favour.

'TIMOTHY WATCHETT.'

'What do you think of that?'

'Good enough to go on,' said Parker. 'At least, we are no longer hampered with horrible doubts.'

'No. And, though she's my sister, I must say that of all the blithering she-asses Mary is the blitheringest. Taking up with that awful bounder to start with—'

'She was jolly fine about it,' said Mr Parker, getting rather red in the face. 'It's just because she's your sister that you can't appreciate what a fine thing she did. How should a big, chivalrous nature like hers see through a man like that? She's so sincere and thorough herself, she judges everyone by the same standard. She wouldn't believe anybody could be so thin and wobbly-minded as Goyles till it was *proved* to her. And even then she couldn't bring herself to think ill of him till he'd given himself away out of his own mouth. It was wonderful, the way she fought for him. Think what it must have meant to such a splendid, straight-forward woman to—'

'All right, all right,' cried Peter, who had been staring at his friend, transfixed with astonishment. 'Don't get worked up. I believe you. Spare me. I'm only a brother. All brothers are fools. All lovers are lunatics – Shakespeare says so. Do you want Mary, old man? You surprise me, but I believe brothers always are surprised. Bless you, dear children!'

'Damn it all, Wimsey,' said Parker, very angry, 'you've no right to talk like that. I only said how greatly I admired your sister – everyone must admire such pluck and staunchness. You needn't be insulting. I know she's Lady Mary Wimsey and damnably rich, and I'm only a common police official with nothing a year and a pension to look forward to, but there's no need to sneer about it.'

'I'm not sneering,' retorted Peter indignantly. 'I can't imagine why anybody should want to marry my sister, but you're a friend of mine and a damn good sort, and you've my good word for what it's worth. Besides – dash it all, man! – to put it on the lowest grounds, do look what it might have been! A Socialist Conchy of neither bowels nor breeding, or a card-sharping dark horse with a mysterious past! Mother and Jerry must have got to the point when they'd welcome a decent, God-fearing plumber, let alone a policeman. Only thing I'm afraid of is that Mary, havin' such beastly bad taste in blokes, won't know how to appreciate a really decent fellow like you, old son.'

Mr Parker begged his friend's pardon for his unworthy suspicions, and they sat a little time in silence. Parker sipped his port, and saw unimaginable visions warmly glowing in its rosy depths. Wimsey pulled out his pocket-book, and began idly turning over its contents, throwing old letters into the fire, unfolding and refolding memoranda, and reviewing a miscellaneous series of other people's visiting-cards. He came at length to the slip of blotting-paper from the study at Riddlesdale, to whose fragmentary markings he had since given scarcely a thought.

Presently Mr Parker, finishing his port and recalling his mind with an effort, remembered that he had been meaning to tell Peter something before the name of Lady Mary had driven all other thoughts out of his head. He turned to his host, open-mouthed for speech, but his remark never got beyond a preliminary click like that of a clock about to strike, for, even as he turned, Lord Peter brought his fist down on the little table with a bang that made the decanters ring, and cried out in the loud voice of complete and sudden enlightenment:

'*Manon Lescaut!*'

'Eh?' said Mr Parker.

'Boil my brains!' said Lord Peter. 'Boil 'em and mash 'em and serve 'em up with butter as a dish of turnips, for it's damn well all they're fit for! Look at me!' (Mr Parker scarcely needed this exhortation.) 'Here we've been worryin' over Jerry, an' worryin' over Mary, an' huntin' for Goyleses an' Grimethorpes and God knows who – and all the time I'd got this little bit of paper tucked away in my pocket. The blot upon the paper's rim a blotted paper was to him, and it was nothing more. But Manon, Manon! Charles, if I'd had the grey matter of a wood-louse that book ought to have told me the whole story. And think what we'd have been saved!'

'I wish you wouldn't be so excited,' said Parker. 'I'm sure it's perfectly splendid for you to see your way so clearly, but I never read *Manon Lescaut*, and you haven't shown me the blotting-paper, and I haven't the foggiest idea what you've discovered.'

Lord Peter passed the relic over without comment.

'I observe,' said Parker, 'that the paper is rather crumpled and dirty, and smells powerfully of tobacco and Russian leather, and deduce that you have been keeping it in your pocket-book.'

'No!' said Wimsey incredulously. 'And when you actually saw me take it out! Holmes, how do you do it?'

'At one corner,' pursued Parker, 'I see two blots, one rather larger than the other. I think someone must have shaken a pen there. Is there anything sinister about the blot?'

'I haven't noticed anything.'

'Some way below the blots the Duke has signed his

name two or three times – or, rather, his title. The inference is that his letters were not to intimates.'

'The inference is justifiable, I fancy.'

'Colonel Marchbanks has a neat signature.'

'He can hardly mean mischief,' said Peter. 'He signs his name like an honest man! Proceed.'

'There's a sprawly message about five something of fine something. Do you see anything occult there?'

'The number five may have a cabalistic meaning, but I admit I don't know what it is. There are five senses, five fingers, five great Chinese precepts, five books of Moses, to say nothing of the mysterious entities hymned in the Dilly Song – "Five are the flamboys under the pole". I must admit that I have always wanted to know what the five flamboys were. But, not knowing, I get no help from it in this case.'

'Well, that's all, except a fragment consisting of "oe" on one line, and "is fou—" below it.'

'What do you make of that?'

' "Is found", I suppose.'

'Do you?'

'That seems the simplest interpretation. Or possibly "his foul" – there seems to have been a sudden rush of ink to the pen just there. Do you think it is "his foul"? Was the Duke writing about Cathcart's foul play? Is that what you mean?'

'No, I don't make that of it. Besides, I don't think it's Jerry's writing.'

'Whose is it?'

'I don't know, but I can guess.'

'And it leads somewhere.'

'It tells the whole story.'

'Oh, cough it up, Wimsey. Even Dr Watson would lose patience.'

'Tut, tut! Try the line above.'

'Well, there's only "oe".'

'Yes, well?'

'Well, I don't know. Poet, poem manoeuvre, Loeb edition, Citroen – it might be anything.'

'Dunno about that. There aren't lashings of English words with "oe" in them – and it's written so close it almost looks like a diphthong at that.'

'Perhaps it isn't an English word.'

'Exactly; perhaps it isn't.'

'Oh! Oh, I see. French?'

'Ah, you're gettin' warm.'

'*Soeur – oeuvre – oeuf – boeuf*—'

'No, no. You were nearer the first time.'

'*Soeur – coeur!*'

'*Coeur.* Hold on a moment. Look at the scratch in front of that.'

'Wait a bit – *er – cer*—'

'How about *percer*?'

'I believe you're right. "*Percer le coeur.*"'

'Yes. Or "*perceras le coeur*".'

'That's better. It seems to need another letter or two.'

'And now your "is found" line.'

'*Fou!*'

'Who?'

'I didn't say "who"; I said "*fou*".'

'I know you did. I said who?'

'Who?'

'Who's *fou*?'

'Oh, *is*. By Jove, "*suis*"! "*Je suis fou*".'

'*A la bonne heure!* And I suggest that the next words are "*de douleur*", or something like it.'

'They might be.'

'Cautious beast! I say they are.'

'Well and suppose they are?'

'It tells us everything.'

'Nothing!'

'Everything, I say. Think. This was written on the day Cathcart died. Now who in the house would be likely to write these words, "*perceras le coeur . . . je suis fou de douleur*"? Take everybody. I know it isn't Jerry's fist, and he wouldn't use those expressions. Colonel or Mrs Marchbanks? Not Pygmalion likely! Freddy! Couldn't write passionate letters in French to save his life.'

'No, of course not. It would have to be either Cathcart or – Lady Mary.'

'Rot! It couldn't be Mary.'

'Why not?'

'Not unless she changed her sex, you know.'

'Of course not. It would have to be "*je suis folle*". Then Cathcart—'

'Of course. He lived in France all his life. Consider his bank-book. Consider—'

'Lord! Wimsey, we've been blind.'

'Yes.'

'And listen! I was going to tell you. The Sûreté write me that they've traced one of Cathcart's bank-notes.'

'Where to?'

'To a Mr François who owns a lot of house property near the Etoile.'

'And lets it out in *appartements*!'

'No doubt.'

'When's the next train? Bunter!'

'My lord!'

Mr Bunter hurried to the door at the call.

'The next boat-train for Paris?'

'Eight-twenty, my lord, from Waterloo.'

'We're going by it. How long?'

'Twenty minutes, my lord.'

'Pack my toothbrush and call a taxi.'

'Certainly, my lord.'

'But, Wimsey, what light does it throw on Cathcart's murder? – Did this woman—'

'I've no time,' said Wimsey hurriedly. 'But I'll be back in a day or two. Meanwhile—'

He hunted hastily in the bookshelf.

'Read this.'

He flung the book at his friend and plunged into his bedroom.

At eleven o'clock, as a gap of dirty water disfigured with oil and bits of paper widened between the *Normannia* and the quay; while hardened passengers fortified their sea-stomachs with cold ham and pickles, and the more nervous studied the Boddy jackets in their cabins; while the harbour lights winked and swam right and left, and Lord Peter scraped acquaintance with a second-rate cinema actor in the bar, Charles Parker sat, with a puzzled frown, before the fire at 110A Piccadilly, making his first acquaintance with the delicate masterpiece of the Abbé Prévost.

14

THE EDGE OF THE AXE TOWARDS HIM

SCENE 1: Westminster Hall. Enter as to the Parliament,
Bolingbroke, Aumerle, Northumberland,
Percy, Fitzwater, Surrey, the Bishop of Car-
lisle, the Abbot of Westminster, and another
Lord, Herald, Officers, and Bagot.

BOLINGBROKE *Call forth Bagot.*
Now Bagot, freely speak thy mind;
What dost know of noble Gloucester's death;
Who wrought it with the king, and who
performed
The bloody office of his timeless end.

BAGOT *Then set before my face the Lord Aumerle.*
KING RICHARD II

THE historic trial of the Duke of Denver for murder
opened as soon as Parliament reassembled after the
Christmas vacation. The papers had leaderettes on
'Trial by his Peers', by a Woman Barrister, and 'The
Privilege of Peers: should it be abolished?' by a Student
of History. The *Evening Banner* got into trouble for
contempt by publishing an article entitled 'The Silken
Rope' (by an Antiquarian), which was deemed to be
prejudicial, and the *Daily Trumpet* – the Labour organ
– inquired sarcastically why, when a peer was tried, the
fun of seeing the show should be reserved to the few

influential persons who could wangle tickets for the Royal Gallery.

Mr Murbles and Detective Inspector Parker, in close consultation, went about with preoccupied faces, while Sir Impey Biggs retired into a complete eclipse for three days, revolved about by Mr Gliberry, K.C., Mr Brownrigg-Fortescue, K.C., and a number of lesser satellites. The schemes of the Defence were kept dark indeed – the more so that they found themselves on the eve of the struggle deprived of their principal witness, and wholly ignorant whether or not he would be forthcoming with his testimony.

Lord Peter had returned from Paris at the end of four days, and had burst in like a cyclone at Great Ormond Street. 'I've got it,' he said, 'but it's touch and go. Listen!'

For an hour Parker had listened, feverishly taking notes.

'You can work on that,' said Wimsey. 'Tell Murbles. I'm off.'

His next appearance was at the American Embassy. The Ambassador, however, was not there, having received a royal mandate to dine. Wimsey damned the dinner, abandoned the polite, horn-rimmed secretaries, and leapt back into his taxi with a demand to be driven to Buckingham Palace. Here a great deal of insistence with scandalised officials produced first a higher official, then a very high official, and, finally, the American Ambassador and a Royal Personage while the meat was yet in their mouths.

'Oh yes,' said the Ambassador, 'of course it can be done—'

'Surely, surely,' said the Personage genially, 'we mustn't have any delay. Might cause an international misunderstanding, and a lot of paragraphs about Ellis Island. Terrible nuisance to have to adjourn the trial – dreadful fuss, isn't it? Our secretaries are everlastingly bringing things along to our place to sign about extra policemen and seating accommodation. Good luck to you, Wimsey! Come and have something while they get your papers through. When does your boat go?'

'Tomorrow morning, sir. I'm catching the Liverpool train in an hour – if I can.'

'You surely will,' said the Ambassador cordially, signing a note. 'And they say the English can't hustle.'

So, with his papers all in order, his lordship set sail from Liverpool the next morning, leaving his legal representatives to draw up alternative schemes of defence.

'Then the peers, two by two, in their order, beginning with the youngest baron.'

Garter King-of-Arms, very hot and bothered, fussed unhappily around the three hundred or so British peers who were sheepishly struggling into their robes, while the heralds did their best to line up the assembly and keep them from wandering away when once arranged.

'Of all the farces!' grumbled Lord Attenbury irritably. He was a very short, stout gentleman of a choleric countenance, and was annoyed to find himself next to the Earl of Strathgillan and Begg, an extremely tall, lean nobleman, with pronounced views on Prohibition and the Legitimation question.

'I say, Attenbury,' said a kindly, brick-red peer, with five rows of ermine on his shoulder, 'is it true that Wimsey hasn't come back? My daughter tells me she heard he's gone to collect evidence in the States. Why the States?'

'Dunno,' said Attenbury; 'but Wimsey's a dashed clever fellow. When he found those emeralds of mine, you know, I said—'

'Your grace, your grace,' cried Rouge Dragon desperately, diving in, 'your grace is out of line again.'

'Eh, what?' said the brick-faced peer. 'Oh, damme! Must obey orders, I suppose, what?' And was towed away from the mere earls and pushed into position next to the Duke of Wiltshire, who was deaf, and a distant connection of Denver's on the distaff side.

The Royal Gallery was packed. In the seats reserved below the Bar for peeresses sat the Dowager Duchess of Denver, beautifully dressed and defiant. She suffered much from the adjacent presence of her daughter-in-law, whose misfortune it was to become disagreeable when she was unhappy – perhaps the heaviest curse that can be laid on man, who is born to sorrow.

Behind the imposing array of Counsel in full-bottomed wigs in the body of the hall were seats reserved for witnesses, and here Mr Bunter was accommodated – to be called if the defence should find it necessary to establish the alibi – the majority of the witnesses being pent up in the King's Robing-Room, gnawing their fingers and glaring at one another. On either side, above the Bar, were the benches for the peers – each in his own right a judge both of fact and law – while on the high dais the great chair of state stood ready for the Lord High Steward.

The reporters at their little table were beginning to fidget and look at their watches. Muffled by the walls and the buzz of talk, Big Ben dropped eleven slow notes into the suspense. A door opened. The reporters started to their feet; counsel rose; everybody rose; the Dowager Duchess whispered irrepressibly to her neighbour that it reminded her of the Voice that breathed o'er Eden; and the procession streamed slowly in, lit by a shaft of wintry sunshine from the tall windows.

The proceedings were opened by a Proclamation of Silence from the Sergeant-at-Arms, after which the Clerk of the Crown in Chancery, kneeling at the foot of the throne, presented the Commission under the Great Seal to the Lord High Steward,* who, finding no use for it, returned it with great solemnity to the Clerk of the Crown. The latter accordingly proceeded to read it at dismal and wearisome length, affording the assembly an opportunity of judging just how bad the acoustics of the chamber were. The Sergeant-at-Arms retorted with great emphasis, 'God Save the King,' whereupon Garter King-of-Arms and the Gentleman Usher of the Black Rod kneeling again, handed the Lord High Steward his staff of office. ('So picturesque, isn't it?' said the Dowager – 'quite High Church, you know.')

The Certiorari and Return followed in a long, sonorous rigmarole, which, starting with George the Fifth by the Grace of God, called upon all the Justices and Judges of the Old Bailey, enumerated the Lord Mayor of London, the Recorder, and a quantity of assorted aldermen and justices, skipped back to our Lord the King, roamed about the City of London, Counties of London and Middlesex, Essex, Kent, and Surrey, mentioned our late Sovereign Lord King William the Fourth, branched off to the Local Government Act one thousand eight hundred and eighty-eight, lost its way in a list of all treasons, murders, felonies, and misdemeanours by whomsoever and in what manner soever done, committed or perpetrated and by whom or to whom, when, how, and after what manner and of all other articles and circumstances concerning the premises and every one of them and any of them in any manner whatsoever, and at last, triumphantly, after reciting the names of the whole Grand Jury, came to the presentation of the indictment with a sudden, brutal brevity.

* The Lord Chancellor held the appointment on this occasion as usual.

'The Jurors for our Lord the King upon their oaths present that the most noble and puissant prince Gerald Christian Wimsey, Viscount St George, Duke of Denver, a Peer of the United Kingdom of Great Britain and Ireland, on the thirteenth day of October in the year of Our Lord one thousand and nine hundred and twenty-three in the Parish of Riddlesdale in the County of Yorkshire did kill and murder Denis Cathcart.'

'After which, Proclamation* was made by the Sergeant-at-Arms for the Gentleman Usher of the Black Rod to call in Gerald Christian Wimsey, Viscount St George, Duke of Denver, to appear at the Bar to answer his indictment, who, being come to the Bar, kneeled until the Lord High Steward acquainted him that he might rise.'

The Duke of Denver looked very small and pink and lonely in his blue serge suit, the only head uncovered among all his peers, but he was not without a certain dignity as he was conducted to the 'Stool placed within the Bar', which is deemed appropriate to noble prisoners, and he listened to the Lord High Steward's rehearsal of the charge with a simple gravity which became him very well.

'Then the said Duke of Denver was arraigned by the Clerk of the Parliaments in the usual manner and asked whether he was Guilty or Not Guilty, to which he pleaded Not Guilty.'

Whereupon Sir Wigmore Wrinching, the Attorney-General, rose to open the case for the Crown.

After the usual preliminaries to the effect that the case was a very painful one and the occasion a very solemn one, Sir Wigmore proceeded to unfold the story from the

* For report of the procedure see House of Lords Journal for the dates in question.

beginning: the quarrel, the shot at 3 a.m., the pistol, the finding of the body, the disappearance of the letter, and the rest of the familiar tale. He hinted, moreover, that evidence would be called to show that the quarrel between Denver and Cathcart had motives other than those alleged by the prisoner, and that the latter would turn out to have had 'good reason to fear exposure at Cathcart's hands.' At which point the accused was observed to glance uneasily at his solicitor. The exposition took only a short time, and Sir Wigmore proceeded to call witnesses.

The prosecution being unable to call the Duke of Denver, the first important witness was Lady Mary Wimsey. After telling about her relations with the murdered man, and describing the quarrel, 'At three o'clock,' she proceeded, 'I got up and went downstairs.'

'In consequence of what did you do so?' inquired Sir Wigmore, looking round the Court with the air of a man about to produce his great effect.

'In consequence of an appointment I had made to meet a friend.'

All the reporters looked up suddenly, like dogs expecting a piece of biscuit, and Sir Wigmore started so violently that he knocked his brief over upon the head of the Clerk to the House of Lords sitting below him.

'Indeed! Now, witness, remember you are on your oath, and be careful. What was it caused you to wake at three o'clock?'

'I was not asleep. I was waiting for my appointment.'

'And while you were waiting did you hear anything?'

'Nothing at all.'

'Now, Lady Mary, I have here your deposition sworn before the Coroner. I will read it to you. Please listen very carefully. You say, "At three o'clock I was wakened by a shot. I thought it might be poachers. It sounded very loud, close to the house. I went down to find out what it was." Do you remember making that statement?'

'Yes, but it was not true.'

'Not true?'

'No.'

'In the face of that statement, you still say that you heard nothing at three o'clock?'

'I heard nothing at all. I went down because I had an appointment.'

'My lords,' said Sir Wigmore, with a very red face. 'I must ask leave to treat this witness as a hostile witness.'

Sir Wigmore's fiercest onslaught, however, produced no effect, except a reiteration of the statement that no shot had been heard at any time. With regard to the finding of the body, Lady Mary explained that when she said, 'O God! Gerald, you've killed him,' she was under the impression that the body was that of the friend who had made the appointment. Here a fierce wrangle ensued as to whether the story of the appointment was relevant. The Lords decided that on the whole it was relevant; and the entire Goyles story came out, together with the intimation that Mr Goyles was in court and could be produced. Eventually, with a loud snort, Sir Wigmore Wrinching gave up the witness to Sir Impey Biggs, who, rising suavely and looking extremely handsome, brought back the discussion to a point long previous.

'Forgive the nature of the question,' said Sir Impey, bowing blandly, 'but will you tell us whether, in your opinion, the late Captain Cathcart was deeply in love with you?'

'No, I am sure he was not; it was an arrangement for our mutual conveniences.'

'From your knowledge of his character, do you suppose he was capable of a very deep affection?'

'I think he might have been, for the right woman. I should say he had a very passionate nature.'

'Thank you. You have told us that you met Captain Cathcart several times when you were staying in Paris last February. Do you remember going with him to a jeweller's – Monsieur Briquet's in the Rue de la Paix?'

'I may have done; I cannot exactly remember.'

'The date to which I should like to draw your attention is the sixth.'

'I could not say.'

'Do you recognise this trinket?'

Here the green-eyed cat was handed to witness.

'No; I have never seen it before.'

'Did Captain Cathcart ever give you one like it?'

'Never.'

'Did you ever possess such a jewel?'

'I am quite positive I never did.'

'My lords, I put in this diamond and platinum cat. Thank you, Lady Mary.'

James Fleming, being questioned closely as to the delivery of the post, continued to be vague and forgetful, leaving the Court, on the whole, with the impression that no letter had ever been delivered to the Duke. Sir Wigmore, whose opening speech had contained sinister allusions to an attempt to blacken the character of the victim, smiled disagreeably, and handed the witness over to Sir Impey. The latter contented himself with extracting an admission that witness could not swear positively one way or the other, and passed on immediately to another point.

'Do you recollect whether any letters came by the same post for any of the other members of the party?'

'Yes; I took three or four into the billiard-room.'

'Can you say to whom they were addressed?'

'There were several for Colonel Marchbanks and one for Captain Cathcart.'

'Did Captain Cathcart open his letter there and then?'

'I couldn't say, sir. I left the room immediately to take his grace's letters to the study.'

'Now will you tell us how the letters are collected for the post in the morning at the Lodge?'

'They are put into the post-bag, which is locked. His grace keeps one key and the post-office has the other. The letters are put in through a slit in the top.'

'On the morning after Captain Cathcart's death were the letters taken to the post as usual?'

'Yes, sir.'

'By whom?'

'I took the bag down myself, sir.'

'Had you an opportunity of seeing what letters were in it?'

'I saw there was two or three when the postmistress took 'em out of the bag, but I couldn't say who they was addressed to or anythink of that.'

'Thank you.'

Sir Wigmore Wrinching here bounced up like a very irritable jack-in-the-box.

'Is this the first time you have mentioned this letter which you say you delivered to Captain Cathcart on the night of his murder?'

'My lords,' cried Sir Impey. 'I protest against this language. We have as yet no proof that any murder was committed.'

This was the first indication of the line of defence which Sir Impey proposed to take, and caused a little rustle of excitement.

'My lords,' went on Counsel, replying to a question of the Lord High Steward, 'I submit that so far there has been no attempt to prove murder, and that, until the prosecution have established the murder, such a word cannot properly be put into the mouth of a witness.'

'Perhaps, Sir Wigmore, it would be better to use some other word.'

'It makes no difference to our case, my lord; I bow to your lordship's decision. Heaven knows that I would not seek, even by the lightest or most trivial word, to hamper the defence on so serious a charge.'

'My lords,' interjected Sir Impey, 'if the learned Attorney-General considers the word murder to be a triviality, it would be interesting to know to what words he does attach importance.'

'The learned Attorney-General has agreed to substitute another word,' said the Lord High Steward soothingly, nodding to Sir Wigmore to proceed.

Sir Impey, having achieved his purpose of robbing the Attorney-General's onslaught on the witness of some of its original impetus, sat down, and Sir Wigmore repeated his question.

'I mentioned it first to Mr Murbles about three weeks ago.'

'Mr Murbles is the solicitor for the accused, I believe?'

'Yes, sir.'

'And how was it,' inquired Sir Wigmore ferociously, settling his pince-nez on his rather prominent nose, and glowering at the witness, 'that you did not mention this letter at the inquest or at the earlier proceedings in the case?'

'I wasn't asked about it, sir.'

'What made you suddenly decide to go and tell Mr Murbles about it?'

'He asked me, sir.'

'Oh, he asked you; and you conveniently remembered it when it was suggested to you?'

'No, sir. I remembered it all the time. That is to say, I hadn't given any special thought to it, sir.'

'Oh, you remembered it all the time, though you hadn't given any thought to it. Now I put it to you that you had not remembered about it at all till it was suggested to you by Mr Murbles.'

'Mr Murbles didn't suggest nothing, sir. He asked me whether any other letters came by that post, and then I remembered it.'

'Exactly. When it was suggested to you, you remembered it, and not before!'

'No, sir. That is, if I'd been asked before I should have remembered it and mentioned it, but, not being asked, I didn't think it would be of any importance, sir.'

'You didn't think it of any importance that this man received a letter a few hours before his – decease?'

'No, sir. I reckoned if it had been of any importance the police would have asked about it, sir.'

'Now, James Fleming, I put it to you again that it never occurred to you that Captain Cathcart might have received a letter the night he died till the idea was put into your head by the defence.'

The witness, baffled by this interrogative negative, made a confused reply, and Sir Wigmore, glancing round the house as much as to say, 'You see this shifty fellow,' proceeded:

'I suppose it didn't occur to you either to mention to the police about the letters in the post-bag?'

'No, sir.'

'Why not?'

'I didn't think it was my place, sir.'

'Did you think about it at all?'

'No, sir.'

'Do you ever think?'

'No, sir – I mean, yes, sir.'

'Then will you please think what you are saying now.'

'Yes, sir.'

'You say that you took all those important letters out of the house without authority and without acquainting the police?'

'I had my orders, sir.'

'From whom?'

'They was his grace's orders, sir.'

'Ah! His grace's orders. When did you get that order?'

'It was part of my regular duty, sir, to take the bag to the post each morning.'

'And did it not occur to you that in a case like this the proper information of the police might be more important than your orders?'

'No, sir.'

Sir Wigmore sat down with a disgusted look; and Sir Impey took the witness in hand again.

'Did the thought of this letter delivered to Captain Cathcart never pass through your mind between the day of the death and the day when Mr Murbles spoke to you about it?'

'Well, it did pass through my mind, in a manner of speaking, sir.'

'When was that?'

'Before the Grand Jury, sir.'

'And how was it you didn't speak about it then?'

'The gentleman said I was to confine myself to the questions, and not say nothing on my own, sir.'

'Who was this very peremptory gentleman?'

'The lawyer that came down to ask questions for the Crown, sir.'

'Thank you,' said Sir Impey smoothly, sitting down, and leaning over to say something, apparently of an amusing nature, to Mr Glibbery.

The question of the letter was further pursued in the examination of the Hon. Freddy. Sir Wigmore Wrinching laid great stress upon this witness's assertion that deceased had been in excellent health and spirits when retiring to bed on the Wednesday evening, and had spoken of his approaching marriage. 'He seemed particularly cheerio, you know,' said the Hon. Freddy.

'Particularly what?' inquired the Lord High Steward.

'Cheerio, my lord,' said Sir Wigmore, with a deprecatory bow.

'I do not know whether that is a dictionary word,' said his lordship, entering it upon his notes with meticulous exactness, 'but I take it to be synonymous with cheerful.'

The Hon. Freddy, appealed to, said he thought he meant more than just cheerful, more merry and bright, you know.

'May we take it that he was in exceptionally lively spirits?' suggested Counsel.

'Take it in any spirit you like,' muttered the witness, adding, more happily, 'Take a peg of John Begg.'

'The deceased was particularly lively and merry when he went to bed,' said Sir Wigmore, frowning horribly, 'and looking forward to his marriage in the near future. Would that be a fair statement of his condition?'

The Hon. Freddy agreed to this.

Sir Impey did not cross-examine as to witness's account of the quarrel, but went straight to his point.

'Do you recollect anything about the letters that were brought in the night of the death?'

'Yes; I had one from my aunt. The Colonel had some, I fancy, and there was one for Cathcart.'

'Did Captain Cathcart read his letter there and then?'

'No, I'm sure he didn't. You see, I opened mine, and then I saw he was shoving his away in his pocket, and I thought—'

'Never mind what you thought,' said Sir Impey. 'What did you do?'

'I said, "Excuse me, you don't mind, do you?" And he said, "Not at all"; but he didn't read his; and I remember thinking—'

'We can't have that, you know,' said the Lord High Steward.

'But that's why I'm so sure he didn't open it,' said the Hon. Freddy, hurt. 'You see, I said to myself at the time what a secretive fellow he was, and that's how I know.'

Sir Wigmore, who had bounced up with his mouth open, sat down again.

'Thank you, Mr Arbuthnot,' said Sir Impey, smiling.

Colonel and Mrs Marchbanks testified to having heard movements in the Duke's study at 11.30. They had heard no shot or other noise. There was no cross-examination.

Mr Pettigrew-Robinson gave a vivid account of the quarrel, and asserted very positively that there could be no mistaking the sound of the Duke's bedroom door.

'We were then called up by Mr Arbuthnot at a little after 3 a.m.,' proceeded witness, 'and went down to the conservatory, where I saw the accused and Mr Arbuthnot washing the face of the deceased. I had pointed out to them what an unwise thing it was to do this, as they might be destroying valuable evidence for the police. They paid no attention to me. There were a number of footmarks round about the door which I wanted to examine, because it was my theory that—'

'My lords,' cried Sir Impey, 'we really cannot have this witness's theory.'

'Certainly not!' said the Lord High Steward. 'Answer the questions, please, and don't add anything on your own account.'

'Of course,' said Mr Pettigrew-Robinson. 'I don't mean to imply that there was anything wrong about it, but I considered—'

'Never mind what you considered. Attend to me, please. When you first saw the body, how was it lying?'

'On its back, with Denver and Arbuthnot washing its face. It had evidently been turned over, because—'

'Sir Wigmore,' interposed the Lord High Steward, 'you really must control your witness.'

'Kindly confine yourself to the evidence,' said Sir Wigmore, rather heated. 'We do not want your deductions from it. You say that when you saw the body it was lying on its back. Is that correct?'

'And Denver and Arbuthnot were washing it.'

'Yes. Now I want to pass to another point. Do you remember an occasion when you lunched at the Royal Automobile Club?'

'I do. I lunched there one day in the middle of last August – I think it was about the sixteenth or seventeenth.'

'Will you tell us what happened on that occasion?'

'I had gone into the smoke-room after lunch, and was reading in a high-backed arm-chair, when I saw the prisoner at the Bar come in with the late Captain Cathcart. That is to say, I saw them in the big mirror over the mantelpiece. They did not notice there was anyone there, or they would have been a little more careful what they said, I fancy. They sat down near me and started talking, and presently Cathcart leaned over and said something in a low tone which I couldn't catch. The prisoner leapt up with a horrified face, exclaiming, "For God's sake, don't give me away, Cathcart – there'd be the devil to pay." Cathcart said something reassuring – I didn't hear what, he had a furtive sort of voice – and the prisoner replied, "Well, don't, that's all. I couldn't afford to let anybody get hold of it." The prisoner seemed greatly alarmed. Captain Cathcart was laughing. They dropped their voices again, and that was all I heard.'

'Thank you.'

Sir Impey took over the witness with a Belial-like politeness.

'You are gifted with very excellent powers of observation and deduction, Mr Pettigrew-Robinson,' he began, 'and no doubt you like to exercise your sympathetic imagination in a scrutiny of people's motives and characters?'

'I think I may call myself a student of human nature,' replied Mr Pettigrew-Robinson, much mollified.

'Doubtless, people are inclined to confide in you?'

'Certainly. I may say I am a great repository of human documents.'

'On the night of Captain Cathcart's death your wide knowledge of the world was doubtless of great comfort and assistance to the family?'

'They did not avail themselves of my experience, sir,' said Mr Pettigrew-Robinson, exploding suddenly, 'I was ignored completely. If only my advice had been taken at the time—'

'Thank you, thank you,' said Sir Impey, cutting short an impatient exclamation from the Attorney-General, who thereupon rose and demanded:

'If Captain Cathcart had had any secret or trouble of any kind in his life, you would have expected him to tell you about it?'

'From any right-minded young man I might certainly have expected it,' said Mr Pettigrew-Robinson blusteringly; 'but Captain Cathcart was disagreeably secretive. On the only occasion when I showed a friendly interest in his affairs he was very rude indeed. He called me—'

'That'll do,' interposed Sir Wigmore hastily, the answer to the question not having turned out as he expected. 'What the deceased called you is immaterial.'

Mr Pettigrew-Robinson retired, leaving behind him the impression of a man with a grudge – an impression which seemed to please Mr Glibbery and Mr Brownrigg-Fortescue extremely, for they chuckled continuously through the evidence of the next two witnesses.

Mrs Pettigrew-Robinson had little to add to her previous evidence at the inquest. Miss Cathcart was asked by Sir Impey about Cathcart's parentage, and she explained, with deep disapproval in her voice, that her brother, when an all-too-experienced and middle-aged man of the world, had, nevertheless 'been entangled by' an Italian singer of nineteen who had 'contrived' to make him marry her. Eighteen years later both parents had died. 'No wonder,' said Miss Cathcart, 'with the rackety life they led,' and the boy had been left to her care. She explained how Denis had always chafed at her influence, gone about with men she disapproved of, and eventually gone to Paris to make a diplomatic career for himself, since which time she had hardly seen him.

An interesting point was raised in the cross-examination of Inspector Craikes. A penknife being shown him, he identified it as the one found on Cathcart's body.

By Mr Glibbery: 'Do you observe any marks on the blade?'

'Yes, there is a slight notch near the handle.'

'Might the mark have been caused by forcing back the catch of a window?'

Inspector Craikes agreed that it might, but doubted whether so small a knife would have been adequate for such a purpose. The revolver was produced, and the question of ownership raised.

'My lords,' put in Sir Impey, 'we do not dispute the Duke's ownership of the revolver.'

The court looked surprised, and, after Hardraw the gamekeeper had given evidence of the shot heard at 11.30, the medical evidence was taken.

Sir Impey Biggs: 'Could the wound have been self-inflicted?'

'It could, certainly.'

'Would it have been instantly fatal?'

'No. From the amount of blood found upon the path it was obviously not immediately fatal.'

'Are the marks found, in your opinion, consistent with deceased having crawled towards the house?'

'Yes, quite. He might have had sufficient strength to do so.'

'Would such a wound cause fever?'

'It is quite possible. He might have lost consciousness for some time, and contracted a chill and fever by lying in the wet.'

'Are the appearances consistent with his having lived for some hours after being wounded?'

'They strongly suggest it.'

Re-examining, Sir Wigmore Wrinching established that the wound and general appearance of the ground were equally consistent with the theory that deceased had been shot by another hand at very close quarters, and dragged to the house before life was extinct.

'In your experience is it more usual for a person committing suicide to shoot himself in the chest or in the head?'

'In the head is perhaps more usual.'

'So much as almost to create a presumption of murder when the wound is in the chest?'

'I would not go so far as that.'

'But, other things being equal, you would say that a wound in the head is more suggestive of suicide than a body-wound?'

'That is so.'

Sir Impey Biggs: 'But suicide by shooting in the heart is not by any means impossible?'

'Oh dear, no.'

'There have been such cases?'

'Oh, certainly; many such.'

'There is nothing in the medical evidence before you to exclude the idea of suicide?'

'Nothing whatever.'

This closed the case for the Crown.

WHEN Sir Impey Biggs rose to make his opening speech for the defence on the second day, it was observed that he looked somewhat worried – a thing very unusual in him. His remarks were very brief, yet in those few words he sent a thrill through the great assembly.

'My lords, in rising to open this defence I find myself in a more than usually anxious position. Not that I have any doubts of your lordships' verdict. Never perhaps has it been possible so clearly to prove the innocence of any accused person as in the case of my noble client. But I will explain to your lordships at once that I may be obliged to ask for an adjournment, since we are at present without an important witness and decisive piece of evidence. My lords, I hold here in my hand a cablegram from this witness – I will tell you his name; it is Lord Peter Wimsey, the brother of the accused. It was handed in yesterday at New York. I will read it to you. He says: "Evidence secured. Leaving tonight with Air Pilot Grant. Sworn copy and depositions follow by S.S. *Lucarnia* in case accident. Hope arrive Thursday." My lords, at this moment this all-important witness is cleaving the air high above the wide Atlantic. In this wintry weather he is braving a peril which would appal any heart but his own and that of the world-famous aviator whose help he has enlisted, so that no moment may be lost in freeing his noble brother from this terrible charge. My lords, the barometer is falling.'

An immense hush, like the stillness of a black frost, had fallen over the glittering benches. The lords in their scarlet and ermine, the peeresses in their rich furs, counsel in their full-bottomed wigs and billowing gowns, the Lord High Steward upon his high seat, the ushers and the heralds and the gaudy king-of-arms, rested rigid in their places. Only the prisoner looked across at his counsel and back to the Lord High Steward in a kind of bewilderment, and the reporters scribbled wildly and desperately stop-press announcements – lurid headlines, picturesque epithets, and alarming weather predictions, to halt hurrying London on its way. 'PEER'S SON FLIES ATLANTIC'; 'BROTHER'S DEVOTION'; 'WILL WIMSEY BE IN TIME?'; 'RIDDLESDALE MURDER CHARGE: AMAZING DEVELOPMENT.' This was news. A million tape-machines ticked it out in offices and clubs, where clerks and messenger-boys gloated over it and laid wagers on the result; the thousands of monster printing-presses sucked it in, boiled it into lead, champed it into slugs, engulfed it in their huge maws, digested it to paper, and flapped it forth again with clutching talons; and a blue-nosed ragged veteran, who had once assisted to dig Major Wimsey out of a shell-hole near Caudry, muttered: 'Gawd 'elp 'im, 'e's a real decent little blighter,' as he tucked his newspapers into the iron grille of a tree in Kingsway and displayed his placard to the best advantage.

After a brief statement that he intended, not merely to prove his noble client's innocence but (as a work of supererogation) to make clear every detail of the tragedy, Sir Impey Biggs proceeded without further delay to call his witnesses.

Among the first was Mr Goyles, who testified that he had found Cathcart already dead at 3 a.m., with his head close to the water-trough which stood near the well. Ellen, the maid-servant, next confirmed James Fleming's evidence with regard to the post-bag, and explained how she changed the blotting-paper in the study every day.

The evidence of Detective-Inspector Parker aroused more interest and some bewilderment. His description of the discovery of the green-eyed cat was eagerly listened to. He also gave a minute account of the footprints and marks of dragging, especially the imprint of a hand in the flower-bed. The piece of blotting-paper was then produced, and photographs of it circulated among the peers. A long discussion ensued on both these points, Sir Impey Biggs endeavouring to show that the imprint on the flower-bed was such as would have been caused by a man endeavouring to lift himself from a prone position, Sir Wigmore Wrinching doing his best to force an admission that it might have been made by deceased in trying to prevent himself from being dragged along.

'The position of the fingers being towards the house appears, does it not, to negative the suggestion of dragging?' suggested Sir Impey.

Sir Wigmore, however, put it to the witness that the wounded man might have been dragged head foremost.

'If now,' said Sir Wigmore, 'I were to drag you by the coat-collar – my lords will grasp my contention—'

'It appears,' observed the Lord High Steward, 'to be a case for *solvitur ambulando*.' (Laughter.) 'I suggest that when the House rises for lunch, some of us should make the experiment, choosing a member of similar height and weight to the deceased.' (All the noble lords looked round at one another to see which unfortunate might be chosen for the part.)

Inspector Parker then mentioned the marks of forcing on the study window.

'In your opinion, could the catch have been forced back by the knife found on the body of the deceased?'

'I know it could, for I made the experiment myself with a knife of exactly similar pattern.'

After this the message on the blotting-paper was read backwards and forwards and interpreted in every possible way, the defence insisting that the language was French and the words '*Je suis fou de douleur*,' the prosecution scouting the suggestion as far-fetched, and offering an English interpretation, such as 'is found' or 'his foul.' A handwriting expert was then called, who compared the handwriting with that of an authentic letter of Cathcart's, and was subsequently severely handled by the prosecution.

These knotty points being left for the consideration of the noble lords, the defence then called a tedious series of witnesses: the manager of Cox's, and Monsieur Turgeot of the Crédit Lyonnais, who went with much detail into Cathcart's financial affairs; the concierge and Madame Leblanc from the Rue St Honoré; and the noble lords began to yawn, with the exception of a few of the soap and pickles lords, who suddenly started to make computations in their note-books, and exchanged looks of intelligence as from one financier to another.

Then came Monsieur Briquet, the jeweller from the Rue de la Paix, and the girl from his shop, who told the story of the tall, fair, foreign lady and the purchase of the green-eyed cat – whereat everybody woke up. After reminding the assembly that this incident took place in February, when Cathcart's fiancée was in Paris, Sir Impey invited the jeweller's assistant to look round the house and tell them if she saw the foreign lady. This proved a lengthy business, but the answer was finally in the negative.

'I do not want there to be any doubt about this,' said Sir Impey, 'and, with the learned Attorney-General's permission, I am now going to confront this witness with Lady Mary Wimsey.'

Lady Mary was accordingly placed before the witness, who replied immediately and positively: 'No, this is not the lady; I have never seen this lady in my life. There is the resemblance of height and colour and the hair bobbed, but there is nothing else at all – not the least in the world. It is not the same type at all. Mademoiselle is a charming English lady, and the man who marries her will be very happy, but the other was *belle à se suicider* – a woman to kill, suicide oneself, or send all to the devil for, and believe me, gentlemen' (with a wide smile to her distinguished audience), 'we have the opportunity to see them in my business.'

There was a profound sensation as this witness took her departure, and Sir Impey scribbled a note and passed it down to Mr Murbles. It contained the one word, 'Magnificent!' Mr Murbles scribbled back:

'Never said a word to her. Can you beat it!' and leaned back in his seat smirking like a very neat little grotesque from a Gothic corbel.

The witness who followed was Professor Hébert, a distinguished exponent of international law, who described Cathcart's promising career as a rising young diplomat in Paris before the war. He was followed by a number of officers who testified to the excellent war record of the deceased. Then came a witness who gave the aristocratic name of du Bois-Gobey Houdin, who perfectly recollected a very uncomfortable dispute on a certain occasion when playing cards with le Capitaine

Cathcart, and having subsequently mentioned the matter to Monsieur Thomas Freeborn, the distinguished English engineer. It was Parker's diligence that had unearthed this witness, and he looked across with an undisguised grin at the discomfited Sir Wigmore Wrinching. When Mr Glibbery had dealt with all these the afternoon was well advanced, and the Lord High Steward accordingly asked the lords if it was their pleasure that the House be adjourned till the next day at 10.30 of the clock in the forenoon, and the lords replying 'Aye' in a most exemplary chorus, the House was accordingly adjourned.

A scurry of swift black clouds with ragged edges was driving bleakly westward as they streamed out into Parliament Square, and the seagulls screeched and wheeled inwards from the river. Charles Parker wrapped his ancient Burberry closely about him as he scrambled on to a 'bus to get home to Great Ormond Street. It was only one more drop in his cup of discomfort that the conductor greeted him with 'Outside only!' and rang the bell before he could get off again. He climbed to the top and sat there holding his hat on. Mr Bunter returned sadly to 110A Piccadilly, and wandered restlessly about the flat till seven o'clock, when he came into the sitting-room and switched on the loud speaker.

'London calling,' said the unseen voice impartially. '2LO calling. Here is the weather forecast. A deep depression is crossing the Atlantic, and a secondary is stationary over the British Isles. Storms, with heavy rain and sleet, will be prevalent, rising to a gale in the south and south-west. . . .'

'You never know,' said Bunter. 'I suppose I'd better light a fire in his bedroom.'

'Further outlook similar.'

16

THE SECOND STRING

'O, *whan he came to broken briggs*
   He bent his bow and swam,
And whan he came to the green grass growin'
   He slacked his shoone and ran.

'O, *whan he came to Lord William's gates*
   He baed na to chap na ca',
But set his bent bow till his breast,
   An' lightly lap the wa''

BALLAD OF LADY MAISRY

LORD PETER peered out through the cold scurry of cloud. The thin struts of steel, incredibly fragile, swung slowly across the gleam and glint far below, where the wide country dizzied out and spread like a revolving map. In front the sleek leather back of his companion humped stubbornly, sheeted with rain. He hoped that Grant was feeling confident. The roar of the engine drowned the occasional shout he threw to his passenger as they lurched from gust to gust.

He withdrew his mind from present discomforts and went over that last, strange, hurried scene. Fragments of conversation spun through his head.

'Mademoiselle, I have scoured two continents in search of you.'

'*Voyons*, then, it is urgent. But be quick, for the big bear may come in and be grumpy, and I do not like *des histoires*.'

There had been a lamp on a low table; he remembered the gleam through the haze of short gold hair. She was a tall girl, but slender, looking up at him from the huge black-and-gold cushions.

'Mademoiselle, it is incredible to me that you should ever – dine or dance – with a person called Van Humperdinck.'

Now what had possessed him to say that – when there was so little time, and Jerry's affairs were of such importance?

'Monsieur van Humperdinck does not dance. Did you seek me through two continents to say that?'

'No, I am serious.'

'*Eh bien*, sit down.'

She had been quite frank about it.

'Yes, poor soul. But life was very expensive since the war. I refused several good things. But always *des histoires*. And so little money. You see, one must be sensible. There is one's old age. It is necessary to be provident, *hein*?'

'Assuredly.' She had a little accent – very familiar. At first he could not place it. Then it came to him – Vienna before the war, that capital of incredible follies.

'Yes, yes, I wrote. I was very kind, very sensible, I said, "*Je ne suis pas femme à supporter de gros ennuis*". *Cela se comprend, n'est-ce-pas?*'

That was readily understood. The 'plane dived sickly into a sudden pocket, the propeller whirring helplessly in the void, then steadied and began to nose up the opposite spiral.

'I saw it in the papers – yes. Poor boy! Why should anybody have shot him?'

'Mademoiselle, it is for that I have come to you. My brother, whom I dearly love, is accused of the murder. He may be hanged.'

'Brr!'

'For a murder he did not commit.'

'*Mon pauvre enfant*—'

'Mademoiselle, I implore you to be serious. My brother is accused, and will be standing his trial—'

Once her attention had been caught she had been all sympathy. Her blue eyes had a curious and attractive trick – a full lower lid that shut them into glimmering slits.

'Mademoiselle, I implore you, try to remember what was in his letter.'

'But, *mon pauvre ami*, how can I? I did not read it. It was very long, very tedious, full of *histoires*. The thing was finished – I never bother about what cannot be helped, do you?'

But his real agony at this failure had touched her.

'Listen, then; all is perhaps not lost. It is possible the letter is still somewhere about. Or we will ask Adèle. She is my maid. She collects letters to blackmail people – oh, yes, I know! But she is *habile comme tout pour la toilette*. Wait – we will look first.'

Tossing out letters, trinkets, endless perfumed rubbish from the little gimcrack secretaire, from drawers full of lingerie ('I am so untidy – I am Adèle's despair'), from bags – hundreds of bags – and at last Adèle, thin-lipped and wary-eyed, denying everything till her mistress suddenly slapped her face in a fury, and called her ugly little names in French and German.

'It is useless, then,' said Lord Peter. 'What a pity that Mademoiselle Adèle cannot find a thing so valuable to me.'

The word 'valuable' suggested an idea to Adèle. There was Mademoiselle's jewel-case which had not been searched. She would fetch it.

'*C'est cela que cherche monsieur?*'

After that, the sudden arrival of Mr Cornelius van Humperdinck, very rich and stout and suspicious, and the rewarding of Adèle in a tactful, unobtrusive fashion by the elevator shaft.

Grant shouted, but the words flipped feebly away into the blackness and were lost. 'What?' bawled Wimsey in his ear. He shouted again, and this time the word 'juice' shot into sound and fluttered away. But whether the news was good or bad Lord Peter could not tell.

Mr Murbles was aroused a little after midnight by a thunderous knocking upon his door. Thrusting his head out of the window in some alarm, he saw the porter with his lantern steaming through the rain, and behind him a shapeless figure which for the moment Mr Murbles could not make out.

'What's the matter?' said the solicitor.

'Young lady askin' urgently for you, sir.'

The shapeless figure looked up, and he caught the spangle of gold hair in the lantern-light under the little tight hat.

'Mr Murbles, please come. Bunter rang me up. There's a woman come to give evidence. Bunter doesn't like to leave her – she's frightened – but he says it's *frightfully* important, and Bunter's always right, you know.'

'Did he mention the name?'

'A Mrs Grimethorpe.'

'God bless me! Just a moment, my dear young lady, and I will let you in.'

And, indeed, more quickly than might have been expected, Mr Murbles made his appearance in a Jaeger dressing-gown at the front door.

'Come in, my dear. I will get dressed in a very few minutes. It was quite right of you to come to me. I'm very, very glad you did. What a terrible night! Perkins, would you kindly wake up Mr Murphy and ask him to oblige me with the use of his telephone?'

Mr Murphy – a noisy Irish barrister with a hearty manner – needed no waking. He was entertaining a party of friends, and was delighted to be of service.

'Is that you, Biggs? Murbles speaking. That alibi—'

'Yes?'

'Has come along of its own accord.'

'My God! You don't say so!'

'Can you come round to 110A Piccadilly?'

'Straight away.'

It was a strange little party gathered round Lord Peter's fire – the white-faced woman, who started at every sound; the men of law, with their keen, disciplined faces; Lady Mary; Bunter, the efficient. Mrs Grime-thorpe's story was simple enough. She had suffered the torments of knowledge ever since Lord Peter had spoken to her. She had seized an hour when her husband was drunk in the 'Lord in Glory', and had harnessed the horse and driven in to Stapley.

'I couldn't keep silence. It's better my man should kill me, for I'm unhappy enough, and maybe I couldn't be any worse off in the Lord's hand – rather than they should hang him for a thing he never done. He was kind, and I was desperate miserable, that's the truth, and I'm hoping his lady won't be hard on him when she knows it all.'

'No, no,' said Mr Murbles, clearing his throat. 'Excuse me a moment, madam. Sir Impey—'

The lawyers whispered together in the window-seat.

'You see,' said Sir Impey, 'she has burnt her boats

pretty well now by coming at all. The great question for us is, is it worth the risk? After all, we don't know what Wimsey's evidence amounts to.'

'No, that is why I feel inclined – in spite of the risk – to put this evidence in,' said Mr Murbles.

'I am ready to take the risk,' interposed Mrs Grimethorpe starkly.

'We quite appreciate that,' replied Sir Impey. 'It is the risk to our client we have to consider first of all.'

'Risk?' cried Mary. 'But surely this clears him?'

'Will you swear absolutely to the time when his grace of Denver arrived at Grider's Hole, Mrs Grimethorpe?' went on the lawyer, as though he had not heard her.

'It was a quarter past twelve by the kitchen clock – 'tis a very good clock.'

'And he left you at—'

'About five minutes past two.'

'And how long would it take a man, walking quickly, to get back to Riddlesdale Lodge?'

'Oh, well-nigh an hour. It's rough walking, and a steep bank up and down to the beck.'

'You mustn't let the other counsel upset you on those points, Mrs Grimethorpe, because they will try to prove that he had time to kill Cathcart either before he started or after he returned, and by admitting that the Duke had something in his life that he wanted kept secret we shall be supplying the very thing the prosecution lack – *a motive for murdering anyone who might have found him out.*'

There was a stricken silence.

'If I may ask, madam,' said Sir Impey, 'has any person any suspicion?'

'My husband guessed,' she answered hoarsely. 'I am sure of it. He has always known. But he couldn't prove it. That very night—'

'What night?'

'The night of the murder – he laid a trap for me. He came back from Stapley in the night, hoping to catch us and do murder. But he drank too much before he started, and spent the night in the ditch, or it might be Gerald's death you'd be inquiring into, and mine, as well as the other.'

It gave Mary an odd shock to hear her brother's name spoken like that, by that speaker and in that company. She asked suddenly, apropos of nothing, 'Isn't Mr Parker here?'

'No, my dear,' said Mr Murbles reprovingly, 'this is not a police matter.'

'The best thing we can do, I think,' said Sir Impey, 'is to put in the evidence, and, if necessary, arrange for some kind of protection for this lady. In the meantime—'

'She is coming round with me to mother,' said Lady Mary determinedly.

'My dear lady,' expostulated Mr Murbles, 'that would be very unsuitable in the circumstances. I think you hardly grasp—'

'Mother said so,' retorted her ladyship. 'Bunter, call a taxi.'

Mr Murbles waved his hands helplessly, but Sir Impey was rather amused. 'It's no good, Murbles,' he said. 'Time and trouble will tame an advanced young woman, but an advanced old woman is uncontrollable by any earthly force.'

So it was from the Dowager's town house that Lady Mary rang up Mr Charles Parker to tell him the news.

17

THE ELOQUENT DEAD

'*Je connaissais Manon: pourquoi m'affliger tant d'un
malheur que j'avais dû prévoir.*'

MANON LESCAUT

THE gale had blown itself out into a wonderful fresh day,
with clear spaces of sky, and a high wind rolling boulders
of cumulus down the blue slopes of air.

The prisoner had been wrangling for an hour with his
advisers when finally they came into court, and even Sir
Impey's classical face showed flushed between the wings
of his wig.

'I'm not going to say anything,' said the Duke obstinately. 'Rotten thing to do. I suppose I can't prevent you
callin' her if she insists on comin' – damn' good of her –
makes me feel no end of a beast.'

'Better leave it at that,' said Mr Murbles. 'Makes a
good impression, you know. Let him go into the box and
behave like a perfect gentleman. They'll like it.'

Sir Impey, who had sat through the small hours
altering his speech, nodded.

The first witness that day came as something of a
surprise. She gave her name and address as Eliza Briggs,
known as Madame Brigette of New Bond Street, and her
occupation as beauty specialist and perfumer. She had a
large and aristocratic clientele of both sexes, and a
branch in Paris.

Deceased had been a client of hers in both cities for

several years. He had massage and manicure. After the war he had come to her about some slight scars caused by grazing with shrapnel. He was extremely particular about his personal appearance, and, if you called that vanity in a man, you might certainly say he was vain. Thank you. Sir Wigmore Wrinching made no attempt to cross-examine the witness, and the noble lords wondered to one another what it was all about.

At this point Sir Impey Biggs leaned forward, and, tapping his brief impressively with his forefinger, began:

'My lords, so strong is our case that we had not thought it necessary to present an alibi –' when an officer of the court rushed up from a little whirlpool of commotion by the door and excitedly thrust a note into his hand. Sir Impey read, coloured, glanced down the hall, put down his brief, folded his hands over it, and said in a sudden, loud voice which penetrated even to the deaf ear of the Duke of Wiltshire:

'My lords, I am happy to say that our missing witness is here. I call Lord Peter Wimsey.'

Every neck was at once craned, and every eye focused on the very grubby and oily figure that came amiably trotting up the long room. Sir Impey Biggs passed the note down to Mr Murbles, and, turning to the witness, who was yawning frightfully in the intervals of grinning at all his acquaintances, demanded that he should be sworn.

The witness's story was as follows:

'I am Peter Death Bredon Wimsey, brother of the accused. I live at 110A Piccadilly. In consequence of what I read on that bit of blotting-paper which I now identify, I went to Paris to look for a certain lady. The name of the lady is Mademoiselle Simone Vonderaa. I found she had left Paris in company with a man named

Van Humperdinck. I followed her, and at length came up with her in New York. I asked her to give me the letter Cathcart wrote on the night of his death. (Sensation.) I produce that letter, with Mademoiselle Vonderaa's signature on the corner, so that it can be identified if Wiggy there tries to put it over you. (Joyous sensation, in which the indignant protests of prosecuting counsel were drowned.) And I'm sorry I've given you such short notice of this, old man, but I only got it the day before yesterday. We came as quick as we could, but we had to come down near Whitehaven with engine trouble, and if we had come down half a mile sooner I shouldn't be here now.' (Applause, hurriedly checked by the Lord High Steward.)

'My lords,' said Sir Impey, 'your lordships are witnesses that I have never seen this letter in my life before. I have no idea of its contents; yet so positive am I that it cannot but assist my noble client's case, that I am willing – nay, eager – to put in this document immediately, as it stands, without perusal, to stand or fall by the contents.'

'The handwriting must be identified as that of the deceased,' interposed the Lord High Steward.

The ravening pencils of the reporters tore along the paper. The lean young man who worked for the *Daily Trumpet* scented a scandal in high life and licked his lips, never knowing what a much bigger one had escaped him by a bare minute or so.

Miss Lydia Cathcart was recalled to identify the handwriting, and the letter was handed to the Lord High Steward, who announced:

'The letter is in French. We shall have to swear an interpreter.'

'You will find,' said the witness suddenly, 'that those

bits of words on the blotting-paper come out of the letter. You'll 'scuse my mentioning it.'

'Is this person put forward as an expert witness?' inquired Sir Wigmore witheringly.

'Right ho!' said Lord Peter. 'Only, you see, it has been rather sprung on Biggy as you might say.

> 'Biggy and Wiggy
>> Were two pretty men,
> They went into court,
>> When the clock—'

'Sir Impey, I must really ask you to keep your witness in order.'

Lord Peter grinned, and a pause ensued while an interpreter was fetched and sworn. Then, at last, the letter was read, amid a breathless silence:

> 'Riddlesdale Lodge,
>> 'Stapley,
>>> 'N.E. Yorks.
>>>> '*le 13 Octobre*, 1923.

'SIMONE, – Je viens de recevoir ta lettre. Que dire? Inutiles, les prières ou les reproches. Tu ne comprendras – tu ne liras même pas.

'N'ai-je pas toujours su, d'ailleurs, que tu devais infailliblement me trahir? Depuis dix ans déjà je souffre tous les tourments que puisse infliger la jalousie. Je comprends bien que tu n'as jamais voulu me faire de la peine. C'est tout justement cette insouciance, cette légèreté, cette façon séduisante d'être malhonnête, que j'adorais en toi. J'ai tout su, et je t'ai aimée.

'Ma foi, non, ma chère, jamais je n'ai eu la moindre illusion. Te rappelles-tu cette première rencontre, un soir au Casino? Tu avais dix-sept ans, et tu étais jolie à ravir.

Le lendemain tu fus à moi. Tu m'as dit, si gentiment, que tu m'aimais bien, et que j'étais, moi, le premier. Ma pauvre enfant, tu en as menti. Tu riais, toute seule, de ma naïveté – il y avait bien de quoi rire! Dès notre premier baiser, j'ai prévu ce moment.

'Mais écoute, Simone. J'ai la faiblesse de vouloir te montrer exactement ce que tu as fait de moi. Tu regretteras peut-être un peu. Mais, non – si tu pouvais regretter quoi que ce fût, tu ne serais plus Simone.

'Il y a dix ans, la veille de la guerre, j'étais riche – moins riche que ton Américain, mais assez riche pour te donner l'établissement qu'il te fallait. Tu étais moins exigeante avant la guerre, Simone – qui est-ce qui, pendant mon absence, t'a enseigné le goût du luxe? Charmante discrétion de ma part de ne jamais te le demander! Eh bien, une grande partie de ma fortune se trouvant placée en Russie et en Allemagne, j'en ai perdu plus de trois-quarts. Ce que m'en restait en France a beaucoup diminué en valeur. Il est vrai que j'avais mon traitement de capitaine dans l'armée britannique, mais c'est peu de chose, tu sais. Avant même la fin de la guerre, tu m'avais mangé toutes mes économies. C'était idiot, quoi! Un jeune homme qui a perdu les trois-quarts de ses rentes ne se permet plus une maîtresse et un appartement Avenue Kléber. Ou il congédie madame, ou bien il lui demande quelques sacrifices; je n'ai rien osé demander. Si j'étais venu un jour te dire, "Simone, je suis pauvre" – que m'aurais-tu répondu?

'Sais-tu ce que j'ai fait? Non – tu n'as jamais pensé à demander d'où venait cet argent. Qu'est-ce que cela pouvait te faire que j'ai tout jeté – fortune, honneur, bonheur – pour te posséder? J'ai joué, désespérément, éperdument – j'ai fait pis: j'ai triché au jeu. Je te vois hausser les épaules – tu ris – tu dis, "Tiens, c'est malin, ça!" Oui, mais cela ne se fait pas. On m'aurait chassé du régiment. Je devenais le dernier des hommes.

'D'ailleurs, cela ne pouvait durer. Déjà un soir à Paris on m'a fait une scène désagréable, bien qu'on n'ait rien pu prouver. C'est alors que je me suis fiancé avec cette demoiselle dont je t'ai parlé, la fille du duc anglais. Le beau projet, quoi! Entretenir ma maîtresse avec l'argent de ma femme! Et je l'aurais fait – et je le ferais encore demain, si c'était pour te reposséder.

'Mais tu me quittes. Cet Américain est riche – archiriche. Depuis longtemps tu me répètes que ton appartement est trop petit et que tu t'ennuies à mourir. Cet "ami bienveillant" t'offre les autos, les diamants, les mille-et-une nuits, la lune! Auprès de ces merveilles, évidemment, que valent l'amour et l'honneur?

'Enfin, le bon duc est d'une stupidité très commode. Il laisse traîner son révolver dans le tiroir de son bureau. D'ailleurs, il vient de me demander une explication à propos de cette histoire de cartes. Tu vois qu'en tout cas la partie était finie. Pourquoi t'en vouloir? On mettra sans doute mon suicide au compte de cet exposé. Tant mieux; je ne veux pas qu'on affiche mon histoire amoureuse dams les journaux.

'Adieu, ma bien-aimée – mon adorée, mon adorée, ma Simone. Sois heureuse avec ton nouvel amant. Ne pense plus à moi. Qu'est-ce tout cela peut bien te faire? Mon Dieu, comme je t'ai aimée – comme je t'aime toujours, malgré moi. Mais c'en est fini. Jamais plus tu ne me perceras le coeur. Oh! J'enrage – je suis fou de douleur! Adieu.

'DENIS CATHCART'.

TRANSLATION

'SIMONE, – I have just got your letter. What am I to say? It is useless to entreat or reproach you. You would not understand, or even read the letter.

'Besides, I always knew you must betray me some day. I have suffered a hell of jealousy for the last ten years. I know perfectly well you never meant to hurt me. It was just your utter lightness and carelessness and your attractive way of being dishonest which was so adorable. I knew everything, and loved you all the same.

'Oh no, my dear, I never had any illusions. You remember our first meeting that night at the Casino. You were seventeen, and heart-breakingly lovely. You came to me the very next day. You told me, very prettily, that you loved me and that I was the first. My poor little girl, that wasn't true. I expect, when you were alone, you laughed to think I was so easily taken in. But there was nothing to laugh at. From our very first kiss I foresaw this moment.

'I'm afraid I'm weak enough, though, to want to tell you just what you have done to me. You may be sorry. But no – if you could regret anything, you wouldn't be Simone any longer.

'Ten years ago, before the war, I was rich – not so rich as your new American, but rich enough to give you what you wanted. You didn't want quite so much before the war, Simone. Who taught you to be so extravagant while I was away? I think it was very nice of me never to ask you. Well, most of my money was in Russian and German securities, and more than three-quarters of it went west. The remainder in France went down considerably in value. I had my captain's pay, of course, but that didn't amount to much. Even before the end of the war you had managed to get through all my savings. Of course, I was a fool. A young man whose income has been reduced by three-quarters can't afford an expensive mistress and a flat in the Avenue Kléber. He ought either to dismiss the lady or to demand a little self-sacrifice. But I didn't dare demand anything. Suppose I had come to you one day and said, "Simone, I've lost my money" – what would you have said to me?

'What do you think I did? I don't suppose you ever thought about it at all. You didn't care if I was chucking away my money and my honour and my happiness to keep you. I gambled desperately. I did worse, I cheated at cards. I can see you shrug your shoulders and say, "Good for you!" But it's a rotten thing to do – a rotter's game. If anybody had found out they'd have cashiered me.

'Besides, it couldn't go on for ever. There was one row in Paris, though they couldn't prove anything. So then I got engaged to the English girl I told you about – the duke's daughter. Pretty, wasn't it? I actually brought myself to consider keeping my mistress on my wife's money! But I'd have done it, and I'd do it again, to get you back.

'And now you've chucked me. This American is colossally rich. For a long time you've been dinning into my ears that the flat is too small and that you're bored to death. Your "good friend" can offer you cars, diamonds – Aladdin's palace – the moon! I admit that love and honour look pretty small by comparison.

'Ah well, the Duke is most obligingly stupid. He leaves his revolver about in his desk drawer. Besides, he's just been in to ask what about this card-sharping story. So you see the game's up, anyhow. I don't blame you. I suppose they'll put my suicide down to fear of exposure. All the better. I don't want my love-affairs in the Sunday Press.

'Good-bye, my dear – oh, Simone, my darling, my darling, good-bye. Be happy with your new lover. Never mind me – what does it all matter? My God – how I loved you, and how I still love you in spite of myself. It's all done with. You'll never break my heart again. I'm mad – mad with misery! Good-bye.'

18

THE SPEECH FOR THE DEFENCE

'Nobody; I myself; farewell.'
OTHELLO

AFTER the reading of Cathcart's letter even the appearance of the prisoner in the witness-box came as an anticlimax. In the face of the Attorney-General's cross-examination he maintained stoutly that he had wandered on the moor for several hours without meeting anybody, though he was forced to admit that he had gone downstairs at 11.30 and not at 2.30, as he had stated at the inquest. Sir Wigmore Wrinching made a great point of this, and, in a spirited endeavour to suggest that Cathcart was blackmailing Denver, pressed his questions so hard that Sir Impey Biggs, Mr Murbles, Lady Mary, and Bunter had a nervous feeling that learned counsel's eyes were boring through the walls to the side-room where, apart from the other witnesses, Mrs Grimethorpe sat waiting. After lunch Sir Impey Biggs rose to make his plea for the defence.

'My lords, – Your lordships have now heard – and I, who have watched and pleaded here for these three anxious days, know with what eager interest and with what ready sympathy you have heard – the evidence brought by my noble client to defend him against this dreadful charge of murder. You have listened while, as it were from his narrow grave, the dead man has lifted his voice to tell you the story of that fatal night of the thirteenth of October, and I feel sure you can have no doubt in your hearts that that story is the true one. As your lordships know, I was myself totally ignorant of the contents of that letter until I heard it read in Court just now, and, by the profound impression it made upon my own mind, I can judge how tremendously and how painfully it must have affected your lordships. In my long experience at the criminal bar, I think I have never met with a history more melancholy than that of the unhappy young man whom a fatal passion – for here we may use that well-worn expression in all the fullness of its significance – whom a truly fatal passion thus urged into deep after deep of degradation, and finally to a violent death by his own hand.

'The noble peer at the Bar has been indicted before your lordships of the murder of this young man. That he is wholly innocent of the charge must, in the light of what we have heard, be so plain to your lordships that any words from me might seem altogether superfluous. In the majority of cases of this kind the evidence is confused, contradictory; here, however, the course of events is so clear, so coherent, that had we ourselves been present to see the drama unrolled before us, as before the all-seeing eye of God, we could hardly have a more vivid or a more accurate vision of that night's adventures. Indeed, had the death of Denis Cathcart been the sole event of the night, I will venture to say that the truth could never have been one single moment in doubt. Since, however, by a series of unheard-of coincidences, the threads of Denis Cathcart's story became entangled with so many others, I will venture to tell it once again from the beginning, lest, in the confusion of so great a cloud of witnesses, any point should still remain obscure.

'Let me, then, go back to the beginning. You have

heard how Denis Cathcart was born of mixed parentage – from the union of a young and lovely southern girl with an Englishman twenty years older than herself; imperious, passionate, and cynical. Till the age of 18 he lives on the Continent with his parents, travelling from place to place, seeing more of the world even than the average young Frenchman of his age, learning the code of love in a country where the *crime passionel* is understood and forgiven as it never can be over here.

'At the age of 18 a terrible loss befalls him. In a very short space of time he loses both his parents – his beautiful and adored mother and his father, who might, had he lived, have understood how to guide the impetuous nature which he had brought into the world. But the father dies, expressing two last wishes, both of which, natural as they were, turned out in the circumstances to be disastrously ill-advised. He left his son to the care of his sister, whom he had not seen for many years, with the direction that the boy should be sent to his own old University.

'My lords, you have seen Miss Lydia Cathcart, and heard her evidence. You will have realised how uprightly, how conscientiously, with what Christian disregard of self, she performed the duty entrusted to her, and yet how inevitably she failed to establish any real sympathy between herself and her young ward. He, poor lad, missing his parents at every turn, was plunged at Cambridge into the society of young men of totally different upbringing from himself. To a young man of his cosmopolitan experience the youth of Cambridge, with its sports and rags and naïve excursions into philosophy o' nights, must have seemed unbelievably childish. You all, from your own recollections of your Alma Mater, can reconstruct

Denis Cathcart's life at Cambridge, its outward gaiety, its inner emptiness.

'Ambitious of embracing a diplomatic career, Cathcart made extensive acquaintances among the sons of rich and influential men. From a worldly point of view he was doing well, and his inheritance of a handsome fortune at the age of 21 seemed to open up the path to very great success. Shaking the academic dust of Cambridge from his feet as soon as his Tripos was passed, he went over to France, established himself in Paris, and began, in a quiet, determined kind of way, to carve out a little niche for himself in the world of international politics.

'But now comes into his life that terrible influence which was to rob him of fortune, honour, and life itself. He falls in love with a young woman of that exquisite, irresistible charm and beauty for which the Austrian capital is world-famous. He is enthralled body and soul, as utterly as any Chevalier des Grieux, by Simone Vonderaa.

'Mark that in this matter he follows the strict, Continental code: complete devotion, complete discretion. You have heard how quietly he lived, how *rangé* he appeared to be. We have had in evidence his discreet banking-account, with its generous cheques drawn to self, and cashed in notes of moderate denominations, and with its regular accumulation of sufficient "economies" quarter by quarter. Life has expanded for Denis Cathcart. Rich, ambitious, possessed of a beautiful and complaisant mistress, the world is open before him.

'Then, my lords, across this promising career there falls the thunderbolt of the Great War – ruthlessly smashing through his safeguards, overthrowing the edifice of his ambition, destroying and devastating here, as everywhere, all that made life beautiful and desirable.

'You have heard the story of Denis Cathcart's distinguished army career. On that I need not dwell. Like thousands of other young men, he went gallantly through those five years of strain and disillusionment, to find himself left, in the end, with his life and health indeed, and, so far, happy beyond many of his comrades, but with his life in ruins about him.

'Of his great fortune – all of which had been invested in Russian and German securities – literally nothing is left to him. What, you say, did that matter to a young man so well equipped, with such excellent connections, with so many favourable openings, ready to his hand? He needed only to wait for a few years, to reconstruct much of what he had lost. Alas! my lords, he could not afford to wait. He stood in peril of losing something dearer to him than fortune or ambition; he needed money in quantity, and at once.

'My lords, in that pathetic letter which we have heard read nothing is more touching and terrible than that confession: "I knew you could not but be unfaithful to me". All through that time of seeming happiness he knew – none better – that his house was built on sand. "I was never deceived by you", he says. From their earliest acquaintance she had lied to him, and he knew it, and that knowledge was yet powerless to loosen the bands of his fatal fascination. If any of you, my lords, have known the power of love exercised in this irresistible – I may say, this predestined manner – let your experience interpret the situation to you better than any poor words of mine can do. One great French poet and one great English poet have summed the matter up in a few words. Racine says of such a fascination:

C'est Vénus tout entière à sa proie attaché.

And Shakespeare has put the lover's despairing obstinacy into two piteous lines:

> *If my love swears that she is made of truth*
> *I will believe her, though I know she lies.*

My lords, Denis Cathcart is dead; it is not our place to condemn him, but only to understand and pity him.

'My lords, I need not put before you in detail the shocking shifts to which this soldier and gentleman unhappily condescended. You have heard the story in all its cold, ugly details upon the lips of Monsieur du Bois-Gobey Houdin, and, accompanied by unavailing expressions of shame and remorse, in the words of the deceased. You know how he gambled, at first honestly – then dishonestly. You know from whence he derived those large sums of money which came at irregular intervals, mysteriously and in cash, to bolster up a bank-account always perilously on the verge of depletion. We need not, my lords, judge too harshly of the woman. According to her own lights, she did not treat him unfairly. She had her interests to consider. While he could pay for her she could give him beauty and passion and good humour and a moderate faithfulness. When he could pay no longer she would find it only reasonable to take another position. This Cathcart understood. Money he must have, by hook or by crook. And so, by an inevitable descent, he found himself reduced to the final deep of dishonour.

'It is at this point, my lords, that Denis Cathcart and his miserable fortunes come into the life of my noble client and of his sister. From this point began all those complications which led to the tragedy of October 14th and which we are met in this solemn and historic assembly to unravel.

'About eighteen months ago Cathcart, desperately searching for a secure source of income, met the Duke of Denver, whose father had been a friend of Cathcart's father many years before. The acquaintance prospered, and Cathcart was introduced to Lady Mary Wimsey at that time (as she has very frankly told us) "at a loose end", "fed up", and distressed by the dismissal of her fiancé, Mr Goyles. Lady Mary felt the need of an establishment of her own, and accepted Denis Cathcart, with the proviso that she should be considered a free agent, living her own life in her own way, with the minimum of interference. As to Cathcart's object in all this, we have his own bitter comment, on which no words of mine could improve. "I actually brought myself to consider keeping my mistress on my wife's money."

'So matters go on until October of this year. Cathcart is now obliged to pass a good deal of his time in England with his fiancée, leaving Simone Vonderaa unguarded in the Avenue Kléber. He seems to have felt fairly secure so far; the only drawback was that Lady Mary, with a natural reluctance to commit herself to the hands of a man she could not really love, had so far avoided fixing a definite date for the wedding. Money is shorter than it used to be in the Avenue Kléber, and the cost of robes and millinery, amusements, and so forth, has not diminished. And, meanwhile, Mr Cornelius van Humperdinck, the American millionaire, has seen Simone in the Bois, at the races, at the opera, in Denis Cathcart's flat.

'But Lady Mary is becoming more and more uneasy about her engagement. And at this critical moment Mr Goyles suddenly sees the prospect of a position, modest but assured, which will enable him to maintain a wife. Lady Mary makes her choice. She consents to elope with Mr Goyles, and by an extraordinary fatality the day and hour selected are 3 a.m. on the morning of October 14th.

'At about 9.30 on the night of Wednesday, October 13th, the party at Riddlesdale Lodge are just separating to go to bed. The Duke of Denver was in the gun-room, the other men were in the billiard-room, the ladies had already retired, when the manservant, Fleming, came up from the village with the evening post. To the Duke of Denver he brought a letter with news of a startling and very unpleasant kind. To Denis Cathcart he brought another letter – one which we shall never see, but whose contents it is easy to guess.

'You have heard the evidence of Mr Arbuthnot that, before reading this letter, Cathcart had gone upstairs gay and hopeful, mentioning that he hoped soon to get a date fixed for the marriage. At a little after ten, when the Duke of Denver went up to see him, there was a great change. Before his grace could broach the matter in hand Cathcart spoke rudely and harshly, appearing to be all on edge, and entreating to be left alone. Is it very difficult, my lords, in the face of what we have heard today – in the face of our knowledge that Mademoiselle Vonderaa crossed to New York on the *Berengaria* on October 15th – to guess what news had reached Denis Cathcart in that interval to change his whole outlook upon life?

'At this unhappy moment, when Cathcart is brought face to face with the stupefying knowledge that his mistress has left him, comes the Duke of Denver with a frightful accusation. He taxes Cathcart with the vile truth – that this man, who has eaten his bread and sheltered under his roof, and who is about to marry his sister, is nothing more nor less than a card-sharper. And when Cathcart refuses to deny the charge – when he, most insolently, as it seems, declares that he is no longer willing to wed the noble lady to whom he is affianced – is it surprising that the Duke should turn upon the imposter and forbid him ever to touch or speak to Lady Mary Wimsey again? I say, my lords, that no man with a spark of honourable feeling would have done otherwise. My client contents himself with directing Cathcart to leave the house next day; and when Cathcart rushes madly out into the storm he calls after him to return, and even takes the trouble to direct the footman to leave open the conservatory door for Cathcart's convenience. It is true that he called Cathcart a dirty scoundrel, and told him he should have been kicked out of his regiment, but he was justified; while the words he shouted from the window – "Come back, you fool", or even, according to one witness, "you b – fool" – have almost an affectionate ring in them. (Laughter.)

'And now I will direct your lordships' attention to the extreme weakness of the case against my noble client from the point of view of motive. It has been suggested that the cause of the quarrel between them was not that mentioned by the Duke of Denver in his evidence, but something even more closely personal to themselves. Of this contention not a jot or tittle, not the slightest shadow of evidence, has been put forward except, indeed, that of the extraordinary witness, Robinson, who appears to bear a grudge against his whole acquaintance, and to have magnified some trifling allusion into a matter of vast importance. Your lordships have seen this person's demeanour in the box, and will judge for yourselves how much weight is to be attached to his observations. While we on our side have been able to show that the alleged cause of complaint was perfectly well founded in fact.

'So Cathcart rushes out into the garden. In the pelting rain he paces heedlessly about, envisaging a future stricken at once suddenly barren of love, wealth, and honour.

'And, meanwhile, a passage door opens, and a stealthy foot creeps down the stair. We know now whose it is – Mrs Pettigrew-Robinson has not mistaken the creak of the door. It is the Duke of Denver.

'That is admitted. But from the point we join issue with my learned friend for the prosecution. It is suggested that the Duke, on thinking things over, determines that Cathcart is a danger to society and better dead – or that his insult to the Denver family can only be washed out in blood. And we are invited to believe that the Duke creeps downstairs, fetches his revolver from the study table, and prowls out into the night to find Cathcart and make away with him in cold blood.

'My lords, is it necessary for me to point out the inherent absurdity of this suggestion? What conceivable reason could the Duke of Denver have for killing, in this cold-blooded manner, a man of whom a single word has rid him already and for ever? It has been suggested to you that the injury had grown greater in the Duke's mind by brooding – had assumed gigantic proportions. Of that suggestion, my lords, I can only say that a more flimsy pretext for fixing an impulse to murder upon the shoulders of an innocent man was never devised, even by the ingenuity of an advocate. I will not waste my time or insult you by arguing about it. Again it has been suggested that the cause of quarrel was not what it appeared, and the Duke had reason to fear some disastrous action on Cathcart's part. Of this contention I think we have already disposed; it is an assumption constructed *in vacuo*, to meet a set of circumstances which my learned friend is at a loss to explain in conformity with the known facts. The very number and variety of motives suggested by the prosecution is proof that they are aware of the weakness of their own case. Frantically they cast about for any sort of explanation to give colour to this unreasonable indictment.

'And here I will direct your lordships' attention to the very important evidence of Inspector Parker in the matter of the study window. He has told you that it was forced from outside by the latch being slipped back with a knife. If it was the Duke of Denver, who was in the study at 11.30, what need had he to force the window? He was already inside the house. When, in addition, we find that Cathcart had in his pocket a knife, and that there are scratches upon the blade such as might come from forcing back a metal catch, it surely becomes evident that not the Duke, but Cathcart himself forced the window and crept in for the pistol, not knowing that the conservatory door had been left open for him.

'But there is no need to labour this point – we *know* that Captain Cathcart was in the study at that time, for we have seen in evidence the sheet of blotting-paper on which he blotted his letter to Simone Vonderaa, and Lord Peter Wimsey has told us how he himself removed that sheet from the study blotting-pad a few days after Cathcart's death.

'And let me here draw your attention to the significance of one point in the evidence. The Duke of Denver has told us that he saw the revolver in his drawer a short time before the fatal 13th, when he and Cathcart were together.'

The Lord High Steward: 'One moment, Sir Impey, that is not quite as I have it in my notes.'

Counsel: 'I beg your lordship's pardon if I am wrong.'

L.H.S.: 'I will read what I have. "I was hunting for an old photograph of Mary to give Cathcart, and that was

286

how I came across it". There is nothing about Cathcart being there.'

Counsel: 'If your lordship will read the next sentence—'

L.H.S.: 'Certainly. The next sentence is: "I remember saying at the time how rusty it was getting".'

Counsel: 'And the next?'

L.H.S.: ' "To whom did you make that observation?" Answer: "I really don't know, but I distinctly remember saying it".'

Counsel: 'I am much obliged to your lordship. When the noble peer made that remark he was looking out some photographs to give to Captain Cathcart. I think we may reasonably infer that the remark was made to the deceased.'

L.H.S. (to the House): 'My lords, your lordships will, of course, use your own judgement as to the value of this suggestion.'

Counsel: 'If your lordships can accept that Denis Cathcart may have known of the existence of the revolver, it is immaterial at what exact moment he saw it. As you have heard, the table-drawer was always left with the key in it. He might have seen it himself at any time, when searching for an envelope or sealing-wax or what not. In any case, I contend that the movements heard by Colonel and Mrs Marchbanks on Wednesday night were those of Denis Cathcart. While he was writing his farewell letter, perhaps with the pistol before him on the table – yes, at that very moment the Duke of Denver slipped down the stairs and out through the conservatory door. Here is the incredible part of this affair – that again and again we find two series of events, wholly unconnected between themselves, converging upon the same point of time, and causing endless confusion. I have used the word "incredible" – not because any coincidence is incredible, for we see more remarkable examples every day of our lives than any writer of fiction would dare to invent – but merely in order to take it out of the mouth of the learned Attorney-General, who is preparing to make it return, boomerang-fashion, against me. (Laughter.)

'My lords, this is the first of these incredible – I am not afraid of the word – coincidences. At 11.30 the Duke goes downstairs and Cathcart enters the study. The learned Attorney-General, in his cross-examination of my noble client, very justifiably made what capital he could out of the discrepancy between witness's statement at the inquest – which was that he did not leave the house till 2.30 – and his present statement – that he left it at half-past eleven. My lords, whatever interpretation you like to place upon the motives of the noble Duke in so doing, I must remind you once more at the time when the first statement was made everybody supposed that the shot had been fired at three o'clock, and that the mis-statement was then useless for the purpose of establishing an alibi.

'Great stress, too, has been laid on the noble Duke's inability to establish this alibi for the hours from 11.30 to 3 a.m. But, my lords, if he is telling the truth in saying that he walked all that time upon the moors without meeting anyone, what alibi could he establish? He is not bound to supply a motive for all his minor actions during the twenty-four hours. No rebutting evidence has been brought to discredit his story. And it is perfectly reasonable that, unable to sleep after the scene with Cathcart, he should go for a walk to calm himself down.

'Meanwhile, Cathcart has finished his letter and tossed it into the post-bag. There is nothing more ironical in the whole of this case than that letter. While the body of a murdered man lay stark upon the threshold, and detectives and doctors searched everywhere for clues, the normal routine of an ordinary English household went, unquestioned, on. That letter, which contained the whole story, lay undisturbed in the post-bag, till it was taken away and put in the post as a matter of course, to be fetched back again, at enormous cost, delay, and risk of life, two months later, in vindication of the great English motto: "Business as usual".

'Upstairs, Lady Mary Wimsey was packing her suitcase and writing a farewell letter to her people. At length Cathcart signs his name; he takes up the revolver and hurries out into the shrubbery. Still he paces up and down, with what thoughts God alone knows – reviewing the past, no doubt, racked with vain remorse, most of all, bitter against the woman who has ruined him. He bethinks him of the little love-token, the platinum-and-diamond cat which his mistress gave him for good luck! At any rate, he will not die with *that* pressing upon his heart. With a furious gesture he hurls it far from him. He puts the pistol to his head.

'But something arrests him. Not that! Not that! He sees in fancy his own hideously disfigured corpse – the shattered jaw – the burst eyeball – blood and brains horribly splashed about. No. Let the bullet go cleanly to the heart. Not even in death can he bear the thought of looking – *so*!

'He places the revolver against his breast and draws the trigger. With a little moan, he drops to the sodden ground. The weapon falls from his hand; his fingers scrabble a little at his breast.

'The gamekeeper who heard the shot is puzzled that poachers should come so close. Why are they not on the moors? He thinks of the hares in the plantation. He takes his lantern and searches in the thick drizzle. Nothing.

Only soggy grass and dripping trees. He is human. He concludes his ears deceived him, and he returns to his warm bed. Midnight passes. One o'clock passes.

'The rain is less heavy now. Look! In the shrubbery – what was that? A movement. The shot man is moving – groaning a little – crawling to his feet. Chilled to the bone, weak from loss of blood, shaking with the fever of his wound, he but dimly remembers his purpose. His groping hands go to the wound in his breast. He pulls out a handkerchief and presses it upon the place. He drags himself up, slipping and stumbling. The handkerchief slides to the ground, and lies there beside the revolver among the fallen leaves.

'Something in his aching brain tells him to crawl back to the house. He is sick, in pain, hot and cold by turns, and horribly thirsty. There someone will take him in and be kind to him – give him things to drink. Swaying and starting, now falling on hands and knees, now reeling to and fro, he makes that terrible nightmare journey to the house. Now he walks, now he crawls, dragging his heavy limbs after him. At last, the conservatory door! Here there will be help. And water for his fever in the trough by the well. He crawls up to it on hands and knees, and strains to lift himself. It is growing very difficult to breathe – a heavy weight seems to be bursting his chest. He lifts himself – a frightful hiccuping cough catches him – the blood rushes from his mouth. He drops down. It is indeed all over.

'Once more the hours pass. Three o'clock, the hour of rendezvous, draws on. Eagerly the young lover leaps the wall and comes hurrying through the shrubbery to greet his bride to be. It is cold and wet, but his happiness gives him no time to think of his surroundings. He passes through the shrubbery without a thought. He reaches the conservatory door, through which in a few moments love and happiness will come to him. And in that moment he stumbles across – the dead body of a man!

'Fear possesses him. He hears a distant footstep. With but one idea – escape from this horror of horrors – he dashes into the shrubbery, just as, fatigued perhaps a little, but with a mind soothed by his little expedition, the Duke of Denver comes briskly up the path, to meet the eager bride over the body of her betrothed.

'My lords, the rest is clear. Lady Mary Wimsey, forced by a horrible appearance of things into suspecting her lover of murder, undertook – with what courage every man amongst you will realise – to conceal that George Goyles ever was upon the scene. Of this ill-considered action of hers came much mystery and perplexity. Yet, my lords, while chivalry holds its own, not one amongst us will breathe one word of blame against that gallant lady. As the old song says:

> 'God send each man at his end
> Such hawks, such hounds, and such a friend.

'I think, my lords, that there is nothing more for me to say. To you I leave the solemn and joyful task of freeing the noble peer, your companion, from this unjust charge. You are but human, my lords, and some among you will have grumbled, some will have mocked on assuming these mediaeval splendours of scarlet and ermine, so foreign to the taste and habit of a utilitarian age. You know well enough that

> ''Tis not the balm, the sceptre, and the ball,
> The sword, the mace, the crown imperial,
> The intertissued robe of gold and pearl,
> The farcèd title, nor the tide of pomp
> That beats upon the high shores of the world

that can add any dignity to noble blood. And yet, to have beheld, day after day, the head of one of the oldest and noblest houses in England standing here, cut off from your fellowship, stripped of his historic honours, robed only in the justice of his cause – this cannot have failed to move your pity and indignation.

'My lords, it is your happy privilege to restore to his grace the Duke of Denver these traditional symbols of his exalted rank. When the clerk of this House shall address to you severally the solemn question: Do you find Gerald, Duke of Denver, Viscount St. George, guilty or not guilty of the dreadful crime of murder, every one of you may, with a confidence unmarred by any shadow of doubt, lay his hand upon his heart and say, "Not guilty, upon my honour."'

19

WHO GOES HOME?

'Drunk as a lord? As a class they are really very sober.'
JUDGE CLUER, *in court.*

WHILE the Attorney-General was engaged in the ungrateful task of trying to obscure what was not only plain, but agreeable to everybody's feelings, Lord Peter hauled Parker off to a Lyons over the way, and listened, over an enormous dish of eggs and bacon, to a brief account of Mrs Grimethorpe's dash to town, and a long one of Lady Mary's cross-examination.

'What are you grinning about?' snapped the narrator.

'Just natural imbecility,' said Lord Peter. 'I say, poor old Cathcart. She *was* a girl! For the matter of that, I suppose, she still is. I don't know why I should talk as if she'd died away the moment I took my eyes off her.'

'Horribly self-centred, you are,' grumbled Mr Parker.

'I know. I always was from a child. But what worries me is that I seem to be gettin' so susceptible. When Barbara turned me down—'

'You're cured,' said his friend brutally. 'As a matter of fact, I've noticed it for some time.'

Lord Peter sighed deeply. 'I value your candour, Charles,' he said, 'but I wish you hadn't such an unkind way of putting things. Besides – I say, are they coming out?'

The crowd in Parliament Square was beginning to stir and spread. Sparse streams of people began to drift across the street. A splash of scarlet appeared against the grey stone of St Stephen's. Mr Murbles' clerk dashed in suddenly at the door.

'All right, my lord – acquitted – unanimously – and will you please come across, my lord?'

They ran out. At sight of Lord Peter some excited bystanders raised a cheer. The great wind tore suddenly through the Square, bellying out the scarlet robes of the emerging peers. Lord Peter was bandied from one to the other, till he reached the centre of the group.

'Excuse me, your grace.'

It was Bunter. Bunter, miraculously, with his arms full of scarlet and ermine, enveloping the shameful blue serge suit which had been a badge of disgrace.

'Allow me to offer my respectful congratulations, your grace.'

'Bunter!' cried Lord Peter. 'Great God, the man's gone mad! Damn you, man, take that thing away,' he added, plunging at a tall photographer in a made-up tie.

'Too late, my lord,' said the offender, jubilantly pushing in the slide.

'Peter,' said the Duke. 'Er – thanks, old man.'

'All right,' said his lordship. 'Very jolly trip and all that. You're lookin' very fit. Oh, don't shake hands – there, I knew it! I heard that man's confounded shutter go.'

They pushed their way through the surging mob to the cars. The two Duchesses got in, and the Duke was following, when a bullet crashed through the glass of the window, missing Denver's head by an inch, and ricocheting from the windscreen among the crowd.

A rush and a yell. A big bearded man struggled for a moment with three constables; then came a succession of wild shots, and a fierce rush – the crowd parting, then closing in, like hounds on the fox, streaming past the Houses of Parliament, heading for Westminster Bridge.

'He's shot a woman – he's under that 'bus – no, he isn't – hi! – murder! – stop him!' Shrill screams and yells – police whistles blowing – constables darting from every corner – swooping down in taxis – running.

The driver of a taxi spinning across the bridge saw the fierce face just ahead of his bonnet, and jammed on the brakes, as the madman's fingers closed for the last time on the trigger. Shot and tyre exploded almost simultaneously; the taxi slewed giddily over to the right, scooping the fugitive with it, and crashed horribly into a tram standing vacant on the Embankment dead-end.

'I couldn't 'elp it,' yelled the taxi-man, ''e fired at me. Ow, Gawd, I couldn't 'elp it.'

Lord Peter and Parker arrived together, panting.

'Here, constable,' gasped his lordship; 'I know this man. He has an unfortunate grudge against my brother. In connection with a poaching matter – up in Yorkshire. Tell the coroner to come to me for information.'

'Very good, my lord.'

'Don't photograph *that*,' said Lord Peter to the man with the reflex, whom he suddenly found at his elbow.

The photographer shook his head.

'They wouldn't like to see that, my lord. Only the scene of the crash and the ambulance-men. Bright, newsy pictures, you know. Nothing gruesome' – with an explanatory jerk of the head at the great dark splotches in the roadway – 'it doesn't pay.'

A red-haired reporter appeared from nowhere with a notebook.

'Here,' said his lordship, 'do you want the story? I'll give it you now.'

* * *

There was not, after all, the slightest trouble in the matter of Mrs Grimethorpe. Seldom, perhaps, has a ducal escapade resolved itself with so little embarrassment. His grace, indeed, who was nothing if not a gentleman, braced himself gallantly for a regretful and sentimental interview. In all his rather stupid affairs he had never run away from a scene, or countered a storm of sobs with that maddening 'Well, I'd better be going now' which has led to so many despairs and occasionally to cold shot. But, on this occasion, the whole business fell flat. The lady was not interested.

'I am free now,' she said. 'I am going back to my own people in Cornwall. I do not want anything, now that he is dead.' The Duke's dutiful caress was a most uninteresting failure.

Lord Peter saw her home to a respectable little hotel in Bloomsbury. She liked the taxi, and the large, glittering shops, and the sky-signs. They stopped at Piccadilly Circus to see the Bonzo dog smoke his gasper and the Nestlé's baby consume his bottle of milk. She was amazed to find that the prices of the things in Swan & Edgar's window were, if anything, more reasonable than those current in Stapley.

'I should like one of those blue scarves,' she said, 'but I'm thinking 'twould not be fitting, and me a widow.'

'You could buy it now, and wear it later on,' suggested his lordship, 'in Cornwall, you know.'

'Yes.' She glanced at her brown stuff gown. 'Could I buy my blacks here? I shall have to get some for the funeral. Just a dress and a hat – and a coat, maybe.'

'I should think it would be a very good idea.'

'Now?'

'Why not?'

'I have money,' she said; 'I took it from his desk. It's

mine now, I suppose. Not that I'd wish to be beholden to him. But I don't look at it that way.'

'I shouldn't think twice about it, if I were you,' said Lord Peter.

She walked before him into the shop – her own woman at last.

In the early hours of the morning Inspector Sugg, who happened to be passing Parliament Square, came upon a taxi-man apparently addressing a heated expostulation to the statue of Lord Palmerston. Indignant at this senseless proceeding, Mr Sugg advanced, and then observed that the statesman was sharing his pedestal with a gentleman in evening dress, who clung precariously with one hand, while with the other he held an empty champagne-bottle to his eye, and surveyed the surrounding streets.

'Hi,' said the policeman, 'what are you doing there? Come off of it!'

'Hullo!' said the gentleman, losing his balance quite suddenly, and coming down in a jumbled manner. 'Have you seen my friend? Very odd thing – damned odd. 'Spec you know where to find him, what? When in doubt – tasker pleeshman, what? Friend of mine. Very dignified sort of man 'nopera-hat. Freddy – good ol' Freddy. Alwaysh answersh t'name – just like jolly ol' blood-hound!' He got to his feet and stood beaming on the officer.

'Why, if it ain't his lordship,' said Inspector Sugg, who had met Lord Peter in other circumstances. 'Better be gettin' home, my lord. Night air's chilly-like, ain't it? You'll catch a cold or summat o' that. Here's your taxi – just you jump in now.'

'No,' said Lord Peter. 'No. Couldn' do that. Not

without frien'. Good ol' Freddy. Never – desert – friend! Dear ol' Sugg. Wouldn't desert Freddy.' He attempted an attitude, with one foot poised on the step of the taxi, but, miscalculating his distance, stepped heavily into the gutter, thus entering the vehicle unexpectedly, head first.

Mr Sugg tried to tuck his legs in and shut him up, but his lordship thwarted this movement with unlooked-for agility, and sat firmly on the step.

'Not my taxi,' he explained solemnly. 'Freddy's taxi. Not right – run away with frien's taxi. Very odd. Jush went roun' corner to fesh Fred'sh taxshi – Freddy jush went roun' corner fesh *my* taxi – fesh friend'sh taxshi – friendship sush a beautiful thing – don't you thing-so, Shugg? Can't leave frien'. Beshides – there'sh dear ol Parker.'

'Mr Parker?' said the Inspector apprehensively. 'Where?'

'Hush!' said his lordship. 'Don' wake baby, theresh good shoul. Neshle'sh baby – jush shee 'm neshle, don't he neshle nishely?'

Following his lordship's gaze, the horrified Sugg observed his official superior cosily tucked up on the far side of Palmerston and smiling a happy smile in his sleep. With an exclamation of alarm he bent over and shook the sleeper.

'Unkind!' cried Lord Peter in a deep, reproachful tone. 'Dishturb poor fellow – poor hardworin' pleeshman. Never getsh up till alarm goes. . . . 'Stra'or'nary thing,' he added, as though struck by a new idea, 'why hashn't alarm gone off, Shugg?' He pointed a wavering finger at Big Ben. 'They've for-forgotten to wind it up. Dishgrayshful. I'll write to *The T-T-Timesh* about it.'

Mr Sugg wasted no words, but picked up the slumbering Parker and hoisted him into the taxi.

'Never – never – deshert –' began Lord Peter, resisting all efforts to dislodge him from the step, when a second taxi, advancing from Whitehall, drew up, with the Hon. Freddy Arbuthnot cheering loudly at the window.

'Look who's here!' cried the Hon. Freddy. 'Jolly, jolly ol' Sugg. Let'sh all go home together.'

'That'sh *my* taxshi,' interposed his lordship; with dignity, staggering across to it. The two whirled together for a moment; then the Hon. Freddy was flung into Sugg's arms, while his lordship, with a satisfied air, cried 'Home!' to the new taxi-man, and instantly fell asleep in a corner of the vehicle.

Mr Sugg scratched his head, gave Lord Peter's address, and watched the cab drive off. Then, supporting the Hon. Freddy on his ample bosom, he directed the other man to convey Mr Parker to 12A Great Ormond Street.

'Take me home,' cried the Hon. Freddy, bursting into tears, 'they've all gone and left me!'

'You leave it to me, sir,' said the Inspector. He glanced over his shoulder at St Stephen's, whence a group of Commons were just issuing from an all-night sitting.

'Mr Parker an' all,' said Inspector Sugg, adding devoutly, 'thank God there weren't no witnesses.'

WIMSEY, Peter Death Bredon, d.s.o.; *born* 1890, *2nd son* of Mortimer Gerald Bredon Wimsey, 15th Duke of Denver, and of Honoria Lucasta, *daughter of* Francis Delagardie of Bellingham Manor, Hants.

Educated: Eton College and Balliol College, Oxford (1st class honours, Sch. of Mod. Hist. 1912); served with H.M. Forces 1914/18 (Major, Rifle Brigade). *Author of:* 'Notes on the Collecting of Incunabula,' 'The Murderer's Vade-Mecum,' etc. *Recreations:* Criminology; bibliophily; music; cricket.

Clubs: Marlborough; Egotists'. *Residences:* 110A Piccadilly, W; Bredon Hall, Duke's Denver, Norfolk.

Arms: Sable, 3 mice courant, argent; crest, a domestic cat crouched as to spring, proper; motto: As my Whimsy takes me.

This re-issue of CLOUDS OF WITNESS *(which has received some corrections and amendments from Miss Sayers) has for postscript a short biography of Lord Peter Wimsey, brought up to date (May 1935) and communicated by his uncle Paul Austin Delagardie.*

I am asked by Miss Sayers to fill up certain lacunae and correct a few trifling errors of fact in her account of my nephew Peter's career. I shall do so with pleasure. To appear publicly in print is every man's ambition, and by acting as a kind of running footman to my nephew's triumph I shall only be showing a modesty suitable to my advanced age.

The Wimsey family is an ancient one – too ancient if you, ask me. The only sensible thing Peter's father ever did was to ally his exhausted stock with the vigorous French-English strain of the Delagardies. Even so, my nephew Gerald (the present Duke of Denver) is nothing but a beef-witted English squire, and my niece Mary was flighty and foolish enough till she married a policeman and settled down. Peter, I am glad to say, takes after his mother and me. True, he is all nerve and nose – but that is better than being all brawn and no brains like his father and brothers, or a mere bundle of emotions, like Gerald's boy, Saint-George. He has at least inherited the Delagardie brains, by way of safeguard to the unfortunate Wimsey temperament.

Peter was born in 1890. His mother was being very much worried at the time by her husband's behaviour (Denver was always tiresome though the big scandal did not break out till the Jubilee year), and her anxieties may have affected the boy. He was a colourless shrimp of a child, very restless and mischievous, and always much too sharp for his age. He had nothing of Gerald's robust physical beauty, but he developed what I can best call a kind of bodily cleverness, more skill than strength. He had a quick eye for a ball and beautiful hands for a horse. He had the devil's own pluck, too: the intelligent sort of pluck that sees the risk before it takes it. He suffered badly from nightmares as a child. To his father's consternation he grew up with a passion for books and music.

His early school-days were not happy. He was a fastidious child, and I suppose it was natural that his school-fellows should call him 'Flimsy' and treat him as a kind of comic turn. And he might, in sheer self-protection, have accepted the position and degenerated into a mere licensed buffoon, if some games-master at Eton had not discovered that he was a brilliant natural cricketer. After that, of course, all his eccentric ties were accepted as wit, and Gerald underwent the salutary shock of seeing his despised younger brother become a bigger personality than himself. By the time he reached the Sixth Form, Peter had contrived to become the fashion – athlete, scholar, *arbiter elegantiarum – nec pluribus impar*. Cricket had a great deal to do with it – plenty of Eton men will remember the 'Great Flim' and his performance against Harrow – but I take credit to myself for introducing him to a good tailor, showing him the way about Town, and teaching him to distinguish good wine from bad. Denver bothered little about him – he had too many entanglements of his own and in addition was taken up with

Gerald, who by this time was making a prize fool of himself at Oxford. As a matter of fact Peter never got on with his father, he was a ruthless young critic of the paternal misdemeanours, and his sympathy for his mother had a destructive effect upon his sense of humour.

Denver, needless to say, was the last person to tolerate his own failings in his offspring. It cost him a good deal of money to extricate Gerald from the Oxford affair, and he was willing enough to turn his other son over to me. Indeed, at the age of seventeen, Peter came to me of his own accord. He was old for his age and exceedingly reasonable, and I treated him as a man of the world. I established him in trustworthy hands in Paris, instructing him to keep his affairs upon a sound business footing and to see they terminated with goodwill on both sides and generosity on his. He fully justified my confidence. I believe that no woman has ever found cause to complain of Peter's treatment; and two at least of them have since married royalty (rather obscure royalties, I admit, but royalty of a sort). Here again, I insist upon my due share of the credit; however good the material one has to work upon it is ridiculous to leave any young man's social education to chance.

The Peter of this period was really charming, very frank, modest and well-mannered, with a pretty lively wit. In 1909 he went up with a scholarship to read history at Balliol, and here, I must confess, he became rather intolerable. The world was at his feet, and he began to give himself airs. He acquired affectations, an exaggerated Oxford manner and a monocle, and aired his opinions a good deal, both in and out of the Union, though I will do him the justice to say that he never attempted to patronise his mother or me. He was in his second year when Denver broke his neck out hunting and Gerald succeeded to the title. Gerald showed more sense of responsibility than I had expected in dealing with the estate; his worst mistake was to marry his cousin Helen, a scrawny, over-bred prude, all county from head to heel. She and Peter loathed each other cordially; but he could always take refuge with his mother at the Dower House.

And then, in his last year at Oxford, Peter fell in love with a child of seventeen and instantly forgot everything he had ever been taught. He treated that girl as if she was made of gossamer, and me as a hardened old monster of depravity who had made him unfit to touch her delicate purity. I won't deny that they made an exquisite pair – all white and gold – a prince and princess of moonlight, people said. Moonshine would have been nearer to the mark. What Peter was to do in twenty years' time with a wife who had neither brains nor character nobody but his mother and myself ever troubled to ask, and he, of course, was completely besotted. Happily, Barbara's parents decided that she was too young to marry; so Peter went in for his final Schools in the temper of a Sir Eglamore achieving his first dragon; laid his First-Class Honours at his lady's feet like the dragon's head, and settled down to a period of virtuous probation.

Then came the war. Of course the young idiot was mad to get married before he went. But his own honourable scruples made him mere wax in other people's hands. It was pointed out to him that if he came back mutilated it would be very unfair to the girl. He hadn't thought of that, and rushed off in a frenzy of self-abnegation to release her from the engagement. I had no hand in that; I was glad enough of the result, but I couldn't stomach the means.

He did very well in France; he made a good officer and

the men liked him. And then, if you please, he came back on leave with his captaincy in '16, to find the girl married – to a hard-bitten rake of a Major Somebody, whom she had nursed in the V.A.D. hospital, and whose motto with women was catch 'em quick and treat 'em rough. It was pretty brutal; for the girl hadn't had the nerve to tell Peter beforehand. They got married in a hurry when they heard he was coming home, and all he got on landing was a letter announcing the *fait accompli* and reminding him that he had set her free himself.

I will say for Peter that he came straight to me and admitted that he had been a fool. 'All right,' said I, 'you've had your lesson. Don't go and make a fool of yourself in the other direction.' So he went back to his job with (I am sure) the fixed intention of getting killed; but all he got was his majority and his D.S.O. for some recklessly good intelligence work behind the German front. In 1918 he was blown up and buried in a shell-hole near Caudry, and that left him with a bad nervous breakdown, lasting, on and off, for two years. After that, he set himself up in a flat in Piccadilly, with the man Bunter (who had been his sergeant and was, and is, devoted to him), and started out to put himself together again.

I don't mind saying that I was prepared for almost anything. He had lost all his beautiful frankness, he shut everybody out of his confidence, including his mother and me, adopted an impenetrable frivolity of manner and a dilettante pose, and became, in fact, the complete comedian. He was wealthy and could do as he chose and it gave me a certain amount of sardonic entertainment to watch the efforts of post-war feminine London to capture him. 'It can't,' said one solicitous matron, 'be good for poor Peter to live like a hermit.' 'Madam,' said

I, 'if he did, it wouldn't be.' No; from that point of view he gave me no anxiety. But I could not but think it dangerous that a man of his ability should have no job to occupy his mind, and I told him so.

In 1921 came the business of the Attenbury Emeralds. That affair has never been written up, but it made a good deal of noise, even at that noisiest of periods. The trial of the thief was a series of red-hot sensations, and the biggest sensation of the bunch was when Lord Peter Wimsey walked into the witness-box as chief witness for the prosecution.

That was notoriety with a vengeance. Actually, to an experienced intelligence officer, I don't suppose the investigation had offered any great difficulties; but a 'noble sleuth' was something new in thrills. Denver was furious; personally, I didn't mind what Peter did, provided he did something. I thought he seemed happier for the work, and I liked the Scotland Yard man he had picked up during the run of the case. Charles Parker is a quiet, sensible, well-bred fellow, and has been a good friend and brother-in-law to Peter. He has the valuable quality of being fond of people without wanting to turn them inside out.

The only trouble about Peter's new hobby was that it had to be more than a hobby, if it was to be any hobby for a gentleman. You cannot get murderers hanged for your private entertainment. Peter's intellect pulled him one way and his nerves another, till I began to be afraid they would pull him to pieces. At the end of every case he had the old nightmares and shell-shock over again. And then Denver, of all people – Denver, the crashing great booby, in the middle of his fulminations against Peter's degrading and notorious police activities, must needs get himself indicted on a murder charge and stand his trial in the House of Lords, amid a blaze of publicity which made all Peter's efforts in that direction look like damp squibs.

Peter pulled his brother out of that mess, and, to my relief, was human enough to get drunk on the strength of it. He now admits that his 'hobby' is his legitimate work for society, and has developed sufficient interest in public affairs to undertake small diplomatic jobs from time to time under the Foreign Office. Of late he has become a little more ready to show his feelings, and a little less terrified of having any to show.

His latest eccentricity has been to fall in love with that girl whom he cleared of the charge of poisoning her lover. She refused to marry him, as any woman of character would. Gratitude and a humiliating inferiority complex are no foundation for matrimony; the position was false from the start. Peter had the sense, this time, to take my advice. 'My boy,' said I, 'what was wrong for you twenty years back is right now. It's not the innocent young things that need gentle handling – it's the ones that have been frightened and hurt. Begin again from the beginning – but I warn you that you will need all the self-discipline you have ever learnt.'

Well, he has tried. I don't think I have ever seen such patience. The girl has brains and character and honesty; but he has got to teach her how to take, which is far more difficult than learning to give. I think they will find one another, if they can keep their passions from running ahead of their wills. He does realise, I know, that in this case there can be no consent but free consent.

Peter is forty-five now, it is really time he was settled. As you will see, I have been one of the important formative influences in his career, and, on the whole, I feel he does me credit. He is a true Delagardie, with little of the Wimseys about him except (I must be fair) that underlying sense of social responsibility which prevents the English landed gentry from being a total loss, spiritually speaking. Detective or no detective, he is a scholar and a gentleman; it will amuse me to see what sort of shot he makes at being a husband and father. I am getting an old man, and have no son of my own (that I know of); I should be glad to see Peter happy. But as his mother says, 'Peter has always had everything except the things he really wanted,' and I suppose he is luckier than most.

PAUL AUSTIN DELAGARDIE.